THE MURDERS

OF

BOYSIE SINGH

DEREK BICKERTON

THE MURDERS OF BOYSIE SINGH

ROBBER, ARSONIST, PIRATE, MASS-MURDERER,
VICE AND GAMBLING KING OF TRINIDAD

INTRODUCTION BY KENNETH RAMCHAND

PEEPAL TREE

First published in Great Britain in 1962
by Arthur Barker Ltd
This new edition published in 2020
Peepal Tree Press Ltd
17 King's Avenue
Leeds LS6 1QS
England

ISBN13: 9781845264492

CONTENTS

LIST OF ILLUSTRATIONS

Photographs are drawn from the Arthur Barker edition of Derek Bickerton's book except those labelled (KR) which Kenneth Ramchand photographed from the archives of the *Trinidad Guardian*. The *Trinidad Guardian* captions are quoted verbatim.

KENNETH RAMCHAND

BOYSIE SINGH: TRUTH AND FICTION

The Murders of Boysie Singh: Robber, Arsonist, Mass Murderer, Vice and Gambling King of Trinidad by English-born Derek Bickerton (1926-2018) is a well-told tale setting out in chronological order the main facts about the life of Boysie Singh (1908-1957), a Trinidadian of Indian origin. The provable facts about Boysie establish him as a record-holder in the annals of criminality. The unverifiable rumours, speculations and other inventions surrounding this figure excited ambivalent commentary in the oral culture, arousing images of fear and loathing, but also casting Boysie Singh as "one of us" – a daring expression of popular resistance, a rebel from the underground making raids upon the establishment. In this respect he resembled the short-lived Kingston rebel, Vincent "Ivanhoe" Martin (1924-48), known as Rhygin, who was later fictionalised in the film, *The Harder They Come* (1972) and in its novelisation published in 1980 under the same title.[1] The apocrypha and charismatic moments are an important part of the Boysie Singh legend. One value of this book is that it doesn't dismiss the shapings of the popular imagination and doesn't want to do so. All the obscene, gruesome and destructive acts attributed to Boysie are acts people thought he was capable of performing. How can we separate the man from the phenomenon people thought he was?

i. The Legend and the Man

Boysie Singh projected himself as Rajah of the Land and King of the Sea. His criminal career on land flourished in downtown Port of Spain and its unsavoury suburbs; on the sea, he ruled the Gulf of Paria, the fishing ground between Trinidad and Venezuela which he made a watery grave for people seeking passage to the Spanish Main or conducting contraband trade between the island and the South American mainland. There is no doubt that when Boysie operated "the chute" in the late 1940s – a shuttle service for illegal immigrants to the largely unprotected Venezuelan coast – many of his passengers never arrived; in his manic period of piracy in the early months of 1950, many Venezuelan boats were burnt and sunk, and their crews shot. According to floating rumours, and to many people professing to have "inside" knowledge, more than 500 victims were sent to join those who had previously perished in Venezuelan revolutionary and counter-revolutionary skirmishes. But there was no proof. When Boysie was charged with the murder of Philbert Peyson in 1950, the newspapers were flooded with stories of murders committed on land and sea by Boysie Singh in the 1940s, including that of the headless corpse of a Norwegian sailor found floating in the same Bayshore area where Peyson's body was pulled out of the water a week or so later. Bickerton claimed to have evidence that could prove Boysie guilty of only two of these killings on the sea, but he estimates, conservatively, that the credible total figure of Boysie's victims was closer to fifty. Nobody had any proof of such a number, and Bickerton advances none. But belief in Boysie's atrocities was strong enough to enhance his reputation and to pass easily into legend.

The land career began in 1932 with his establishment of a gambling club for playing whappie at 59, Prince Street and with the selection of secret whe-whe "turfs", or "schools" as Bickerton called them, for "bussing the mark", that is, ceremonially revealing the winning number in the popular and illegal game. This was a pastime separate from the card and dice games in the clubs, and although it was Boysie who chose and sealed the winning number, he enacted the bussing of the mark as if what Fate had decided was as much a mystery to him as to the other devotees.[2] Whe-whe was a somewhat esoteric Chinese game involving the interpretation of dreams, the reading of signs, and the potency of numbers. The lower classes believed with all their souls in the fragments of this cabalistic rite, and many others at all levels in the society had residual feelings about its supernatural echoes.

By the end of the 1930s, Boysie's network of whe-whe schools had spread further into Port of Spain's surrounding neighbourhoods. Playing his usual cat and mouse with the police, he would inform on those who held schools where he wanted to place his own school, and bully or intimidate others till they cleared out. He owned three clubs in addition to the original at 59 Prince Street with its double-filtered entrance and cocooned back room – the Sunrise and the Baltimore on the corner of Prince and Charlotte Streets, and the Dorset at 55 Queen Street, which was to become the most notorious of all. From 1944, the Dorset became the centre of operations and was a haunt well-known to the tough and the prurient. In this period, Boysie frequented Hell Yard in East Dry River where he engaged in gambling, fighting war with kites, and becoming familiar with hardy types. Bickerton writes (p. 127; page references are to this edition) that just before Christmas 1949, three fellows "from behind the bridge" came to no. 55, "looking for trouble". The trio, unnamed by Bickerton, included the famous pannist 'Spree' Simon who was wounded by one of Boysie's henchmen called Fire Kong. 'Spree' limped for the rest of his life as a result. It was two years before Fire Kong was charged and convicted of shooting with intent.

The clubs gradually diversified their offerings, beginning, logically, with the sale of rum. Later, gin and whisky, purchased from American soldiers on the black market, were sold back to them in single drinks at a good profit. Soon Boysie owned facilities that can be described as night-clubs with music for dancing, gambling dens, brothels, safe havens for other kinds of "adult" entertainments, and nonstop drinking. At the twenty-four-hour-a-day Dorset, Boysie accumulated guns for no special purpose at this time other than profit (many he sold to exiled Venezuelans), and established networks for receiving and disposing of stolen property. As a minimally profitable courtesy he sold opium that came from India, and marijuana from Venezuela.

He had on call thugs whom he could dispatch both to execute strong-arm services and carry out insure-and-burn schemes for respectable people – if the requests were too many for him to handle personally, or if he wasn't in the mood. His care-nothing toughs sometimes served as bouncers at the clubs, keeping order and adding to the sense of security that arose from Boysie's having policemen on the payroll from time to time. It wasn't long, however, before there were also policemen who wanted to catch him out. He was never able to purchase for himself and his clientele at the Dorset the kind of immunity he enjoyed at 59 Prince Street.

In one of the earliest childhood Woodbrook episodes, Bickerton relates how, having brutalised a schoolmate, the ten-year-old Boysie ran more than three miles across the district with police in pursuit, circling back to his parents' house and scrambling into a hiding place under the roof that he had prepared in advance for occasions like this. It was like a version of "Police and Thief", a game children played in which "thief" found ingenious places to hide, and "police" did all they could to catch them. After a while, the players exchanged roles, and the true-to-life game continued smoothly. Boysie's whole life was a game of police and thief, from that ten-year-old's three-mile flight, to his final capture for the murder of Thelma Haynes.

Just as Ernest Hemingway always felt the taxman was closing in on him, so Boysie felt that the police were out to get him one way or the other. At the end of the second "Floating Corpse Trial", when he was found guilty, Boysie wept: "I am innocent of this act, and I have been framed. Since 1925, the police is behind me either to kill me or get me a long sentence in prison… I have been framed…" (p. 170). The Appeal Court judges who reversed the guilty verdict confirmed Boysie's view of how the law operated. Later, when he was found guilty of another murder, Boysie returned to his complaint, saying that the police, "tyrants existing in this country, have the country corrupted. For wanting promotion they will do anything in this country."

Although Boysie professed to admire Hitler, he had as little interest in world affairs as he had in the politics of the island. It was a period that included labour unrest, the formation of trade unions, echoes of Negritude and Garveyism, the first glimmerings of the formation of an Indo-Trinidadian political identity, and progress towards universal adult suffrage, but Boysie seems to have had no interest in what was going on. This marked his difference from another Trinidadian Indian figure who attracted popular and ambivalent celebrity, Bhadase Sagan Maraj (1919-1971).[3]

Boysie wanted to be a boss, but taking part in political activity never crossed his mind. He seems to have operated his business without any thought either that the War was going to make his fortune or that its end would threaten his money-making capacity. The infamous ships-for-bases deal between the British Government and the USA led to the posting of thousands of American soldiers to the island and the frequent visits of seamen. Boysie had the reflexes to corner opportunity when it arose, but not the vision to plan for what was not in plain sight. During the years of the American occupation, thousands of idle soldiers, far from home and not directly involved in any of the fighting, spent, lost, and were in other ways relieved of their dollars in or near Boysie's clubs and brothels. By 1944 he possessed more money than he had ever expected. He was, to all appearances, at the height of his physical powers. He became a dresser with a suit for each occasion, setting a style of having the outfit and all the accessories in the same colour.

What he called "the glamour days" in his diary had arrived. The "badjohn"[4] shape-shifted at will into the "sagaboy".[5] He donned the ostentatious Cab Calloway jacket, pleated trousers, with long gold chains passing round the neck and hanging from the waist partly draping his legs. At the height of his fortunes and bizarre glory, Singh owned a fishing fleet of around thirty pirogues, and three or four launches with inboard engines. He invested in houses for rent around the city, and was regularly adding to his portfolio; he was now receiving and disposing of stolen property on a large scale; and there was an expansion of personal services like the administering of beatings and the burning of cars and buildings on behalf of well-insured persons.

He was a flamboyant figure at race meetings. In his staged strolls around the Savannah he would parade with his retinue as "Rajah of the Land". He developed a good name for always being willing to give "a raise" to hard-up persons and for the ostentatious distribution of dollar bills in public places. In this he can be seen as anticipating the activities of the Jamaican dons and don gorgons who ensured the loyalty of their garrison ghetto communities by a mixture of terror and largesse, though unlike the dons, his influence was never connected to any political role.

Boysie hardly smoked or drank, but he was addicted to gambling. When the Americans started to leave Trinidad in 1945, his incon declined. The Dorset was still highly profitable, however, anc ture of the American soldiers would not have been so bad fo hadn't lost almost half of his cash fortune to rich Syrians whose [illegible] of him as a player in their prestigious club meant so much to his self-esteem. In order to be admitted to gamble with them he was obliged to play poker instead of the lower-class game of whappie, at which he was adept. These "socialites" (so Boysie considered them) did not take the Indian to their bosom. They saw him as a man who had money to lose. But if he had learnt a lesson about where he did not belong, that did not turn him off gambling. He returned to familiar haunts, playing whappie to recoup his massive losses. He lost even more. His luck was failing.

The second half of *The Murders of Boysie Singh* is held together by four sets of events. The first was Boysie's dominion over the Gulf of Paria. This was a kind of return to the past. In the late 1920s, Boysie had humbled himself to work as a jostler (fisherman's shore assistant), and as junior crew on fishing pirogues, until, still a teenager, he bought his own boat, *The Perseverance*. It looked then as if he was preparing to make his way in the world by relatively honest means. But he could not commit to a regular job or life, and soon events were to take him to Port of Spain where he could be larger than life.

When his funds started to boil down after the war, he returned to fishing in the Gulf of Paria from a base in Cedros in south-west Trinidad. From 1947 to 1949 he ran a profitable fishing operation[6] but could not be satisfied by that, and he could not abandon his Port of Spain operations. It was from Cedros that he used his mastery of the Gulf and his knowledge of the wild Venezuelan coast to conduct the profitable and infamous shuttle service called "the chute". Troubled by the Cedros fishermen who raided his fishpots and damaged his seines, and raging at the Venezuelan authorities who confiscated three of his boats, he shifted his base from Cedros to Cocorite, west of Port of Spain, in 1950. In what sounded like "gun talk" (bravado) he declared personal war on Venezuela. He turned his launch, the *Marie Louise*, into a weapon of war, costumed his men, and donned black. The erstwhile saga boy metamorphosed into the Pirate of the Gulf, seizing goods and personal possessions, burning boats, and killing crews and passengers. His main target was Venezuelan boats involved in the lucrative trade of buying goods in Trinidad and smuggling them duty-free into Venezuela. But what began as a rationally directed criminal operation turned into an orgy of violence, and even Trinidad fishermen fell victim to his blood-lust. Thus did the Rajah fulfil his destiny as Master of the Sea.

The second of the four sets of events was the three trials connected to the murder of Philbert Peyson, a gang member deemed a police informer by Boysie and peremptorily sentenced to death. The discovery of Peyson's corpse on April 20, 1950 brought an abrupt end to the piracy days. The detailed reporting of "The Case of the Floating Corpse" in the newspapers through 1950 and into early 1951 made Boysie a household headline, and flushed out a chorus of crimes and misdeeds that the oral culture had been waiting to amplify when it became safe for tongues to wag. A hung jury in the first trial necessitated a retrial in which Boysie was found guilty. This was followed by an appeal that concluded with an acquittal on January 25, 1951. The three trials and his gambling took all his money and brought down his empire.

The third startling event was the spectacle of a repentant Boysie Singh dressed all in white as a wayside preacher at the Croisee in San Juan, or travelling on his motorbike to crossroads, popular junctions, eaves of rumshops and other suitable spots. He canvassed repentance and the possibility of the forgiveness of sins. The blessing bestowed upon him, could be sought in prayer by all contrite sinners.[7] Though his mission was interrupted by a jail sentence for offences committed before he had gained salvation (forgiven by God but not forgotten by the less divine courts), he resumed his ministry as soon as he finished serving his prison term. The preaching career only came to an abrupt end when, according to his diary as quoted by Bickerton, "The Police arrest me for riding my Autocycle in 1954 late, and that made me go back into the ordinary life".

Back in "the ordinary life" meant not being in the public eye. He did not have the wherewithal or the zest to open another club. He did not have the pull to attract a following from amongst those who would once have rushed to be his henchmen. In 1954, a clumsy arson job with a substandard assistant showed to anybody who needed services that Boysie was no longer the man for them. Boysie boiled down to being a semi-retiree with a diminished practice, doing low-profile jobs at low prices. His body was deteriorating. He was suffering from diabetes and advanced gonorrhoea. Gambling and "The Case of the Floating Corpse" had sucked away his money, but he was still gambling. He was impotent. His wife, Doris Leon, had left him for her lover, PC Harry Seurattan of the Besson Street station. Boysie may have been depressed, or worse, as the highlightings in his Bible of Job 19, 17 and 18 seem to suggest: "My wife hath abhorred my breath and I entreated the children of my womb. Even fools despised me, and when I was gone from them, they spoke against me." In Bickerton's book, there is an undertone suggestive of tragedy, as the author highlights the pathos of Boysie's lonely fate.

The fourth and final event was Boysie's participation in the murder and disappearance of a woman, the love partner of a handsome Maracas Bay lifeguard called Boland Ramkissoon. Boland had separated from his legal wife Dorothy to whom he was paying maintenance. Thelma Haynes was a beautiful woman from British Guiana who gave up a promising career with Geoffrey Holder's dance troupe to live with Boland in his tapia house at Ramkissoon

Trace in San Juan. All the thrills and romance of a union across racial lines. By all accounts they were still in love.

Boland, though, became a fervent member of the evangelical Church of Pilgrim Holiness[8] and he appears to have been convinced that in living with Thelma he was not living in accordance with holy scripture. To be sure of salvation and perhaps to give himself a chance of promotion to an attractive position as a minister in the church, he was told he must "put Thelma away". He took this injunction literally. "Uncle" Boysie would help him to put away Thelma if Boland asked him. The subdued Boysie was living in San Juan at the time and Boland had been showing him respect and admiration. Did Boysie come out of retirement to do this last job because Boland played upon their shared Indianness?

Thelma Haynes's body was never found. The trial of Boysie and Boland in "The Case of the Missing Dancer" brought Boysie onto the front pages again.

But Boysie had gone down in the world. Though there were crowds in the precincts of the Court, swarms in the hangman's cemetery when he was being buried after the execution, the people were no longer in awe of him. He no longer represented them in their opposition to injustice and unfairness. They came only to bear witness to the taming of an amoral force that had once seemed to be carrying out their own buried apocalyptic wishes to bring down the network of colonial institutions and interest groups that stood in the way of their liberation.

At the end of his Introduction to *The Murders of Boysie Singh*, Bickerton states: "To the best of my belief... this book constitutes the only full and true account ever published of one of the most remarkable characters in the recorded history of crime". For its suggestive and absorbing portrait of the flamboyant and lethal Boysie Singh, and for Bickerton's honest efforts to see the man in his social and cultural context, *The Murders of Boysie Singh* is an important work. It adds to and complicates our understanding of its time and holds portents of the dire conditions that exist in Trinidad today. It deserves and needs to be laid before the people of Trinidad and Tobago.

ii. A Sociologist's Nightmare

With the passing of time, *The Murders of Boysie Singh* has become a major social document, a rich source of information about the lifestyles and psychology of the Port of Spain proletariat, including the barrack-yard dwellers who comprised a kind of community, as well as other lower working-class persons striving to rise with the help of God and invisible wages. Perhaps without knowing he was doing so, Bickerton also takes us below this layer to the roots of the country's anarchism. His book helps us to identify an underclass (below the barrack-yard dwellers but not totally cut off from them) resembling the Indian tribals or "janglis" inhabiting the novels of Harold Sonny Ladoo.[9] The book gives us, then, insight into the existence of a floating underclass, below the conventional proletariat, made up of immigrants from the countryside, from other islands, from the suburbs and other oppressed urban pockets. They formed a loose band of individuals, without home, without work, without community, without hope. They were impervious to a sound colonial education or any kind of nurture, deracinated individuals with nothing to lose, who moved into and around the darker zones of the city. They lived off gambling, petty crimes and women, and doing odd jobs for crime bosses like Boysie Singh. Some of them became regulars who slept in Boysie's clubs and became his toughest henchmen. For all that, it is a spirited life full of graphic nicknames (Bamboozie, Geronimo, and Bag of Rice – who made jail for stealing that commodity) and backchat that gave spark and depth to some of the exchanges between them as witnesses and the attorneys in the Boysie Singh trials. When Wilkie (a man with over 40 convictions who had spent more than half his years in jail) was asked if he didn't feel sorry about the death of Bumper, he didn't pause to think: "Sorry? I am not sorry over nobody's death. Who dead dead. I know I have to die" (p. 163).

The book's focus on the relationship between Boysie and the police gives us a vantage point from which to understand the continuing difficulties of managing crime in Trinidad. The several chapters giving detailed coverage of the investigations, the conduct of the trials, and court and police-station procedures could serve as an informal handbook of malpractice in the administration of justice, and idiosyncratic policing. There are many instances of justice delayed or foregone. In spite of his reputation, Boysie was granted bail on an arson charge and he was never called to trial. There was strong evidence that Boysie killed two Trinidad fishermen and stole their equipment, but the matter was not pursued because he was already being tried for another murder. There was no attempt made to see if there was any truth in the rumours of Boysie's piratical activity in the Gulf of Paria. The reports of the floating corpse trials show police suborning witnesses, training them to stick to their story and coaching them into a frustrating series of "I don't remember" (a speciality of a 14-year old state witness called Loomat). The guilty verdict arrived at in the retrial of the Floating Corpse case was achieved by police concealment of the station diary, the compulsory purchase of witnesses, the deportation of a key defence witness and Inspector Bleasdell's fabrication of cases against Boysie's four co-accused in a comprehensive frame-up. The two henchmen who helped Boysie to commit the alleged crime were not even questioned by the police. The Appeal Court statement overturning the guilty verdict was very clear about the tainted quality of the witnesses, the corruption of the inspector and the bias of the judge.

The book also allows us to see the contempt/ distrust felt by the ordinary offender for a system which more often than not gave the impression that it existed to protect the status quo and the interests of those who had property and possessions to defend. Discrimination by class is very noticeable in the trials, and the official participants like judges, prosecuting counsels and the defence shared the attitude of the respectable that the accused and the witnesses were contemptible low life. Cross-questioning the star witness, Loomat, Mr Isaac Hyatali addresses him as "Boy", "My boy" and sarcastically as "Mr Loomat". When the defence counsel tried to impress upon the jury that a particular witness was unreliable, Judge Kenneth Vincent Brown intervened to remind everyone that particular instances of incredibility would need to be proved since, in general, it was unreasonable to expect any of the witnesses in the case to be credible, given the class of people involved and the places they came from.

Commendably, Bickerton begins his book with a descriptive analysis of Trinidad in the period of Boysie's career. He understood that Boysie's Trinidad is "a background without some knowledge of which he can never be properly understood". He offers the kind of analysis you can find in V.S. Naipaul's work, though Naipaul wrote out of a deeper understanding of Trinidad and a perverse love for it. Bickerton's instincts are generally right, though sometimes the reader may feel that knowledge alone will not do if there is not a feel for the place being written about. Bickerton describes a brash, traffic-clogged, materialistic, modernistic, America-infiltrated British colonial city, with dark beds of sin and vice, without values and standards (of Europe, one wonders). What he records of this side of the city was undoubtedly true, though he ignores other sides of Port of Spain, as if the city did not have the history and traditions unearthed by writers such as Gerry Besson, V.S. Naipaul, Stuempfle and others.[10] He recognises the rich mixture of races but he sometimes uses his knowledge recklessly, rushing in to pronounce on subjects that Trinidadians understand to be bewilderingly complex. For instance, he asserts that the races "mix but do not mingle, for in spite of the propaganda about dwelling in unity together, the nerve-jangling suspicion and distrust that exist between the various races can be felt all the time, and erupt occasionally in acts of meaningless violence" (p. 48).

Writing in 1960, Bickerton does not acknowledge the upsurge of dance around Beryl McBurnie and the Little Carib Theatre in the same Woodbrook where Boysie was brought up; the emergence of Trinidadian writers such as Sam Selvon and V.S. Naipaul; intellectuals such as C.L.R. James, Eric Williams and Lloyd Best; the excitement of the Federal period; Carnival, calypso and the inventiveness of pan; the magnificent built heritage around the Savannah and other examples of architectural art. Apart from the hosay in St James, and although he is quick to notice African-Indian tensions, he does not show any wish to understand Indian and African cultural practices, and offers as regular Indian practice at least two barbaric behaviours for which there is little or no evidence to be found.[11] Bickerton's knowledge of Trinidad is not deep and, to put it bluntly, there is a certain amount of patronizing Eurocentricity as well as occasional instances of superior dismissiveness in the book. He describes the brashness of Port of Spain of the early 1960s and then he states: "Yet, embedded like fossils in these neon-age strata, one finds *Indian tribal customs, primitive African rites and beliefs*, [my italics] proletarian attitudes and patterns of behaviour more typical of the nineteenth than the twentieth century, all mixed incongruously together in a sociologist's nightmare, presenting contrasts as violent as the physical surroundings of the city themselves" (p. 49).

For all that, there is nothing intentionally unsympathetic in Bickerton's attempt to present the background for understanding Boysie. The book does describe "a sociologist's nightmare" with its attendant demons, and it does give a sense of contrasts in the human and physical surroundings. There is, as Poynting has written, "a refreshing curiosity about Trinidadian society which is always, ultimately, sympathetic to the people rather than the elite."[12] Because there are to be found in him many of the contradictory currents in the Trinidad of the 1930s and 1940s, Bickerton's Boysie Singh emerges as a representative of these times, a pre- figuring of the lawlessness, the brutality, the crimes against the person, the unfeeling violence, the lack of respect and reverence, the cynicism and anarchy of twenty-first century Trinidad.

iii. The Making of the Book

Bickerton only heard about the crime lord in 1958, about a year after Singh and Boland Ramkissoon were hanged for the murder of Thelma Haynes. He was living in Barbados and writing a column for the *Barbados Advocate*. With United Kingdom readers in mind ("they had had Heath, Haigh and Christie crammed into them *ad nauseam* and might well be glad of a change"), he was thinking of doing "a book of Celebrated Caribbean Crimes, a more or less virgin field as far as the British public was concerned". It was then that editor Ian Gale brought up the name of Boysie Singh. The conversation led Bickerton to pay a preliminary visit to Trinidad where he was astonished by the things he was told and by what he found in the newspaper files about Singh's career. He concluded that he didn't need to write a book on Caribbean crimes after all, for Boysie Singh seemed to have committed "all the crimes there were, except blackmail and simony." Bickerton's subsequent research visits could not have been very lengthy, but he took the opportunity to talk to Trinidadians and build a store of information about the ethnic groups and come to his own conclusions about the kind of society Trinidad was.

In his other life, Derek Bickerton became a linguist with a serious interest in Creole languages and he went on to have a distinguished professorial career in this field from his base at the University of Hawaii.[13] Before writing *The Murders of Boysie Singh*, he had written two gripping thrillers, one of which was made into a movie. (Long ago, a film option was taken out on *The Murders of Boysie Singh,* but it has yet to be made). In 1963 came his third novel *Tropicana* which he must have been finishing off around the time that he began to work on Boysie Singh. *Tropicana* is set in Barbados where Bickerton lived for several years. He writes about its people and social arrangements with insight, lived familiarity and considerable sociocultural knowledge. The language and feelings of both his White and Black Barbadian characters are represented convincingly and, in the latter case, without condescension.

Bickerton was clearly fascinated with a continuing Trinidad characteristic, the popularity of gambling at every social level in Trinidad, and he took the trouble to find out about the main gambling games. He explains whappy, sebby-lebby (a dice game), all-fours,[14] the ring game and the vertical roulette Boysie set up when he went to the races, boat racing, stickfighting, and everything that was capable of being bet on. Such activities were at the heart of social life in and around the city and in towns and villages far from Port of Spain. Bickerton's descriptions of these activities bring the games and the players to life in ways especially interesting to Trinidadians who played them or witnessed them in the past.

There was probably more social, religious and cultural significance in gambling among the lower classes than either Bickerton or the participants could consciously articulate. The games we think of as profane are relics and fragments of the sacred. There has to be some significance to the stalking of the jack in all-fours and the excitement when he is cornered and hung (vengeance, justice, the cornering of the knave); and there can be little doubt that in addition to the magic numbers in "sebby-lebby", the rolling of the dice (bone, stone, grain, seed etc) is a relic of divination practices common in Africa and the East. In whappie, the relentless willing of designated cards to turn up when the player wants them must belong to some forgotten tradition of devotees summoning the gods by laying down gifts to secure an apparition. The cabalistic nature of the Chinese whe-whe is better understood if it is remembered that the game brought to the island by the Chinese in the mid-1800s was originally called "chinapoo", an oracle game like I-ching, and that Chinapoo is the name of the Chinese jumbie that is the symbolic figure of the game. What Bickerton's book sees clearly are the attempts by the disadvantaged to bring luck or chance into their lives as a rescuing force.

All the narrative gifts of a writer of thrillers and the insights of a novelist representing social and psychological realities are evident in *The Murders of Boysie Singh,* not least in the author's engagement with its phenomenal protagonist, a real, often inhuman and exasperatingly unknowable creature. But this is not a novel, and Bickerton affirms that he did his best to ensure that none of the persons and events in his book are fictional. Unfortunately, there is no listing of specific sources, and the absence of citations when crucial events are written up, as if by an eye-witness, can raise questions.[15] It appears, too, that Boysie's only son, Chuncie, was one of the main informants, but this is not acknowledged anywhere. We can only presume that Chuncie may have been the person who lent Bickerton his father's death-cell diary and annotated bible.[16]

Bickerton tells us that the story emerging from research and interviews in Trinidad was one "which I would never have had the nerve to write as a novel." He does, however, give his book some of the qualities of the most readable of novels. There is no lack of striking incidents and intriguing episodes. The main figure engages us in the way the central character in a novel holds a reader. Although the end of the story is known, the reader still has a what-happens-next appetite, since Bickerton releases the stories in Boysie's crowded life with dramatic skill, teasing the reader with little "cliff-edge" statements, inviting wonder over what the next chapter might hold. The ends of the chapters are written in such a way as to suggest that the book might have been published serially in a magazine or newspaper.

Like the English novelist Henry Fielding, whose ur-true-crime morality, *The Life and Death of Jonathan Wild, the Great* (1743) he refers to as an inspiration, Bickerton uses the convention of the omniscient narrator to set up the action and to offer commentary, and he does this with a fair amount of success. Sometimes though, he is a little too omniscient for his own good, and some of his potted comments on the ways and "psychologies" of Africans and Indians, for example, have a greater investment in differences than in similarities. This can lead to howlers such as his declaration that on the basis of "the facts" he has proposed about the different criminal patterns of Africans and Indians, "one could have prophesied that Trinidad's first successful gang would be composed of Africans and controlled by an Indian" (p. 233).[17]

At any rate, Bickerton is not quite correct in his assumptions about the nature of Boysie's gang. Boysie had henchmen who did his bidding, but there was no organisational structure. There was no mafia-type operation as the omniscient Bickerton theorises, contrary to the evidence that he himself provides. When Boysie lost most of his money in gambling and had to sell almost everything he had in order to win acquittal in "The Case of the Floating Corpse", the gang was finished. No money to pay salaries instantly meant no gang. With Boysie unable to be present as Chief Whip, and lacking in funds to be Paymaster, everything crashed.

It is lucky for us that Bickerton worked on his book at a time when there were people alive who knew Boysie well, either because they worked with him or had significant personal relations with him. There were many others who remembered the murder trials of 1950 and 1957 and some of the officials and characters in them. Many ordinary citizens had stories of the years (1947-1949) when Boysie carried on a fishing business in Cedros, and Bickerton heard accounts and rumours of Boysie's operation of "the chute". He also heard unbelievable tales about those frenzied days in the early months of 1950 when he was making "mas'" as a pirate *sans humanite* in the Gulf of Paria. Bickerton does his best to pick his way through the mass of conflicting "information" coming from different segments of the society, all of whom had their own obsessions. The Whites and the well-off looked down upon the upstart knave and saw him as a threat to order and property in the society. Aspiring Blacks felt that his doings would affect their progress and their being accepted in society – though many of them secretly agreed with the majority of the oppressed who saw Boysie – from a safe distance – as someone who was on their side, a cavalier rebel against all the forces that were keeping them down.

Bickerton conscientiously explains how he made decisions about what to include and what not to put in the book ("the highest common factor of agreed detail"), and what to include but with a warning. The process he describes is not foolproof, but as far as he was concerned, what he was recording was all true and any resemblance to fiction was purely coincidental. He may have been fooled or misled in some instances, but the facts presented are either reliably evidenced or are consistent with the nature of the man being written about.

Bickerton had the good fortune to get hold of the two now lost documents referred to above, the Bible and the diary. The bible is the one Boysie used in his prison reading and carried around when he operated as a preacher between 1952 and 1954. In this, Boysie highlighted passages that referred to the troubles he had seen and pointed to biblical figures like Job, Joseph and Jesus, with all of whom he identified – especially Job and Jesus. Bickerton also had in his hands the diary addressed to Chuncie that Boysie began to keep in the months before his execution. Among other tantalizing samples, Bickerton quotes these instructions to Chuncie: "Son, you will Put in the Life of P.O.S. Yankey days. Paricey [piracy] days. Preaching days. Glamour days. Fishing days. Fighting days. Prison days". Bickerton wrote the book that the son was expected to write about the life of the father.

iv. Loomat Say He See Boysie

This section looks at the commentary in calypso about the murder trials. Given the apparent nonexistence of court transcripts, the detailed reports in the printed newspapers of the day and the "newspapers in verse" are the main available records for any study of how Trinidad represented the life of Boysie Singh.

Not many people today remember the bloody violence of the Christina Gardens murders carried out in the early 1970s by Abdul Malik (born Michael De Freitas, aka Michael X), fictionalised in V.S. Naipaul's *Guerrillas* (1975). Fewer still know much about Boysie Singh, but it is not true to say, as Bickerton does, that "his crimes had received surprisingly little publicity, considering their variety and their remarkable nature".

The name of Boysie Singh spread sensationally to all the towns and villages of Trinidad in the 1950s because of the two murders for which he was tried. The trials were covered every day in great detail by two daily newspapers and an evening tabloid from which Bickerton drew extensively. The trials also generated calypsos that spread the word throughout the country. The calypsonians read the newspapers avidly and they listened to the voices of the man and woman in the street. They covered the news pithily from their own angles and with the insight of the folk.[18]

Bickerton shares some of this calypsonian spirit when after Philbert's body floated up between the boats anchored off the jetty of the Trinidad Yacht Club, he remarks on the arrival of the corpse in the club's yard, that this was "the only way in which he could ever have gained access to that select institution". Bickerton was undoubtedly alert to Trinidad's race, class and colour system – clinically set out in Edgar Mittelholzer's 1950 novel, *A Morning at the Office*.

When the first of three trials commenced at the Central Criminal Court (which was then situated in the Red House) on July 17,1950, the public gallery was packed, and Woodford Square overflowed with thousands who came just to be there to catch a glimpse of the accused parties and public figures going in and out. They gossiped, gambled and placed bets on the outcome. They brandished newspapers as text to comment on, to argue over and to prove their points. *The Port of Spain Gazette, The Evening News, and The Trinidad Guardian* were daily publishing long reports of each day's proceedings,[19] the *Guardian* using catchy subtitles and inserting photographs of the accused, the judge, the crown prosecutor and the outstanding criminal lawyers of the day.

With three trials of this case, the calypsonians had plenty to share. In the "Floating Corpse Murder Case", Viking sang about the guilty verdict, to which an unreliable state witness and the judge's biased summing up had contributed:

Not me who say, is the paper publish
So I had to read it from start to finish (Repeat)
I talking 'bout the floating corpse murder case
That cause a lot of gossip in the place
Yes, the case lasted long to please the public
But from the time Loomat talked I knew they get stick

The key witness for the prosecution was Loomat, a 14-year-old Indian associate of Boysie who had turned state witness. The first two lines of the chorus ran:

Loomat say he see Boysie
Don't blame the Judge and the Jury

The line, "Don't blame the Judge and the Jury" pointed to the instrumentality of Loomat. Viking sometimes varied it to "Tie the iron on Bumper body". As Bumper was a known homosexual, Viking also voiced a sexual innuendo:

Loomat say he see Boysie
Tie **he** iron on Bumper body

The calypso was not the official road march, but in the 1951 Carnival, wining and chipping revellers made it so, singing the chorus with less subtle variations that incorporated the sexually suggestive words "wood" and "battie".[20] One of the most interesting variations suggests a popular partiality for Boysie, and contempt for the other Port of Spain Indian who is reviled as a "coolie" and a liar.

Loomat say he see Boysie
Loomat is a liard Coolie

Boysie seems to have been told about the calypso while the trial was going on; at one point he told the Court, "Loomat say he see Boysie, but Boysie ain't see Loomat."

Loomat was in a triangular homosexual relationship with Bumper and one of the accused, John Durant. Stanza 4 of Viking's second Boysie calypso "Floating Corpse Acquittal" did some suggestive signifying on the affair:

Bumper, Loomat, and Durant were friends I know
Playing a game of kokioko [21]

For more than six months, the spectacle outside the Court and the dialogue and the drama inside it provided excitement for all classes in the society. The Whites, the Coloureds and the growing number of aspiring Blacks on the weary road to whiteness were anxious to see the end of public enemy number one. Some of the most idiosyncratic witnesses in the trial were members of the under-class fighting their own little wars of survival.

Then on July 25, 1951, after three trials stretching over the period July 17, 1950 to January 25, 1951, the Court of Appeal reversed the verdict of the lower Court and ordered that the accused be set free immediately. The respectable classes enhanced Boysie's sinister reputation by noising it about that the appeal court judges had been intimidated and/or bribed.

Viking was quick off the mark with "Floating Corpse Acquittal". He does not condemn the people's delight with the decision, but there were obvious questions. Since nobody had killed Bumper, Bumper must have killed himself: "They were innocent it can't be denied/ So the whole floating corpse was suicide". The rest of the song points to piquant elements in the case while the chorus and the closing lines of two of the stanzas repeat the conceit that this was not a murder case: "Bumper, Bumper, I wish you could hear me/ Bumper, Bumper why you throw yourself in the sea". Viking ends two of the stanzas with a supplementary refrain: "Bumper, you are greater than Houdini/Tying your own foot with iron below the sea", and "Bumper was trying out his stamina / To see how he could keep iron under water".

It was as a down-and-out and has-been that, in July 1956, Boysie was tried with Boland Ramkissoon for the murder and disappearance of Boland's common-law partner, Thelma Haynes. This trial lasted three weeks and the accused were found guilty on February 25, 1957. They were hanged on August 20, 1957. Once again, the *Guardian* reported the trial every day and in full, this time as "The Case of the Missing Dancer". The calypsonians chimed in.

Although Thelma's body was never found, Boland and Boysie were doomed. They had loudly borne witness against each other in the police station; there were several eye-witnesses as well as evidence of their being together on the day of the murder. Circumstantial evidence established that Thelma was murdered, everything indicated that Boysie and Boland were involved.

Before the trial ended, Lord Eisenhower sang: "Thelma was a Dancer", giving a resume of the matter before the court and identifying the accused as "That man Singh again" and "Ramkissoon from Ramkissoon Trace" who "Saved sixty-four lives but couldn't save Thelma" – alluding to the fact that Ramkissoon was a lifesaver on Maracas beach. He touches on the rumour that "Boland and Pappie" were trying a screw to get some money and had Thelma hidden safely in Venezuela. Eisenhower reports that Ramkissoon came to the police with dreams about where Thelma's body lay, "But he better dream good to get away". All this was presented as evidence at the trial. The calypso ends with Eisenhower awaiting the verdict. But it was Lord Melody with "The Thelma Haynes Story" who best read the signs of the times. The calypso begins by sounding the alarm to the neighbourhood with the repeated shriek, "Murder! Cold-blooded murder", and linking this murder with other crimes which were turning the island into "a dead man's territory". After consulting with his own seer-man grandfather, the singer is sceptical about the meanings of Ramkissoon's dreams and visions that only came to him "after she dead". The calypso closes with the sociologically apt outrage of his immigrant neighbour. "Heng dem" she declares, "Without a trial, I do not care". She is an immigrant woman as Thelma was, and she is now living in fear: "Before me husband dream similar/ I think I am going back to Grenada."

This time round, there were no significant stirrings in the crowd. They did not wonder how you could hang a man for murder when no body had been found. If anything, they rejoiced in the judgment passed on a pathetic and diseased man whose physical gifts and criminal network had shrivelled. He was now the Rajah who had no clothes.

v. "Fighting Days"

In his well-organised book, Bickerton lays out Boysie Singh's career in a chronological set of chapters that follow his life and career. The chapters, titled "The Early Days", and "Apprenticeship in Crime", describe many actual fights that Boysie engaged in during his childhood and teens, which he literally called his "Fighting Days". I could have stolen a subtitle from Seepersad Naipaul's *Gurudeva and Other Indian Tales* (1943) and called an account of the early years "The Making of a Badjohn".

In the diary Boysie kept in his last days in prison, "Fighting Days" is one of the topics he wanted his son Chuncie to include in a biography. The examination of fighting as a cultural practice offers interesting insights into social continuities deriving from a history of brutality during slavery and indentureship, and the circumstance of peoples struggling (sometimes against one another, like the proverbial crabs in a barrel) to survive and grow in pressing circumstances. "Fighting" has resounding application to Boysie Singh, a combative and striving character, longing to be visible, from his earliest days.

Bickerton's outline of the terrain in which Boysie grew up between 1908 and 1932 is effectively done. In those days, there was still a beach (Crows Beach) and wetlands at the end of the Seigert streets, and Wrightson Road was a single-lane coastal road running from the foot of Charles Street to the sewerage pumping station at Mucurapo. He mentions Boysie's crab-catching in the swampy land at the bottom of Rosalino and Luis Streets and in the mangroves that stretched west to the pumping station, reporting that Boysie boosted his income by stealing crabs from other boys' traps. He describes others of Boysie's activities: kite-flying near the pumping station; pitching marbles for gain; liming with "bad company" and making the transition from marbles to dice; bullying and intimidating; and convictions for disorderly behaviour and obstruction (resisting arrest?).

Boysie mauls a schoolmate; he beats back an attack from five of the boys in his Woodbrook circle whose crabs he used to steal; he fights repeatedly with an older boy for "leadership" of the informal Woodbrook gang. Bickerton describes Boysie and Harris Timson engaging in a series of drawn encounters, the first of which was sparked by an argument over a game of dice. In addition to Bickerton's account, there is a more awed memory of these fights in "Boysie Wanted To Be A Boss", a feature article in the *Trinidad Guardian* of 4 August 1957, by Lenn Chongsing. Chongsing's article is based upon "facts" supplied by a boyhood friend and later key associate of Boysie Singh.

According to Chongsing, Boysie's reputation as a fighter started in a cow yard at Luis Street. This cow yard was "a communal cow pen, an open space used also for weddings and other celebrations among the East Indians living on the street." Bickerton discusses the fighting between Timson and Boysie, but does not mention a cow yard or communal space. He does record, without elaboration, that Boysie's mother kept cows to supplement the family income.

According to Chongsing, a regular dice game was run in the cow yard "by the only Negro there, a man called Harris", who had a leader's authority over those who took part in the game. Although younger and smaller than Harris, Boysie clashed with him often, because "Boysie wanted to be boss, an early trait". According to Chongsing, an old habitué of the cow yard told him: "He was a hell of a fighter, ... He always used to get beaten by Harris. People used to be sending for the Police everyday. It was a hell of a thing between the two of them. He fight Harris until one day he beat him". There is a story that after this fight, Boysie spent some time with the Peru brothers in St. James, after which he returned to San Juan.

Closely connected with "fighting" was "licks" or strokes which you could get from the police (the boy Boysie was sentenced to six official strokes with a tamarind rod at least twice). At school you got detention, and if you got a certain number of detentions you qualified for licks. You also got licks from a marauding dean of discipline for being "duncie" or disorderly. At home, you could get licks for an offence committed at home and as a punishment for getting licks at school. Bickerton's reference to the brutalization that getting licks at home sometimes involved misses the ordered varieties and the levels of severity of corporal punishment dealt out at home. As recorded in note 11 below, Bickerton's gratuitous attempt to specify how licks happened in Indian homes is so misinformed that it is offensive.

Boysie lived the whole cluster of terms relating to violence against the person in his early Woodbrook days. As noted above, fighting, and a series of convictions for petty thefts, gambling, and violent behaviours were giving him a much desired reputation as a badjohn. An armed attempt to steal a purse from an old man sleeping on a verandah at a house in or near Rosalino Street signalled that the apprentice days were over. He was charged with assault with intent to rob, and he was sentenced to four years hard labour on the prison island of Carrera, a finishing school from which the badjohn graduated in 1930. Fighting led to Boysie's first known killing and to the formal commencement of his career as a criminal in Port of Spain. Bickerton does not supply sources for his account of the clash between Boysie and a man called David Leach, but the main elements are supported by Chongsing's "Boysie Wanted to be a Boss".[22]

In 1932, Woodbrook boys went to town for Carnival. They were ambushed by a Port of Spain gang led by a whore-master and gambling operator called David Leach. Leach was waiting to fix up Boysie, because Boysie had been sleeping with one of Leach's girls, an Indian called Popo, without paying. The Woodbrook boys scattered and the Port of Spain boys found and savaged a straggler who happened to be a relative of Boysie. Although Boysie's arm had been put in a sling at hospital as a result of the ambush, he decided that the time had come to put a good beating on Leach. He left his hospital bed and went home where he disguised himself in kurtah and dhoti as an Indian beggar. His two companions lured Leach into the street whereupon Boysie sprang at him from his hiding place. He was armed with his talismanic "Three Little Trees", a stick mounted by an obeah man. He put such a savage beating on Leach that he died of his injuries a few days later. Boysie's doctor confirmed that Boysie was not in a condition do what had been done to Leach and no witnesses dared to come forward. It was his first murder.

The Woodbrook out of which Boysie drifted to begin his criminal career in 1932 had been a 348-acre sugarcane estate purchased from the William Burnley Company in 1899 by the prospering children of the Siegert family. The brothers had crossed over from the small town of Angostura in Venezuela with their father's formula and had been producing Angostura bitters in Trinidad since 1875. The Seigerts moved quickly to level the estate and develop it as a residential area. They laid out eight streets running south from the general area of Tragarete Road down towards the seashore. The streets were named after members of the Seigert family, beginning with Carlos Street immediately west of Murray Street and continuing to Petra Street near to today's Audrey Jeffers highway. In 1911, the Woodbrook development was sold to the Crown, after which the Town Board made regulations that restricted the inflow of the lower classes who were being flushed out by slum clearances elsewhere in the city. This deliberate exclusion enabled the settlement to achieve a lower middle-class to middle-class identity very quickly.[23]

Bickerton gives the Capildeo house at 17 Luis Street as the birthplace of Boysie Singh. This house was purchased by V.S. Naipaul's grandmother Soogie Capildeo Maharaj in 1936, and Savi Naipaul Akal says in *The Naipauls of Nepaul Street* that the house had a "tricky" reputation and that its previous owners were members of Boysie Singh's family. She does not give the name of the previous owner nor does she say that Boysie was born there. Vidia Naipaul came with his parents to live in 17 Luis Street around 1938. Naipaul turned Luis Street into the Miguel Street of his 1959 short story collection *Miguel Street*. It would be a striking coincidence if the greatest Trinidadian writer and the greatest Trinidad gangster lived at different times in 17 Luis Street. But there is some uncertainty about Boysie Singh's exact birthplace, so we must settle for there being a Woodbrook association of some sort between the two.

vi. Big Orchestra was Playing

There is no uncertainty about a fabulous social event in Woodbrook – Boysie's wedding in 1941. It was held at 13, Rosalino Street where Boysie had been living since 1932, if not before. At the time Boysie was operating three or four gambling clubs and taking part in all-fours competitions all over the country, winning tournaments, winning bets on results, making contacts for recruiting young Indian girls for his brothels, and in general living up to his growing notoriety. Things were going well for him. He was a man with a good income; he was therefore in need of a wife.

The wedding came about because a friend called Tinsingh,[24] who was managing the Sunrise Club for Boysie, was planning to get married to a Roman Catholic girl. Boysie had been in a relationship with Doris, an Afro-Trinidadian from Toco, since 1938. On impulse, he decided to be officially joined with Doris on the same day that Tinsingh was taking his bride. The wedding took place on July 27, 1941 and it made news. The light-skinned members of the church choir swallowed their revulsion and obediently sang for Boysie and Tinsingh.

Bickerton's account of the grandeur of the wedding does not include the fact that in addition to John 'Buddy' Williams's band (Trinidad's best) who played on the first two nights of the week-long party, there was an Indian orchestra from British Guiana. Bickerton gives a fine description of an event that Boysie hoped would give him respectability and social standing. It was held in an RC Church, the Rosary Church in Port of Spain on the corner of Park and Charlotte Streets and, according to Bickerton, the wedding party arrived in fifty-six cars and "a hundred and sixty odd cars" lined Rosalino Street for the reception. Significant for future business was that many American soldiers from nearby Docksite were allowed to join in the celebrations and expressed amazement at the splendour of the fete. "Rich Man, Poor Man", Lord Brynner's calypso of 1976 summed it up:

Rich man had a wedding/ High society wedding
He invited the Governor/ And all he spend was twenty dollar

But the poor man had a wedding/ Big expensive wedding
One hundred motor car/ And he spend a thousand dollar

Chorus

Rich man, poor man
Who says I'm a poor man
I have plenty dough
And I spreading joy for so.

vii. The Weary Road to Doris

When Boysie's unnamed mother died in March 1932, he was on the Woodbrook seashore selecting mangrove wood to make fishpots. Bickerton reports (p. 61) that the hardened 24-year-old Boysie "covered his face with his hands and said 'I've got no money – no work – and now God take my mother too'." His father had died around 1926. As a baby, Boysie had been wet-nursed by an Indian lady at 15 Luis Street, and since his mother had to go to work, it was his sister, older by eighteen years, who more or less mothered him. Boysie may have loved his mother and he showed deference to his older sister, but this did not make him have any respect for women.

It did not stop him from running brothels, though he made sure by his brass-knuckled presence that prostitutes in his establishments were not physically abused or cheated. Like a slave-owner or animal farmer , he took care of the stock. From time to time he selected one of the girls for personal use.

The Murders of Boysie Singh does not attempt to examine Boysie's relationships with women, but it gives enough information to make us wish Bickerton had focused more on the subject. The first association was with an Indian girl called Rosie from the orphanage (Belmont or Tacarigua) whom he picked up in 1926. For some reason he could not take her home, "either to his mother's or sister's house" and they could only have sex in the bush at the bottom of Luis and Alberto Streets. The connection did not last long. The orphan Rosie comes and then goes. How many more Rosie's were there in those days? After Rosie, Boysie met another Indian called Mana Lala who apparently used to sell in the market. But within a year, Boysie was taken away to serve his four years in prison at Carrera. When he returned in 1930, Mana Lala was still around, waiting for him, and on April 15, 1931, she gave birth to Boysie's only child, a boy, Anthony, who came to be known as Chuncie (a term of endearment, usually for a chubby, "choonksie" child). Then Boysie drifted into Port of Spain in 1932, leaving Mana Lala behind.

Mana Lala was not active in Boysie's life after he went to Port of Spain, but some kind of relationship continued. There is a *Trinidad Guardian* photograph of August 20, 1957, the day of the execution, showing Mana Lala and an unidentified woman going to pay a final visit to Boysie in the Royal Jail.[25]

Anthony Singh (centre without hat)... stands outside the Royal Gaol yesterday for the last visit to his father, Boysie Singh, who will be hanged this morning. ... In picture at left, Anthony Singh's mother is assisted by an unidentified woman as she walks into the Royal Jail to see Boysie for the last time.

Chuncie stayed in contact with his mother, presumably with Boysie's approval. By 1950, the young man had developed a routine of spending the eve of his birthday with Mana Lala. At least, this is what he testified in the first Bumper trial: Boysie could not have used his jitney on the night of April 14 to take Bumper to his death in Cocorite because he (Chuncie) had the jitney and had used it to go to his mother where he ate roti rather than ice cream and cake. The vehicle was parked outside her place all night.

There is as yet no documentation of the presence of young Indian women in and around Port of Spain in the 1930s and 1940s, and little serious or informed speculation. More immediately relevant to Bickerton's project, however, is that knowing more about Mana Lala and Popo, and finding out from them what it was like to be with Boysie would have added significantly to our knowledge and understanding of this impenetrable being.

Chuncie was the author's main informant. If Mana Lala was dead when Bickerton spent time in Trinidad collecting information, Chuncie would have been able to tell him things about this faithful woman. Did Boysie just pick up and leave her without a word? What might she have said to Chuncie about "your father"? If she was still alive in 1960, Chuncie would have been able to introduce Bickerton to her. There was also Boysie's oldest sister who was still alive in 1957, and whose name at least Chuncie might have been able to supply. Chuncie might also have been able to say more about the sister who Bickerton mentions as being four years old when Boysie was born.

Bickerton reports that the Indian prostitute, Popo, took care of Chuncie and lived with Boysie at 59 Prince Street from 1932 to 1938. He doesn't go into how this arrangement came about, but in the article "Boysie Wanted to be Boss", Lenn Chongsing says that Popo "gave him a start when she staked him to his first gambling shop after he drifted out of Woodbrook".[26] It was Boysie's relationship with Popo that had led to the battle with Leach the brothel-keeper, and to Boysie's setting up of a base in Port of Spain in 1932 in the first instance.

The Murders of Boysie Singh tells a little of Popo's story but it does not wonder where she came from or where she went when she fled from Boysie in 1938. Did she follow "The Case of the Missing Dancer" in the papers? Was she among the spectators outside the Royal Jail when he was hanged? How did she begin in prostitution? To what extent was she a "free agent", not amenable to any form of arranged marriage or any of the controls of the Indian family or community from whom she had cut herself off? What we do know invites speculation. Boysie accused Popo of ill-treating Chuncie, Mana Lala's son. Was Popo bitter that Chuncie was everything to Boysie and that after six years with him there were no children? Was she less and less there for Chuncie because she had resumed her profession? Did they quarrel about who gave who gonorrhoea? Did she remind Boysie that she had given him her earnings to make a start in his gambling business?

Bickerton relates factually that when Boysie fell in with Doris in 1938, he decided to murder Popo. The zwill-wielding kite-flyer of Woodbrook put ground glass in a roti for Popo and when that did not finish her off, he tried with a smile to get her to swallow a capsule containing more ground glass to hasten her "recovery". Popo evidently knew the beast she was dealing with. As soon as she was able to move, she packed her bags and vanished. Twenty years later, Bickerton would have had to be ingenious and persistent if he wanted to find her. The starting point would have had to be Chuncie.

Popo's fate encapsulates Boysie's brutal and exploitative attitude to women, his ruthlessness, his sociopathic narcissism and the unpredictability not so much of his purposes, but of the capricious action he would take at any given time. It seems significant that the women he got involved with before Doris were Indian women who might have had some inclination to accept that a man was lord and master. Was Boysie so insecure about where he stood in the city at large that he had to bolster himself by dominating them? Did his contempt for them indicate a self- contempt that he covered over with bravado and display? It never crossed Boysie's mind to marry any of these women. In fact, he never thought of marrying anybody at all until it seemed to offer a way of giving him more visibility.

Doris wasn't backward. She moved into 59 Prince Street as soon as Popo departed. It is not impossible that she pushed Boysie to get rid of Popo. In his article "The Personal Life of Boysie Singh" (*Trinidad Guardian*, Thursday August 8, 1957), Lenn Chongsing provides more details about Doris than Bickerton had gathered. Doris was a buxom "Creole", part African, part Spanish, with "a big head of hair". In time, Chongsing writes, " her teeth glittered with gold". Doris was different. She was not a passive woman. She had come from Toco and was a servant in Woodbrook. If she missed the breathtaking countryside and the sea, she wasn't ready to go back as some of her friends had done.

Bickerton asserts that the period from 1938-1941, before the arrival of the Americans, was "perhaps the most peaceful in Boysie's life". In these years, he intimates, Boysie didn't go roaming in search of sex or trouble, but stayed home with Doris and Chuncie in the evenings talking, or listening to the wireless. Boysie Singh spending quality time with his child and his new woman is hard to imagine, but we have no grounds for challenging Bickerton's claim that this was "the nearest to domesticity that he ever came" (p. 76). If we believe Chongsing's account, however, things were different once the wedding came. Chongsing's article is based upon "facts" told to him by Tinsingh.

As described above, Boysie's wedding was a lavish one, a showy grab for visibility. Whilst he did not wish to be White and he had contempt for the respectable (many of whom visited his clubs surreptitiously), there is no doubt that he wanted them to see him.

Boysie agreed to abide by the conditions imposed when a Roman Catholic marries a non-Catholic, but, on the day before the wedding he petulantly declared that he was not going to go through with any ceremony. All he would do was be a guest at Tinsingh's wedding. Chongsing relates that before the wedding, Boysie told Doris that he intended to leave Chuncie all that he owned before marrying her. Because Doris did not give the answer he wanted, he called off the wedding , accusing her of wanting to marry him for his money. On what was now just Tinsingh's wedding day, however, Doris turned up with an unnamed companion. Boysie changed his mind.

Chongsing quotes Tinsingh as follows: "She come in a car with a man... I call Boysie. She was dress in short white dress and round white topee hat. Boysie come and he hook her and walk right back in the church. So he get married." We don't know who was the man accompanying Doris.

Of the honeymoon, Chongsing writes: "Doris Singh did not have an ordinary honeymoon, and she barely escaped being his first floating corpse victim, five days after the wedding." On the road back from Stauble's Bay, Boysie ordered the driver to stop the Buick. He stood on the edge of the road at the cliff top and invited the others to make use of what he warned them would be the last stop before the long drive to Port of Spain. When this transparent strategem failed, he dragged open the back door of the car and grabbed his bride. "You are a dangerous woman. You don't want me. You want me money," raged the operator of the nefarious chute. "I going to throw you overboard." The driver and Tinsingh held him down till he stopped raving. Back in civilization, Boysie went to his club, and that night Doris headed out for Toco. It was six months before Boysie decided he wanted her back.

A delegation went to Toco in the Buick to negotiate Doris's return. Doris's two sisters came to live with the reconciled couple. When 13 Rosalino Street was sold in 1946 – before the move to 192 Western Main Road in Cocorite (sisters and all) – the deed showed that the owners of 13 Rosalino Street were B. Singh and D. De Leon. It may well be that Doris De Leon laid down certain terms and conditions before agreeing to come back from Toco.

That Boysie went to bring Doris back from Toco after six months of separation suggests that there was something about her that held him. One or two references to her leaving him in 1950 suggest regret. In his death cell diary, he wrote appreciatively: "She was a very good wife to me. If I had taken her Advice I would Be a better man... my wife told me that if I leave the life I am living and my Friends, and live a better life I will be a better man. And she said if I sick she will Work and mind me." (p. 220). Doris was evidently different from the line of Indian women who preceded her in her ready assumption of the freedom to be explicit about her thoughts and feelings. For the first time Boysie had become involved with a woman who would not bend to his will as a matter of course. His stress about getting married and getting married to an African would have been aggravated by the suspicion that supposedly comes to men who are about to marry women who have no money and want money. Doris's account of her life with Boysie would have been a valuable addition to Bickerton's book.

Boysie's personal and ethnic uncertainties show in Tinsingh's reproduction of four sentences Boysie blurted out that evening as he tussled with Doris: " I am an Indian. What you want me for? You don't want me. You want me money".

viii. I am an Indian. What you want me for?

According to Bickerton, Boysie's father, Bhagrang Singh was a Chatri from the Punjab who served in the Indian army and brought with him "a cavalry sabre, its fine steel scarcely rusted by a century in the tropics, its hilt wrought into the shape of a falcon's head with red stones for eyes." The sword seems to have had some supernatural or religious significance for Bhagrang: "On a certain day each year it was his custom to pray over it." He was earning very little at the time of Boysie's birth; his mother was contributing to the family income by minding cows, selling Indian condiments by the wayside, and travelling to "Indian" areas, selling haberdashery and household items with boy Boysie in tow. The family lived in a part of Woodbrook around Luis Street which was apparently the focus of a small settlement of Indians. It was not far from Coolie Town (later St James) on the Western Main Road where Indians from the old Peru Estate had been settling since the 1860s.

There would have been a certain amount of "Indianness" in Boysie's childhood environment but, on the surface at any rate, little seems to have stuck. When the unorthodox Bhagrang Singh was approaching death, he instructed his family that his sabre should be thrown into the sea. On no account should it be kept or sold: "There were no people left, he said, who understood the old things; he feared that the sword would fall into evil hands and be used to commit acts of violence" (p. 59). Among the "no people left ... who understood the old things" were his children, who did not honour the patriarch's dying wish. Boysie was eighteen years old. Aware of the violence his son had already espoused, was Bhagrang anxious for the sword not to fall into Boysie's hands?

The Woodbrook-born Boysie can be described as one of the Port of Spain Indians who knew next to nothing about any Indian religion. The criminal associates with whom he interacted at his base in downtown Port of Spain were drawn from all the island's ethnic groups and included immigrants from neighbouring islands. For all practical purposes, there was a working acceptance by the Trinidadians around him that he was one of them, a Trinidadian, not a "small islander" or an Indian. Terms and concepts like "Indo-Trinidadian ", or "Creole" or "creolized Indian" were not part of their apparatus. They were familiar enough with "coolie" and with the associated stereotypes, but those who were familiar with Boysie's ways were not moved to apply the term to him. This seemed to be good enough for the aggressive and crooked entrepreneur to live with.

As noted above, the Indians and Africans in Boysie's Port of Spain were at the bottom of the social scale, whether barrack-yard dwellers or people without fixed abodes. They were gamblers, prostitutes, thieves, schemers, casual labourers and convenient spare parts, some of whom fitted more or less regularly into Boysie's operations. A select few graduated to being permanent members of his organization. In these circumstances, to contradict Bickerton, Boysie's "gang" could only have been multi-ethnic. An Indian gang member called Rammie, who was sent to San Juan to deal with Joseph Maynard alias "Bam Bam", shot Bam Bam in the face, and took a five year jail term without incriminating the boss. An African called Bamboozie also known as Guangosir, who worked with Boysie for many years, including the Cedros years, would have done the same.

Writing in the early 1960s, and with a predisposition to analyse, Bickerton had learned what he could about Indians in general, including rural Indians, and he was quite aware that there were Indians, especially in downtown Port of Spain, who did not conform to the social arrangements and systems of self-regulation from India that were only partly functional in Trinidad. He generalized, nevertheless, that Indians who had moved to the city "became, as they say in Trinidad, 'creolised' – that is to say they abandoned their religious beliefs and with them a large part of their customs... in their attempt to appear, in manners, dress, and possessions, as Western as they could" (p. 58). But people like Boysie and Loomat had little or no Indian culture to abandon. Bickerton's unsubtle theory of Indian creolisation seems to be more applicable to aspiring middle-class Indians in general than to the lower-class Indians in downtown Port of Spain. Their "creolisation" or mixing came from their proximity to lower-class urban Blacks. The calypsonian Atilla the Hun reproduces in his book, *Atilla's Kaiso*, a calypso by Killer, "What's Wrong With These Indian People", that describes some of the changes taking place among lower-class Indians in the city, more so among the women who adopt Western names, go to dances, and can be seen "fighting in the road for their Yankee man" or pushing through the crowd surrounding the butcher to buy their piece of pork.[26]

There are shortcomings in its account of Indians in general that can give offence, but *The Murders of Boysie Singh* does document the different existence of lower-class Port of Spain Indians (and perhaps a handful of others, trafficking with downtown Port of Spain from their bases in San Juan, St James, and Woodbrook). The Indians at this level were different as regards occupations, and in their un-traditional attitudes to family, sexuality and religion. The lost Loomat and the hysterical Boland Ramkissoon, who succumbed to the call of American evangelicalism, are particular instances of deracinated Indians.[27]

The case of Boysie Singh is more subtle and surprising. Throughout the book, Bickerton keeps trying to pin down his man by inserting interpretations and anticipations. In Chapter 29, "Portrait of a Murderer", he works at summing him up. He puts Boysie on the winners' podium as one of the highest-scoring murderers in the world, tries to work out exactly in what category of murderer Boysie might be placed, and then, vain task, he seeks to explain the man. But it is notable that although Bickerton says a lot about Indians in Trinidad and in the city, his subject's Indianness does not come into any of his attempts to explain Boysie.

On his visit to Boysie's unmarked grave (Chapter 30), he is still wondering what kind of man Boysie had really been. He fixes on the words of Boysie's son Chuncie as a possible epitaph: "He was not a man like you or I", casting an ambiguous light on all the plausible solutions to the mystery of Boysie Singh that he himself had proposed. This retreat brings him and the reader back to the words of a *Guardian* Staff Reporter David Renwick. After listing the many faces of Boysie Singh and referring to many versions of the story of Boysie Singh, Renwick escapes into existential despair: "Will the truth of Boysie Singh ever be known? I doubt it: you see there is no truth."[28] In this article, Renwick also reports, without comment, what Boysie's sister felt at the time of his marriage to Doris: "He leave the Hindu people, then he come Catholic for the wedding." Boysie's interest in Catholicism was in part at least a function of his wish to be seen by the other world – the high society of White Creoles and the respectable classes. Doris's Catholicism may have influenced him(in spite of the Hinduism of his family) to make a surrender to Roman Catholicism at the end of his life.

Boysie Singh was a Port of Spain "badjohn", listed in Sparrow's calypso "Badjohns" along with Mastifay, Fire Kong and other distinguished members of the pantheon. It is interesting to note, however, that young Boysie Singh had all the traits and motivations of the Indian village badjohn that, in 1943, Seepersad Naipaul ascribes to Gurudeva in his short story of that name. Gurudeva appoints himself leader of the young men in the village who must defend the village's honour against other villages. He is obsessed with a craving for fame. He is inspired by the praise-songs of old Jaimungal recalling the exploits of dead and gone bad-Johns:

> Now, at twenty-two, his whole ambition was to be noticed. It was not enough that he had made his presence felt and feared in the house. It was not enough that his father, his mother, his two elder brothers and their wives stood in awe of him. He wanted to be looked upon with awe by the whole village. He hankered to be popular but he wanted to be popular in a spectacular way. He wanted people to point at him and whisper, "See that fellow going there? He is Gurudeva the bad-John!" [29]

When Gurudeva is sentenced to twelve months in jail for wounding old Sookwah and a policeman, he tells the magistrate in true badjohn style "'Wait until I come back'. To his sad father, the puffed out chest of Gurudeva declares: 'Is orright, Bap, I is a man.'" In Woodbrook, Boysie Singh was a badjohn like Gurudeva, belonging to a tradition of badjohnism among Indians in Trinidad that was in existence since the middle of the nineteenth century.

But the badjohn leader of the Woodbrook Boys started off as an unknown

Indian in Creole Port of Spain. Extravagant criminal activities, casual violence, and eruptions of coldblooded and reckless actions were the self-assertion of an outsider determined to be seen and felt. In this phase of manufacturing a self and making an impression, he took on many roles and wore many masks. At 55 Queen Street, he kept brass knuckles and a mounted poui stick for keeping order; at the height of his fame he had dozens of suits and shoes for going out; on special occasions he wore the extravagant accoutrements of the dandy or saga boy; and in the piracy days he wore black. He started off the first series of murder trials by wearing a different suit and tie each day. A number of significant occurrences suggest that behind the masks there was a reality the Indian in Port of Spain might not have realized he was effacing with intent. It is reasonable to infer, also, that behind the many role selves, there was no concept of a real or foundational self.

After parading in the streets as an Indian prince one Carnival, Boysie adopted the sobriquet "the Rajah", much as a calypsonian might call himself "Lord Kitchener", "Atilla the Hun" or "King Austin". Boysie was not making a conscious assertion of Indian identity when he chose to play "Indian Prince" in the Carnival, or when he took the name "Rajah" in real life. The mas' of the Rajah was a declaration of ambition, a marker of achievement, and an advertising of class. It is more than likely that "Rajah" came naturally to him as a synonym for Emperor or Czar or King. But that is the word that came, carrying something from a distant area of darkness that, it must be said, he never consciously acknowledged or tried to discover.

Yet he shared certain tastes with Indians. He took part in Hosay as a skilful stick-fighter, not indeed as someone caught up in a funeral ceremony, but as something he took part in with almost religious regularity. The "bad tribe of Indians" in San Juan who wanted to ambush him for associating with their enemies, the Peru brothers, knew where he could be found during the Aranguez Hosay festival.[30] It seems that Boysie Singh liked Indian music and singing. Before the 1939-1945 War he was often in the crowd at a place in San Juan called Noon's Hall where concerts and singing competitions were regularly held. It was at Noon's Hall that what Bickerton calls "The Feud With San Juan" began. It can be argued that this was not a feud, but a dance with natives of his person. The city mobster's stubborn preoccupation with San Juan may have had a deep origin and was perhaps an expression of a contorted sense of affinity.

Given Boysie's urge to be boss, it as inevitable that he would get into an argument with Mano Das, the leader of San Juan Indians. Boysie wanted to be regarded as the leader of the Indians! The competition with Mano Das took the form of a dispute about who was the best singer in a particular competition, and it led to a fight that had to be broken up by the police. Boysie's reaction to the unfinished encounter was to advertise his power to the hard-working Indian farmers of San Juan. He went to the

Port of Spain market where they brought their produce and he and his toughs inflicted heavy beatings on them. The donkey-carts bringing San Juan produce to the market had to stop making the dangerous journey. Thus provoked, Mano Das went to town to finish the fight with Boysie Singh. To Boysie, victory over Mano Das meant that San Juan Indians now knew who was man. The embargo on the farmers was lifted. But this brought no peace.

As city Indian could not leave San Juan alone, and San Juan folk could not forget a displaced icon. In his youth he had helped with the cows and even toted manure on his head. Was there something about the hard-working Indian farmers that stirred him against his will? We can't know. The simmering tensions flared up again during the War when Boysie thought San Juan was his space to set up whe-whe stations and to pursue amorous activities as he pleased. He started sleeping and eating at the house of Zena and Rosie, two Indian girls belonging to San Juan and, it seems, to the San Juan gang, until Boysie came. "One afternoon", Bickerton writes, "when Boysie was in bed with one or both of the sisters" the San Juan boys surrounded the house, rained stones on it, and waited with sticks to finish him off once and for all. The brawny dodger fought his way out and, ever ready to summon the law to his aid, came back with a police escort.

By 1946, the house at 13 Rosalino Street had been sold and Doris and her two sisters had moved to 192 Western Main Road, Cocorite. For most of 1947-50, Boysie divided his time between Cedros (fishing and the transporting of would-be immigrants to Venezuela), Port of Spain (the Dorset Club and gangster operations), and Cocorite (the base of the pirate activities of 1950). Doris left him in 1950 as soon as he was charged with the murder of Bumper.[31] From jail he instructed Chuncie to sell 192 Western Main Road and thenceforth his address became Bridge Road, San Juan. It was a neighbourhood where his sister, his niece and other relatives, Mana Lala, and Indian friends of the old days lived.

Boysie did not regress into Indianness. But the Creole world he had entered so brashly and conquered with such cold-blooded efficiency did not finally take him in. After the Bumper acquittal, he had no money. His gang members had long deserted the leaking pirogue. He was in and out of hospital suffering from diabetes. His gonorrhoea was well advanced. The Port of Spain world he had bossed in the War years offered him none of the comforts and memories of a loved place. His clubs had been shut down and his cronies had moved off. He may have thought, in the prosperous times, that marriage to Doris would cement his standing as a Creole. But her abandoning of him in 1950 seems to have added to the depression that came with the shutting down of his clubs, desertion by lady luck, and the failing of his instincts as a gambler. The Boysie magic was gone, his revels ended, the Creole world he ruled had faded. He had already learnt from his experience with the Syrian gamblers that there was no way of breaking into the world of the Whites and the well-to-do.

He had nowhere to turn but to the Indian people with whom, without thinking about it, he had once experienced the sense of being a natural part of an entity larger than himself. In his last weeks, before being held for the murder of Thelma Haynes, Boysie was being taken care of at the home of Mrs Jagroop Ramsumair of 84 Eastern Main Road, Arouca. Boysie gifted expensive jewellery to Mrs Ramsumair and bought dresses for her four daughters. Interviewed by *Trinidad Guardian* reporter David Renwick,[32] Mrs Ramsumair spoke of Boysie as if he was her best friend. Two photographs of Boysie's last devoted Indian friend appeared in Renwick's *Trinidad Guardian* articles, one with her clutching a framed photo of Boysie, in his saga boy outfit, and the other with her daughter stringing around her neck the solid gold chain given to her by Boysie.[33] During their investigations connected with the murder of Thelma Haynes, the police came to Mrs Ramsumair's house with a search warrant and found personal items belonging to Thelma Haynes. They also found Boysie's wardrobe of ten suits, five ties and six pairs of pants. It was the nearest he would get to home in the years of despair .

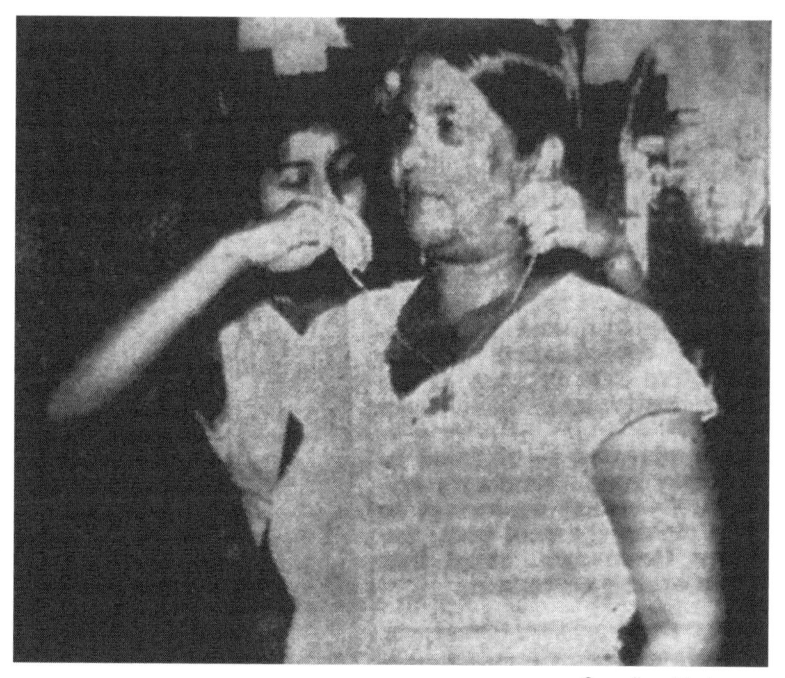

Guardian Photonews

BOYSIE THE BENEFICIENT... here is evidence of it. This expensive gold chain, inset with a precious stone, was given to Mrs. Jagroop Ramsumair by Boysie "as a gift one morning." Her daughter strings it around her neck. Still in Mrs. Ramsumair's house in Arouca (where, incidentally, Thelma Hayne's jewelry was found): Boysie's entire wardrobe of 10 suits, five ties and six pairs of pants.

Guardian Photonews

Mrs. Jagroop Ramsumair stands in her yard at Arouca and holds aloft a picture of the dandy Singh. It is her prize possession, depicting Boysie in the Cab Calloway outfit he entranced the crowds with one races day. It shares pride of place alongside others of Dalip Singh [a Trinidadian wife murderer] and Mahatma Ghandi [sic].

In V.S. Naipaul's *A Bend in the River* (1979), Indar presses his fellow Asian Salim to free himself from a crippling allegiance to family and ancestral traditions. It is necessary to trample on the past, Indar stresses, to escape from a sense of inferiority and the sense of being fated to be a loser that was inflicted by long subjugation to "superior" nations. But Indar professes to understand the world and his possibilities in it: "I am tired of being on the losing side. I don't want to pass. I know exactly who I am and where I stand in the world. But now I want to win and win and win." Later in the novel, we find him a defeated and deflated man. The world did not allow him to win and win and win.

He withdraws from it. The simple idea comes to him that it is time to go home: "And that's how it has been with him. From time to time, that is all he knows, that it is time for him to go home. There is some dream village in his head."[34]

The Port of Spain Indian, too, wanted to win and win and win. His late association with San Juan and familiar bodies of Indian people suggests that the defeated adventurer wanted to go home. This was an instinctive reflex. It could not satisfy the longing that had come with his discovery that there was no accommodation for him as an eventual loser in the Creole world. The house in Arouca was like home for a few months, and San Juan may have comforted him in his misery, but there was nothing that could promise to deliver the dream village in his head.

Boysie's sermons and his theology during his preacher days may have been an expression of this tough man's longings. He drew upon Doris's Catholicism and his own readings in the Bible. His wayside meetings began with a prayer, the Litany of the Sacred Heart of Jesus. In the dreams and visions that came to him in his death cell, Jesus and the Virgin Mary figure largely. In the first page of his diary, written while awaiting execution, he tells his son that he used to "look through the iron bars in the cells and Pray to the virgin lady to take me to Jesus". While he was in No 10 cell he saw the sun rising, and "on the side of the sun was a block of mooroune [maroon] colour and Jesus was going into the block."

Not even in extremis was the son of Bhagrang Singh visited by a sound, colour, smell or image from the religion of his father. In his last days the forlorn Port of Spain Indian requested instruction in the Catholic faith, and was handed over to the prison chaplain. On the day before his execution he was officially received into the Catholic Church. As he walked in silence towards the hangman's rope next morning, only the prayers of the ever present Father Tiernan could be heard, commending Boysie's soul to the dream of a Holy Kingdom that trampled on the dream village in his head.

Endnotes

1. The Perry Henzell movie starred reggae singer Jimmy Cliff. The book based on the movie was written by Michael Thelwell and was first published by Grove Press in 1980.
2. Bickerton took the trouble to learn the rules and the playing practices of whe-whe, all the dice and card games, and other ways of gambling popular among the urban proletariat and the poor people of Trinidad. This preparation enhances the social and cultural significance of the book. His descriptions evoke actual games and the actions and emotions surrounding the business and rituals of gambling. He also describes the war-like kite-flying of the period and evidently found out about the different techniques and kinds of fishing practiced by Trinidad fishermen.

3. Like Boysie, Bhadase Sagan Maraj, made money off the Americans during the war. He rose from petty village gangsterism between Hindus and Muslims to become a towering and influential figure in the Hindu community through trade unionism, and religious and political leadership – until brought low by drug addiction. Through the Sanathan Dharam Mahasabha which he founded in 1952, Maraj made an outstanding contribution to the provision of education to descendants of Indians in Trinidad. Unlike Boysie, he became leader of a political party in the island and at the Federal level. In Hugh Robertson's film *Bim* (1974), written by Raoul Pantin, some of the scenes involving the young Indian Bhim Singh in the clubs and brothels of downtown Port of Spain could have come out of Boysie's milieu. When Bhim has to leave the city because the police are after him, he goes to Cedros and lives as a fisherman in Icacos, a move that is similar to Boysie Singh's shift to Cedros in the late 1940s. The character of Bhim in the movie resembles a composite of Boysie Singh and Bhadase Sagan Maraj.
4. A badjohn is a person who uses violence or the threat of violence to intimidate a community or individuals into giving him recognition and paying deference. He acts with impunity, takes people's goods and possessions as tributes, and considers himself exempt from making payments for goods and services. This is how he satisfies his wish to be seen and respected in his community. The known history of badjohnism is quite long, and there are two ethnic streams that converge in the 1940s and 1950s. One stream has its origins in the Black barrackyards, and it is from this stream that the word badjohn came into being. The term was first used to refer to a Barbadian, John Archer, who came to Trinidad from Barbados via Panama in 1887. When he died in 1916, he had 119 convictions in the magistrates courts to his name. A detailed summary of Archer's life and behaviours can be found in Kim Johnson, 'How Badjohn Became a Word' http://massassination.blogspot.com/2010/03/legend-of-bad-john. html#axzz2bmKiSQmx. The other stream, which was to lead to the Poolool Brothers and Dole Chadee, to name the most famous, is connected with largely unacknowledged traditions of obscenity, rum-drinking, violence, and other lawless behaviours among Indians no longer subject to the forced discipline of indentureship. In Chapter 2 of his doctoral dissertation *The Hidden History of Trinidad: Underground Culture in Trinidad 1870-1970* (2007), Raymond Ramcharitar describes badjohnism and other lawless, violent and subversive behaviour in the Indian "underground". He cites newspaper articles from the *Port of Spain Gazette*, including April 18, 1890, 'Capture of the Desperado Macoon' (a badjohn gang leader) and August 15,1893, "Coolie Gambling House" in Port of Spain long before Boysie Singh's enterprise began. The early badjohns in both streams used cutlasses and Macoon had guns, but in general the early badjohns were stickmen and hand-to-hand fighters. This was to change by the 1940s when bottle and stone contests started to use guns, knives, cutlasses and bombs. One badjohn in a famous calypso made use of the same hammer that he used when tuning pans. Badjohns of both ethnicities had warrior roles in the steelband clashes with one another and with the police. A flavour of the activities of badjohns is given in Sparrow's "Ten to One is Murder", and famous badjohns are named in the same singer's "Badjohns", which lists Boysie Singh and Boysie's henchman Fire Kong.
5. A saga boy is not so much a gigolo as a (normally) good-looking man

who is kept by a woman who fits him out with clothes, shoes, jewellery etc . This brands him as her man and she will fight any woman who trespasses. As for the sweetman, if he is unfaithful he faces the wrath of his keeper, and dismissal. The sweetman appears in many calypsos. "Sweetman" by Alfred Mendes is the most spectacular short story about the phenomenon. At the climax, the offending sweetman is humiliated by his keeper who strips him of clothes and jewellery and all the other effects she had supplied to make him look good. The term has also come to be used for any man who dresses sharply in the latest style to strut his way into the eye and heart of women. The saga boy and his owner are sensuously represented and translated into figures of energy and desire in Peter Minshall's giant mobile puppets of 1990. For a discussion of Boysie Singh and "saga", see Harvey R. Neptune *Caliban and the Yankees* (2007), p.123-124.

6. The fishing industry in Cedros was controlled by the Ramjohn brothers Alfred, Bull, and Willie who were entrenched when Boysie arrived. Boysie innovated outrigging – a way of having more lines in the water than the Cedros fishermen had managed up to that point. This allowed him to bring in larger catches, as did the boldness with which he defied the Guardia Nacional and fished in Venezuelan waters. But he was no match for the Ramjohns, and he did not dominate the fishing as Bickerton suggests. There is a story that Bull Ramjohn went to Boysie's base in St Marie and threatened to expel Boysie if Boysie's Port of Spain crews, partly made up of thugs from the clubs, continued to harass the Ramjohn people. It was at this time that Boysie began operating his fatal ferry to Venezuela.
7. The question of the genuineness of Boysie's repentance has often been raised. Bickerton reports being told that Boysie would sometimes run a card game for gamblers at the preaching venue as soon as his prayer meeting was over. In an interview with a *Guardian* reporter, a self-satisfied Loomat sniggered that the prayer meetings were just a way to distract the police from his other shady activities. Boysie wrote intensely about God's mercy in his death-cell and was admitted into the Roman Catholic Church the day before his execution.
8. In the second half of the 20th century, radio evangelism from America began to sweep Caribbean and African countries. Many Pentecostal-type churches have been established and they continue to draw in Hindus and Christians from the more conventional churches. In their zeal to convert Indians such churches have tended to disparage Hinduism, but religion continues to be an area of undiscriminating coexistence in Trinidad.
9. *No Pain Like This Body* (Toronto: Anansi, 1972) *Yesterdays* (Toronto: Anansi, 1974).
10. See for example: *The Book of Trinidad* by Bridget Brereton and Gerard Besson (Paria Publishing Company, 2010); Michael Anthony, *The Making of Port of Spain* (two volumes, 1978 and 1985); and Stephen Stuempfle's monumental *Port of Spain: the Construction of a Caribbean City 1888-1962* (UWI Press, 2018).
11. See Boysie Singh, p. 58 where the brutal killing of a young girl is given as the traditional punishment for adultery imposed by the panchayat; and p. 52 where Bickerton states that it is the custom in many Indian families for the physical punishment of children to be left to mothers and that Boysie's mother used to beat him often with "that favourite West Indian instrument of chastisement , the bull's pizzle..." The latter

could inflict the most damaging wounds and was rarely found in domestic circumstances.

12. Jeremy Poynting, personal communication, August 2019.
13. Derek Bickerton (1926-2018) was a linguist who was interested in creole languages, and in the evolution, acquisition and development of language more generally. He is the originator of the famous bioprogram hypothesis for creole language genesis, which confers a special status on creole languages and their syntax by virtue of the fact that they are acquired under conditions of impoverished input. If creoles originate from pidgins, Bickerton reasoned, and if pidgins do not possess the full richness and complexity of structural patterning that fully fledged languages do, then how could creoles possibly arise? There is a gap here which, he argues, is filled in by the young human's developing cognitive intelligence and its predisposition for language. In other words, the child is simply incapable of acquiring just a pidgin, but internalizes instead something infinitely richer and more flexible, a fully formed language, the Creole. Because of their unique genesis and the short distance between genesis and synchronic state of the language, Creoles constitute an exciting window into what is cognitively basic and necessary for human language systems. They represent in the purest form, most unadulterated by history, the features of language that emerge from human cognitive universal tendencies. As such, this work is compatible with Chomsky's early views on Universal Grammar and many early generativists considered creole languages an important empirical ground in the search for typological universals for the reasons adduced by Bickerton. His work is at odds with other creolists who seek explanations for the commonalities across creole languages in terms of a common substrate or origin, and is nowadays considered controversial. (Note on Bickerton as linguistic scientist supplied by Gillian Ramchand.)
14. According to Charles Cotton's *Compleat Gamester* (1674) all-fours was played in Kent in the seventeenth century, where it probably originated. It is still played in Yorkshire and Lancashire. It was popular in America in the 19th century where it was called 'Old Sledge' or 'Seven Up'. It seems to have been superseded there by 'Pedro' and 'Pitch', also known as 'High-Low-Jack'. It is assumed that the game was brought to Trinidad by the British. In the twentieth century, Trinidad is the country in the world where all-fours is most played in homes and neighbourhoods, where regional and national competitions are enthusiastically supported.
15. The account of the encounter with a Venezuelan pirogue on pp. 130-131, and the treatment of Leonard Olivera pp. 134-135 read like eye-witness accounts, but there is no reference to any source; and Chapter 22, "How Bumper Died" is plausible, but how does Bickerton know "the truth" about the killing of Bumper?
16. Boysie's grandson, Ashram, does not remember seeing either the bible or the diary loaned to Bickerton by Chuncie. Bhangrang's sabre, however, is in the possession of a family member.
17. Bickerton's attribution of racial characteristics to Africans and Indians resembles the classificatory scheme proposed by the White West Indian Deschampsneufs in V.S. Naipaul's *The Mimic Men* (1967). He divides the three main races in the island into the long-visioned (the Indians), the short-visioned (Africans) and the medium-visioned – the White Creoles whose destiny it is to keep the society in balance.

18. Calypsos involving Boysie that were sung close to the time include: “Floating Corpse Murder Case” (Viking on the first guilty verdict) “Floating Corpse Acquittal” (Viking); “Pirates in the Gulf of Paria” (Kitchener); “Thelma Was a Dancer” (Lord Eisenhower) and “Thelma Haynes Story” (Lord Melody). I was unable to locate: “The Thelma Haynes Tragedy” by Tiny Terror, 1957.
19. The trials as reported in the newspapers include: i. Boysie Singh Trial for Murder of Philbert Payson, “The Floating Corpse Murder Trial”, begun in Central Criminal Court, July 17, 1950 before Mr Justice Kenneth Vincent Brown. Trial ended August 22,1950. Jury cannot agree.
    ii.Retrial began November 6, 1950, the Second “Floating Corpse” Trial before Mr Justice S.E.Gomes. Trial ended December 6, 1950. Verdict: Guilty.
    iii. Appeal began January 10, 1951, heard by Sir Cecil Furness-Smith, Mr Justice W. H. Irwin and Mr Justice E. Mortimer Duke. Ended January 25,1951. Verdict: Reversal of previous verdict. Boysie and his fellow-prisoners to be immediately set at liberty.
    iv. Trial of Boland Ramkissoon and Boysie Singh for the murder of Thelma Haynes (“The Case of the Missing Dancer”). Begun in Central Criminal Court, February 4, 1957 before Mr Justice F.J. Camacho. Ended February 25, 1957. Verdict: Guilty.
    v. Appeal heard May 6, 1957 (before Mathieu-Perez, Archer, and Watkin-Williams). Appeal dismissed.
    vi. Appeal to Privy Council made in “forma pauperis”, July 1957. Heard by Judicial Committee July 1957. Appeal dismissed.
20. Personal discussions with Hollis Liverpool, September 2019.
21. “Kokioko” is onomatopoeic for the crowing of a cock. It also refers to carrying someone, usually a child or handicapped person on one’s back. The calypso is more sexually suggestive. The three men played the game of riding on one another’s backs.
22. *Trinidad Guardian*, 4 August, 1957.
23. For the rapid development of Woodbrook into middle-class status, Google Dylan Kerrigan: “Woodbrook on the Path to Independence”. Kerrigan argues that Woodbrook was “essentially Creole” and that its “nationalist culture and politics... essentially marginalized the Indians...” Among the oral documents on which the article is based, there is this memory of resident Mary Cain: “Miguel Street, as Naipaul named his first novel, was Luis Street. It was re-named Cowpen Street when Indians moved in to staid Woodbrook. They kept cows. We kept ducks, chickens or turkeys.”
24. Tinsingh was not an Indian. His real name was Michael Arno (Arneaud?). Boysie and Michael were friends since childhood, and were often referred to as “the two Singhs”. Since Arno was the thinner of the two Singhs, he was called Tinsingh.
25. See page 28 for photo of Mana Lala.
26. *Atilla’s Kaiso* (Trinidad: UWI Extra-Mural Dept, 1983), p. 88. Killer also sang “Grinding Massala”. According to Atilla, “he wove the Indian rhythm cleverly into the kaiso and even while singing English words, simulated the speech of the average person of Indian origin...”
27. The best place to begin researching the Indians of Port of Spain especially downtown Port of Spain is the three novels and short stories of a Port of

Spain Indian Ismith Khan (1925-2002). Khan wrote about cultural resistance, ancestral legacies, cultural evolution over generations, becoming Trinidadian, and the discovery of self through action, thought and artistic expression. See *The Jumbie Bird* (1961) *The Obeah Man* (1964) *The Crucifixion* (1987) and *A Day in the Country and Other Stories* (1994). His most memorable character is the old Pathan warrior Kale Khan who took part in the resistance to the colonial repressing of cultural expression at the time of the Hosay riots and whose spirit fails when a political representative of newly-independent India summarily dismisses the longing of overseas Indians for a connection with the ancestral land.

28. David Renwick, "Boysie Singh Now Living on Borrowed Time", *Trinidad Guardian*, 4 August 1957.
29. *Gurudeva and Other Indian Tales* (Trinidad, 1943), p. 4.
30. The Hosay or Mohurrum festival was originally a Shia Muslim religious festival of mourning for the slain grandson of the Prophet Mohammed. In Trinidad, the festival was considerably secularised and attracted participants of other ethnic groups and religions. Stick, gatka-fighting was an important part of the dramatic street theatre.
31. There was a suggestion that it was Doris who caused Boysie's defence to requisition the police station diary that showed the extent of Inspector Bleasdell's lying and inventing, which was mainly responsible for Boysie's acquittal in "The Case of the Floating Body" by the Court of Appeal. The Indian policeman for whom she left Boysie was suspected of telling Doris about the suppressed diary.
32. See "Talk of the Town", *Trinidad Guardian*, Thursday, August 1, 1957; and "Boysie Singh Now Living on Borrowed Time", *Trinidad Guardian*, Saturday, August 4, 1957. "The Rajah Preached: The Spots Remained" (Loomat exposes Boysie Singh), *Trinidad Guardian*, August 11, 1957. "The Rajah and the Floating Corpse", *Trinidad Guardian*, Sunday, August 4.
33. See p. 37 and 38 for photos of Mrs Ramsumair with captions.
34. V.S. Naipaul, *A Bend in the River* (London: Andre Deutch, 1979), p. 167 and p. 261, respectively.

DEREK BICKERTON

THE MURDERS OF BOYSIE SINGH

INTRODUCTION TO BOYSIE

I FIRST HEARD of Boysie Singh in the editorial office of the *Barbados Advocate.* I had been discussing with Ian Gale, the editor, a serial I was then writing for the paper, and the conversation drifted first to the possibility of running some local crime serial and then to West Indian crime in general. Both of us thought it would be a good idea if someone produced a book of Celebrated Caribbean Crimes, a more or less virgin field as far as the British public was concerned; they had had Heath, Haigh and Christie crammed into them *ad nauseam,* and might well be glad of a change.

It was at this stage that Gale asked me if I'd ever heard of Boysie.

I had not. His execution had taken place a year before I arrived in the West Indies, and his crimes had received surprisingly little publicity considering their variety and their remarkable nature. Possibly the very efficiency with which they had been committed had created the atmosphere of doubt, ignorance and conjecture which seemed to surround them. For although, according to Gale, Boysie had committed possibly forty or fifty murders, and been tried for murder three times, only one of his victim's bodies had ever been recovered, only two murders were ever mentioned in the various prosecutions brought against him, and, as he had eventually been found "not guilty" of one of them, and had obstinately refused, until the last minute – when this right was dramatically withheld from him – to confess to any others, the world was left with the picture of a man who, despite his evil reputation, had only one legally certified victim to his credit. That this picture was false, Gale, like most West Indians, felt certain. But in the three years that followed Boysie's death, no one had come forward with any tangible proof, and in consequence his full story had never yet been told.

It so happened that the following week I had arranged to join a geological survey party on a trip into the unmapped, scarcely explored Southern Pakaraima Mountains, on the boundary between Brazil and British Guiana. To get there I had to pass through Trinidad, the scene of Boysie's activities, and Gale suggested that if I had time I might stop over a couple of days. He could use a short series of articles on the man, if I felt like doing them. After what I had just heard, I did. New mass-murderers do not turn up every day.

To the average Englishman, Trinidad is the home of the calypso. It has a Pitch Lake. Some people once threw bottles during a Test Match there. Princess Margaret likes it, and when she arrives she is greeted by happy flag-waving crowds. It sounds like somewhere quaint, exotic, a tropical backwater into which the tensions of European life scarcely intrude.

Trinidad is not like that at all.

In Trinidad there are three-quarters of a million people. They constitute what is perhaps the most mixed population in the world. Africans, Indians, Spaniards, Chinese, Syrians, French, English, Portuguese and Americans, together with every conceivable – in a literal sense – combination of these, mix in its streets; mix, but do not mingle, for in spite of the propaganda about dwelling in unity together, the nerve-jangling suspicion and distrust that exist between the various races can be felt all the time, and erupt occasionally in acts of meaningless violence.

Trinidad's murder and road accident rate is one of the highest in the world.

Most towns and cities in the West Indies still have the air of somnolence instantly recognised by readers of Somerset Maugham. But Port of Spain is like a modern American city dropped suddenly and complete on the tenth parallel, a pocket Detroit fighting ninety-degree heat and ninety per cent humidity to realise its own portion of the American Dream. On one side of it lies uncut jungle; on the other, Shanty Town, a sodden mudbank on the edge of a mangrove swamp where the submerged tenth lives in petrol-can shacks and the refuse problem is handled by moulting black vultures. It has no history to speak of – a hundred and fifty odd years ago, when it was annexed from Spain, the population was only a few hundreds – and because of this and its mixture of exiled races it has few shared standards and traditions and no measure of success save material wealth. The split-level house in Belmont or Cascade, the Impala and the Bel Air, the electric gadgets and the wife or mistress starlit with jewels – these are the only valid symbols of achievement, and, once they are obtained, there are few who trouble to ask by what means.

In the city proper, traffic jostles bumpers through the gridiron of streets, races three abreast down the one-ways to beat the lights, clogs into honking, cursing jams hundreds of yards long. Everywhere new office blocks are going up; despite the continuous guerilla warfare waged by the unions, business is booming. A car over two years old is a rarity worth comment; like Americans, Trinidadians seem sold on the idea of expendability, on the swift expansion of the economy which alone can make this possible. Every clerk has a manager's Corona in his briefcase. Even the skies have a tense, anxious air, are taut with a nervous crosshatching of overhead power lines that gives suburban intersections the look of early Klee. At night, as in so many American cities, there are streets where no law-abiding citizen dare walk. Back of the waterfront, gaudy cabarets pump a vitriolic calypso-tinged jazz into the hot night, offer prostitutes of all colours to seamen from every port in the world. Yet, embedded like fossils in these neon-age strata, one finds Indian tribal customs, primitive African rites and beliefs, proletarian attitudes and patterns of behaviour more typical of the nineteenth than the twentieth century, all mixed incongruously together in a sociologist's nightmare, presenting contrasts as violent as the physical surroundings of the city themselves.

This is the Trinidad against which Boysie must be seen; a background without some knowledge of which he can never be properly understood. For he, as much as anyone, embodied the divergent impulses – the backward drag of the racial group tradition, the forward push of the American success-dream – which have made modern Trinidad; indeed, he himself played no small part in its making. For much as the respectable might wish to deny it, their island would not have been quite the same if Boysie had never lived.

After a day of reading through old newspaper files on Boysie's bloody career, I realised that his story was one which deserved, and in fact needed, far more than a short series of articles in a local newspaper. Even my Caribbean Crime Calendar faded into limbo. It was superfluous; Boysie himself seemed to have committed all the crimes there were except blackmail and simony. I could not extend my two day stay in the island, but I could, and did, return to continue and complete my researches.

The story that gradually emerged from these is one which I would never have had the nerve to write as a novel. Yet, fantastic as it seems, I have erred if anything on the side of caution. One of the disadvantages of dealing with a criminal as successful as Boysie is that there is not the amount of official documentation that exists on most convicted mass-murderers. For many of his exploits, even for some that may easily be inferred from undisputed facts – the disappearance of a fishing-boat and its crew, for example, and the subsequent sale by Boysie of the boat's equipment – there is no source of information save the memories of people actually involved in the incidents or in whom Boysie had personally confided. Now to the natural untrustworthiness of memory there may be added the desire to avoid self-incrimination (though most of my informants were very decent about this) and, in some cases, the truth-corroding habits of a lifetime spent in dodging the law.

For most of the incidents in this book I have confirmation from at least two independent sources, both claiming to be eyewitnesses of the events described. In some cases, from the private nature of the crimes, these have proved impossible to obtain; in every instance I have made this fact clear in the text. For some incidents I have three or four distinct versions; here I have taken the highest common factor of agreed detail, or, where agreement was minimal, relied on the version which seemed (from the reliability of the person giving it and its congruence with known facts of Boysie's character) most likely to be correct. Some reputed crimes of Boysie's could not be confirmed, and have therefore been omitted; one or two stories about him which are dubious have been included either for their intrinsic interest or because on internal evidence they stand some chance of being true, but again this has invariably been indicated in the text. To the best of my belief, then, this book constitutes the only full and true account ever published of one of the most remarkable characters in the recorded history of crime.

2: THE EARLY DAYS

JOHN BOYSIE SINGH was born on the 5th April, 1908, at 17, Luis Street, Woodbrook – a northwestern suburb of Port of Spain.

His parents were both pure-blooded Indians. In the later years of the nineteenth century, a large number of Indians were brought to Trinidad and British Guiana as indentured labourers. They were originally intended to work on the sugar plantations in place of the Negroes, who after Emancipation preferred to scratch a bare existence as peasant proprietors, or to drift to the towns and seek work they felt less degrading than manual labour on the land.

As soon as their indentures had expired, however, most Indians too acquired land of their own, bought a small wayside stall, or, in their turn, moved to Port of Spain in the hope of bettering themselves.

Among these men was Boysie's father, Bhagrang Singh. Bhagrang Singh came from the Punjab; he was originally a member of a Hindu caste known as the Chatri. Unlike most Hindus, the Chatri had a reputation for prowess in war, and at one stage of his life Bhagrang served in the Indian Army, probably in a cavalry regiment.

The circumstances under which he left the army are rather obscure. Most of the Indians who came to labour in the canefields were moved simply by the desire to escape from semi-starvation in their own country, but in Bhagrang's case there seems to have been a darker reason. The story goes that he killed a man of high rank – some say, a prince – and had to flee for his life. What is certain is that he brought with him only one relic of his past – a cavalry sabre, its fine steel scarcely rusted by a century in the tropics, its hilt wrought into the shape of a falcon's head with red stones for eyes. On a certain day each year it was his custom to pray over it.

Yet by the time of Boysie's birth his swashbuckling days were over. He was still tall and powerfully built (most of the Singh family were physically well above average, especially for Indians, who tend to be shorter and slighter in build than Africans or Europeans) but a natural reserve in his manner was increased by an almost total ignorance of English. He was employed as a night watchman on a sugar estate. The work, though poorly paid, was regular, and the household in which Boysie grew up was one of respectable poverty.

Of his mother little is known. She seems in some ways to have been a more enterprising character than her husband, for she kept cows to eke out his meagre income, and later on travelled with a pedlar's pack of haberdashery to the Indian villages in the countryside round Port of Spain.

Boysie was the youngest of four children. These were remarkably widely spaced in age. His elder brother was twenty-eight when Boysie was born, his two sisters eighteen and four respectively. He was born, it is said, on a night of thunder, lightning and heavy rain – though perhaps this is merely one of those retrospective legends which attach themselves to those of a sinister eminence. His mother had no milk for the first three days of his life – I am told that this is by no means uncommon amongst Indian women – and Boysie had to be suckled by a foster-mother.

In those days when Trinidad was merely a sleepy and half-forgotten backwater of the British Empire, Woodbrook was the outermost suburb of Port of Spain, and Luis Street almost the last street in Woodbrook. It consisted, and still very largely consists, of weathered wood, single-storey houses, set on tiny plots of land on which one or two coconut palms and perhaps a few fruit trees grow. It runs at right angles to the seashore, and ends nowadays in an open, grass-grown stretch beyond which are quays where the small coastal steamers moor. Before the First World War, however, this land was a mangrove swamp – an expanse of waterlogged grey mud and muddy grey water, over which the many-legged mangroves straddled on crooked, corky stilts – such as can still be seen bordering the Eastern Main Road and the shoreline at Cocorite, a few miles west of the city.

It was in and around this swamp that the child Boysie had his earliest adventures.

As the youngest in the family, he was spoilt both by his parents and his sisters. His father never corrected him. It is the custom in many Indian families to leave physical punishment of the children to the mother. As he grew more and more mischievous, however, his mother came to beat him with greater frequency, using for the purpose that favourite West Indian instrument of chastisement, the bull's pizzle – made flexible by hanging a stone on it to stretch it and then drying it in the sun. But whether they indulged or beat him, his parents seemed to have little influence over Boysie. It was not that he was a rebellious child, though his career was soon to be marked by acts of rebellion against authority; his attitude towards his parents seemed to be one of indifference. From an early age he went his own way. The only person who had any authority over him, or for whom he had any respect, was his eldest sister. She had married as a child, before Boysie was born, and had offspring of her own, but in Indian families the elder children are expected to take their share in the upbringing of the younger ones. It was with her more than with his mother that Boysie spent his earliest years.

He had little schooling. For a few years he attended elementary schools

– Ackal and Newtown – but he seems to have been an intractable pupil, and there is no evidence that he learnt anything beyond the rudiments of the three R's. At one of his trials, for the purpose of his defence, he claimed to be illiterate; in fact he could read adequately and write a fair hand, though with numerous mistakes of spelling, grammar and punctuation.

It was at Newtown school that his fighting career began. One Friday, just before the August holidays, while on the way home from school, he beat one of his classmates so badly that the police were called. Boysie threw his schoolbooks to his nephew, Mano his eldest sister's son, only a few years younger than he – and took off with the police in hot pursuit. In those days open country stretched to the north as well as the west of Woodbrook, and it was north – away from home – that Boysie ran, across the Queen's Park Savannah, the grassy open space which now contains Port of Spain's racecourse and cricket ground, and on into forest-covered hills which rose steeply beyond, past Cushie Hill and then bearing off to the left towards Maraval. The police still toiled in pursuit. Unable to shake them off, Boysie swung yet further left and doubled back towards Woodbrook – a circuit of some three or four miles.

Once he reached home he would be safe. He had a hiding place prepared for just such an occasion – a space under the roof which was entered by pushing aside a loose board. A ladder was placed ready against the wall. Boysie clambered up, kicked down the ladder, and waited. Below, the police hammered on the door, demanding that Boysie be produced. His parents denied that he lived there. In the end the police gave up and went away, and nothing further was heard of the affair.

Boysie can have been no more than ten or eleven at the time. He had learnt the first of his lessons – that it is sometimes possible to defy the law with impunity.

It was at about the same time that he learnt a rather sharper lesson – that if one does get caught, the consequences are likely to be unpleasant.

Some time in 1919 – when he was eleven – he was arrested for flying a kite on the Woodbrook Savannah. This may seem a trivial offence; it should however be remembered that in Trinidad, until quite recently, kite flying was more than a mere children's pastime; it was a complex and highly aggressive sport in which contestants, many of whom were grown men, aimed, with the aid of such exotic accessories as slacking mange and zwill, at cutting loose and capturing the kites of their opponents. Occasionally these contests degenerated into gang fights, and it was for this reason that the police tried to prevent kite-flying within the city limits.

The punishment, however, was grossly disproportionate. He was taken to Port of Spain Police Headquarters, held there overnight in a cell, and the next morning brought before a magistrate – this was of course before the days of Juvenile Courts – who sentenced him to receive six strokes from a tamarind rod.

In the diary he kept in his death cell, Boysie claimed that this incident made him a criminal. Whether one accepts that or not (and the claim has a somewhat fictitious ring) it would understandably breed in him a bitterness against police and all those in authority.

Yet though his outlook might have been warped by this injustice he could hardly claim that his character was radically changed. He had already begun to show many of the traits which were to distinguish him in adult life. He would not tolerate opposition. In every sport he had to excel; in every enterprise he had to be the first. He had developed a love of money, and had learnt to gamble at marbles – it is said that at this game he learnt the manual dexterity that was to serve him so well as a card-player later in life. When things went well for him, he was generous and sunny-natured, but his temper was violent and easily roused.

His chief pastime – or for that matter, source of income – during his early teens was the catching of land-crabs in the swamps round the Pumping Station. The crabs were caught in traps which consisted of crude wooden boxes with one end open, inside which pieces of coconut husk were placed as bait. The crabs, sometimes nearly a foot across, would enter the box and in so doing dislodge a trapdoor which fell, locking them in.

Boysie, however, was not satisfied for long with the proceeds of his own traps. He began to steal from those of the other boys. He stole even from his nephew Mano, who was at this time his closest companion. But there was nothing that they could do. Boysie was bigger and tougher than any of them. Already people were beginning to be afraid of him.

One day, five boys whose traps he had robbed ganged up on him. He fought all five of them. Someone ran to his sister and told her, and she came down to the mangrove swamp to find Boysie still valiantly defending himself against the odds. She told him to stop fighting, and he obeyed her; reluctantly, but he obeyed. However, she did not trust him, and throwing the youths a rope which she had brought for the purpose, told them to tie his hands. This was too much for Boysie. The fight broke out all over again. But still the five could not master him. At last his sister called him again, and he came meekly to her and let her tie his hands. She dragged him home after her like a tethered beast. He was twelve years old when this happened.

But by this time no one else had the least vestige of control over him. He used to accompany his mother on trips into the country. His mother would take her pack of haberdashery and go by train to Caroni, a town largely inhabited by Indians, and from there they would travel on foot for a week at a time, selling in markets, visiting the sugar estates on paydays. While his mother was selling, Boysie would disappear. He would be gone for hours at a time and no one would ever know what he was doing.

When they returned to Woodbrook, he would disappear again, returning to the house only for meals.

On Wrightson Road there stood a fustic tree – a variety from whose extra-hard wood the naves of cartwheels are made. The bare space under its wide-spreading branches was the Woodbrook boys' "liming place". "Liming", in Trinidadian slang, means hanging around the streets gossiping and waiting for any mischief that may turn up. It was here that Boysie began to gamble seriously. The boys would set up pennies in the dusty earth and flick marbles at them. If you hit a coin, you won it. From that they went on to rummy at a penny a hand. And from that to dice.

The dice game which the Woodbrook boys played is known as sebby-lebby, and the rules are as follows. Two dice are thrown. If the thrower scores two, three or twelve, that is "crop" – he loses instantly, and the throw passes to the next player. If the thrower scores seven or eleven, that is a straight, and he wins. If he throws any of the remaining numbers – four, five, six, eight, nine or ten – further betting takes place. Anyone can bet against the thrower that he can "bring back" – that is, throw again – the number originally thrown. He can keep rolling until he either brings back the number, and wins, or throws a seven – and loses.

Not all the dice players under the fustic tree were boys of Boysie's age. It was the custom in those days for youths and young men of widely differing ages to gamble together. One of the young men – a fellow called Harris Timson – was eight or nine years older than Boysie. During the day he worked in a lumber yard, but in the evenings and on Sundays he would come down and gamble on Wrightson Road. He was not only older, he was bigger and stronger than the rest of the gang. A group so amorphous could hardly be said to have a leader, but Harris exercised at least a kind of negative authority – all were in awe of him, none dared oppose him.

To Boysie, Harris represented a challenge. The difference in age and size meant little to him. Harris held a place which he felt should by right be his. The only way he could win that place would be by beating Harris. For a boy of fourteen that might seem an absurd ambition. But Boysie at fourteen had a man's growth, strength, determination. Moreover by beating Harris he would do more than merely achieve leadership of the Woodbrook boys; he would be laying the foundations of a formidable Reputation.

To gain a Reputation was the chief aim of most working-class youths in his day. They had little to look forward to but a life of monotonous labour at starvation wages – and they would be lucky to get that. There were no politicians to flatter them with promises. There were no unions to teach them self-respect. Their only way of escape was to gain a Reputation. Only the man with a Reputation was respected. People were quiet when he spoke. When he entered a bar, drinks would be thrust on him and he would not have to pay. If he cheated in a gambling game, no one dared accuse him. If he saw something in a shop that he fancied, he would take it and no one would challenge him.

The clash came one evening. It started with an argument over a sebby-lebby dice game. Boysie threw the dice and Harris stopped him and told him to throw again. Boysie's quick temper flared. Within seconds the two of them were fighting.

Men who claim to have been eyewitnesses swear that the fight lasted over two hours. At the end of that time, when both combatants were covered in blood and scarcely able to stand, some of the Woodbrook fishermen who had been watching the fight – Gowdie, Black Joe, Freshkin and Blood – decided that they'd had enough and separated them by force.

Within fifteen minutes they were firm friends. At this age Boysie seems to have had none of the malice which made his enmity so deadly later in life. They remained on the best of terms for several years afterwards. However, this did not stop them from fighting. Time and time again they contested the leadership of Woodbrook. Their fights became a legend throughout the district. Yet all these battles were drawn. Neither could decisively defeat the other, and when the fight was over they would resume their normal friendly relations.

In 1922 Boysie had his second conviction – for gambling. He received a further six strokes from the tamarind rod. This time however the punishment was wholly without effect; gambling now had a hold over Boysie that it was to retain, whether he was in luck or out of it, until the day he died.

But he did not gamble all the time. He had already discovered the second great love of his life – the sea.

It was the custom for the Port of Spain fishermen to race their boats on Sundays. One boat would challenge another; the stake was often as high as fifty dollars – a large amount for those days – though this sum had to be raised by contributions from the skipper, his crew, and sometimes outsiders as well. No doubt it was the gambling angle which first appealed to Boysie. When, one Sunday, the fisherman Black Joe found himself a hand short, and asked Boysie to join him, Boysie jumped at the chance. Black Joe won his race, and Boysie received his share of the stake money.

But a strange thing had happened. Until that time he had cared for nothing save easy money and an unbeaten record in fighting.

Now, during that race, something about the sea – its sense of freedom, perhaps, or the excitement of fighting a force far stronger than man – had seized his imagination. Later on he was to desert the sea, stay away from it for years at a time. Yet he returned to it again and again, until the last years of his life.

For the right to go to sea he was ready, for the first time in his life, to put up with menial and ill-paid work. He took to "jostling" boats – that is to say, getting them ready for sea, loading and unloading them, making sure they were securely beached on their return, washing them down, looking after and repairing the fishing tackle, and so on. His wages depended on the catch. If the catch was a good one, he might receive as much as sixty cents – half a crown. If not, he would have to rest content with whatever was given him.

After a few months of this work he was allowed to go out on fishing trips.

He sailed first with "Gowdie", whose real name was Captain Doyle. Fishing boats normally carried a crew of three – the captain and two hands. Boysie was the third man, and as junior had the smallest share of the takings.

The Port of Spain fleet fished – and for that matter still fishes – the stretch of sea that lies between Trinidad and Venezuela, and is bounded on the north by the Bocas, the series of narrow channels which links the Gulf of Paria with the Caribbean. It is a shallow sea, nowhere more than a few fathoms deep, and stained an ochreous yellow by the vast outflow of the Orinoco river, which streams up to the Bocas from the flat, jungle-covered delta to the southwest of the island. Boysie would come to know that sea better than his own backyard. Now, however, it was still an adventure. The boats would leave Woodbrook under sail and travel with the steady easterly trades, past Cocorite and Chaguaramas to the string of islands which extend from the northwestern tip of Trinidad. There they would put down lines for redfish, kingfish and barracuda. They would have to row back against the wind. Here was where Boysie came into his own. Even in his youth he had the strength of two normal men. He seemed never to tire.

Every Sunday there were more wagers, more races. The boat that had Boysie in it usually won.

He was also a strong swimmer. In stormy weather he would swim out to salvage any boats or fishing equipment that was seen drifting. This was not done purely from kindness of heart. He enjoyed showing off his prowess in any field, and the things he salvaged he sold, the money going to increase his stakes in the gambling ring. Yet he swam for pleasure also. He would often go out alone to ships anchored as much as three miles from the shore. Even in middle age he could stay submerged for more than a minute at a time.

After some months with Gowdie he transferred to Freshkin's boat. Despite his gambling, or perhaps because of its success, he had managed to put a little money to one side, and in another three or four months he was able to buy a boat of his own – the twenty-two footer, *Perseverance.* It was an achievement indeed for a boy still in his 'teens. It seemed then that Boysie might really be going to make something of his life.

3: APPRENTICESHIP IN CRIME

UNTIL HIS LATE 'teens, Boysie's life, for all its wildness, did not differ materially from the lives of other youths of his own class and background. Many of them gambled and fought; many were not above a little occasional stealing when opportunity offered. Moreover their behaviour must be seen in the wider context of the social changes then taking place in Trinidad.

For many years after the introduction of indentured labour, the structure of the transplanted Indian communities changed little. Like most immigrants, the Indians tended to stick together, and many of the place names in southern Trinidad – Fyzabad or Siparia – indicate the extent to which they founded towns and villages of their own. Even today, with their white-onioned mosques, bullock-carts and greybeards in dhotis, many of the remoter villages seem nearer the Ganges than the Gulf of Paria.

Until the turn of the century – and in many cases a good deal later – these communities continued to be ruled by the village elders, in accordance with the laws and customs they had known in India. English colonial rule, like the Western standards on which it was based, made little headway in such surroundings. As late as the twenties and thirties it was not uncommon for the police to find, in country districts, the bodies of young girls who had been killed by having their sexual organs pierced by a broom handle. This was the traditional punishment for adultery; it would have been imposed by a full session of the village council, and it would be impossible for the police to find a single member of the community to give evidence against those who had carried it out.

In a cosmopolitan city like Port of Spain, however, the system could not work so easily. The Indians who moved there were daily spectators of a way of life – the way of the white and high-colour classes – which materially at least seemed preferable to their own. They became, as they say in Trinidad, "creolised" – that is to say they abandoned their religious beliefs and with them a large part of their customs (such as survived did so in the form rather than the spirit) in their attempt to appear, in manners, dress, and possessions, as Western as they could. Yet they were still far from understanding the complex of social, moral and religious forces that had gone to shape the civilization they admired; they could do no more than imitate its outward forms. They had cast off the moral restraints of the East without accepting those of the West. They were lost in a wasteland where there seemed no guide but their own interest. It is hardly surprising that there was – and still is – a high percentage of lawlessness amongst the less successful sections of the Indian community.

It does not seem as if Boysie ever had any form of religious instruction. If such had been offered to him, it is interesting if somewhat unprofitable to speculate on its possible effect. The strange, late and exotic flowering of religion in Boysie's life may have sprung from some untapped layer of his personality which under earlier cultivation might have produced more fruitful results.

But as things fell out, the chance of a worthwhile life Boysie had when he bought *Perseverance* was doomed to be wasted. Soon he had further convictions for assault and obstruction; but what was most fateful to his development was his rooted belief – shown at many stages in his later life – that anything that he wanted was his for the taking. It was this belief which led him, even at the height of his success, to commit innumerable trivial thefts, thefts of things which he could have afforded a hundred times over. But it was too much trouble to pay. And he was the strongest. So why should he bother?

Needless to say, paying at the cinema he regarded as beneath his dignity. He was an expert at "poping" – getting in free – but one evening at the London Theatre, Woodbrook, he wasn't quite expert enough. The film, appropriately enough, was part of the Tarzan saga – Tarzan in those remote days being played by the late Elmo Lincoln. But the caretaker, an ex-constable called Hazelwood, spotted Boysie sneaking in. Constables in those days were chosen for size alone; this did not, however, prevent Hazelwood from getting soundly beaten. Boysie was arrested and charged with wounding; the charge was subsequently reduced to assault and battery, but he now had a string of minor convictions, and he received his first prison sentence – twenty-one days hard labour.

Shortly after he came out, his father died. Although he had never reproved his son he seems to have had a good idea how Boysie was shaping. Calling his family to his bedside, he begged them to take the sword which he had guarded for so long and throw it into the sea. They were not to keep it and on no account to sell it. There were no people left, he said, who understood the old things; he feared that the sword would fall into evil hands and be used to commit acts of violence. It was better to throw it away. But his wishes were ignored. His eldest daughter kept the weapon, and it remains in the family to this day.

Boysie showed no signs of grief at his father's death. He is said, however, to have been depressed and ill-tempered for some time afterwards.

It was about this year – 1926 – that he met the first woman in his life, an Indian girl called Rosie, who came from an orphanage. Little is known of her, save that she was good-looking – Boysie, I was told, "never loved an ugly woman". Boysie could not take her home, either to his mother's or his sister's house, so they made love in the open, on the waste ground round the bottom ends of Luis and Alberto Streets. After a year or so he quarrelled with her and took up with another Indian girl, Mana Lala, who was to be the mother of his only child.

But in the meantime, the convictions were coming thick and fast. Late in 1926 he was arrested for stealing a purse; convicted, he was made to put up a £20 bond and placed on probation. A few days later he was caught in the act of picking a man's pocket – the pocket contained one dollar – and received his second prison sentence, this time a six-month term of hard labour. The bond was of course forfeited; to pay the money his sister had to sell her cows. On leaving gaol, Boysie went to sea again, determined to raise sufficient to pay her back; but the fishing was poor that season. He decided that there were quicker and easier ways of making money.

An Indian farmer from Chaguanas – a friend of the late Bhagrang Singh – had come into Port of Spain to buy a cow. He was staying at a house in Luis Street, where it was his custom to sleep out on the gallery. He had not so far found a cow to his liking, so the purchase money, over a hundred dollars, remained intact. He slept with it in a bag tied round his waist, under his dhoti.

One night Boysie crept up to the house. In his hand he held a razor; he was going to cut through the dhoti and the string which attached the bag. Silently he approached the sleeper, but in the darkness he did not see that the latter's hand was clutching the moneybag with a peasant's determination. Boysie cut, and the man woke and screamed out loud. His fingers were laid open to the bone.

Boysie fled – without the money. But the man had recognised him.

Once more he was arrested. This time the charge was assault with intent to rob, and the matter too serious to be dealt with by a magistrate. Boysie was remanded to the next Assizes. There he was convicted and sentenced to four years hard labour.

This term he served in Carrera prison.

Carrera is on a rocky island off the coast of Trinidad. A mile and a half of muddy, shark-infested water separates it from the mainland. It is the prison where long-sentence men and difficult cases are sent.

There is a quarry on Carrera, and in those days prisoners used to split the rocks with a crowbar and then use a sledgehammer to break them into smaller pieces. As a change from this they would pound coconut fibre, smashing the husks up with a wooden mallet and then separating the strands which were used to stuff the cheaper grades of mattress.

Boysie did not take kindly to either task. During the earlier part of his sentence he was a troublesome prisoner. One of the gaolers in particular kept coming behind him while he worked in the quarry, needling him with sarcastic remarks until one day Boysie snatched up a shovel and lashed out blindly at his tormentor. For this he was put into solitary confinement.

Solitary at Carrera was no joyride. Prisoners had leg irons and were kept for three or four days at a time in water-oozing, rat-ridden cells under the gaol. Water and a small ration of bread was all that they received. Boysie had several more spells in solitary, mostly as the result of disputes between him and the kitchen staff. He had quickly grasped the law that applies in all prisons – the kitchen staff are the only prisoners who eat well. The staff at Carrera, however, did not want Boysie amongst them. He was, they said, too young and hungry. He would take more than his share.

Boysie, as usual, took the refusal of a privilege as a personal insult. But a course or two of solitary cured his impetuous nature. Instead of lashing out the moment he was provoked, he would plan his assaults in advance, saving each day a small piece of bread from his ration and hoarding it under his shirt, so that when he was placed in the punishment cell he would have a reserve of food to fall back on.

Anyone who had surveyed Boysie's life at this point would have had little difficulty in prophesying the rest. The pattern was already clear – the chronic aggression, the series of unplanned petty crimes, the inevitable convictions each of which brought a heavier penalty than the last. He seemed set for the career of the hardened recidivist, never making more than a handful of dollars from his compulsive thefts, in and out of gaol for the rest of his days.

Perhaps thoughts of this kind occurred to Boysie himself. No one can know; one can only look at the facts. During the latter part of his four-year term his behaviour must have improved, for he was released on ticket of leave early in 1931 with ten months of the sentence still to run. He did not return to gaol – except for a four-month spell in 1934 for unlawful wounding – until 1950. Yet in that period he built up an almost impregnable empire of crime. He must have learnt a great deal in Carrera.

Mana Lala, who seems to have had the most agreeable nature of Boysie's mistresses, was waiting for him when he came out of gaol. Soon she was carrying his child.

In the following year – 1932 – there occurred three important events in Boysie's life. That March his mother died. He was down on the seashore collecting wood to make fishpots when another fisherman brought him the news. For once he seemed moved by grief. He shed no tears – he cried only twice in his life, and each time they were tears of rage – but covered his face with his hands and said, "I've got no money – no work – and now God take my mother too." But at the funeral he had recovered his normal composure.

The following month Boysie's son was born; Anthony, or "Chuncie", as he was called, for in his early childhood he was delicate and almost feminine in appearance.

Until the birth of his son Boysie had shown no real affection for anyone. He respected his sister; he looked on his nephew Mano with good-humoured tolerance; for his mistresses it is doubtful if he felt more than the purely physical desire of a healthy and highly-sexed young male. But for Chuncie he revealed a depth of feeling which was in sharp contrast with the callousness of his normal behaviour.

Before these two events, however, there had occurred one which was to have a still greater influence on Boysie's career.

Trinidad was originally a Spanish colony, and even after the British occupied it the Catholic influence persisted. As in most Latin countries, Carnival is still celebrated on the three days prior to Lent. In its original form, Carnival was a last fling before the Lenten austerities – from "carne vale", a farewell to meat – but in Trinidad the feast has become wholly secularised, and is now merely an excuse for ostentatious display. People save all year in order to have a costume more elaborate than their neighbours', often spending hundreds of dollars which they can ill afford. During the days of Carnival they form up in bands, representing Indian princes, Egyptian kings, Roman gladiators, or other exotic figures of history, and parade through the streets and round the Queen's Park Savannah. Those too poor to take part flock to watch the fun. The vast majority who celebrate Carnival are of course law-abiding people, but in the confusion that prevails, violence frequently breaks out.

On the Tuesday of Carnival, Boysie and some of his Woodbrook friends went into Port of Spain to see the festivities. In George Street they encountered a man called David Leach and his followers.

Leach was at that time the "favourite", the acknowledged leader of the Town Boys. That does not mean that he was a gang leader in the modern sense. It was not until Boysie's heyday that American-style gangsterism came to Trinidad. But in the twenties and thirties there was great rivalry between the young men of the various suburbs. They did not deliberately look for trouble, but if one of their number became involved in any dispute with someone from another territory, then they would take his part, and a sporadic gang warfare would develop.

Leach had a score to settle with Boysie. Leach was not merely the Town Boss, he ran a string of prostitutes from whom he derived a considerable income. One of these prostitutes was an Indian girl called Popo, with whom Boysie had been sleeping – and, what was far worse in Leach's opinion, not paying. On that Tuesday, Leach's men outnumbered Boysie's. They attacked with knives and sticks, and the Woodbrook boys scattered, Boysie's right arm all but broken by blows from Leach's stick. At the hospital where he went for first aid, the doctor put his arm in a sling and told him he could not use it for another week.

While Boysie was being patched up at the hospital, the Leach boys were roaming the streets in search of further prey. They soon found it. One of Boysie's nephews was flushed from hiding, and though he defended himself with a three-foot iron picket snatched from a coconut vendor's cart he was soon overpowered and beaten into unconsciousness. He arrived at the hospital just as Boysie was leaving.

Hurt as he was, Boysie decided that Leach must be taught a lesson, and that immediately. He reached home – he was living now at 13 Rosalino Street, Woodbrook – around seven that evening. The first thing he did was to remove the sling and bandages. Then he dressed himself in a dhoti and courta – a type of vest – so as to resemble an Indian beggar; to this day many Indian beggars wear native costume, perhaps in the hope of arousing racial sympathy. Then he sent for George Harper, one of the Woodbrook fishermen, and a fellow called Edgar. The three of them set out for Leach's George Street headquarters.

Boysie was carrying his stick, "Three Little Trees". This stick was made of an exceedingly hard wood called poui, and was said to have been "mounted" – that is to say, a certain magical ceremony had been performed over it so that its blows would have more than normal force.

Edgar, a small and inoffensive-looking man, went ahead to 33 George Street and called Leach. Suspecting nothing, Leach came out into the street, alone. He took no heed of the old beggar crouched in a gateway, leaning on his stick.

"All right, Leach," Boysie said. "I've come for you."

Leach whirled round, but he was too late. Boysie, seemingly unimpeded by his crippled arm, swung "Three Little Trees" high in the air and brought it down once, twice, three times. The first blow struck Leach on the head. He staggered backwards. The second crashed into his chest. He doubled up. As he fell, the third stroke descended, breaking his back.

Leach lay senseless in the roadway. The running figures of Boysie and his two companions were swallowed up in the night.

The next day the police came for Boysie. They found him in bed, pale and dishevelled, his head swathed in bandages, his right arm once more in a sling. Despite his protestations he was taken to the police station. But the doctor who had treated Boysie testified that in his condition he could not possibly have delivered the blows which crippled Leach. Moreover there were no witnesses, or at any rate none had come forward. Reluctantly the police let him go.

Leach lingered for several days in hospital; then he died.

The killing of Leach was a landmark in Boysie's career. Before, there had been nothing to distinguish him from a dozen local strong-arm boys. Now

Leach's mantle fell upon him and in addition to being leader of the Woodbrook boys, he was accepted as boss of the Town Mob. He no longer needed to eke out a living by petty crime. For a man in his position, he was soon to find, there were far easier and safer ways of making a living – illegal though they might be.

His apprenticeship in crime was over. He was heading for the big time now.

4: PRINCE STREET

ONE OF LEACH'S most lucrative occupations had been the running of a gambling school. Gambling was then as much against the law as it is nowadays in England – though soon the authorities were to acknowledge the passion for gambling that rules the Trinidadian proletariat, and the police began to license certain clubs for the playing of whappie and other games. But as Boysie was soon to learn, there were ways of getting round the law.

Moreover for as long as he could remember, Boysie had been a gambler himself. It was only logical that he should take over Leach's school.

Soon after Leach's death, Boysie moved into town. His first gambling shop was in an upstairs room on Queen Street – a street which some years later was to gain a lurid fame from his activities. Soon, however, he received notice to quit from the owner of the premises, and moved to nearby Charlotte Street. A short time afterwards he moved again, this time to 59, Prince Street, which was to remain his headquarters until the end of the thirties.

It was at Prince Street that Boysie laid the foundation of his personal fortune and began to draw round him the nucleus of what was to become the most bloodthirsty gang of cutthroats in the Caribbean.

No. 59 consisted of a long, narrow single-storey building extending back from the street, and flanked by an open yard. The building was divided into three sections. The first, which gave on to the road, was sublet; the second, or central section, was occupied by Boysie and Popo – the Leach ex-prostitute with whom he was now living – and his son Chuncie; the third section, which consisted of a single barn-like room, was the gambling shop. One gained access to the shop and the yard through a passageway four feet wide and about twenty feet long which passed between the sublet section and the charcoal shop next door.

In this passage there were three gates. The outer one was kept locked. If you wanted to go in and gamble you knocked on it. The tenants in the front of the building would then tell Boysie or his deputy. The latter would come to the gate and examine you through a circular spy-hole provided for the purpose. If you were known personally you would be admitted; if not, not.

Once you had been accepted and had passed down the dark passageway, you found yourself completely cut off from outside observation. On two sides, the yard was bounded by high stone walls, on the third by a galvanised iron paling. Frequently when a school of thirty or forty men had been accumulated, all three gates would be locked, and no-one else admitted. Gambling went on at all hours of the day and night.

In later days, when Boysie's ruthless killings spread terror through Port of Spain, many stories were spread of the innumerable fights, beatings-up and even murders which were supposed to have taken place at Prince Street and others of Boysie's clubs. Nearly all of these are without foundation. At this period of his life, Boysie was primarily a businessman. That his business was illegal makes no difference; he was intelligent enough to realise that he could make far more money running well-organised and well-conducted gambling clubs than by doping or clubbing the odd rich customer. Such tactics would not merely land him in trouble and disrupt the good relations he was gradually establishing with the Trinidad police – they would scare off his more respectable clients, whose dollars were as good as a hoodlum's and probably more plentiful.

This is not to deny that a great many roughnecks and criminals did patronise Boysie's clubs, as they patronised any place where they could gamble without interference. But Boysie knew them all and kept them under control. In other gambling joints, fights over welshing, cheating or disputed bets were a common occurrence. Boysie's reputation, however, together with the fists, feet, head and stick which he was ready to unleash on the least provocation, was sufficient to keep even the roughest in order.

He developed his own way of settling disputes over debts. If he heard that one of his regulars was owed money, he would pay him out of his own pocket. Then the debtor would be called to account. Boysie would ask him, "When can you pay?" If the man explained that he was hard up, that he couldn't pay for two or three weeks, or even months, Boysie would accept that; but woe betide the man who promised to pay the next day and failed.

The card game most commonly played at Prince Street was whappie. At whappie any number can play. The game is managed by a man called the "casa" who, as the name indicates, looks after the interests of the house as well as regulating the play. Sometimes Boysie himself was the casa, sometimes Cecil Forbes, Tinsingh or some other of his close associates. It was part of the casa's job to collect the house percentage – five cents on bets of up to a dollar, ten cents on bets of between one and ten dollars, and twenty-five cents on anything higher.

The game begins by the casa "brewing" – shuffling – the cards. He then asks, "Who's nicking?" Whichever player accepts becomes the "nicker". The nicker has in whappie a certain fractional advantage, as will be seen in a moment. He can now if he wishes brew the cards a second time. He then passes them to the player on his left who cuts and is known henceforth as the "cutter". He also can brew if he likes. After this neither nicker nor cutter handle the cards. The pack is handed back to the casa who places the first card, face uppermost, in front of the nicker, the second in front of the cutter.

The game resembles baccarat or chemin-de-fer in that the real struggle is between these two players, though as in the better-known games the other players can join in. The nicker can bet only on "his" card – the first turned up. Similarly the cutter must bet on the second card. The other players can bet on either side, but it should be pointed out that their bets are against each other and not against the house. In whappie, the house cannot lose, unless the casa appoints a deputy and takes a hand in the game himself – as Boysie frequently did.

Suppose that the nicker's card is a seven, the cutter's an ace – or "ess" as it is invariably pronounced by Trinidadian gamblers. The next stage of the game consists of seeing whether ace or another seven will come up first. To this end the casa deals, placing the cards alternately on two separate piles. If the seven comes first, the nicker wins – the odds throughout the game are of course even – if the ace, the cutter wins. Suppose it is the seven. There are now two sevens and an ace on the table. This stage of the game is called "single". Now the nicker has the option of betting the cutter that his card – the seven – will come up again in a certain number of cards – say three or four. Odds on this chance are longer, but no longer than two or three to one because if the card doesn't come up in the stated number, the nicker doesn't lose – the casa simply goes on dealing as before until ace or seven appears again, and the odds revert to even.

There are now two possibilities. Either an ace will come up, making two aces against two sevens, or the seven will reappear, making three sevens against a single ace.

When there are two pairs, the stage of the game is known as "albo". The casa proceeds as before until a third ace or seven appears. Suppose it is the seven. The players now have the option of betting "diviné" or "défini". To bet "diviné" means that you pick one of the two aces outstanding – the ace of hearts or clubs, for instance, if spades and diamonds are already on the table – to appear before the remaining seven. To bet "défini" means that you back the seven to appear before either of the aces.

On the other hand, if at the two-one stage a third seven crops up, the diviné-défini phase is reached a stage earlier, that is all.

In the final stage of the game, there will either be three sevens and three aces on the table – in which case the last bet is decided like the first, by which of the two comes up – or there will be four of one kind out, and two sevens or two aces still in the pack. Suppose the seven of spades and the seven of diamonds have not yet been played. The nicker has first pick and can back either against the other. Or as a variation he can play "in front or behind". That is to say, if the first of the two outstanding sevens falls on the heap nearest him – "in front" – he wins, while if it falls on that nearest the cutter – "behind" – he loses.

When this stage is completed, the casa rebrews the cards and a new nicker takes over.

Whappie is a fast game, and even with low stakes large sums of money can change hands in a short space of time. One day Boysie was to find this out to his cost. But in the Prince Street period, his luck was good, and most days he had a sizeable sum from his own winnings to add to the house percentage.

It must not be supposed that the police were ignorant of Boysie's doings. A club so well patronised in the heart of town was bound to draw their attention sooner or later. No action, however, was taken against the Prince Street premises.

The police might have argued that, as there were bound to be such clubs, it was better that they should be well-run and well-organised. They might have argued that it was sometimes a positive advantage to know where certain persons were to be found. They might have argued that on occasions Boysie himself passed on pieces of information that were of use to them. But these arguments would have borne little weight with anyone who had taken the trouble to conceal himself near the Prince Street entrance on a Friday evening, and had watched the policemen slipping in one by one to receive their weekly stipend – five dollars for a constable, ten for a sergeant. Some of these men were to be promoted and to hold high rank in the police force when Boysie was in his heyday.

At this period he was still in his late twenties. Physically he was at his peak; still free of the diseases which were to plague him later, and with no sign of the grossness which the good living of the fat years was to bring. The only weak parts of his body were his wrists, which he usually protected with leather straps; they were not strong enough to absorb the shock of his sledgehammer blows, and always after a fight he would complain of pains in them. He was not yet the pace-setting dandy of the war years. He appeared almost invariably in white shorts and a white silk sleeveless vest of the type known in Trinidad as a "merino", with a broad belt of dark brown leather. "Three Little Trees" was his inseparable companion whenever he sallied forth from Prince Street.

His usual destination on these jaunts was Hell Yard.

Hell Yard lay on the banks of the Dry River – the huge stone conduit, fifteen feet deep and thirty feet across, which carries storm water from the hills behind Port of Spain through the low-lying sections of the town and out to sea. The Yard is abandoned now, partly built on and partly overgrown with weeds and bushes, but in those days it was a fair-sized expanse of waste ground on which the rougher characters of the neighbourhood, particularly from "behind the bridge" – the slums on the wrong side of the Dry River – used to congregate for gambling, arguing, "liming", or flying kites.

Kite-flying, as mentioned before, was a serious business in those days. The aim was to capture as many kites as possible. If you flew a kite at all it was no use saying you didn't want to play; all kites were considered fair game, and in self-defence you would be forced to arm your kite with the various accessories which were used in kite-fighting.

The most common of these was a mixture known as mange. This came in two varieties – slacking mange and pulling mange. The base for both types was made by grinding soda-water bottles into a fine dust, and mixing it with rasom – a powdery substance which, I was assured, could be bought in any self-respecting Port of Spain store. The purpose of this was to make the glass cut better.

To make pulling mange, this base was mixed with dasheen, an Indian root vegetable rather like a yam which when boiled produces a gluey substance. In slacking mange this was replaced with "bread pit" – the soft crumbs from the inside of a loaf – mixed with water, or boiled rice. The purpose of these substances was to make the mange stick to the kite string. To do this it was often necessary to moisten the mixture with saliva. When the mange had been applied to the string it was left to dry, care being taken to avoid touching it.

Pulling mange is so called because it is used by the school of thought which holds that the best method of kite-fighting is to let your kite overrun your opponent's and then cut his string by pulling it back towards you. Slacking mange is preferred by those who allow the wind to do the job for them and drag their kite over their opponent's string, severing it on the outward journey. The majority of kite-flyers in Boysie's day used slacking mange, but Boysie had great success with the pulling variety.

A further refinement is to use zwill. Zwill is made by breaking up bottles and allowing the fragments to dry thoroughly in the sun. They are then chipped with an iron barrel-hoop so as to produce thin slivers of glass like razor-blades. These slivers are inserted into the tail of the kite in the following manner; a paste made with flour and lime is spread over the cloth of the tail (the lime is to prevent the paste being eaten by cockroaches) the slivers thrust through the cloth, and the cloth then folded over and stuck down with the paste so as to hold the zwill in position.

Zwill is especially useful in the manoeuvre known as touchiné zwill. This one is for experts only. Normally the kite-fighter aims to work his kite so that it crosses his opponent's string at an angle, so that the cutting of it – whether with zwill-barbed tail or mange-covered thread – is made comparatively easy. In touchiné the aggressor flies his kite above but a little to one side of the enemy kite, then slacks his string suddenly so that the tail cuts forward instead of across.

Boysie was a master of this and indeed of all kite techniques. His wrists may have been weak, but they were flexible, perhaps from the constant pulling in of fish-lines. He often came back from Hell Yard with half-a-dozen captured kites under his arms.

His jaunts were the more frequent at this time as he and Popo were not getting on well. Trouble arose because of his intense love for his son; he believed that Popo was ill-treating Chuncie, and beat her frequently with his thick leather belt. In 1938 there came a further cause of disagreement. Boysie met the woman who was to become his wife, and he determined to get rid of Popo for good.

He decided in fact to murder her. He took some of the ground glass he used in his pulling mange and mixed it in a roti – one of the thin pancakes which form the staple diet of Indians in Trinidad. Popo ate it, was taken violently ill. Boysie came to her as she lay writhing in bed and handed her a capsule which contained more ground glass, telling her, not without truth, that this would cure her for good. Popo however refused it. As he had offered it to her he had been laughing – and laughter was with Boysie an invariable sign that he was plotting mischief. The effect was in the end as satisfactory for Boysie as if she had taken it, for no sooner had she recovered than she packed her belongings and left Prince Street for ever.

5: THE GAMBLING GAME OF DREAMS

THE Prince Street gambling shop, however, was far from being Boysie's sole source of income during the thirties. As the "favourite" of Port of Spain he was in great demand as a hired bravo; his normal charge for a beating was thirty-five dollars. Sometimes he might delegate the work to one of the many followers he was already accumulating. Often he would do the job himself. In fact one of the points which distinguish Boysie from the average Soho or Chicago gang leader was his readiness to do his own dirty work even when help was available. To the end of his days he was proud of his reputation as a fighter.

But the income derived from this source was irregular and quite negligible compared with the sums which he made from operating whe-whe schools.

Whe-whe – pronounced "way-way" – is a gambling game which has marked affinities with the American numbers racket and the "animal game" of Brazil. Like them it is based on a series of numbers, in this case from one to thirty-six, each of which corresponds to some animal, person or thing. The correspondences in Trinidad go as follows: –

1. Centipede
2. Old Lady
3. Carriage
4. Dead Man
5. Parson Man
6. Belly
7. Hog
8. Tiger
9. Cattle
10. Monkey
11. Corbeau (Carrion crow)
12. Tie Pin
13. Crapaud (Frog)
14. Money ears
15. Sick woman
16. Jammet woman (Prostitute)
17. Pigeon
18. Water boat
19. Horse
20. Dog
21. Mouth
22. Rat
23. House
24. Cocobey (Cold in eye or sores on body)
25. Morocoy (a South American tortoise)
26. Fowl
27. Little Snake
28. Red Fish
29. Opium man
30. House cat
31. Parson wife
32. Lolo (man's penis)
33. Spider
34. Blind man
35. Big snake
36. Cat pan (any utensil used for the purpose of a bidet)

The importance of their names is that many, perhaps most whe-whe punters select their number according to their dreams. If they dream of a tiger, they bet on number 8; of a blind man, number 34. One might think that the chance of dreaming certain numbers – morocoy, for instance, or cat pan – are somewhat slight; but here the science of dream-interpretation comes into its own. Not merely the name of a particular number, but anything, however remotely connected with that name, or anything which may be interpreted as representing that name, is considered an augury of fortune, and the whe-whe addict will stake his bet in accordance.

The whe-whe banker operates like a street bookie, collecting his bets through a network of runners. Whe-whe was and still is as illegal as street betting in England, so every day the banker chooses a new site – a shop, a bar or a street-corner – as a rendezvous for his runners and for the process known as "busting the mark".

The "mark" is the winning number. No element of chance enters into its selection; it is simply chosen by the banker, who usually writes it on a slip of paper, folds the paper in half and pins it up in some conspicuous spot before collecting bets from the runners. The procedure is repeated daily. In the first week or so of any whe-whe bank there is nothing to guide him in his selection. It is said that many bankers, like punters, rely on their dreams for their choice. "And suppose they have no dreams one night?" I asked. "Oh, they'll make sure they dream something, don't you worry." But from the second week on there exists a more reliable guide.

This is the "abstract" which every enterprising banker keeps or has his clerk keep. In this abstract are entered the totals staked on each number on every day of the week; soon patterns begin to emerge; some numbers are found to be favoured by the punters and others unaccountably ignored. The banker picks his mark accordingly.

The odds given in whe-whe vary from bank to bank, but whenever Boysie bust a mark – opened the slip of paper to reveal the winning number – he paid off at twenty-nine to one. These odds, while giving the bank a pronounced edge, do not prevent it from being wiped out by a bunch of lucky punters. In the thirties, though, the luck all ran Boysie's way.

His first schools – which developed concurrently with the whappie at Prince Street – were held on Laventille, a hill behind Port of Spain. Soon he had made enough to buy his first property, a house in Belmont which he promptly rented out. Seeking fresh fields to conquer, he tried to set up a second school on nearby Fort George Hill. Here, however, another banker was already established, and warned Boysie off. Angry words passed between the two men. For once Boysie did not resort to violence to prove his point. An easier means lay to hand; he simply informed on his rival, and accompanied in person the squad sent to raid Fort George. The banker was arrested, charged and convicted. He took the hint. Boysie's whe-whe territory continued to expand.

It was as a result of this affair that Boysie contracted a short-lived alliance with the Peru brothers, for the Fort George banker was their enemy also. The Peru brothers, Jogie and Hani, who were shortly to be hanged for murder, had a somewhat ambiguous reputation. Many regarded them as desperate gangsters, but on their being so described in a recent newspaper article, a surviving relative wrote bitterly, complaining that they were honest men who had merely defended themselves against hooligans.

There is perhaps some truth in this contention. One evening, Jogie Peru, who at that time was employed by the City Council, was cycling home from work along Mucurapo Road, when two or three men in ambush beneath a bridge leapt out and beat him up so severely that he was in hospital for several weeks. When he came out of hospital he did not return to work, but roamed Port of Spain with brother Hani looking for his assailants.

Eventually they spotted a man Jogie claimed was one of them, a fellow called "Dolly" Hope. "Dolly" fled with the Peru brothers in hot pursuit. Cornered, he took refuge in a private house, but the brothers smashed their way in and hacked him to pieces with their cutlasses. For this murder both were convicted and executed. Although Boysie was never closely associated with them, some of their notoriety rubbed off on him and helped to increase his "Reputation".

Informing on whe-whe, Boysie soon found, was not a one-way business. Soon one of his runners – a man called "Nugget" – informed on him. As a runner, Nugget naturally knew where the mark was to be bust. On the day in question it was observed that all the runners save Nugget were present. Suddenly a lookout spotted the police approaching. The gang scattered in time and none were arrested.

Boysie took no immediate action. Even when Nugget approached him, the following week, and asked him for a "raise" – Trinidadian for a non-returnable loan – Boysie said nothing, even gave him a couple of dollars. Perhaps there was someone there he did not trust; more likely it was his malicious sense of humour, which would delight in lulling Nugget into a sense of false security, playing with him as a cat plays with a mouse. A week later, Nugget, emboldened by his apparent immunity, came to Prince Street to ask for another raise. This time Boysie told him to wait in the shop, and went quietly and locked all three of the gates in the passageway. Then he came back with "Three Little Trees" and beat Nugget insensible. When Nugget came round he beat him again. The process lasted the best part of two hours, at the end of which time those present dragged Boysie bodily from his victim for fear he would kill him. Nugget recovered, but he will limp to the end of his days.

At least two other men who informed on Boysie received the same treatment. One of them had his chest battered with a hammer; according to an eyewitness, it was as if Boysie was pounding coconut fibre in Carrera again. Somehow they survived, and none of them ever reported the incidents to the police; people were becoming afraid to report him, for fear that still more savage reprisals would follow.

His reputation was increased still further by the Hosein night stickfights in which, during this period, he took part.

The Hosein Festival, which is annual, and, like Easter, moveable by the moon, is a festival of Mohammedan Indians which corresponds to the better-known Middle Eastern Ramadan. Believers fast for ten days prior to the appearance of the new moon, whereupon the festival begins and lasts for three nights – Flag Night, Small Hosein and Big Hosein. As with Carnival, the religious significance is now largely ignored or forgotten, but the outward forms of the feast persist, and amongst these the most striking is the ritual stickfighting at which Boysie excelled.

During the festival, drums beat all the time, gradually building up an atmosphere of tension while the celebrants drink and dance, until one of them is sufficiently inflamed to issue a general challenge. This he does by flinging his stick down on the ground. Immediately a circle is formed while the challenger performs a dance of defiance around the stick. Anyone who wishes to take up the challenge then throws his own stick into the circle. Nowadays the two fighters are often friends who have no intention of hurting each other, but merely wish to show off their prowess with the stick. In the thirties, however, these contests were often a serious affair, especially if the combatants came from rival districts. There were no fixed rules, although it was considered unsporting to hit one's opponent in the back or after his stick had fallen to the ground; there was no referee either; the spectators were sole arbiters of fair play. The fight went on till one or other of the combatants had his head broken open and blood drawn.

Boysie never lost one of these fights.

It was at an Indian festival – though not a Hosein night – that Boysie began his feud with the leader of the San Juan Indians, Mano Das.

San Juan is a working-class suburb of Port of Spain – perhaps satellite town would be a better description, for it lies several miles from the city along the Eastern Main Road, in a narrow trough between hills. An asthmatic railway pants through it, and from its decrepit main street there branch off twisting side-roads where tough bars and clubs rub shoulders with Chinese groceries and plaster-white Indian temples. Boysie was to have a lot of trouble in San Juan before the finish; one of his henchmen would be killed there, he himself would come within an ace of death, and it would be a San Juan killer who brought him to his last fatal journey.

The feud began in a building then known as Noon's Hall, which was a place where Indian singing competitions were frequently held. It often happened at such competitions that the judges' decisions caused disputes to break out among the audience. Boysie considered himself something of an authority on Indian music – which he often played to himself between five-thirty and seven in the morning – and on this particular evening he got into an argument with Mano Das over who was the best singer. A fight began, which, however, was soon broken up by the police. The combatants fled, but from that time on, Boysie, annoyed perhaps at being deprived of victory, nourished an implacable hatred against all residents of San Juan.

Many of these make their living by growing market-garden crops and bringing them into Port of Spain market by donkey cart. Boysie now took to visiting the market in company with the tougher of his boys – among whom was already listed the terrible Fire Kong – and beating up any San Juan people he saw there. It got so that no one from San Juan dared to bring his cart into Port of Spain any more.

At length, Mano Das came to town to do battle for his people. This time the fight was not interrupted and Boysie was victorious.

Satisfied at last, he lifted his embargo on the produce carts. But the truce which followed was an uneasy one. The San Juan boys bitterly resented Boysie's attempts to extend his activities – amorous as well as financial – into their district, and a few years later the feud flared up more violently than before.

But that was during the war years. The last years of peace were drawing to their close when Boysie got rid of Popo and took in her place the woman who was to become his wife.

Her name was Doris. She was a Creole – part Negro, part Spanish – who came originally from a village called Toco on the northeast coast of Trinidad. I have never been to Toco, but from what I have been told about it, it sounds like an earthly paradise. Above the boiling Atlantic surf the hills are covered with rich coconut plantations; everyone has a little land, no one ever goes short of food, and there is none of the strife and bitterness of class or race that are so common in Trinidadian villages nowadays. But the inhabitants of Toco breed large families, and there is not work for all of them. So the young people come to Port of Spain, to find work as yardboys or maids; but all the time they are there – and they seldom stay long – they dream of their distant home, and the day when they will have saved enough to return there, even if only for a while.

Doris was one of the few who stayed. She worked as a house-maid in Woodbrook, and it was there that her exotic looks caught Boysie's eye. She in her turn was fascinated by the tough, free-spending young Indian, and as soon as Popo departed she moved into Prince Street. The period which followed – from 1938 to the arrival of the Americans in 1941 – was perhaps the most peaceful in Boysie's life. There were none of the rows and beatings which had marred his earlier liaisons. His fellow gamblers and strong-arm men were no longer welcome in his home, with the exception of Cecil

Forbes, a quiet young man whom Boysie trusted implicitly and who in his turn was utterly loyal to his employer. During this period he seems to have been faithful to Doris. Instead of roaming the town in search of sex or trouble he would stay at home in the evenings with her and Chuncie, talking or listening to the wireless. It was the nearest to domesticity that he ever came.

About this time Boysie had two brushes with the supernatural – one explicable, the other inexplicable. The first concerned a haunted house in Woodbrook. A poltergeist was supposed to be functioning there; stones were hurled at passers-by; no one dared go near the place. Boysie, however, was no more afraid of ghosts than of his fellow men. One evening he paid a visit to the house. Stones were hurled at him. Boysie, unlike the others, did not take flight. To him, flying stones could only have one explanation. He walked in the direction from which they had come, and sure enough found some fellows hiding in the bushes behind the house. Boysie grabbed a handful of stones and returned their fire, and the haunting ceased forthwith.

The second manifestation was less easily dispelled.

One evening at about eight o'clock, Boysie and Doris were sitting listening to the news of the war which had just broken out in far-off, mythical Europe. Boysie was a staunch supporter of Hitler – partly out of antipathy to the Colonial government, but mainly because Hitler, like Boysie, was born under Aries and operated with the Aries-type ruthlessness which Boysie so admired and sought in his smaller way to imitate. Chuncie, who at this time was seven, was playing on the floor. The room opened directly onto the yard – the yard in which Nugget and his fellow-informers received their punishment – by means of a type of door common enough in old tropical houses, divided horizontally so that the upper part can remain open for coolness while the lower remains shut. Of the three gates in the passageway, two were locked. The gambling shop was for once empty; there were only the three of them in the building.

Suddenly, looking up from his game, Chuncie saw the figure of a man in a hat and a white jacket pass across the open, upper half of the door. He cried out, but by the time he had attracted Boysie's attention the figure – which had been coming as if entering from the street – had disappeared. Boysie snatched up "Three Little Trees" and ran out into the yard. It was empty. He searched the entire building, but there was nobody there. He accused Chuncie of making the story up, and soon the incident was forgotten.

The next day Doris saw the same man in the bathroom. She recognised him at once by his white jacket and hat. She ran to call Boysie, but by the time Boysie arrived the figure had once more disappeared. Still Boysie would not believe. He told Doris she must have imagined it.

The same evening all three of them saw the man. He passed the half-open door a second time, in his hat and white jacket, without a sound, but this time going out towards the street. Boysie cursed and ran down the passageway towards the gates which he knew perfectly well were locked. Of course there was no one. None of them ever saw the man again.

A few days afterwards Chuncie fell ill. A doctor was called, but had no idea what was the matter with him. During the day his fever was slight but in the evening it would soar regularly to 103. He remained thus for nearly two months until one day the sickness left him as suddenly and inexplicably as it had come.

6: GANG WEDDING

IN EUROPE THE WAR was spreading. Poland went under; in the icy north, Finland struggled alone; Denmark vanished in a matter of days, and Norway followed scarcely less swiftly. Holland, Belgium and France were about to be overrun, and England, aware at last of her vaunted Navy's weakness and the threat of unrestricted submarine warfare, was preparing an agreement by which certain bases were to be leased to the United States in return for forty obsolescent destroyers.

Of this agreement, which was to alter the whole course of his life, Boysie naturally knew nothing. The war excited little interest in Trinidad, except among the ruling class, which felt that its own interests and perhaps its very survival were involved. Among a minority of Trinidadians – those who had taken part in the 1937 riots, in which a hated policeman was drenched in kerosene and burnt alive – an opposite view prevailed, the view that a German victory was to be welcomed if it meant the end of the colonial system. But to most the war was like a distant, involved, interminable test match, the veering fortunes of which gave a passing interest to their days, but which, it seemed, could have little effect on their lives beyond the ever-lengthening list of shortages that they had to endure.

Yet if Boysie had been a soothsayer, he could hardly have prepared better for the days that were to come. Already, late in 1939, he had realised the inadequacy of his Prince Street premises, and had opened another gambling club on the corner of Prince and Charlotte Streets. This was known as the Sunrise Club. The police had by now introduced the practice of issuing licences for bona fide members' clubs, where gaming was allowed to take place. Boysie was able to secure such a licence for the Sunrise.

Shortly afterwards he acquired the premises next door, which became known as the Baltimore Club. For licensing purposes it was treated as a separate establishment, but soon after opening it Boysie knocked holes in the dividing wall and ran the two clubs as one.

He began to attract a better class of customer than had been willing to brave the locked gates of Princes Street. In those days, apart from a few cinemas and the stuffy lounges of hotels, there was nowhere to go in Port of Spain after dark. Now to the thrill of gambling, Boysie added the attraction of being able to see, in perfect safety – for he maintained as strict a discipline as in Prince Street – a representative cross-section of the

Trinidadian underworld. Sailors, sightseers and respectable citizens on the spree began to frequent his two clubs. Some came to gamble, some to watch, some to look over the prostitutes who were beginning to flock mothlike around the irresistible beacon of money. To all three categories, Boysie realised, nothing would be more welcome than a drink.

He installed bars in both clubs, and the bars in their turn drew still more custom, so much that a year after the opening of the Sunrise he was able to start a third club, the notorious Dorset, at 55 Queen Street. In the early days of the war the Dorset took second place to the other two, but Boysie was to retain it when the others had to be relinquished, and it would serve as warehouse, brothel and arsenal for his pirate crew.

Guardian Photonews

This is 55 Queen Street, Port of Spain, where the Dorset Club flourished. Where Singh called the tune at Whappie and All Fours, where smoke lay heavy in the air, where broken bottles were crunched underfoot, where laughter, noise and bustle filled the air... heavy with the scent of rum and crime.

That phase of his career, however, still lay in the future. The early war years – 1939-41 – were for Boysie a time of preparation, during which he was gradually feeling his way towards the combination of gambling, drink, sex and drugs, which by the end of the war would bring him to the height of his fortune.

However, the clubs did not occupy the whole of his time. Since the middle thirties he had been playing another card game, known as all fours. All fours, a four-handed game like bridge or whist, was extremely popular throughout Trinidad at this time, and was in fact to the middle and lower-middle classes what whappie was to the proletariat. Tournaments used to take place every weekend, for stakes as high as three or four hundred dollars.

All fours is played as follows. Scoring is based on a series of points, known as "chalks". Two pairs of players take part and the first pair to score fourteen "chalks" wins the game.

Six cards are dealt to each player; the dealer deals anticlockwise. He then "kicks" – turns up – a card to indicate trumps. If he kicks a jack or six of any suit he immediately gets three or two chalks respectively. Only two players are allowed to look at their cards – the dealer and the player on his right. The latter can then "beg", that is ask for three more cards. But the decision rests with the dealer; if he wishes to stand he can refuse the extra cards but must forfeit a chalk. Otherwise he must deal three cards to each player and kick again for trumps. Should the same suit come up, the process must be repeated. This however is the limit; the dealer cannot increase the number of cards beyond six extra ones, or a total of twelve.

The game then follows the same pattern as bridge; tricks being played and taken, with the odd difference that in all fours it is not necessary to be out of a suit in order to trump – one can trump and then follow suit in the next round. When the hand has been played, the tricks of each pair are examined, and four chalks are awarded; for "high", "low", "jack" and "game". The pair whose tricks include "high" – the highest trump – win a chalk; those whose tricks include "low", the lowest, win another. Whichever pair wins a trick containing the Jack of Clubs wins a third chalk, while the fourth – "game" – is decided by adding up the cards on a points basis, ace being equal to four, king to three, queen to two, jack to one, and the others having their face value.

In all fours, as in any other game where it was feasible, Boysie was not above supporting his luck with a little practical assistance.

He used to mark the key cards in the pack with a needle, punching a pattern into their backs which even if visible was meaningless to the uninitiated. His own hand he kept palmed, to avoid others taking advantage of the code. A certain amount of polite tipping-off between partners is quite permissible in all fours. The disadvantage is that the normal signs are known to all regular players – first finger stretched out for an ace, second for a king, cards tugged several times at the corner to indicate number of trumps, and so on. Boysie developed a system of his own with his regular partners, tipped his hand by minute movements of his head, which to the opposing pair looked like natural, involuntary gestures.

In the course of these tournaments Boysie travelled throughout the island. He became known personally to people in almost every town and village; this was to serve him well when wartime shortages caused him to plunge heavily in the black market. If a bar or shop was closed when he wanted service, all he had to do was to knock and say, "You know who I is?" and the place would open immediately for him.

With his income soaring from all these sources – the clubs, the whe-whe, the all fours, the occasional strong-arm work, which he would still undertake – he began to look for a safer source of income: property. One of the first houses he purchased was 13 Rosalino Street, which his mother had owned and which had passed on her death to his elder sister. Other properties in the Laventille district were quickly rented out, but 13 Rosalino Street, with its old associations, he decided to make his home.

There was only one thing needed to complete the domestic picture: marriage.

Marriage was in the air. Tinsingh – former casa of Prince Street, now managing the Sunrise, and despite his nickname, no Indian (his real name was David Arno) – was already engaged to a girl who was a Catholic – as for that matter was Doris. It is supposed to be Tinsingh who gave Boysie the idea of a double wedding.

Boysie agreed. He had come a long way from the impulsive young hoodlum who had been discharged from Carrera ten years before. Although he was far from being accepted by polite society, most people nowadays treated him with a cautious respect. There was no better way in which he could mark the extent of this advance than by holding a slap-up wedding. For weddings in the West Indies have a far greater importance than they have in England – perhaps because they are so much rarer. In many islands marriage is still the exception rather than the rule, and the illegitimacy rate exceeds fifty per cent. This is not because West Indians are immoral. It is partly a legacy of the slave days – when any impediment however slight to the breeding of slaves was sedulously removed by manpower-hungry planters – and partly a result of the widespread belief that to be truly married the prospective partners must beggar themselves with ostentatious display. It is not uncommon for a couple to live together for twenty or thirty years before they can save up enough – or what in their opinion is enough – to get married.

The wedding was fixed to take place on July 27th, 1941, at the Rosary Church in Port of Spain. Boysie was quite willing to accept the proviso that goes with all weddings between Catholics and non-Catholics – that children of the marriage will be brought up in the Catholic faith. As things happened, this didn't matter, for there weren't going to be any children.

To Boysie the most important thing was not the ceremony itself but the party which preceded and followed it.

Preparations began a month or more beforehand. The yard behind 13 Rosalino Street – an area about fifty feet square – was completely roofed in with galvanised iron. Chuncie, Doris and her sisters and many neighbours sat up night after night making streamers and paper chains. On the eve of the wedding, the yard was filled with chairs and trestle tables, and decorated with orchids, ferns and palm fronds.

That night the party began, was interrupted briefly the following afternoon for the official ceremony, and went on for a further week without pause.

Fifty-six cars took Boysie, his friends and relations to the Rosary Church in downtown Port of Spain. Boysie had changed from merino and shorts into a grey herringbone suit; he changed back again as soon as the party got back to Rosalino Street. The wedding itself passed off without incident, though I heard of one respectable lady who is still teased by her family because she sang in the choir at the wedding of "that awful gangster, Boysie Singh". When it was over, Boysie and his gang wasted no time in getting down to the serious business of the day.

Nine hundred guests were invited to the wedding party, and well over a thousand attended at one time or another during the week. A hundred and sixty odd cars were parked outside the house. All Boysie's henchmen were there, together with a large part of the population of Woodbrook. There was a barbecue pit with three cooks working in shifts. On each table there were two or three bottles of whiskey – already a prestige drink in the Caribbean – and if these ran out, all you had to do was to call one of the barmen who were in constant attendance and he would supply you from the fifty-five cases of Scotch that Boysie had bought. If your tastes were more exotic, you could choose from among the contents of the ten cases of punchacreamer – a Trinidadian speciality consisting of rum, milk and eggs – eight cases of Gilbey's wine, and six cases of champagne. Or if you had a thirst there were three thousand bottles of beer. No one remembers how much rum was ordered. So plebeian a drink was beneath the notice of a "favourite" such as Boysie.

If you wanted to dance, John "Buddy" Williams and his Orchestra, at that time the best band in Trinidad, were there to play for you on the night of the wedding and the following Sunday; a local combo filled in on other nights. If you felt hungry, there were a dozen goats and a limitless supply of chickens to be consumed; pork, unclean to Moslems, and beef, sacred to Hindus, were conspicuously absent, so as not to give offence to guests of those denominations.

Boysie did not drink at the party; in fact he seldom drank at all, and was a nonsmoker throughout his life. He had his hands full keeping everyone in order.

This was the year in which the American army first came to Trinidad. The Lend-Lease agreement had been signed, and the Americans had set up their first base at Docksite. Some of the earliest arrivals, wandering aimlessly through the quiet streets of Woodbrook, saw the long line of cars and heard the dance-music and the noise of the crowd. Curious, they approached and enquired what was going on. A wedding, they were told. Could they join in the fun? Boysie, with a shrewd eye to the future, said they could. On succeeding nights a large number of Americans came to Boysie's party. One of them was greatly impressed by it, and told Boysie, "I saw Henry Ford's son get married, but this party has his beat by a mile."

Boysie was not overwhelmed by the compliment. "Eat and drink what you like," he replied cautiously, "but don't take anything away."

Three of the Americans ignored this advice and tried to slink out with bottles of whiskey. They were spotted, forced to disgorge their loot, and given a thorough beating.

Their fellow-countrymen did not interfere; they reckoned the three had got what they asked for.

Otherwise the party passed off without bloodshed. The drink alone cost Boysie more than three thousand dollars. Including food, staff, the two bands and all extras, the total must have exceeded five thousand by the time the last fuddled guest staggered home.

Yet the beginning of Boysie's married life was hardly auspicious. From some time in the middle thirties, Boysie had suffered from chronic gonorrhoea. Probably he had contracted it from Popo; he foolishly refused to have it treated, preferring to doctor himself with an iron tonic and blood purifier called Ferrol Compound. Useful though this mixture may be in the treatment of less stubborn diseases, it failed to purify Boysie's tainted blood. It seems likely that he became sterile from this cause; certainly neither Doris nor any of the women with whom he subsequently slept ever conceived by him. In the later years of his life he was practically, if not totally, impotent. Among his more offbeat ideas was one that in its advanced stage his gonorrhoea somehow converted itself into syphilis; but there is no evidence that he ever suffered from the latter disease.

7: YANKEE DOLLARS

THE G.I.'s WHO PEERED curiously at the high jinks in Rosalino Street were merely the advance guard of a vast tide of Americans poised ready to sweep over the island.

Nobody, not even Boysie, could have foreseen the impact they were to have on Trinidad's way of life. Until their arrival, Trinidad, in common with most other out-of-the-way British colonies, had been dragging along with one foot in the nineteenth century. All of a sudden it found itself invaded – that is not too strong a word – by the brashest and least inhibited section of the world's most self-consciously modern state. Each night hundreds of these men, dollars burning their olive-drab pockets, were turned loose on Port of Spain. But what was there for them to do? At eight p.m. the rum-shops closed. The few hotels there were in those days served as officers' stamping-grounds. The G.I. would do anything, go anywhere for a drink.

As it was, his only available recreation lay in the dubious embraces of the drab, unimaginative prostitutes who hung around Marine Square, or in the grimy network of streets that made up the heart of the city. To see what they were like one has only to inspect the brothel quarter of almost any other West Indian city – say Georgetown or Bridgetown. Dressed rather worse than housemaids, without make-up, their hair tortured into bizarre shapes by an inadequate course of straightening, such women could hardly excite desire; their sole advantages were cheapness and availability.

But demand magically produces, if there does not already exist, supply. One of the most popular songs of this period, a pastiche calypso, sung I believe by the Andrews Sisters (one marvels sometimes at the frankness of songs which still somehow get past the Auntie of Portland Place) went as follows:

Drinkin' rum an' coca-cola,
Goin' down Point Cumana,
Both mother and daughter
Workin' for de Yankee dollah.

No one worked more wholeheartedly for the Yankee dollar than Boysie, who was quick to realise that a steady supply of rum 'n' coke and mothers and daughters was the shortest and swiftest way to empty those overfilled pockets. Not a great innovator, he was quick to pick up a hint in any subject which interested him, whether it was gambling, fishing or the nightclub business. Rapidly he began to make over the bare, somewhat barn-like structures of Queen and Charlotte Streets into something that was recognisably an American's idea of a dive.

Perhaps because it was the latest to develop, the Dorset Club – 55 Queen Street – came closest to this idea. No. 55 was a three-storey building of a type common in downtown Port of Spain; the top floor was really a series of garrets with dormer windows let into the steep-pitched roof. The ground floor of 55 was a restaurant, nothing to do with Boysie, who had only the two upper floors; for these he paid the not exorbitant rent of forty dollars a month. On the top floor were rooms where gambling was carried on, but the main part of the club lay on the first floor. Here there was a combined bar and dance-floor, together with a few rooms rented off by the hour to the stable of regular prostitutes Boysie quickly collected. At this stage none of these lived on the premises, and many of them took their men elsewhere; all of them, however, had to pay Boysie a cut on any pick-ups they made in the club – a dollar-fifty, for example, on a five-dollar short time.

For this they got their money's worth in protection from a Tarzan-like thug called Fire Kong, a wiry newcomer from Barbados known as Bage, and others on the strong-arm squad; in fact Boysie himself, obedient to his own maxim, "She is we and we is she", would often sally forth in person to settle any customer who got out of line. The girls adored him. He was always willing to give them help and advice, to encourage them to dress better and make the most of themselves; the modern Trinidadian prostitute, with her high heels, skintight dresses, elaborate hairdo and sophisticated manner is very largely Boysie's creation.

In prostitution there is always a high staff turnover. But this was no worry to Boysie. Through his all-fours matches he had contacts all over the island. Many of these were ready, for a small consideration, to inform him of any likely-looking girls in their districts. Boysie himself or one of his henchmen would then approach the girl and offer her a job in town; the nature of the job would not perhaps be exactly specified. Many jumped at the chance, for in the villages there was little future for a girl save an early marriage and years of drudgery and childbearing. Indeed most of those who accepted seemed to have raised no objections when the nature of their work became plain to them. Sometimes outraged parents would come in from the country to remonstrate with their erring daughters, seldom however with much success.

Drink, oddly enough, caused Boysie more trouble than prostitution. The latter was ignored by the authorities – as it still is, apparently, throughout the West Indies; legislation, if it exists, seems never to be invoked – and the police were not unwilling to permit gambling, but drink was a different matter. It may be that the American army sparked action against places where its troops were allowed to get incapably drunk, encouraged to have intercourse with uninspected and often infected women, and sometimes relieved of their wallets at the same time; whatever the cause, from 1942 on, Boysie had increasing difficulty in getting the Sunrise and Baltimore relicensed, and in 1944 he was refused licences altogether and closed both clubs. Henceforth all his activities were concentrated in the Dorset.

Unlike the other two clubs, the Dorset had never had a liquor licence, yet despite brushes with the law it kept open without a break – literally, for it worked on a twenty-four-hour basis, and could boast, with more justice than the Windmill, "We never closed" – until in 1947 he shut down bar and dance-floor and converted the premises into a full-scale brothel.

The closest of these brushes occurred one evening when some police officers entered the club. Boysie himself was behind the bar at the time and assumed, with good reason, that the call was a social one; he had already picked up the half-bottle from which he would pour them a convivial "snap". He was not to know that this time the police were under orders to raid the club, orders too stringent to be ignored. Before Boysie could move one of the police had leaned over the bar and snatched the bottle. Boysie struck it from his hand; it smashed on the floor. This did not worry the police, however. On the shelves behind the bar whole rows of rum bottles were prominently displayed. They seized several of them and told Boysie he would be charged.

In the court proceedings which followed, these bottles were prominently displayed. The case seemed a foregone conclusion until Boysie's counsel rose and asked counsel for the prosecution to sample their contents. Puzzled, the lawyer eventually consented. A glass was produced and filled; but as the lawyer tasted it his mouth twisted in a grimace of disgust, and he spat the liquid out on the floor. Boysie had been prepared for just such an eventuality; the real rum and whisky were hidden under the bar, and the bottles on the shelves contained merely cold tea.

It was widely believed – probably by people who had never been in his clubs – that Boysie's drinks were often replaced by potions far less innocent than tea. I was even given the recipe for one of the knockout drops allegedly used; peel and grate some potatoes, then squeeze the gratings and add potato juice to 3/4 rum – the taste excites no suspicion and two normal-sized drinks should be ample especially if the subject has been drinking already. (I have not tried the above mixture so can take no responsibility for the results, lethal or otherwise). It is of course likely, almost inevitable, that in the long career of his clubs one or other of Boysie's customers was given a doped drink, but this was far from being standard practice. The legitimate or semi-legitimate returns of the business were so huge that it just was not necessary. Of course, not even Boysie could control the actions of all those who used the clubs. It was – and for that matter still is – quite common for a prostitute who has felt a big roll on her client to give the "rake" – tip-off – to her ponce who will then lurk outside the premises till the client appears and apply the classic West Indian technique known as "lockneck" – locking one arm round the victim's windpipe from behind while running the free hand through his pockets. But Boysie himself never organised these assaults, and in fact tried as far as possible to prevent them; they were bad for business.

Drink did, however, lead Boysie into the black market. The only alcoholic drink that Trinidad produced in those days was rum. Everything else had to be imported, but at a time when the Western world was struggling for survival, and enemy submarines were sinking vessels even in the Caribbean, little shipping space could be spared to haul gin and whisky to the smaller colonial islands. Boysie set to work to corner what was available, scouring the island, paying fifty per cent over the odds; on these trips he used the car he had bought shortly after his wedding, a big grey chauffeur-driven Buick. (It had to be chauffeur-driven because Boysie had failed his driving-test; he managed the car well enough but he omitted to make any signals, and although he pulled the examiner across his own desk and punched his head soundly, the verdict remained unchanged.) Another source of supply was the Americans themselves, who smuggled the stuff in or stole it from their own bases, only to have it sold back to them at double or treble the price. The clubs could absorb all that Boysie could gather.

But it was not only drink that Boysie bought from the Americans. He had never been averse to receiving stolen property if the price was right; now he began to deal extensively in rings, watches, cameras – and guns.

To Boysie, at that time, guns were no more than a portable and easily saleable commodity. There is not the slightest evidence that he began to accumulate them deliberately. There were usually a dozen or so revolvers hidden in the attics of Queen Street, but as yet Boysie had no use for them; for his vendetta with the San Juan mob, which was shortly to break out again, he preferred "torpedoes", small home-made hand-grenades which maimed and terrorised but did not normally kill.

The narcotics trade was another profitable sideline. Frequented as it was by sailors from all over the world, 55 Queen Street made a natural clearing-house. Marijuana came in large quantities from nearby Venezuela; opium from India, brought in by swarthy seamen who spoke not a word of English and who concluded their deals in sign language. Boysie paid up to forty dollars an ounce for raw opium. But although these drugs – along with every other form of diversion, legal or illegal, normal or perverse – were available to the clientele of No. 55, the market was never large enough for Boysie to make big profits in this field.

He scarcely needed them; his net income from the clubs – after paying a wage bill estimated at around four hundred dollars – was now three thousand dollars a week.

His peak year was 1944. In that year he had nearly a quarter of a million dollars in hard cash, not to mention some thirty-three properties which included a dozen houses bought for mistresses and ex-mistresses and a twenty-acre market garden at Toco managed by his mother-in-law.

Gone now were the merino and shorts which he had worn in the old Prince Street days. A visit to the Cab Calloway film, *Stormy Weather*, is supposed to have influenced his style of dressing; he blossomed out in the shoulder-pads, drape-cut jackets and voluminous trousers that set the style for a whole generation of saga-boys. He wore a different-coloured suit for every day of the week. This presented no difficulty; he had at one time a hundred and twenty. Despite his habit of buying them six at a time, he never had more than a hundred pairs of shoes. These he bought in colours to match his suits; if they did not match he painted them himself, for he also initiated the vogue for wearing completely matching outfits – hat, suit, shirt, tie, socks, shoes and cane all in an identical shade – which has lately been feebly imitated by the Barbadian King Dyall and others. Once, when supplies were scarce, he bought an entire shipment of hats for his own use.

His accessories were still more startling. From his fob pocket a gold chain swooped dizzily to within inches of the floor, almost tripping him as he walked; this chain had cost him fifteen hundred dollars. Another chain with a gold star hung round his neck. On each finger were two gold rings, each ring worth eighty or ninety dollars. A gold-topped walking-stick – one of a set of forty – had usurped the place of the too-rugged “Three Little Trees”.

Thus attired he would set out, to the races, which he never missed, or merely to parade the streets. Wherever he went crowds of youths and children would follow him; sometimes when he grew tired of this he would fling handfuls of silver on the ground and walk on while his entourage scrambled for the coins. Wherever he went, men came to him, flattering him, begging for a raise; usually they were successful; they addressed him as “Rajah”, but to himself he was “the Vagabond King”, a title which summed up aptly enough the persona at which he aimed; king of the vagabonds, uncrowned ruler of the underworld, gay, rash and generous, yet obeyed with as much trembling diligence as the most arbitrary despot of the east.

Yet even at the height of his success there were certain signs that the run of fortune would, before long, be reversed. Among the first of these was the fight with the American.

There are in existence at least four completely different versions of this

Boysie Singh at the height of his success

fight; so different that one would assume there were four different fights, if the storytellers had not denied this so vehemently. I will tell the one which seems to me the most convincing: –

One evening an American soldier from the base at Chaguaramas was drinking alone at 55 Queen Street. He had made himself comfortable by placing both his feet on the table. Suddenly Boysie appeared; he had just returned from a day at the races. He asked the American quite politely to take his feet off the table. The American did not move and answered, "I buy my drink, I sit where I want." Boysie made no reply but went into one of the top-floor rooms where he stripped off his Cab Calloway finery and changed into merino and shorts.

Back in the bar, he asked the American a second time to remove his feet. The American ignored him. Boysie told him if he didn't move them they'd be moved for him. The American yawned and said, "You and who else?" Boysie's lips tightened and he pushed the American's feet off the table.

The American leapt to his feet and swung a right. It was the first and the last blow he landed, for Boysie instantly closed with him. The American seized Boysie's arm and got a hammerlock on him. Boysie tried desperately to break the American's grip, hitting him in the chest and stomach, but the American was a giant of a man and held on. Boysie's neck was wrenched and all but broken in his grip. Several of the boys came forward and tried to break up the fight but Boysie called out to them not to interfere; he would never willingly admit that he might need help to end a fight in his favour.

They remained thus, locked together and almost motionless for some ten or twelve minutes. Then Cecil Forbes, who had been watching the fight, said, "This is damned foolishness," lifted his stick and struck the American. The American loosed his grip.

Forbes handed the stick to Boysie, who struck the American twice more. The American turned to run but Boysie hurled the stick after him, splitting open his back so that his shirt was oozing blood as he ran downstairs and out into the street. Boysie sat down abruptly, rubbing at his stiff and swollen neck.

Within minutes an American patrol car screamed to a halt outside the club and the Military Police came storming upstairs, pistols in their hands. They were greeted with bland denials and glasses of free whisky (all M.P.'s in the American Army were entitled to as much free drink and as many free women as they wanted, provided they didn't make things troublesome for Boysie).

Eventually, happier but no wiser men than they had arrived, they left the club empty-handed.

But for Boysie it was a pyrrhic victory. Shortly after the fight he began to complain of severe stiffness in his neck, which he could hardly move. His condition grew rapidly worse and he was obliged to enter a nursing home, where he was given a course of injections. During the first week of his stay he improved considerably, but in the third week a relapse set in, and Boysie, whose opinion of medical or any other experts was not high, accused his doctor of deliberately retarding his recovery so that the nursing home would benefit by the extra fees. Sending for Cecil Forbes, he ordered him to give the doctor one of his own injections. This was too much even for the faithful Cecil, who indignantly refused, and Boysie finally gave up the idea and asked Cecil to take him home.

Gradually he mended. But in his absence business had been going badly. He had left the Dorset in the hands of henchman Tomkin, and he immediately assumed that the latter had been fiddling the till. Tomkin was promptly called to account. He indignantly denied the charges, and had the temerity to "talk fight" to Boysie and threaten what he, Tomkin, would do to him if Boysie were capable of defending himself.

For the first recorded time in his life Boysie wept; wept tears of rage, for he was too weak to strike Tomkin, and for the first time in his life had to swallow an insult without returning the instant retribution it deserved. He did not forget this humiliation. Around Christmas of 1943, when he was at once more able to walk about, he met Tomkin on the Queen's Park Savannah, and challenged him to make good his boasting. Tomkin had to accept. Although he was not yet fully recovered, Boysie swung Tomkin clean off his feet, lifted him high in the air and dashed him to the ground.

When Tomkin came to his senses he moved out of Port of Spain for good.

So Boysie came back to the club life, and went on as before. He should have learnt from this experience that no one can win all the time, whether in fights or at cards. But he did not. He was at the height of his wealth and power. Nothing could stop him now – or so it seemed.

8: THE FEUD WITH SAN JUAN

IN THE EARLY FORTIES, the clubs did not provide the whole of Boysie's income. He still kept his whe-whe banks in action, and he made a great deal of money at the races.

This he did not obtain through betting. Boysie hardly ever played the horses; he preferred a gamble whose outcome he could to some extent control. At every race meeting he ran at least two gambling games – the Ring Game and the Wheel Game.

The Ring Game, which was legal provided one had a licence to play it (which Boysie did; he ran up to three Ring Games at every meeting) required an enclosure about eighteen feet square surrounded by a bamboo fence some four feet in height. In the centre of this enclosure there stood a table five feet square on which a large number of notes had been spread, notes of one, two and five dollar denominations. Each note was weighted with a sixty cent piece, which was equal in value to the English half-crown; Trinidadian currency was then in an uneasy halfway stage between decimal and duodecimal coinage. In the centre of the table lay a twenty dollar note, similarly weighted.

The game consisted of throwing a brass ring, with a diameter slightly greater than that of the sixty-cent piece, over one or other of the coins. If this was done successfully, the player won, not the coin itself, but the note beneath it – one, two, five, or twenty dollars as the case might be. The ring of course had to cover the coin exactly; if not the player forfeited his stake which was the humble one of a penny a throw. However the very smallness of the stake ensured that the games would be well patronised, and every race day Boysie would collect a certain and worthwhile profit.

However his real favourite was the Wheel Game – so much so that he used to leave the management of the Ring Game to his deputies and handle the Wheel Game himself. This was partly because it was extremely profitable, partly because he had invented it himself and was rather proud of it.

The Wheel Game was really a kind of crude, do-it-yourself roulette. The apparatus required consisted of a box about three feet square; when this box was opened it revealed a large wheel divided into segments, each segment bearing the name of some card – say, the three of diamonds, or the ace of clubs. The inside of the box lid, which would be left facing upwards next to the wheel, was divided into sections which correspond to the segments of the wheel. Those wishing to bet on, say, the seven of hearts, would place their bet – which could be as little as a cent, and rarely rose above a shilling – in the corresponding section on the lid of the box.

Boysie then spun the wheel. It was slowed down by a bamboo strip which was fastened to the side of the box above the wheel and projected horizontally so that as the wheel revolved it struck against a ring of nails driven in round the wheel's circumference. As there was a nail at the corner of each segment, the bamboo strip had to rest within one segment when the wheel stopped, and thus, in addition to slowing down the wheel, it served as a pointer to indicate the winning number. This paid off at odds of only twelve to one, so the scales were definitely weighted in favour of the bank, and the game was in fact completely illegal. However, the low stakes, and the fact that it depended on pure chance, without the slightest element of skill, drew to it even bigger crowds than patronised the Ring Game.

For his whe-whe schools he was no longer content to work Port of Spain; satisfied that the San Juan mob was by now whipped into shape, he opened a bank on Locust Hill on the outskirts of San Juan. His chief assistant in this enterprise was a man called Harris (no connection with the Harris he had fought so often in Woodbrook) and Harris's house in San Juan became a kind of local headquarters where the busting of marks was planned and the abstract kept.

It was through this Harris that he met two sisters, Indian girls, known as Zena and Rosie, who shared a house and were, it appeared, communal girlfriends of the San Juan gang. This, however, did not worry Boysie. He became a frequent visitor to their home, and soon he was not merely visiting but eating and sleeping there.

This was too much for the San Juan mob. One afternoon, when Boysie was in bed with one or both of the sisters, sixteen or eighteen of the boys surrounded the house, armed with sticks, cutlasses and iron bars. This time they were determined not to let Boysie escape; they would finish him off once and for all.

The first Boysie knew of the siege was a fusillade of stones that came smashing through the windows. He was alone, unprepared and unarmed; pulling on his clothes he seized the only available weapon, a cocoa-knife – a type of knife with a long handle and a hook at the back of the blade for pulling down cocoa-pods and ran out of the house. How he fought his way through the besiegers, nobody knows, but a little while afterwards he was seen coming down a San Juan street, dishevelled but not seriously hurt, carrying in place of the cocoa knife a cutlass and stick which he must have wrested from his pursuers. He was never slow in calling on the aid of the police when things were going against him, as he had proved in the affair of the Fort George banker; now he went to the San Juan police station and reported the assault.

In the meantime, news of the affair, magnified by rumour, had filtered back to Port of Spain. By the time it reached 55 Queen Street, it had hundreds of bloodthirsty San Juanese scouring the town for Boysie. Of Boysie's henchmen the only one ready to go to his assistance was Cecil Forbes; without troubling to collect help, Forbes got a car and drove out to San Juan.

At a junction in San Juan known as the Croisée – one which was to have a sinister meaning for Boysie twelve years afterwards – Forbes met the police jitney which had set out in search of Boysie's assailants. In the jitney (Trinidadian for pick-up truck, usually with canvas cover) were Boysie, four or five policemen, and the man who had met Boysie after his escape from the ambush, whom we will call X.

Forbes climbed into the jitney, and they set off. By this time the day was drawing to its close. It had rained heavily in the afternoon; the roads were glassy with rain, and clouds like smoke were swirling low over the steep banana-green hillsides that rise at the end of nearly every San Juan street. One at least of the passengers in the jitney – X – was feeling nervous; the night before he had had a dream, and in the dream he was riding in a car and the car crashed and someone – he didn't know who – was killed. But the jitney driver didn't seem to be worrying. With Boysie leaning over his shoulder giving directions, he drove fast – faster perhaps than he should have done – down the El Socorro Road.

Suddenly ahead of them they saw a knot of men standing by a parked car. As the men in the car saw the jitney, they started up and accelerated away. The police driver slammed down his accelerator and gave chase. The men left stranded by the wayside scattered and ran – but not before one of them had rolled an empty oil-drum into the road, in the path of the speeding jitney.

The driver saw it too late and swerved, his brakes screaming uselessly as the tyres failed to grip the oil-slick surface. The jitney missed the drum, but it was swinging wildly out of control from one side of the road to the other, its passengers flung about like peas in a tin. It glanced off a telegraph pole on the right-hand side, mounted the left-hand shoulder, and overturned.

Most of the men in the jitney had only minor injuries. But Forbes' neck was broken. He died in hospital a few hours afterwards.

Boysie never forgave the San Juan mob for Forbes' death. He would load up his car with "torpedoes"; these do-it-yourself grenades consisted of charges of gunpowder mixed with sharp-edged flints which were then wrapped in layers of brown paper and fastened with twine. They exploded on impact, with a force that, unless the victim was in a confined space, was damaging but hardly lethal; at least there is no record of anyone having been killed by them. Thus armed, Boysie and his henchmen drove through the San Juan streets; whenever they saw a member of the rival outfit they hurled torpedoes at him and then drove away. Soon none of the San Juan boys dared show themselves, and Boysie was able to go on practising whe-whe and adultery without interruption.

Once he was caught red-handed by the police flinging torpedoes from his car. None of his targets, however, dared to come forward and give evidence; the police had to content themselves with charges of throwing missiles and being "armed with a weapon to commit a felony". For the past thirteen years, Boysie's record – apart from a few trivial gambling and fighting cases – had been clean. He was bound over for two years on a fifty-dollar bond.

The main danger to his whe-whe schools was – now as in the days of Nugget – the informer. A man called Joseph Maynard – better known as Joe Bam-Bam – reported the San Juan school to the police. This time Boysie felt that a beating would not be a sufficient deterrent.

One of Boysie's gang, an Indian known as Rammie, went to Joe Bam-Bam's house one night and knocked on the door. When Joe Bam-Barn opened it, Rammie aimed a pistol at his head and fired. Unluckily for Rammie, Joe Bam-Bam had his mouth open, perhaps being about to wish his visitor "Good evening", and the bullet that had been meant to kill him passed through it. He lived to testify against Rammie, whom he had recognised, and Rammie drew a five-year term of imprisonment, which he accepted philosophically; if he had denounced his employers it wouldn't have lessened his sentence, but it would have decreased his chances of survival when he was let out.

So Boysie finally imposed his will on the recalcitrant suburb of San Juan. Apart from Forbes, his forces received only one serious casualty, and that not in battle. One night one of Boysie's gang, who had just emerged from a brief prison sentence, found another of the mob had taken over his woman. She, her new protector, and some of their friends were in fact laughing and drinking in the bar at 55 Queen Street when he entered. He rushed upstairs to the garret where he found Boysie and asked him for a couple of torpedoes. He didn't tell Boysie what the bombs were for, and Boysie didn't ask; he had plenty, and he was used to giving them out to his followers so they could settle private scores. He gave the man a couple.

The man ran downstairs. Halfway down he was stopped by his brother, who guessed what was happening, and told him not to be a fool. The two men struggled on the narrow stairway; suddenly one of them slipped and in his fall brought down the other on top of him. There was a flash and a deafening roar as the torpedoes exploded.

The brother had one of his hands blown off; the jealous lover, both. Fingers were scattered the length of the staircase. Boysie, the first down, somehow bandaged their wrists and prevented them from bleeding to death. The whole affair was hushed up.

In a grimy upstairs club I saw the man with no hands. The place was just an empty cage of a bar with a bare room beyond it in which men with hats crushed over their eyes were playing whappie and more men were standing around watching. It was gone midnight. My companion left me at the bar and went over to the group. Under a flyblown lamp that seemed to give off darkness visible I saw him speak to a tall man in the group. The tall man turned and stared at me with a bony expressionless face. As he did so he put two stumps of arms behind his back.

My companion returned to the bar, shaking his head. "He doesn't want to talk to you."

I didn't press the point. No one could blame him. "He hardly makes a living," my companion said as we stumbled down the black stairway. "After all, there isn't much that a man with no hands can do."

Yet in a way, I thought, he hadn't done so badly. Unlike so many of those who were close to Boysie, he was still alive.

9: POST-WAR SLUMP

WHILE THE FEUD with San Juan was still in progress, however, Boysie was suffering a series of defeats in other spheres.

The first was the closing down of the Sunrise and the Baltimore. It may be wondered why Boysie did not persist in running these clubs after licences were refused for them; also why, if he was forced to close those two, he was able to go on running the Dorset which had never been licensed at all.

The answer is that it was not so much the police as the respectable burghers of Port of Spain who wanted Boysie out of business. They could forgive him for encouraging vice; what they could not forgive was that he so blatantly made it pay. The Sunrise and Baltimore, once having been licensed as clubs, could hardly survive long in face of a determined police offensive; it is possible that something of the sort was hinted to Boysie, coupled with the suggestion that if he was co-operative in the matter, blind eyes might be turned in the direction of Queen Street. Whether or not this is so, the Dorset was never disturbed, despite periodic complaints of the immoral and even criminal goings-on there. For after all, those in authority could declare there never had been a club registered at 55 Queen Street, so why should there be one there now; he would be a brave Prodnose who would investigate the place in person.

Boysie could console himself with the thought that he had skimmed the cream of the American trade. Already the theatres of war were moving further and further from the Caribbean, and the U.S. bases in Trinidad had lost a good deal of their strategic value; within months, the conflict would be at an end, and the forces stationed there would be still further reduced.

Still, there was no use disguising the fact that the closure was a severe financial blow to him. Overnight his income dropped by two thousand dollars a week, and though this loss was soon partially offset by the increased trade of the Dorset, he never again – except for brief periods when the American fleet visited the island – equalled the takings of the peak 1944 days.

But it was from another and unexpected quarter that the severest blows came.

All through the club period Boysie had continued to gamble at all fours and whappie. He was still lucky, though perhaps not quite as phenomenally so as he had been in the Prince Street days. Now on occasion he lost, sometimes more money than he had on his person. When this happened he would give his hat to one of the hangers-on who invariably accompanied him and the man would hurry to Rosalino Street where Boysie kept a large trunk stuffed with notes. Doris, or whoever was there, would recognise the hat and give the messenger the required sum. For however much Boysie lost, it was a point of honour with him never to give an IOU. – all debts had to be settled promptly and in cash.

Until the end of war, however, he still won more often than he lost.

Snobbery – an incongruous failing in one so earthy as Boysie – led to his gambling downfall. Perhaps he felt that as a man with a hundred and twenty suits, thirty-three properties and a quarter-million in the sock he was entitled to something better than the shirt-sleeved whappie clubs which till then he had frequented. As has been mentioned before, this attitude was not one which would cause either surprise or opposition in Trinidad. Certainly the exclusive gambling club which he now took to frequenting made no bones about accepting the notorious gang-leader and whoremaster into its gilt-edged ranks. If he had money to spend – and he had plenty – he was welcome.

The other members of this club were mostly rich businessmen; many of them were Syrians, a minority in Trinidad which has succeeded out of all proportion to its numbers. Plebeian games such as whappie were of course beneath the notice of such sophisticates. Poker was their game, and especially short-pack poker – a murderous variant in which the cards of lower denominations (sometimes from eights down, but depending of course on the number playing) are removed from the pack. Apparently the sole advantage of this move is to avoid those hands when everyone has pairs or nothing, and either the players throw in or one of them scoops the pool without even a raise. Money changes hands fast in short pack.

Boysie had never before played poker, but he reckoned that anything with cards in it was his meat. After all, he was not bound by the curious moral scruples which handicap the chances of so many card players. The glamour of his new associates, however, seems to have blinded him to the fact that they were no more scrupulous than he. Moreover Boysie was a mere novice at the game; his Syrian opponents had cut their milk teeth on poker-chips. For once the roles were reversed; skilfully they played him, letting him win just enough to restore his confidence, then going in ruthlessly for the kill.

He lost 58,000 dollars in a single disastrous week.

In an attempt to recoup his fortunes he turned again to his favourite whappie. But even here it seemed that the luck which he had enjoyed for so long had finally deserted him. He became involved in a whappie game in a rum shop in Tunapuna – a village a few miles beyond San Juan, notorious for its toughness – which belonged to a man named Carey. The game lasted three nights. Boysie began to lose steadily. Time and time again he sent a messenger back with his hat, but often by the time the latter returned he had already lost the money he had sent for, and had to despatch the man immediately for a further supply. One of the nights his hat went back to Rosalino Street sixteen times.

When the game was over, Boysie had lost 72,000 dollars. Most of the money had gone to Carey, who spent it on a fleet of eighteen Fiat taxis. Nor was he the only man to get a start in life from Boysie's débâcle, for even these two losses were merely episodes in a steady losing streak. The quarter-million vanished like snow in August. When it was gone, the properties followed – even 13 Rosalino Street was sold, and Doris and Anthony had to move temporarily into No. 55 until Boysie bought a house for them at Cocorite on the Western Main Road.

Boysie faced the situation with his customary resilience. He developed in the course of his life a remarkable capacity for switching from one mode of existence to another at a moment's notice. Those who knew him well say that throughout his life he liked to finish any piece of business before night fell; for the morning after, finished or not, he would have no recollection of it; his head would be full of some new idea which he would have to put into practice at once.

Now he proceeded to reorganise his life in accordance with his new and unwelcome poverty. The gambling and the whe-whe had to be sacrificed. 55 Queen Street ceased to exist as a club; partitions were put up and the dance-floor divided into thirty-three rooms, each of them rented out to prostitutes by the week. Although this reduced his income from the premises he was able to keep a check on the returns as he would never have been able to do had he left the place as a club in the hands of a manager. For his new scheme involved his leaving Port of Spain altogether.

Even while he was running his three clubs, Boysie had not entirely forgotten the sea. He had always kept a boat, and had even gone out fishing at weekends, purely for pleasure. Now he was faced with the choice which was facing wartime racketeers all over the world: either go straight or plunge into hundred per cent crime. Boysie decided to go straight – at any rate for the time being. Fishing was the only legitimate trade at which he had ever had any success. He had been doing well at it when his four-year term in Carrera had diverted him to other paths. Now, with the little capital that remained to him, he decided to take it up again.

At the time – early in 1947 – the prospects looked good. Post-war food shortages had raised the price of fish, and the wartime submarine scare had kept local fishermen well within home waters, so that for those who were willing to go further afield there were good hauls to be had. Boysie looked over the Port of Spain fleet and decided that in the narrow waters of the Bocas it represented too much competition. He decided to base himself on the village of Cedros, a few miles from the southwestern tip of the island. He still had sufficient money to buy himself the nucleus of a fleet. By the end of the year his boats were fishing far out in the Gulf of Paria, within sight of the low poison-green mangrove swamps that bordered the Orinoco delta on the coast of Venezuela.

10: FISHING DAYS

BY 1948 BOYSIE had accumulated a fleet of thirty fishing boats – the largest individually-owned fleet ever to operate in these waters. Most of them were twenty-three footers, pirogue-type craft powered by outboard motors and manned by a crew of three, a "captain" and two hands. In addition he usually had two or three larger launches with inboard engines and crews of five or six.

The design of the pirogue boat is based on that old Amerindian standby, the corrial. The corrial is merely a hollowed-out log, though the more sophisticated indigenes improve it by heating the wood and then hammering in crosspieces so as to spread out the sides and enlarge the capacity of the boat. In the pirogue this idea is developed further; the log supplies only the keel and the base of the sides, which are then built up with planks. Pirogues ride higher in the water than conventional, keel-built boats; they are highly manoeuvrable but need considerable skill to handle, especially in bad weather. Yet though they are easily enough overturned, they are virtually unsinkable – a fact which was to have a profound influence on Boysie's piratical techniques.

The engines which drove these boats were hard to come by. Fishermen bid desperately against one another for the miserable export quota which Trinidad was allowed. Boysie now found himself on the receiving rather than the delivering end of the black market. He paid up to six hundred dollars for a nine-horse Johnson engine, whose list price was at that time three hundred. But it was money well spent, for within a year of starting operations Boysie's personal gain from the business was seldom less than two hundred dollars a day.

There were five types of fishing which Boysie's fleet practised: filleting, banking, trolling, fish potting and seine netting.

"Filleting" means fishing with drift nets by night. The net used is a long narrow sleeve of four-inch mesh, two and a half fathoms wide and extending as much as two hundred fathoms in length. Boats usually set out in the evening, and on reaching the fishing grounds one man handles the boat while the other two slack out the net. The boat is then allowed to drift through the greater part of the night; towards dawn the net is pulled in and the boat returns to port at the hour known in the West Indies as "foreday morning".

Banking is a daytime operation. The boat is taken out to the fishing banks where large numbers of fish are known to congregate; there it is anchored and devices known as "banking spellars" are put down. The banking spellar consists of a rough cross made out of stiff wire. To each corner of this cross a more flexible piece of wire with a hook is attached. The cross is weighted with a lead weight which varies from half a pound to five pounds depending on the strength of current on the bank and the depth of the water – for the banking spellar is aimed at large, slow-swimming fish such as redfish and grouper which stay close to the bottom. The whole apparatus is lowered on a length of 15 or 24 gauge fishing twine. Most fishermen handle only one spellar at a time; Boysie, with his usual desire to excel, fished with two, one line in his hand, the other hooked nonchalantly round his big toe. If the toe line was the first to meet with success he would simply switch lines and haul it in in the normal fashion.

Even 24 gauge was not always strong enough for the larger fish. Grouper – ugly creatures with flattened toad heads, director's paunches and a bite like a rat-trap – can run up to a hundredweight or more. For these Boysie would put down a special grouper line, gauge 36 or upwards, with a lighter lead so that the line would drift well away from the boat and not become entangled with the spellars.

Trolling was carried out with hand-lines and artificial bait. Caper spoon bait was the type Boysie used when it was obtainable; for these metallic lures, like everything else in the late forties that came from England, were hard to obtain. I have myself seen some imitation spoons which he had forged for him; though their finish is crude they are an excellent likeness, and even incorporate some improvements of his own. A keen student of the habits of fish, he had noticed that for Trinidadian waters the placing of the hook on the orthodox spoon was unsuitable; he even went to the length of detaching and reversing the hooks on the spoons he bought from England.

This type of fishing was Boysie's own favourite. As with the clubs, his fertile mind was quick to think up and put into practice any improvement which would make business cheaper to operate or more lucrative to run. Formerly, the Cedros fishermen had trolled with as much as fifty fathoms of line, which they considered necessary in order to reach the depth at which troll-caught fish – fast-swimming species such as carite (Spanish mackerel), kingfish and cavalli – are normally found; for although they swim in the upper levels of the sea, the speed of a motor-driven boat draws out the line almost level with the surface. Like so many innovations, Boysie's looked obvious – once it had been thought of. It was simply to increase the weight on the lines, so that instead of trailing far behind the boat they plunged at a steep angle to the fish-zone, and ten fathoms instead of fifty would suffice. This not only cut drastically the amount of fishing twine used – no small item in a fleet the size of Boysie's – it also greatly reduced the amount of time taken to pull in a line, detach the fish and recast. Anyone who has seen the speed at which a school of cavalli can move will appreciate the advantage this gave him over his competitors.

But Boysie's most revolutionary invention was that which became known as outrigger fishing. In normal trolling, one man handled the engine while the other two held single lines either side. Boysie took two long bamboo poles and lashed them down firmly amidships so that they projected over opposite sides. They were further secured by ropes which connected the outward ends of the poles to the bow of the boat. From the ends of the poles hung fishing lines equipped for trolling; a short length of twine at water level connected these lines to the operator in the boat, who was thus able to pull in the outrigger line as well as his own hand line which he would be manipulating at the same time. Each boat thus carried four lines instead of two, and covered a much larger area of sea.

The catches increased proportionately. Before Boysie's innovations a good average for a single fisherman was two to three hundred pounds a day. Boysie himself caught up to fifteen hundred pounds of fish a day, and averaged between eight and nine hundred. On one occasion, in his launch *Pat Baron* with a five-man crew, he brought in a record-breaking catch of 5,915 pounds.

Boysie's fourth method, fish-potting, is practised in most tropical waters. The term "fish-pot" is perhaps misleading. In the Caribbean, at any rate, the "pot" is a roughly box-shaped structure, the skeleton of which is made of wood, and the sides filled in with anything from plaited bamboo shoots to chicken wire. When the latter material is used, the result looks rather like an underwater hen-run in which bemused-looking fish can be seen swimming aimlessly about. For the fish gain access to the interior through a funnel-shaped entrance, wide at the mouth but narrow at the throat, so that while entrance is a simple process, egress is next door to impossible.

There are two types of pot, differentiated not by their structure but by the method of marking their position; buoy – in patois, "buey" – pots, and drag pots.

Buoy pots are, as their name indicates, attached to buoys. Though this is by far the safest and simplest way of locating the pots, it has, as Boysie was to find, one grave disadvantage – it is as easy for some unscrupulous rascal to find the pots as it is for their rightful owners. Boysie, with that touching faith in the honesty of the law-abiding which is often evinced by professional criminals, brought down from Port of Spain the buoy-marking method, and in his early days at Cedros used it in preference to the accepted drag-pot technique.

This, to which Boysie was reluctantly compelled to revert, consisted of attaching to each fish-pot a rope which corresponded in length to the depth at which the pots were to be sunk. The other end of the rope would be attached to a master-rope so that all the pots would be linked together. The crew would then drop the pots on a straight line, one after the other, uncoiling the master rope as they went and allowing it to sink to the bottom after the pots. There was thus nothing on the surface to indicate their presence, save the "marks" which were known only to the owning crew and which would – they hoped – enable them to recover the pots in due course.

Once these marks – which could be cliffs, houses, trees or any other outstanding feature on shore – were properly aligned, the crew would know that they were somewhere near the place where the pots had been dropped. To recover them they would lower a small anchor known as a "creep" and drag to and fro with it until it fouled the master rope. The pots could then be hauled in one by one – at least that was the theory. Movement of tide and current – currents are generally swift and strong off the coast of Trinidad – could move the rope or even the pots themselves, and in consequence a good many pots were never recovered.

Seine fishing, though possible only for a short period of the year, was while it lasted perhaps the most reliable source of big catches. The net used was the Italian seine, a combination of large and small meshes. Three-man boats could handle a seine, but during the season the launches were invariably put on to this work. Two of the men would pay out the net while the launch turned in a wide circle. When the circle was complete the buoyed end of the net would be hauled on board again. The top of the net would now be in the shape of a capital letter omega with the boat placed horizontally across the foot of the letter; the net itself would form an enormous bag, still open below and at the side nearest the boat.

Two men would then station themselves near the stern of the boat and start to haul in one end of the net; two more near the bow would haul in the other. The fifth man would stand between them and with an oar violently agitate the water close to the boat to prevent the fish from escaping beneath it. Gradually the ring of fin-threshed, silver-flashing water would shrink, the tightening of the net would prevent escape from below, and in a storm of pelicans, gulls and sea eagles the heaving slippery bag of cold life would be swung inboard.

But seine fishing off the coast at Cedros is only possible in May, June and October. In fact the various fishing seasons depend on two factors; local rainfall and the volume of water that flows out from the Orinoco river, which in its turn depends on the rainfall in the Guiana highlands.

When the Orinoco is flowing strongly, the fish are driven down the Trinidad coast past Cedros where they can be caught by trolling. In the Guiana Highlands, from which the Orinoco and most of its tributaries flow, there are two rainy seasons, May-July and October-November. There is a time-lag of a month or so before this increased rainfall makes itself felt in the outflow from the Orinoco delta, so that the trolling seasons of Cedros are July-September and November-December.

When the flow is less – in the three seine-fishing months – the fish do not move so far, and tend to congregate in shoals off the banks below Cedros, where they fall easy prey to the big Italian seines. But from January to April the continental and Caribbean dry seasons coincide; in Trinidad and the lesser Antilles weeks pass by with scarcely a shower. In this dry cloudless weather, fish seek the bottom, and trolling and seining are alike useless. It is at this time that the fish-pots come into their own.

Boysie was the first to extend the normal fishing seasons by following the fish away from Trinidad towards the South American continent. Before his time the local fishermen had never ventured further than Soldier Rock, seven miles southwest of Icacos Point. Boysie sailed on to the west to the mouth of the Rio Pedernales, one of the northern distributaries of the Orinoco, and on northwestwards into the innermost recesses of the gulf, into a region unknown, not merely to Trinidadians, but to the world at large, for the Venezuelans have only a handful of outposts on the jungle-choked gulf coast, and even on the Admiralty chart there are large white patches without even a sounding. This strange and forsaken corner of the sea, with its shark-ridden, alluvium-stained waters, its baffling currents, its shifting, treacherous shoals and its far western horizon of impenetrable green, Boysie made his own and knew as "The Hole" – a hole into which several of his victims were to vanish without trace.

The shore side of his business Boysie organised with the efficiency of his club management. All repairs and maintenance work on the boats was handled in the workshop which he set up at Cedros. Two lorries packed with ice commuted between Cedros and the Port of Spain fish market, where the bulk of his catch was sold to wholesalers. Unlike the other dealers, however, he was always willing to sell to the local people, even if this involved him in some financial loss. On occasions, when fish were plentiful, he would present his own personal catch to the villagers free of charge.

His motives for these displays were probably the typical Boysie mixture – part generosity, part showmanship, part a desire to keep the locals on his side. He never fought or beat anyone up in Cedros. He was always ready with a handsome subscription for local charities. He even lent a lorry to the village cricket team for its away fixtures. Yet the Cedros fishermen never really accepted him. To them he was always the interloper, the big city boy; in his early days at Cedros they must have sniggered behind their hands, daily expecting his ruin; when instead he had the impertinence to beat them at their own game they were consumed with a bitter envy. Whenever he set out, boats would shadow him, seeking the new fishing grounds which had brought him his success. His fishpots would be lifted and mysteriously emptied of their prey.

But his own fishermen idolised him. Many of them were the same men who had served him as bouncers, barmen, casas or general runabouts in the club days; they adapted themselves with remarkable ease to the vastly different life at Cedros. He paid them well, protected them if they ran into trouble with the local police; he even had hot meals prepared for those who were going out early, for as he himself said, "A hungry man can't work".

The work had its difficulties and its dangers. Besides the attitude of the locals, there was the weather to contend with. The coast at Cedros is flat and open, exposed to the north wind. In the Christmas of 1948, three of his boats were driven on to the lee shore and wrecked. There were also the Venezuelan coastguard patrols, who had a somewhat elastic conception of the three mile limit. But fish were still plentiful, he was making good money, and once more, as in his fishing days with the old *Perseverance*, there seemed no reason why he should not live down his past and succeed in establishing a profitable and legitimate business.

But it was not to be. A true Aries subject, Boysie served always as a magnet for trouble. Or perhaps it was that, meeting the troubles that anyone must encounter who shoulders his way through life, he lacked the patience either to endure or circumvent them. Faced with a barrier of any kind, he knew nothing else but to smash his way through it, regardless of the cost to himself or others. This was the method which had served him well enough in the past; its few failures were easily forgotten.

11: FIRST STEPS IN FREEBOOTING

YET IN A WAY it could be said that Boysie drifted into piracy, just as he had drifted into gambling, gang leadership, the nightclub business, by a series of imperceptible stages. The saying that none goes so far as he who knows not where he is going is exemplified by this phase of Boysie's career; for although the time would come when he would figuratively, if not literally, nail the skull and crossbones to his mast, and openly announce his piratical intentions, a series of events which began long before he went to Cedros had by then effectively committed him to a life of crime on the high seas.

In 1945, the fishing boat Boysie kept for his pleasure in Port of Spain came into collision with a larger boat owned by one Cadell. Boysie's boat was swamped and damaged in the collision. Boysie blamed Cadell but said that he would be satisfied provided Cadell made good the damage. This, Cadell, disclaiming all responsibility, refused flatly to do. Boysie said nothing, but waited.

His time came late in 1947, when big catches off Cedros lured a number of Port of Spain boats to the south of the island. One of them was Cadell's launch. Although Boysie himself was an intruder in the Cedros fishing-grounds, he resented intrusions by other fishermen from the capital, and the presence of Cadell was doubly offensive. Two or three days after Cadell's arrival, he rowed out by night, cut loose three of the invading fleet, and towed them to the windward side of a nearby reef. Waves and tide did the rest; all three boats were wrecked. They were not discovered until two days later, and by that time they were beyond repair. Nothing was ever proved against Boysie, though no doubt Cadell at least had his suspicions.

For his next bout of trouble afloat Boysie himself was hardly to blame. As soon as he had introduced his buoy pots, the locals had begun to steal from them. But a greater menace than casual thieving was the seine-fishing which two other fleets carried on in the same area. Their seine-nets used frequently to foul on the buoys, and either tear or have to be cut loose. In revenge the rival fishermen would smash the buoys, often haul up and empty the pot beneath. Boysie, who at this time had some three hundred and fifty pots out, complained to the owners of the fleets. These denied that they had given any instructions for the removal or damage of Boysie's equipment, and put the blame on their men, who of course could not be supervised all the time. But the destruction went on, until one day some fishermen reported to Boysie that they had just seen a boat actually engaged in lifting his pots.

Boysie, half-mad with rage, took his largest boat and ten men armed with revolvers and set out in pursuit. If he had caught the raiders there can be little doubt that they would have been his first maritime victims. Luckily for them, however, they had moved away, and when Boysie reached the site of his pots the sea lay bare and empty to the horizon. He cruised around for some time without sighting any suspicious craft, then returned reluctantly to Cedros.

The news had spread, and a small crowd was waiting for him on the beach. Backed by his phalanx of henchmen, Boysie marched to the centre of the village with the locals straggling after him. When he arrived there he turned and addressed the assembled company. Anyone he caught raiding his fish-pots, he told them, he would kill without a moment's hesitation. The threat was effective for the rest of that season – 1948. But in the early part of the next year the trouble broke out again – despite the fact that he now kept a thirty-six-foot launch permanently stationed in the potting area to watch over his equipment – and was one of the main causes for his leaving Cedros in the middle of 1949 and returning to Port of Spain.

It was pique rather than financial embarrassment which led him to make this move, His profits from fish-potting cannot have made up more than a small proportion of the total, and he never used more than four boats in the laying of pots. But his dispute with the Venezuelan authorities was to have more far-reaching consequences.

In recent years many readers in England must have been puzzled by the harsh treatment which Venezuela meted out to any Trinidadian fishermen unfortunate enough to drift into Venezuelan waters. Many of these men were imprisoned, for weeks or even months at a time, without any form of trial and, as far as one could tell, for no offence other than the purely inadvertent and technical one of trespassing on Venezuelan territory without the necessary documents. This state of affairs lasted for several years, and was the cause of several minor diplomatic incidents; it was ended only recently by an exchange of goodwill missions between the governments of Dr. Eric Williams and President Betancourt. The Jimenez dictatorship may have contributed to the severity of the treatment – gaoled fishermen usually complained of dungeon-like cells, inadequate food, brutal handling – but the original aim of the Venezuelan authorities was to limit the vast amount of smuggling that went on – and still goes on – between Trinidad and Venezuela.

The basic cause is the difference in the cost of living between the two countries. Prices in Venezuela are two or three times higher than those in Trinidad. For this reason, smuggling is a one-way affair; the contraband, chiefly textiles, is bought in Trinidad, usually by Venezuelan dealers, shipped across the Gulf, and landed somewhere on the desolate east coast of Venezuela, where customs posts are few and far between. The Trinidadian authorities turn a blind eye to this, for, as one high official told me, "They aren't breaking any of our laws; it's no concern of ours what they do in Venezuela." He might have added that the trade is extremely profitable to the Trinidadian merchants who supply the contraband goods.

Boysie did not do much in the way of smuggling. He lacked contacts in Venezuela through whom to dispose of the goods, although in the political underworld he found a good market for the cache of guns he had collected at 55 Queen Street. Venezuelan revolutionaries were prepared to pay a hundred dollars for a revolver; as Boysie had bought most of his for around twenty it was a profitable transaction.

But there was another form of contraband which did not require continental contacts; the running of illegal immigrants.

There were many reasons why a man might want to enter Venezuela without the cognisance of the authorities. He might be a Venezuelan citizen who for some reason or other was obnoxious to the current Venezuelan government. He might be a Trinidadian who had heard of the rich pickings to be obtained in Caracas, but was unable to secure an entrance visa. He might be a criminal of any nationality who was on the run from the police and had heard the good news that Venezuela did not practise extradition. Who or what he was did not trouble Boysie, for Boysie would take anyone who could pay his price.

No one was better suited than Boysie to handle this dangerous trade. From his fishing experience he knew every creek and inlet of the Venezuelan coast, knew them better than the Venezuelan coastguards themselves. As soon as he realised the possibilities he set up the escape route which became known, throughout the Trinidadian underworld, as "the chute".

It functioned as follows: the intending passenger would hear via the underworld grapevine of the existence of the chute, and make contact either with Boysie himself on his frequent visits to the capital, or the members of his entourage who, flies round the jampot, were always to be found "liming" in the vicinity of No. 55. These would pass on the news, and, if the client were particularly hot, put him up at the Dorset until Boysie was ready for him. Boysie would then send one of his cars and the client would be driven the seventy miles to Cedros. If he arrived before dark he would be lodged in a shoreside building which Boysie rented, and if necessary meals would be provided for the duration of his stay; this was all part of the service and no additional charge was made.

When dark came, he would be taken on board one of Boysie's boats. Boysie generally handled these assignments personally and alone, at least in the early days of the chute; he saw no reason to share the proceeds with any of his followers, for even in one of the outboard-driven boats, and single-handed, he could in reasonable weather make the Venezuelan coast well before dawn.

So Boysie and his passenger would cruise through the long hours of the night across the black stillness of the Gulf, the only sound the sputtering of the Johnson engine, the only visible thing the plume of white spray from the propeller, phosphorescent under the starlight. Once clear of the coast, Boysie would swing on to a west-north-west bearing, crossing the Gulf diagonally towards the base of the long, rugged Peninsula of Paria which thrusts out like a finger pointing at Trinidad. By the small hours of the morning they would have arrived off the dropping-point. This was a beach a few miles southwest of the little town of Guiría, which lies on the southern coast of the peninsula and is in fact almost the only civilised settlement on it.

Still in thick darkness and silence the passenger would scramble from Boysie's boat into the surf, clutching the case or cases which contained all of his worldly goods that he could take with him, wade up over a bank of small rounded stones to the sand above, and walk on for a hundred yards to the road that passed by the beach. In a short while he would come to the Amerindian village of Cocal, where the white man's writ did not run and the indigenes were willing enough to help the weary traveller on his way – at the right price, of course.

But what happened to him after he left the boat was no concern of Boysie's. His own price for the services he rendered varied according to his estimate of the passenger's means, but it averaged around three or four hundred dollars. This was of course paid in advance, and provided that he got his boat away in time – which he invariably did – it didn't matter to him if his passengers were picked up immediately by the Venezuelan police. In fact at least one of them was subsequently arrested. What if anything he told the police is not known, but it is certain that the Venezuelan authorities soon had a pretty shrewd idea of what was going on, though they lacked the means to stop it.

He had already had trouble with Venezuela. In 1947, two of his boats had engine breakdowns and drifted before the trade winds till they fetched up on the Venezuelan coast. There the crews were detained and the boats impounded. After a few weeks the fishermen were allowed to return, but not the boats. There is no reason to suppose that this high-handed action was in any way connected with Boysie's Operation Chute, or even that any link was established between the immigrant runner and the owner of the stranded vessels; such behaviour is all too typical of the cavalier disregard with which a certain type of Latin civil servant treats the property of others. But to Boysie, quick as always to take offence, it seemed a deliberate personal insult, and he spent the next two years in futile expostulation with both the Colonial Government and the Venezuelan Consulate in Port of Spain.

While he was still trying to recover his boats he became involved in another imbroglio with the Venezuelans.

In 1947, twenty-two fishermen, including some of Boysie's employees, were arrested and imprisoned, some of them for as long as seven months. The Colonial Government, as sluggish as usual when it came to protecting its subjects against outsiders, finally bestirred itself and at the end of the year despatched an official deputation to enquire into the circumstances of the fishermen's imprisonment and arrange if possible for their release. This deputation consisted of a member of the Legislative Council, Chanka Maharaj, two county councillors Man Mohansingh and Brig Mohansingh (no relations of Boysie), a local headmaster called Mr. J. P. Kalloo, an interpreter, and, of all people, Boysie himself.

Possibly on no other occasion in the history of the Raj has His Majesty's Government been represented on a diplomatic mission by a convicted felon. To be fair, his inclusion was due mainly to a combination of circumstances; the arrested fishermen were held at Guiría; Guiría was not connected with the rest of the world by any regular transport service, and Boysie was the only resident of Cedros with a boat which was considered worthy of such an august mission. It was in Boysie's largest launch, the *Pat Baron,* that they eventually embarked. Mr. Kalloo, a Boy Scout leader, had dressed for the occasion in full scout uniform complete with badges, and caused quite an impression among the crowd which watched the *Pat Baron's* departure; the rest of the deputation were more conservatively garbed.

After a roughish passage the *Pat Baron* moored at Guiría jetty and the Trinidadians disembarked. None of them spoke more than a word or two of Spanish, and the interpreter seems to have been totally disregarded. The impression created by Mr. Kalloo's uniform was as marked as at Cedros, but differed in kind; here it was greeted, first with stares of disbelief, then with snorts of ribald mirth. Chanka Maharaj, whose estimate of his own importance did not seem to be shared by his uncomprehending audience, launched into an impassioned diatribe in English. Boysie, smelling trouble, stayed by the jetty.

Of the incidents that followed, there exist two versions. The politicians stoutly deny that anything untoward occurred. But Boysie, who came back alone, had a different story to tell. According to him, Maharaj's harangue was suddenly interrupted by the arrival of the Venezuelan police, rifles at the ready. Someone must have blundered; the authorities at Guría could not have been informed of the mission, and in the eyes of the police these were simply some more of the weird Trinidadians – spies, smugglers or whatever they might be – who seemed so unaccountably fond of Venezuela's rugged hospitality. Threats and protests were of no avail. The deputation was rounded up at gunpoint, marched off to the calaboose and installed in cells next to the fishermen it had come to rescue.

Boysie claimed that he alone got away. Loitering by the jetty, he had a gun-muzzle stuck in his ribs and a blue-chinned policeman warned him that if he set foot in Venezuela again he would be shot on sight. Stormy though the day had become, he was only too glad to cast off the *Pat Baron* and make course for Cedros.

The deputation returned several days later, with eight fishermen whose release they had secured. Despite their denials, Boysie continued to insist that his version was the true one. If Maharaj and his followers claimed otherwise, it was merely their unwillingness – natural enough in politicians – to admit to a humiliating episode in their careers.

Whatever the truth of the matter, the incident ended – almost as soon as it had begun – Boysie's diplomatic career. But his brush with the Venezuelan authorities did not cause him to abandon the chute. On the contrary, any course of action which would embarrass and frustrate those authorities seemed to him only just. Not many weeks after his mission to Guiría he contracted to drop two Chinese "on the Main" – the Trinidadian fisherman's term for the South American continent.

At dusk one evening they set out. There were only the Chinese and Boysie in the boat. As was usual on nights selected for these trips, there was no moon. The Chinese, who had brought aboard several bulging suitcases, seemed rather nervous; they chattered continuously in their high-pitched, gabbling voices. Boysie steered in silence, and the boat's wake extended, faintly gleaming, losing itself in the blackness of the Gulf night.

Halfway across, at a point about ten miles south of Patos Island, he stopped the engine, and the boat glided to a standstill and lay rocking gently in the swell.

This was standard practice. A Johnson engine could not cross the Gulf on a single filling of its tank. On all his journeys Boysie stopped to refuel, but the Chinese were not to know this. They broke out once more into a sibilant chattering; Boysie could not understand what they were saying, but from what happened afterwards they must have thought he had stopped to rob and kill them.

The outlines of the three men were barely visible in the darkness; Boysie in the stern, the Chinese amidships. The latter sat tense, expectant. Unseen by Boysie, one of them drew a gun. Boysie, relaxed, still unaware that anything was amiss, reached down for the petrol cans that were stowed under his seat.

The Chinese thought he was going for a gun. The armed one lifted his weapon and fired.

The first Boysie knew of it was the flash and roar, the whine of the bullet past his head. His reaction was instinctive, immediate; before the Chinese could fire again he threw himself sideways, rocking the boat to throw out the man's aim, and then, while the boat was still violently in motion, plunged over the side. He dived deep, turned under the keel, and surfaced on the far side. The Chinese were still peering into the darkness, wondering what had happened. They were taken completely by surprise; Boysie's arm snaked over the gunwale, gripped the man with the gun and gave a savage jerk. The Chinese hit the water and disappeared. Perhaps his neck was already dislocated by the force and suddenness of Boysie's pull. It was over before he had time to cry out.

Boysie climbed back in the boat, picked up the second Chinese and threw him after his companion.

The whole affair was over in seconds. Soon even the ripples of their fall had spread and vanished and the boat was once more rocking gently, almost imperceptibly in the Gulf swell. It was not until this moment that Boysie realised the suitcases were still on board. He opened them, and found, hidden among the clothes, three thousand dollars. He filled the tank, restarted the engine, and set course for Trinidad.

At least that was Boysie's story, and in default of any other it must be accepted or rejected entirely. It seems unlikely that he would have set out deliberately, alone, with the intention of killing two grown men, even if in reality it was he and not the Chinese who had the pistol. But the Chinese could not tell their side of the story; no trace was ever seen of them again.

12: SHIPMATES ASHORE

DURING THE CEDROS days Boysie paid frequent visits to Port of Spain, to check on the running of the Dorset and to handle some even less legitimate sidelines he was developing. It was on one of these trips that he met with a nasty accident. He was returning to Cedros in his Ford pick-up with several of his confederates. Lulled by the long, flat, straight stretches of road, sleepy perhaps after a night with one of his many mistresses, he was dozing over the wheel when the pick-up swerved suddenly and left the road. By the roadside was a standpipe from which a small boy was drawing water. The pick-up rolled over him and he was killed instantly.

The police came. Boysie had of course no driving licence – after failing his test he made no further attempt to obtain one – and when the police decided that the only licensed occupant of the pick-up, one Randolph Martin, must have been driving, neither Boysie nor Martin made any effort to disabuse them. Martin was charged with manslaughter and committed for trial.

His trial never came off. Like a subsequent case in which Boysie was concerned, it was postponed time and time again. There may of course have been good and sufficient reasons for this. Whether or not that was so, the postponements were certainly very fortunate for Boysie; and while the case was pending Martin had the misfortune to die.

Boysie's enemies swore that he had been deliberately put to work on Boysie's ice lorry so that his health would be destroyed; when at last he was forced to take to his bed, Boysie finished the job by poisoning him. Boysie's apologists, on the other hand, claim that his death was quite accidental. He was in the habit of getting drunk, and when he had drunk himself incapable he would lie down on the ice in the back of the lorry, separated from it only by a few layers of sacking, and in this somewhat uncomfortable position sleep off his debauch. As a result of this habit he contracted tuberculosis from which he eventually died. Far from wishing to kill him, Boysie had supported him throughout his last illness and finally paid for the funeral.

The reader can take his choice. Whatever the truth of the matter, Martin's death saved Boysie from an investigation which might have been awkward for him.

Back in Cedros, more trouble was waiting for him in the shape of a series of disputes between his men and the locals. A typical one took place at the Hosein festival of 1948, where some of his men got involved in a fight. Such was Boysie's reputation in the district that the local police called on him to help restore order, and in particular to pacify a man called Douglar who had broken a local man's head and was threatening violence to anyone who approached him. Boysie reasoned with Douglar and discovered his chief fear, a not unreasonable one in the West Indies – was that if he "went quietly" the police would use third degree methods on him. Boysie assured him that he personally would see this did not happen. Douglar finally agreed to accompany the police to the station, but as a sign of his resentment removed all his clothes and got into the police car stark naked.

No sooner had he done so than he screamed out loud. He had been sitting in the back of the car between two policemen, and he told Boysie that these men had hit him with their elbows and stamped on his bare feet. Boysie didn't trouble to hear the police side of the story, but wrenched open the car door, pulled Douglar free, and cursed and abused the police, after which he took Douglar home. The police made no effort to prevent him, but the following day an Inspector called and formally charged him with obstructing the police in the execution of their duty.

For some reason this charge was never pressed; or at least I could find no record of a conviction. But the good relations Boysie had built up during his time at Cedros were still further impaired. Henceforth the police kept an unfriendly eye on all his activities; this was a further factor that influenced his move the following year to Port of Spain.

Even before his return to the capital, however, he had stepped up his criminal activities there. He was in fact rapidly developing a new and profitable sideline – arson.

Boysie's arson was of two kinds – the burning of buildings and the burning of cars. The former was carried out either on the instructions of the owners, who might wish to collect insurance money or merely get rid of an otherwise immovable tenant, or on occasion at the behest of business rivals who were prepared to carry the principles of competitive free enterprise to their logical conclusion.

The first of his major "fire jobs", as he called them, took place in 1948. This was the burning of the Crystal Palace nightclub, which was completely gutted, fortunately without loss of life. Arson, though probably suspected, was never proved, and Boysie collected two thousand dollars for his services. He had already by this time perfected his fire-raising technique, which was based on a simple mechanical device of his own invention.

This was in effect a delayed-timer incendiary bomb. The parts required were a cheap alarm-clock, of the type in which a vibrating clapper strikes a bell, a box of matches, some paper, an inflammable plastic container and a gallon or so of petrol. A bundle of match-heads would be tied to the clapper and the box placed so that when the clapper vibrated it would rub the heads on the phosphorus, striking side. Paper would then be soaked in petrol and wrapped around the clock. The alarm would be set for a few hours ahead, and then the clock placed in a box together with the plastic container full of petrol. One of the gang would secrete the box on the doomed premises.

When the alarm went off the matches would strike, igniting the petrol-soaked paper which in turn would melt the plastic and send the petrol up in an explosive rush of flame. There would be no trace left, except perhaps the heat-twisted, barely recognisable skeleton of the clock. And in those days the Trinidad police lacked the experience and the laboratory facilities to interpret that piece of evidence – even if they had noticed it.

The firing of cars was invariably carried out for insurance purposes.

Boysie's clients in this racket were often respectable citizens who were anxious to make a few foolproof dollars on the side, for the whole beauty of the offence is that it is one virtually impossible to prove. The prospective insurance-twister simply contacted Boysie and informed him that at a certain time and date his car would be left unattended – and of course unlocked – in such-and-such a street. One of the boys would then get in, disconnect the ignition leads, start the car and drive it to some unfrequented spot in the country outside Port of Spain. There, of course, one of Boysie's own vehicles would be waiting. The stolen car would then be stripped of dynamo, coil, starter-motor and anything else removable that had a resale value – sometimes even the door-handles would be unscrewed. As soon as these had been transferred to Boysie's car, the other would be destroyed by soaking it in petrol and setting light to it. This method had the dual advantage of turning the car into a complete write-off for the insurance company while removing any clues such as fingerprints which the gang might have inadvertently left behind.

An hour or so after the car had been stolen, the owner would put in an appearance, express suitable surprise at the absence of his vehicle, and report the matter to the police. It would be quite safe to do so, for the car would already be a twisted, smouldering skeleton. In due course it would be found, the insurance money collected, and a proportion of it handed to Boysie, who would also realise on the looted parts. As long as Boysie kept quiet, no breath of suspicion could attach to the owner, for in Trinidad bona fide car thieves usually adopt the same technique; the smallness of the island makes it too dangerous to dispose of complete vehicles.

His reputation was such that people knew he would keep quiet, that the service he provided was safe, efficient, and with no kickbacks. One of his customers was the proprietor of a filling-station who had actually bought one of Boysie's old cars for six hundred dollars. He did the car up, insured it for seventeen hundred, and then got Boysie to burn it. The price asked was two hundred dollars, nothing to Boysie, of course, but it was one of his characteristics that he would take as much trouble over a small job worth a few dollars as over a large one involving thousands. Extravagant as his living might be, he still had something in common with the Indian small trader who knows, better than anyone, that all a millionaire has is a hundred million cents.

At the last minute, however, the proprietor offered Boysie an old jeep instead of the dollars, and Boysie accepted; the gang could always do with an extra runabout.

Boysie never bought when he could steal, even if the object he required was trifling in value or at any rate well within his means. One of the most remarkable instances of this trait arose from his acquisition of the jeep. If it had led to his arrest and conviction – as it very nearly did – Boysie might never have embarked on the career of full-scale piracy which commenced shortly afterwards.

The jeep needed some new parts for the front-end differential and, rather than buy these, Boysie decided to steal them from the scrap-yard of a dealer called Keyser. He himself kept the night-watchman in talk while his Mapp truck glided to the entrance and his gang lifted an entire, nearly-new jeep engine from its chassis and loaded it on the truck. But someone from a nearby house must have spotted them, noted the number and phoned the police; for hardly had they reached Boysie's house than the police arrived.

They had not even had time to finish unloading; the differential was still on the truck, while the rest of the stolen engine was in the backyard. One of them kept the police talking while another ran to a club a little way down the road, where Boysie had gone to play poker. Boysie had just time to fix an alibi before the police arrived. He accompanied them back to his house, and they began to search.

Unfortunately in their haste, and doubtless also their premature glee at having finally caught Boysie red-handed, the police had omitted to check with Keyser and find out what was actually missing. Now they realised suddenly that they were not sure what they were searching for. They glared suspiciously at the jeep engine in the yard, but as luck would have it this had been placed next to two marine engines which were almost identical in appearance. Boysie was able to persuade them that all three were from his boats. The differential, hidden under sacking, they never noticed at all. They were left with no alternative but to accept Boysie's story – for that night at any rate.

But the engine was now too hot to handle. Early next morning it was dismantled and the parts dumped in the Macaque River in Diego Martin. By the time the police had checked with Keyser, Boysie was in the clear.

He continued to levy toll upon the world. Immediately after his return to Port of Spain he had set about stripping the partitions in 55 Queen Street and reconverting it from brothel to club. He also started another club in a building scheduled for demolition at the corner of Macdonald Street and Tragarete Road – the owner of the site was a friend of his who lent it him free of charge. Both these clubs were furnished by the simplest expedient of stealing furniture. He would go out in the small hours with his jitney or the Mapp truck and drive through the better-class residential suburbs. Whenever he saw a porch or verandah with any chairs or tables left out he would stop, his men would leap down and pad soft-footed over the lawns, and the furniture would be removed with a speed which Joe May might envy. He even stole five dozen folding metal chairs from the Queen's Park Oval cricket ground.

The clubs were soon doing a roaring trade – better perhaps than before. The postwar period of slack trade was now over; oil and American investment were rapidly turning Port of Spain into the noisy, neon-lit city which it is today. The base at Chaguaramas might have declined as a source of customers, but the American fleet paid frequent visits, and whenever it dropped anchor Boysie's machine threw itself into high gear. The entire mob would be sent out to scour the streets for sailors, who were lured to No. 55 with promises of unlimited drink and women. The veteran whores of Boysie's stable would each take on upwards of twenty Yanks a day, and the best-looking of them – those whom Boysie normally reserved for his own use – would be getting twenty dollars for a "short time". Such was their erotic prowess that it was by no means uncommon for young and naïve sailors to empty their pockets and give the girl everything they possessed. For the poorer or stingier there were the old bags who would rent out their withered charms for five dollars or less. Whatever the price, Boysie took his cut, and Boysie's muscle squad stood around to see that there was no cheating.

If your tastes were more exotic, they too would be catered for. In these last monstrous days of No. 55, Boysie's floorshows blossomed into spectacles seldom before seen west of Suez. A striptease was the most innocuous entertainment on the bill. It served merely as an hors d'oeuvre to the programme of perversion which followed, and which could be varied to suit the most recondite tastes. The complete sexual act, with all its conceivable variations, would be performed by a woman and a man whose member was more than double the normal size; between two women whose clitorises were so overdeveloped as to equal in proportions the male organ; between two adult males. Often on the receiving end of the latter spectacle was a homosexual crook on the fringe of Boysie's circle who rejoiced in the not inappropriate nickname of Bumper.

It is ironic to think that the prime mover in this saturnalia was by this time almost completely impotent. Overindulgence and gonorrhoea had between them ruined Boysie's manhood. Night after night, in the garrets of No. 55, the most seductive of his women would dance naked before him, their gold, copper or ebony bodies twisted in grotesquely lascivious postures; but all to no avail. The discovery of penicillin had come in time to halt or at least hide the ravages of his disease, but for the thing that mattered most to Boysie it had arrived too late.

13: THE LAST OF THE FISHING

DESPITE ALL THESE ACTIVITIES on shore, which filled up the latter half of 1949 and the first quarter of 1950, Boysie still carried on with his fishing. When he left Cedros he disposed of the greater part of his fleet and transferred the remaining six boats from the southwestern corner of the island to the narrow strip of flat coast that borders the hills to the northwest of Port of Spain.

This was conveniently near 192 Western Main Road. The boats themselves were usually anchored off a battered wooden quay known as the Leper Asylum jetty. The asylum itself was situated about a hundred yards away on the landward side of the Western Main Road, which runs parallel with the coast. Nowadays the lepers, the few that are left, are settled on the island of Chacachacare in the Bocas, and the high corrugated iron fence of a warehouse borders the jetty on one side; but ten years ago the spot was relatively unfrequented, and Boysie had it pretty well to himself.

Chuncie was playing an increasingly important part in the business. As the most skilful of his father's mechanics he was kept busy repairing and servicing the engines of Boysie's fleet; yet he still found time to accompany his father on the more legitimate trips.

For these, Boysie had produced yet another innovation.

The local waters were being overfished, and the only place where Boysie could be certain of good catches was the "Hole" – the cul-de-sac of gulf west of the Pedernales-Guiría line. But the journey there and back consumed fourteen hours out of a sixteen-hour trip, leaving only two hours actual fishing. It was impossible to fish longer than that, not because Boysie or his men begrudged themselves sleep, but because if they stayed any longer the fish would rot and become unsaleable on the long voyage home.

To avoid this Boysie loaded two of his boats with ice; eighteen hundred pounds of it in each boat. He was thus able to fish the Hole for two or three days at a time. During that period, of course, a great deal of ice would melt, but enough remained to keep the fish at a low temperature.

He fished in this manner during the last three months of 1949. Just before Christmas of that year he set out on what was to be his last fishing trip.

Boysie handled one of the boats alone; in the other were Chuncie and a fisherman called George Harper. Harper, who had a big part left to play in his employer's life, was an old associate of Boysie's; they had known each other from *Perseverance* days. Boysie's boat was equipped with a new sixteen-horse power Johnson engine; Chuncie's had an older sixteen-horse job and a nine-horse spare. They left Cocorite in bad weather which lasted the whole trip. The seas pitched continuously and none of them could sleep much in the snatches of rest they took between hauling in and casting the nets. With his usual ruthlessness, however, Boysie kept them at it. When at five in the evening of the third day, they finally left the Hole and turned homewards, all three of them were on the verge of exhaustion.

They were driving into a strong easterly wind. It took them three hours to draw level with Guiría, and as they did so the wind freshened almost to gale force. Soon they sighted two other Trinidadian boats homeward bound, hailed them, and told them to stay close in case of accident. All this time the seas were rising higher, and the four boats made scarcely any headway. At 11 p.m. the other two decided that arrest, imprisonment and confiscation were preferable to the dangers ahead; they turned tail and headed downwind for the Venezuelan coast.

Boysie thought of following, then decided against it. From his last trip to Guiría he had a pretty good idea of the reception he would get. The loss of his boats and catch was likely to be the least of his troubles; he stood a good chance of losing his life whichever course he took. He decided to go on. His engine was running better than Chuncie's, but he kept it throttled down so that the other boat would not lose sight of him. He was running perhaps some fifty yards ahead.

Suddenly the engine of Chuncie's boat cut out.

The boat, pirogue-built, high in the water, swung like a weathercock broadside on to the waves. Water poured over the side, filling the bilge in the space of seconds. Clinging desperately to the wallowing boat, Chuncie realised what had happened; dizzy with fatigue, he had forgotten to refuel, and the engine had simply run out of petrol. It was a simple mistake, but one that looked like proving his last. True, the pirogue would take a lot to sink, but a few more waves would overturn it, and the shallow, muddy waters beneath were swarming with shark. Fighting to keep his balance, he struggled towards the stern of the boat. If he could get the engine going again, he could turn the bows into the wind. There might still be time for this manoeuvre – though he doubted it.

Suddenly, close at hand, over the noise of the storm, he heard the throb of another outboard. Boysie had seen, even through the pitch darkness, that the other boat was no longer following, had swung his own boat round, brought it back, and was now fighting to keep level with the drifting, disabled hulk of his son's vessel. Chuncie, from the stern, shouted to Harper to catch the rope that Boysie was now preparing to throw. But Harper, cowering in the bows, either could not or would not hear him.

Chuncie dragged himself the length of the boat, shook Harper by the shoulder and told him to go to the stern and try to start the engine. Then he grasped the rope that his father threw him and made it fast to the bows of his own boat. Gradually, as Boysie's engine took the strain, the three-parts swamped pirogue turned into the wind.

Harper meanwhile had filled the tank. Now he got ready to start, but failed in the darkness to notice that the starting cord was wrapped round the ignition lever. He pulled, and the lever went to full retard and jammed there. The engine could not start.

Chuncie yelled curses at Harper and told him to bail out the boat while he tried to fix the engine. It was impossible. Reluctantly he was compelled to unfasten it and replace it with the nine-horsepower spare. But this had got wet when the boat filled and started on one cylinder only, firing and missing and firing again. At last Chuncie was satisfied that it would work well enough to drive them. He told his father that they could make it alone, and gave orders to Harper to cast off.

They had not been going very long before the new engine cut out altogether.

Once more the boat swung broadside to the seas. This time it was already waterlogged, and their plight was desperate. Chuncie remembered all the tales of the fishermen who had been caught in gulf storms and never seen again. He knew well enough how they would die. In that warm sea they could live and cling to the upturned boat indefinitely, but before very long the sharks would come, curious, nosing after any garbage of the sea, slashing with their fierce mouths that saw and tear but do not bite cleanly, leaving great gaping wounds through which the victim's blood would ooze gradually away, leaving the corpse white and waxy. There was only one chance and that was to throw out the anchor and hope it would hold and pull the boat bows-on to the sea while Chuncie freed the jammed lever on the sixteen-horse engine. He let go the heavy anchor; rope reeled out, sixty fathoms of it, before the iron caught and the labouring, gunwale-deep boat shuddered its head round into the wind. Madly he began bailing.

Harper had reached his limit. Hunched up, soaked to the skin, shaking with cold, he crouched in the swirling water and would not or could not move.

As the boat slowly emptied, the danger of actually capsizing retreated, though their position was still perilous in the extreme. Chuncie stopped bailing and began to struggle with the starting-cord of the sixteen-horse. In the absolute darkness of the night and the storm he could not see how the cord was twisted, had to feel out its tangles knot by knot with his numbed fingers. He told Harper to go aft and take off the nine-horse in readiness. Harper did not budge. Chuncie cursed him viciously, but he might as well have cursed the waves that were pounding them. Somehow he got the cord loose, staggered again to the stern, and unfastened the smaller engine himself.

While he was doing this his father's boat once more drew alongside. Chuncie called to him to go on, he would ride out the night somehow and, if he survived it, follow on when the seas had gone down. Boysie insisted that he should go with him, sacrificing the anchor if need be. The two men shouted angrily at one another over the noise of the storm, and in the end Chuncie gave in, caught the rope Boysie threw him and made it fast to the bows, then cut loose his precious sixty fathoms of anchor-rope, replaced the nine-horse with the sixteen-horse, and jerked at the cord until at last the engine sprang into life.

Slowly the two boats moved off to the east, with Chuncie's engine running at half-speed and the towrope taut between them as Boysie's boat took the strain. As soon as they were moving Chuncie began to bail once more, for the pirogue was still dangerously low in the water. So they went on, with Harper still prostrate and semiconscious in the bilge, and Chuncie bailing like an automaton, until after four hours the sky began gradually to lighten and the seas to decline as the two boats drew in under the lee of Trinidad. By the time they drew level with Chacachacare, the sea lay as calm and unruffled as if the storm had never been.

Several times on that last stage of the trip Chuncie shook Harper and tried to rouse him from his stupor, but the most he got was a scarcely audible mutter of "Can't make it", between chattering teeth. Chuncie himself was by now so exhausted that he could no longer see well enough to steer, but had to turn his own engine off and let Boysie tow. At last, around seven in the morning, they drew into the Leper Asylum jetty at Cocorite.

Chuncie went across to the house to collect the jitney so that they could off-load their catch. He decided that before he collected it he would change his sodden clothes. Halfway through this he fell down on the bed and lost consciousness and remembered nothing until the following morning.

After a couple of days rest all three recovered from their ordeal – even Harper, who had been hauled ashore half-dead from exposure. But Boysie never went fishing again. From henceforth, when he put to sea it would be the others who ran the danger of death. Boysie wasn't going to hazard his life for the price of a boatload of fish. The richest prey lay on the surface of the sea, not in its depths.

14: THE PIRATE OF THE GULF

EVEN WHEN HE RETURNED to Port of Spain, Boysie continued to operate the chute.

According to many Trinidadians, those who made a safe passage through the chute were lucky indeed. Estimates of the numbers who vanished between 1947 and 1950 vary, but usually enter double figures. There are even those who will solemnly assure you (on what evidence they themselves find it hard to say) that Boysie killed and threw overboard anything up to a hundred luckless travellers.

No one will ever know for certain; Boysie often worked alone, and doubtless many of his crimes are buried with him. Although most of the estimates are, I feel certain, wild exaggerations – the majority of his victims were murdered in genuine acts of piracy, not illegal crossings – it is easy to see how they have come about. The temptations of the illegal emigration racket are obvious enough; even though few people in Trinidad can have heard of Petiot, the French mass-murderer who claimed at least twenty-seven victims with his bogus escape route during the German occupation. It took no great acumen to see that a person travelling illicitly, with everything portable he possessed, to a country with which communications were at the best of times difficult and from which he might have good reason not to communicate at all, made something pretty close to the ideal murderee. The only surprising thing is – if Boysie's own account is to be believed – that he took so long to find out, and did so purely by accident.

Certainly, no sooner was Boysie indicted in his first murder trial than the disappearance of every missing person over the previous five years was fathered upon him. Amnesiacs, ne'er-do-wells, henpecked husbands and adulterous wives – they might have had the best reasons for leaving home and staying away; but common report had them all going down the chute. Circumstantial details were not lacking – the woman, for instance, who begged Boysie for her life and was let off, the child whose brains he dashed out against the stern of his launch.

Yet if one considers Boysie's character, these stories stamp themselves as inventions. On his pirate-raids Boysie never let anyone off; he was not fool enough to leave any witnesses alive. But nor would he dash out a child's brains; not for humanitarian reasons but because such a method was clumsy and inefficient; the cold-blooded precision of his killings was precisely what made them more horrifying than any display of brutality or sadistic violence.

Moreover, though an accurate schedule is hard to establish, it seems likely that the vast majority of Boysie's killings occurred within the space of a few weeks in the spring of 1950 – a period in which, for all his blood-chilling control, he seems to have been moved by a fury as irrational, and unassuageable as the feeding mood of a shark.

I have only been able to trace – with any degree of certainty – one of Boysie's passengers who was definitely and deliberately thrown over the side. He was a Portuguese crook, called Gouveia, on the run with over two thousand dollars worth of stolen gold. This time there were others on board besides Boysie. They included the two men who had now become his closest lieutenants – Fire Kong and Bage. As soon as the boat reached mid-gulf, it stopped and Fire Kong held Gouveia at gunpoint while the others stripped him of cash and gold. Then he was prepared for disposal in the manner which Boysie was to make peculiarly his own.

There are almost as many stories about Boysie's corpse-removing methods as there are people he is supposed to have killed. One is that he gutted the bodies so that expanding stomach gases would not force them to the surface – as was done by Boysie's namesake, Dr. Dalip Singh, in 1955. Another is that Boysie always kept on deck a tubful of quick-setting cement; the victim would be made to stand in it till it set and then flung over, still alive, on an express trip to the seabed. My favourite is the one which tells that Boysie never sailed without a dead donkey on board. In mid-gulf the donkey would be cut up and the raw and bleeding pieces flung into the sea. These would soon attract sharks, and served as hors d'oeuvres to the human meal which would follow.

In fact Boysie's method was less sensational but a good deal more reliable. He would simply tie the victim's hands and feet, and then lash the still living body to some heavy metallic object. With Gouveia this was an iron anchor-chain, but anything would do; a boat's engine-plate was the most usual. Then, praying, screaming, or simply paralysed with fear, the victim would make his final, vertical journey.

Gouveia's gold was hot and had to be dropped at half-price, but in addition to the loot there was of course his passage money, which Boysie had prudently made him pay in advance. It is possible that the proceeds of this crime went to pay for Boysie's death ship, the infamous *Marie Louise.*

The *Marie Louise* belonged to two brothers, John and Leonard Olivera. The Olivera brothers were of Portuguese extraction, descendants of the immigrants from Madeira and the Azores who were brought in during the eighteen-thirties to make up the acute labour shortage that followed the freeing of the slaves; they picked up a living by fishing on their own account and helping Boysie in his legitimate and some of his less legitimate activities. John in particular was an excellent mechanic, and he serviced Boysie's engines in the latter part of the Cedros period. At this time Boysie was frequently buying new boats, but it seemed likely, from an incident that preceded the purchase, that he had already decided on the purpose for which the *Marie Louise* was to be used.

To the casual eye there was nothing to distinguish the *Marie Louise* from any of a dozen other launches in the vicinity of Port of Spain – and that too was a big advantage. She was a plain straightforward thirty-footer, with neither deck nor superstructure; the keener observer might however have noticed that she had the low, rakish lines of a boat that is built for speed. Originally she was powered by a Grey Ordinary marine engine of fifty-two horsepower. This was not enough for Boysie. Before even the boat had changed hands, he decided to replace it with a Grey Fireball, which develops five thousand revs to the Ordinary's three thousand five hundred.

Moreover he knew where a Grey Fireball was. The only disadvantage – a trifling one from Boysie's viewpoint – was that it belonged to someone else and Boysie didn't intend paying for it. It was indeed fixed in another launch that was anchored in Stauble's Bay. One night Boysie set out with John and some of his other henchmen in one of his outboard-driven boats. A hundred yards from the spot he anchored, and one of the men climbed overboard with one end of a hundred-yard rope round his waist. Noiselessly he swam to the doomed launch, cut its mooring-rope and attached his own. Then he gave the signal – three pulls on the rope – and Boysie's crew slowly reeled in their biggest catch so far.

The original rope was now replaced with a stronger one, and Boysie lost no time in towing his prize into deeper waters. As the two boats got under way, a couple of the gang were already hard at work dismantling the Fireball. It took them half an hour, by which time the boats were out of sight of the shore.

Boysie now had the gutted launch to dispose of. He could have left it to drift, but it would then have been discovered minus engine and the reason for the crime would have been clear; Boysie didn't want the Port of Spain police checking his fleet for Fireball engines. If he sank it the owner would probably assume it had been cut adrift by hooligans. But a pirogue-built boat is almost unsinkable. Boysie however had come prepared; his boat was loaded with cans of petrol, and as soon as the engine had been transferred, his men drenched the captured vessel and set light to it. It burnt down to the waterline before its heavy, loglike bottom sank finally with a hiss and sparks into the oily waters of the Gulf. But by that time Boysie was already on his way home.

Not long afterwards the purchase of the *Marie Louise* was completed. Boysie – after equipping it with its new engine – now had a boat that could outrun pretty well anything in the Gulf; he also had the men to handle it, men who would do his bidding, whatever it might be. These men were Fire Kong and Bage.

Fire Kong, whose real name was Gerald Miller, was a black giant who turned the scale at 220 pounds; a Colt forty-five looked like a toy in his hands. It was indeed his size and the ferocity of his appearance that provided the second half of his nickname, originally King Kong but altered to Fire Kong because of his addiction to the type of behaviour known as "Fire" or "Grand Charge" – in an argument he would bluster and threaten his opponent without the slightest intention of backing his words with deeds. For Fire Kong was at heart a coward. He would go to any lengths to avoid a fist-fight; he had a neurotic fear of having his skin cut or bruised in any way.

Nor was this the only odd facet of his character. Although he almost always wore pyjamas, he was hardly ever seen to sleep, and on the rare occasions when he slept he did so in a sitting position, wedged in a corner of the staircase at No. 55, his head propped on his arms. If he assumed this posture when he was not sleeping, it was a bad sign, a sign that he was plotting trouble for someone. His whole manner was that of a man haunted by some evil he could not comprehend.

Neurotic or cowardly he might be, but he was formidable enough with a gun in his hand. Just before Christmas 1949 he was drinking at No. 55 when three fellows from "behind the bridge" came in, drunk and looking for trouble. They should have known better than to find it with Kong, who ran to his room and came back with a revolver in each hand. The three dived for the stairs, but not quickly enough. Kong emptied both guns at them. The place was so full of smoke that you couldn't see, and perhaps this explains why all three survived; though two of them were hit in the hand and one in the foot. The case was investigated by the police, but although they knew Kong was responsible they could get no one – not even the wounded victims – to testify against him.

Fire Kong had been associated with Boysie from his early days; Bage was a more recent recruit. His real name was Duncan Trotman. His nickname was derived from his place of origin; he was a Bajan, a native of Barbados, but that law-abiding island did not give him enough scope for his criminal propensities. Travel between the islands, which in those days were separate Crown Colonies, was far from easy; the unit governments feared (and even under Federation still fear) that if free movement were allowed, an influx of landless labourers would depress their peoples' already low standard of living. Bage, an early disciple of free movement, solved the problem in 1942 by taking passage on one of the numerous boats which thrived on the black market in citizens created by these restrictions. He was an illegal immigrant – a fact which was to have some influence on his future career.

In character and appearance he differed so much from Fire Kong that the two of them might almost have made up a vaudeville act. Bage was five-foot six in height and weighed a skinny 125 lbs. While Kong was sunk in neurotic gloom, Bage was all the time smiling and cracking jokes. His whole personality was flighty and unpredictable. He would commit crimes, especially thefts, without planning or even anticipation. When he had money he spent it freely. He was fond of women. But he resembled Kong in the absolute and unquestioning obedience he gave to Boysie. Boysie appreciated their loyalty and rewarded it by giving them, in addition to their regular wage and the bonuses they received for their jobs, the freedom of No. 55; they could do whatever they wished there, drink as much as they liked, have all the women they wanted, free of charge.

Perhaps Boysie would have turned to piracy eventually, whatever had happened. He had already looted and destroyed boats, he had already killed at sea and found what looked like a foolproof method of corpse disposal; to complete the piratical equation it was only necessary to link these two processes. But according to Boysie himself there was one particular incident that launched him on his bloody career.

Since 1947 he had been trying to get back the two fishing boats that had been confiscated by the Venezuelan authorities. The Venezuelan consulate had hedged and procrastinated throughout that time; now, late in 1949, they informed Boysie that his nets had rotted and were useless and the boats had been taken over by the Venezuelan government in order to defray the expenses incurred in shipping the crews back to Trinidad. To add insult to injury, they informed him of the purpose to which they had been put – coastguard patrol.

Boysie was mad with rage. Publicly he stated his intention to sink any Venezuelan boat that he met in the Gulf. Nobody believed him or took him seriously at the time; they assumed it was the kind of hotheaded speech that anyone of his temperament might make in the circumstances. They should have realised that Boysie was no Fire Kong. What he said he would do, he did. They should have taken warning from the fact that he once more changed his style of dressing.

Boysie had a strong consciousness, uncommon among criminals, of the periods into which his life divided itself. In his prison diary he wrote of his "Yankey days, Fishing days, Fighting days, Prison days" – and of course his Piracy days, or "Paricey" as he preferred to spell it. Each period he marked deliberately by adopting a particular type of dress – the shorts and merino of the fishing days, the Cab Calloway outfit of the Yankee days, and so on. Now he took to wearing the pirate's colour, black; black shirt, black trousers, black hat, black shoes; no touch of another colour was allowed to soften the grimness of his apparel.

Thus dressed, and with his brace of murderers at his back, he set out on the spree of ruthless killing which was to make him the most feared man in the Caribbean.

The first pirate voyage was in March 1950. He set out in broad daylight in the *Marie Louise,* with Fire Kong and Bage and two other men. The launch was loaded with iron for the disposal of bodies and petrol for the disposal of boats.

They had not gone very far when they sighted another boat. It was big for a pirogue, forty or fifty feet long, decked in and with cabins both above and below deck. Its course was the same as that of the *Marie Louise* – westwards towards Venezuela. There were four or five men on deck. None of them paid much attention to the *Marie Louise;* to them it was merely another of the many fishing-boats scattered across the Gulf.

Boysie, in the bows of the *Marie Louise,* laughed and ground his teeth together. The man at the engines opened the throttle on the Fireball and the *Marie Louise* swung round to intercept.

15: THE KILLING TIME

THE VESSEL which the *Marie Louise* was speeding to overtake was a contraband boat. Its owners had bought large quantities of textiles in Trinidad and were now returning to land them on some deserted part of the Venezuelan coast. Perhaps some of their friends had accompanied them for the ride; certainly the complement – eleven men – was high for a boat of that kind. But whether their main object was business or pleasure, most of them had had all too good a time in Port of Spain, and were sleeping off the party below deck.

Boysie of course had no idea there were so many people on board. He assumed the men he could see were the entire crew. He began to put into effect the plan which he had worked out for such an occasion.

The *Marie Louise* drew level with the Venezuelan boat, and standing up in the bows Boysie hailed her. They had been out fishing, he said, and were short of water. Could the Venezuelans spare some? One of the crew answered in broken English that they could. Bage brought the *Marie Louise* alongside, and Boysie's men each picked up a tin pan or jug and with these innocent looking articles filed aboard the larger boat.

No sooner were they all on deck than at a signal from Boysie they threw down their pans and drew revolvers. The Venezuelans had not time to resist or even cry out. The boarding party, led by the giant Fire Kong with a Colt .45 in each hand, opened fire with a fusillade of bullets which killed or wounded every Venezuelan on deck.

Then a cry from below told them that their work was not yet over.

Kong plunged down the companionway. Of the men below deck, some were awake and scrambling from their bunks, others were still asleep. That made no difference. Kong and his men shot them all down, the sleepers and the waking alike. No one resisted; though afterwards the gang found three revolvers on board, no one even had time to draw. Within a matter of seconds half the Venezuelans were dead. The others were either too severely wounded to move, or thought it best to pretend to be so, in the hope that Boysie would content himself with removing the contraband and let the survivors live.

If they thought that, they were due for a bitter disappointment.

On deck, Boysie's men were already lashing and weighting their victims. The assortment of old iron they had brought with them – anchor chains, engine plates and the like – was sufficient for the victims Boysie had anticipated, four or five at the most, but wholly inadequate for the number that were now dragged from the cabins. To weight these, the engine of the captured boat had to be dismantled. By the time all eleven were securely trussed, every scrap of metal on the two boats, with the exception of Boysie's own engine, had been commandeered for the gruesome task.

The gang worked with desperate haste, for all this time the burning sun of the Caribbean beat down upon them, and at any moment another boat might cross the horizon and come to investigate. Some of those still living begged for their lives, others prayed, or so it seemed from their gestures, for most spoke only Spanish; but no matter what tongue they had used, the result would have been the same. In Boysie's sombre, deep-set eyes there was no trace of pity; he was determined that no one should live to testify against him, and his will was hardened by the sense of grievance, magnified a hundredfold in his twisted mind, against his victims' fellow-countrymen. Possibly he even derived a sense of power, a sense that he had put himself beyond all moral law, at the sight of human beings utterly at his mercy. Certainly he never again afforded his victims the dubious privilege of a revolver shot; all the rest save one were sent to the bottom alive.

When the business of tying was complete, Boysie told his men to throw their captives – dead or alive, wounded or not – into the sea.

If anyone had been minded to disobey him, the sight of Fire Kong with his two revolvers at Boysie's side, ready to send any mutineer to join the other victims, would have been enough to deter the strongest. The command was obeyed. Soon the deck was clear again, save for the blood that was swiftly drying in the sun.

Below deck they found seventeen thousand dollars' worth of merchandise. This loot was divided up on the basis of one-third to Boysie, the remaining two-thirds to be divided between the members of the crew. The captured boat was then fired and turned adrift. Neither it nor the members of the crew were ever seen again.

It is impossible to be certain how many pirate trips Boysie made in March and April 1950. Although Fire Kong and Bage invariably accompanied him, the other members of his crew were frequently changed; it seems almost as if he wished to blood his entire gang, either to involve them in his own guilt and thus bind them the closer to him, or perhaps merely to give himself the macabre pleasure of observing their reactions to the atrocities he forced them to commit.

That this idea is not fanciful is borne out by Boysie's own behaviour. When he picked a new man to accompany him on these voyages, he never told him what they were going to do. He would say, "We're going to test out the boat," or, "We're just going for a little ride." The green crewman would of course have his suspicions; although not all the gang were privy to

Boysie's latest venture, they all suspected that something very much out of the ordinary was going on. These suspicions would be deepened by Boysie and those of his henchmen who were in the know, who as soon as the voyage had begun would snigger unpleasantly and ask if he'd ever killed anyone; when he answered no, there would be another outburst of winks and nudges, wisecracks from Bage and tooth-grindings from Boysie. But the whole enormity of the proceedings would not be revealed to him until he was ordered to truss up the still-living victim and attach the weights. By that time it was too late to back out.

But this policy of Boysie's makes it difficult to check on the actual total of his victims, the more so since the Venezuelan boats he intercepted were probably all engaged in smuggling, and their contacts on shore might have had the best of reasons for not reporting their loss. Certainly statements in the press which appeared after Boysie's arrest indicated that at least seventeen Venezuelans were reported missing in the Gulf during the period of his activities, and even including the eleven on the big pirogue I have only been able to account for fourteen of them. Nor were Venezuelans the only ones to suffer.

Naturally, not every trip Boysie made proved fruitful. At the beginning of April there seemed to have been several voyages on which no prey was found. Also at this period Boysie was deeply involved in a series of events on shore which were to have the gravest consequences for him. But on April 16th he was at sea again, and this time sailed far into the night without sighting anything.

Then, on his way back to Cocorite he saw lights and, on approaching more closely, found a fishing boat with two men in it. The boat was powered with an outboard motor, and the sight of this decided Boysie. The outboard was worth only a few hundred dollars, but it was better than nothing, better than returning empty-handed once more – even though the price would be two men's lives.

The two men in the boat were Port of Spain fishermen, Philbert Wilson and Sonny Cook. They had a drift-net out and were moving slowly on the current. Neither of them showed any alarm when the *Marie Louise* veered towards them; it was not uncommon for fishermen to exchange a few words when their paths crossed, and Boysie's boat was in all probability familiar to them already.

The *Marie Louise* drew alongside. All the four men on board her had revolvers, but Fire Kong was the only one who troubled to draw. Too bewildered as yet to feel fear, Cook and Wilson raised their hands. Bage scrambled aboard their boat and made it fast to the *Marie Louise.* Kong and the other man followed him while Boysie looked on. Bewilderment changed to blind panic as they bound the fishermen's hands and ankles and then forced them to lie down and lashed on the heavy iron bars. But by that time it was too late, and neither tears nor curses availed them. In a matter of minutes they too had been hurled overboard.

Boysie took their engine and their net, and burned their boat; then he set course for Cocorite once more.

Here the loot from Boysie's raids was unloaded, but he was too cautious to unload directly onshore. Returning by night, he would transfer his spoils to a boat which was anchored some distance from the jetty; then, a day or two later, and openly, in broad daylight, he would transfer them from the anchored vessel to the shore.

This stratagem was the more effective for two reasons. The vessel Boysie used as his depot ship was one which was known to have no engine, and could not therefore be suspected of having taken part in piracy. Moreover, it did not even belong to Boysie, though Boysie had the best of reasons for using it, and his passage between ship and shore, with or without equipment, would not excite the slightest comment.

To realise how this advantageous state of affairs had come about, it is necessary to recount the history of the depot ship. Named *Sam Super I,* it was one of a pair of big launches owned by an Indian business man and bus company owner called J. W. Samaroo. Samaroo had originally intended using them to start a passenger service between Trinidad and Tobago, but he had had constant trouble with the engines and had eventually – some three months before the piracy began – anchored them off the Leper Asylum jetty and asked Boysie to look after them, keep them baled and look out for a buyer. They were solidly built craft, a hundred and twenty feet in length, with a superstructure in the centre which housed two cabins, and fore and aft of this a fixed wooden awning with rows of seats for passengers. The engines had been housed in an engine-room below the cabins, and it was in this place that the loot was generally stored.

Sam Super I had only recently been salvaged from the sea bed.

It happened in this fashion. For a long while John Olivera had been planning to go to South America. His genius was one which inclined towards fiddling rather than downright crime, and he sensed that for one of his type the moneymaking possibilities on the other side of the Gulf might be much greater. However, at that time – February 1950 – he was hard up, and needed about a hundred dollars to obtain his visa and pay the balance of his passage money.

Accordingly, he hatched a plot with his brother Leonard. On board *Sam Super I* was a large copper tank, for the storage of fuel; John suggested that they should steal this tank and sell it, dividing the proceeds between them. They agreed, and the tank was removed one dark night and sold to an engineering firm in Port of Spain for five hundred dollars. To conceal the theft, John knocked a hole in the bottom of *Sam Super I* and scuttled it.

Before the salvage operations could begin, John had left for South America.

It was not until Boysie had the boat raised that he realised what had happened. The police were informed – not the first indication of Boysie's touching faith in them when something was done unto him – and very soon ran the tank to earth. The firm which had unwittingly bought it, assuming it to be the seller's property, furnished them with a description of Olivera which was soon passed to Boysie.

Boysie decided that this action could not go unpunished. Samaroo's boats were under his protection, so that if anything happened to them he was responsible; the sinking of the *Sam Super I* was a grave reflection on his efficiency, one moreover that might prejudice the contacts with more respectable society which were a source of income as well as prestige and protection to him. Moreover John and his brother, as members of the organisation, had been guilty of treachery, and treachery unavenged might set a dangerous precedent for other ambitious members of the gang. Clearly, according to Boysie's lights, an example had to be made.

John, already in South America, was beyond his reach; his brother, however, was still in Port of Spain. Boysie sent word to him that he wanted him to come on a trip, a trip such as they had taken to Staubles Bay when they stole the Fireball. On the night of April 18th – two days after the slaying of Cook and Wilson – Leonard appeared promptly at the rendezvous.

They set out in the *Marie Louise* – Boysie, Fire Kong, Bage, Leonard and another man whom we will call Z. Z did not know any more than Leonard, any more than Boysie's other green hands, what was scheduled to happen.

The night was moonless, and very still. Not a ripple stirred the oily swell of the Gulf. When the boat stopped, a match-flame held in the hand burnt vertically into the warm air. The *Marie Louise* circled off Staubles Bay, but this time there was no launch, and the crew contented themselves with stealing a few oars from moored fishing-boats. Then they set course to Moros Island, but still found no prize worthy of their trouble. Leonard however suspected nothing, even though they were moving into unfrequented waters, where the chance of a capture was remote indeed.

At last, on the far side of Cronstadt or Doctor Island, Boysie stopped the engine and called Leonard to him. Still unsuspecting, Leonard sat beside him. "Are you hungry?" Boysie asked solicitously, and Leonard admitted that he was. Boysie gave him a roti, which he ate. Then suddenly, without warning, Boysie said "Put your hands behind your back."

Leonard stared at Boysie, whose face was only dimly visible in the starlight, with astonishment and disbelief. "What's happening?" he asked.

"Put your hands behind your back," Fire Kong roared at him. He turned and saw the dim outline of the revolver in Kong's huge hand. Slowly, still hardly believing what was happening to him, he obeyed.

"Tie his hands," Boysie said to Bage.

Bage came forward with a length of cord and tied Leonard's hands. Only when he felt the cord bite into his wrists did Leonard realise the utter hopelessness of the situation. He began to weep.

"Say your prayers," Boysie said curtly to him.

"What happened? What happened?" Leonard, delirious with fear, kept asking over and over again. Bage ignored his pleas and went on with the work. Leonard's wrists were by now securely fastened; Bage turned to his ankles. As soon as he had finished Boysie told Fire Kong to bring the engine plate they had stowed in the bottom of the launch. Roughly, Kong jerked the trussed Leonard to his feet and made him sit over the plate; Bage brought more cord and began to lash Leonard's legs to it.

Leonard had stopped crying now and had begun to pray. He said first the Lord's Prayer and then the Magnificat while Bage and Kong worked on him. Then at last he was ready. Boysie gave the word, and they lifted him. He stopped praying. In tying his legs to the iron Bage must have pulled the cord too tight, for even as he was lifted into the air he cried out, "Oh, God, my foot!" They were his last words. Bage and Kong heaved, the waters parted for him, and in a swirl of foam he vanished from sight for ever.

The engine started up and the *Marie Louise* was soon swallowed in the blackness of the night.

Two days later – April 20th – Boysie set out on what was to be his last pirate trip.

This time he sailed with his regular crew and a man whom we will call Y., who was told that Boysie was going to "test the boat". Y., however, guessed something of what was toward when soon after leaving Cocorite, Boysie, grinning evilly, turned to him and asked him, to the accompaniment of a snigger from Bage, "Did you ever kill a man?"

This time they were heading southeast, towards the area off Waterloo (a village south of Port of Spain), which any contraband boat would have to pass en route from Port of Spain to the Rio Pedernales. But the first boat they sighted was not a Venezuelan – it was the boat of two more Port of Spain fishermen, Hilary Taitt and Reynold Mayers. This, however, did not worry Boysie. After all, they had an engine, and that was by now enough to sign their death-warrant.

The sun was setting, but the evening was still clear – it was around half-past five – when the *Marie Louise* drew alongside Taitt's boat. The elder of the two – Taitt, a man of sixty – called out to them, called Boysie by name, and Boysie realised suddenly that he had known him well during his childhood at Woodbrook. However he did not hesitate for an instant, but called to Fire Kong to cover the two men.

Fire Kong drew both his guns and told the fishermen to get into the *Marie Louise*. Trembling, they obeyed. Boysie ordered Y. to tie their hands. Y. hesitated, took one look at Kong, who jerked the barrel of a .45

menacingly in his direction, and then, scarcely less frightened than the two victims, began to tie their legs. Even so he made such a mess of the job that Bage had to come and retie them afterwards. All this while Taitt was pleading with Boysie, for he knew now the fate that was in store for them. "Boysie," he kept saying. "Don't kill me, Boysie. Just give me a drop on the Main. I won't tell on you. I'll never tell on you if you'll only drop me on the Main."

By this time the engine, the object of the whole operation, had been removed from Taitt's boat and put in the *Marie Louise.* Still lashed together, the two boats began to move away into deeper water, towards the hidden Venezuelan coast.

"All right, man." Boysie said. "I'll drop you on the Main."

Taitt's face was bathed in tears of relief, but his companion, Mayers, a young man of about twenty-five, was not so easily deluded. Throughout the ordeal he had maintained an air of calm composure, as if disdaining to give his captors the satisfaction of tears or entreaties, aware that these would never move them; aware also perhaps that Boysie, far from taking them to Venezuela as Taitt believed, was merely playing with them, was taking them out from the coast because the waters where they had been captured were too shallow for the job. Coolly, he asked Y. for a cigarette, then began to speak quietly about his family; he had just got married, things were going well for him; it was a pity to have to die at such a time. Y. "broke down morally"; Mayers' courage made the job harder than any tears would have done, yet he knew that even a word of opposition would cause him to share the fishermen's fate.

Then the engine stopped, the boats drifted, Bage and Fire Kong fastened on the irons. Taitt screamed and wept, reviling Boysie for his treachery, but Boysie's expression never changed. "Say your prayers," he said. But neither man prayed, or if Mayers did he did so silently, in his mind; for Taitt was still shrieking as he went over the side, but Mayers went to his death without a word.

The men then cast off Taitt's boat and set fire to it.

No sooner had they done so than there came a faint droning from the clear blue dry-season sky, and a plane appeared. It was a Venezuelan airliner on the regular run from Maturin to Piarco; it passed only a few thousand feet over their heads. The pilot and the passengers must surely have seen the long smear of smoke from Taitt's burning boat, but if they did, it does not seem as if any of them reported the matter.

They were not the only ones who saw the fire. The throb of another engine spread across the still waters, and bearing down on them Boysie saw a long, cumbersome-looking boat, a thirty-five-foot corrial with an in-board engine. The crew of three – one older man and two younger, a father and his two sons the pirates assumed – had seen the drifting smoke and altered course so as to render assistance to what they in their innocence must have thought was a vessel in distress.

By the time they realised their mistake it was too late. The *Marie Louise,* which no doubt they thought was on a similar errand, swung across their bows, and Fire Kong levelled his forty-fives at them. One of them tried to dive for the small cabin amidships.

"Go down there and you're a dead duck," Kong roared at them.

The three men stood erect, their hands raised. Bage and Kong crossed to the corrial and began tying them. None of them, it seemed, spoke much English; the older man began to pray rapidly in his native tongue, but the others tried to calm him and, when they failed to do so, fell into an obstinate silence. Within three minutes they had all gone over the side.

The corrial was a better prize than the boats of poor fishermen. The Venezuelans had spent most of their cash in Trinidad, and had only about 700 bolivares – 360 dollars – left. They had, however, well over three thousand dollars worth of goods on board – shoes, shirts, lengths of material, all of which they had hoped to smuggle back into their own country.

Boysie was pleased with his haul. All the way back to Cocorite through the gathering darkness he kept teasing Y., saying, "How do you like killing people, eh?" and "What does it feel like to be a murderer?"

He might have been more subdued if he could have seen the object, sodden with a week's immersion but still recognisable for what it had been, which at that very moment lay in the yard of the Trinidad Yacht Club, only a mile or two from his home on the Western Main Road.

16: THE TROUBLE WITH BUMPER

THE STORM which was about to burst over Boysie's unsuspecting head had its origin in a series of events which began a fortnight before the last pirate trip.

Bumper – front man in No. 55's invert show – has already been mentioned. His real name was Philbert Peyson. A heavily-built man in his early thirties, he had supplemented his pickings from the Dorset by odd jobs and occasional thieving, and had recently become very friendly with a fourteen-year-old Indian boy of similar tastes called Rahamut Ali – better known as Loomat.

Loomat, who was to play a vital part in Boysie's future, had got completely beyond his parents' control and used to commute between their home and his aunt's, both of which were near the Dorset, so that if he were missing each would think he was at the other's house. In fact he was probably out thieving, or consorting with Bumper or another man of the same type, John Durant. If one is to believe Loomat himself, he also spent a great deal of time at No. 55, where he was treated as a kind of mascot by Boysie's girls.

Boysie himself always denied this, claimed that he never met Loomat until April 6th or 7th 1950. The truth is hard to ascertain, for as events were to turn out it was as much in Boysie's interests to assert that he hadn't known Loomat as it was in Loomat's to assert that he had. Neither, however, denies that they met at Easter that year in connection with the robbery at the Mico Shirt Factory.

Loomat, Bumper and a third man called Leo did the Mico job. Originally it was Loomat's idea, for the factory premises adjoined his aunt's house, and it was only necessary to climb a wall to gain access to them. An outside staircase led up to a doorway under the roof of the building, and this was where Loomat came in, for though the door was a strong one and firmly bolted there was a narrow aperture between the top of it and the lintel, too narrow for any normal man to pass, but just wide enough for the lath-thin, eel-like Loomat to squeeze through. Once inside, he let in the others, and with their knives they began to cut through the celotex ceiling to reach the workshops below. There was then no night-watchman on the premises, so they could work without fear of disturbance.

Even when they had made a hole in the ceiling and dropped through, their work was not over, for the made-up shirts and materials were stored in a locked room, and they had to cut through a partition to get at them. Then a problem arose, for, with an irresponsibility common among West Indian criminals, they had gone into the job without any idea of how they would dispose of the loot.

A brief conference followed, during which Bumper suggested Boysie, and as no one else had any suggestions, he and Loomat now left the factory and went round to No. 55. Boysie listened with interest to their story. He could not give them a price without seeing the goods, but he agreed to send a car round to collect them, and to pay a good figure if they proved satisfactory.

Everything went off successfully, and the three men received their payment. Reports vary as to how much this was, though it seems that Bumper's cut was two hundred or two hundred and fifty dollars. According to his own story, Loomat received five hundred and fifty which, if true, would certainly explain Bumper's subsequent dissatisfaction; as Loomat's protector he would certainly have expected the larger share. On the other hand, it seems odd that Boysie should give such a large sum to a boy of fourteen whom (he claimed) he had never seen before.

Such an action might, however, have had the object of weaning Loomat away from Bumper. Boysie seems to have been impressed by the burglarious expertise Loomat had demonstrated in the Mico job; a thief who could wriggle through narrow openings would be most useful in the crimes he was planning. He made up his mind to take Loomat for his own. This was a further cause of annoyance to Bumper. Up till then, the latter had been hogging the proceeds of Loomat's robberies and doling out only a small percentage to his protégé. If Boysie succeeded, Bumper, who had never had it so good, would lose the greater part of his income as well as his "friend".

Matters were complicated still further by Durant. Durant, alleged third leg in the paederastic triangle, also aimed to use Loomat as his tame thief. Rivalry between him and Bumper was bitter.

It was in this involved context that Boysie, two or three days after the Mico break-in, began to plan a raid on a combined grocery and beerhall in Woodbrook called the Brooklyn Bar.

For the Brooklyn Bar job, Boysie had intended to use Loomat; though a large quantity of cash was supposed to be kept on the premises, access to the place where it was kept was likely to be difficult. Loomat, however, was not available, for reasons which will be indicated later. Boysie, unwilling to give up an idea once he had conceived it, decided to go ahead with Bumper, Leo, Fire Kong and Bage. On the night of the robbery he himself drove them to Woodbrook, dropped them there, and went on driving round the district until such time as they might have completed the job; he was too old a hand to leave a car parked near the scene of the crime.

In the course of his circuit he had occasion to pass Woodbrook Police Station. Glancing into the station yard he saw to his surprise that a police jitney parked there was rapidly filling up with uniformed constables. Smelling trouble, Boysie hit the accelerator. Through his rear-view mirror he could see the jitney swinging out into the road and following him.

The Brooklyn Bar lay at the far end of the road. As Boysie raced towards it, his headlights picked up a swiftly-walking figure. It was Bumper – Bumper, who was supposed to be acting as lookout man at the Brooklyn – but he was walking *away* from the Bar. Seconds ahead of the police, Boysie's car screamed to a halt outside the building. Bage and Fire Kong were on the pavement, waiting; Leo was still inside.

It was a sheer fluke that Boysie's two most loyal henchmen were in the clear. They had been supposed to help Leo in the actual break-in, but once inside the building they found they had to force another door at the end of a passage so narrow that only one man at a time could work. Bage had pointed out that it was foolish for all three of them to remain inside where they would be trapped without a hope of escape if anything went wrong; he and Kong therefore told Leo to let them know when he was ready for them, and went to wait in the street.

Boysie yelled to them to jump in, and, without a thought for the unfortunate Leo, they did so. Already the headlamps of the police jitney were blazing in Boysie's mirror. As the doors crashed shut, he hurled the car into motion again. The jitney braked only long enough to shed some of its uniformed men, who swiftly threw a cordon around the bar; then it raced in pursuit of Boysie. But Boysie, driving with his customary disregard for the public safety, soon outdistanced the more cumbersome vehicle. Leo was the only one to be arrested. He did not seem to hold it against Boysie that he had been left behind, or perhaps he thought that in the long run it would be wiser to keep quiet. Whatever the reason, he took his three-year rap without talking.

Back at No. 55, Boysie held a council of war. It was pretty obvious that someone had informed on the Brooklyn job; it was equally obvious to Boysie who that someone was. All were agreed that a police investigation at that time would be fatal; they were at the height of their piratical activities, a raid on their hideouts would reveal actual loot from their victims, and although they all confidently believed that a successful murder prosecution without a body was a legal impossibility, they were well aware that once under arrest they would have to face charges far more serious than mere breaking and entering.

The situation was as old as gangsterism itself. Bumper could not be allowed to live.

17: THE CASE OF THE FLOATING CORPSE

THE OBJECT which Vernon Levy, boatman, saw on the morning of the 20th April, 1950, floating off the Trinidad Yacht Club, was still recognisable as human – though that was about all you could say for it.

The Trinidad Yatch Club, taken from approximately the position where Bumper's body was found floating.

Levy, an employee of the Yacht Club, was baling out boats anchored off the jetty when he first saw it. At first he took it for the body of a white man, for though Bumper had been black enough when he entered the water, several days' immersion had stripped off most of his skin, and a Negro's flesh is as white as that of a Caucasian. The gases of decomposition which swelled his chest and stomach were bubbling gently through the ravaged tissue of his right cheek. The top of his scalp was hairless, his eyes had been destroyed, probably by fish, and in his legs were deep lacerations caused by fishes' teeth. His wrists were lashed behind his back and his ankles bound together. Attached to his body by a thicker rope was a seven-foot-long piece

The corpse of Philbert Peyson (Bumper) being towed into the Trinidad Yacht Club

The disintegrating corpse of Philbert Peyson on the Yacht Club jetty. Prolonged immersion has removed the upper pigmented layers of his skin, thus rendering him white enough for entry into that august establishment.

of iron which was subsequently found to weigh eighty-nine pounds; even this weight had been insufficient to prevent the stomach gas formed by decay from forcing the corpse to the surface.

Levy called the police, who dragged what was left of Bumper ashore and laid him out in the yard of the Yacht Club – the only way in which he could ever have gained access to that select institution.

Five days later Boysie was arrested and charged with the murder of Philbert Peyson, alias Bumper.

Charged with him were four other men: Eldon Coggins, alias "Paka Beyer", 26, Augustus James, alias "Frisco", 24, David Bruce, alias "Tobago", 21, and John Durant, 36. After several adjournments the preliminary hearing took place in the Port of Spain Third Police Court before Mr. B. W. Celestain, magistrate, on the 5th, 6th and 7th June, 1950. All five defendants were committed for trial at the next assizes.

But long before the hearing, the whole of Trinidad had been plunged in a fury of speculation. The discovery of Bumper's corpse was immediately linked in the public mind with the killing of a sailor whose body, minus hands and feet, had surfaced off the U.S. base at Chaguaramas four days before Bumper's corpse was found. This body was never definitely identified. A week earlier, the captain of the Norwegian ship S.S. *Alar* had reported the disappearance of a crew member, whose name was given as Arneaud Suite, aged 20. By the 16th this ship had left Trinidad. The corpse however corresponded in age, colour and probable length of immersion with the missing man, so it was generally assumed that it was in fact Suite.

From these bare facts sprouted a monstrous legend. Hands and feet somehow became transmuted into head and penis; the latter organ, it was suggested, had been removed by Boysie so that he could eat it, presumably to restore his potency by sympathetic magic. Another version had Boysie a collector of male organs, which he removed from all his victims and preserved in alcohol in a glass sweet-jar. (This one perhaps grew from the tale of the handless man's severed fingers, which were also supposed to have been preserved in this manner.) Two version of how the "Norwegian Sailor" met his end – one, by stabbing, the other, by decapitation with a "Hooked sword" – blatantly fail to conform with the findings of the postmortem: that the cause of death was suffocation. But these facts did not stop large numbers of Trinidadians from believing one or other of these stories, both of which agreed that the man had been killed at No. 55 Queen Street.

After careful investigation I have come to the conclusion that Boysie did not kill the sailor. Not only do the stories fail to tally with even the few facts that are known, but they are categorically denied by those who were closest to him at the time. As these people were quite ready to admit his other murders, it seems unlikely that a concern for his reputation prompted their denials. Who killed Suite (if it was indeed Suite) will probably never be known.

Rumour was on firmer ground when it associated Boysie with the disappearance of the four Port of Spain fishermen, Wilson, Cook, Taitt and Mayers, which until that time had received scant attention, and with the reports of missing boats which were just beginning to come in from Venezuela. Strangely enough, it was not until a week after the arrests that the piracy story broke in the local press, and by then the Floating Corpse case (as it came to be described) was already *sub judice,* so that any references to Boysie and his gang were precluded. Still the papers made up in sensationalism what they had lost in delay; despite the shortage of facts, the *Guardian* – Trinidad's leading daily – filled its front page with the gruel of conjecture, and managed to keep the story (fed intravenously with rumour and vivid imagination) alive for over a week.

The whole Port of Spain waterfront, it was said, was paralysed with fear; a photograph showed the entire fishing-fleet voluntarily confined to harbour, its crews too terrified to put to sea. Police launches swept the Gulf, searching for any trace of the missing men or their boats. And, as usually happens at such times, the usual horde of anonymous crackpots came forward with their inside stories. Most of these dealt with the pirates' *modus operandi.* They were said to wear masks; they were all disguised in customs officers' uniforms; they were so chary of even their voices being recognised that they did not communicate with one another by speech, but by tapping in code on the sides of their boat with pieces of wood. It was obvious from these stories that Boysie's full ruthlessness was still not recognised; for why disguise yourself, why knock on wood, when you knew that no witnesses would be left alive?

The search for the missing fishermen was abandoned on 11th May, and the piracy story died for lack of further sustenance. In the hands of the police, however, there were now articles which would have soon revived it had the press been permitted to tell of them. In the course of investigations all Boysie's haunts had been thoroughly searched, without result, for the gang had had time to conceal what loot was left; but there was nothing they could do about goods which had been sold already. At the home of another fisherman the police found nets and an engine which had belonged to Wilson and Cook, victims of the April 16th raid. The authorities could now have prosecuted Boysie for piracy and perhaps the murder of the two fishermen, but they decided against it; they had what seemed the cast-iron case of Bumper to work on, and a man can only be charged with one murder at a time.

So, on July 17th 1950, there opened what was to prove the longest and most sensational murder trial in the history of Trinidad.

The Central Criminal Court, where the Port of Spain Assizes are held, is situated in a building known as the Red House. A sombre chunk of Edwardiana, painted a dull terracotta shade, the Red House dominates the whole of one side of Woodford Square, in the centre of Port of Spain. The Square itself might almost be described as a park, for it spreads over an area of two or three acres, iron-fenced, grass-covered, and dotted with trees; it has a dusty, sinister, Purdyesque air, looks the kind of place where they might kill people by night; even in the daytime, with grim-eyed layabouts sprawled on its benches and clumped around its rusty iron bandstand – in which it is almost impossible to imagine a band actually playing – it is a place where the respectable citizen does not care to linger. On the morning of the 17th, the environs of the Red House and Woodford Square were packed with the thousands who had failed to gain admittance to the public gallery of the courtroom, and who now milled round arguing and gambling on the probable result, or simply hoping to catch a glimpse of the defendants on their way to or from the Red House.

Boysie Singh, bible in hand, on his way to court during the Floating Corpse Trial

The case was tried before Mr. Justice Kenneth Vincent Brown. The acting Solicitor-General, Mr. C. T. W. E. Worrell, led for the prosecution; for the defence, Boysie had retained Mr. Rupert C. Archbald, K.C., and Mr. Edgar Johnston, while each of the other accused had his own counsel.

All five looked confident and calm as the trial opened. A *Guardian* reporter described Boysie as "the best-dressed accused ever to face trial on a capital charge". He had discarded his all-black pirate outfit as clearly unsuitable for the occasion; on each of the first nine days of the trial, he wore a different-coloured suit, with shirts, ties, socks and shoes to match. As the case wore on and the outlook grew blacker, he paid less attention to his appearance, whether through indifference or lack of suits is not known.

Eleven jurymen were challenged – ten by the defence – before the jury could be empanelled. The Solicitor-General then opened the case for the Crown.

The Crown case was that Bumper, a known member of Boysie's gang, had last been seen alive on Friday 14th April. On the evening of that day, witnesses had seen Bumper, the five accused and the boy Loomat leaving 55 Queen Street in Boysie's jitney, T 1001. The jitney was then driven to Cocorite, and stopped at a point where the road ran close to the sea, not far from the Aquatic Club. Boysie then went and fetched his launch from its anchorage off the Leper Asylum jetty. On his return he spoke to Coggins, who struck Bumper down with a blow to the head. Bruce and Durant had then fetched rope and a piece of iron and lashed Bumper to it. Bumper, still alive, was placed in the launch, which set out to sea, while Loomat waited in the jitney. The five men returned about half an hour later, without the launch, which they had moored in its usual anchorage. The party then returned to No. 55, where they drank and sang for the rest of the night.

The day after the discovery of the body, Boysie went to Besson Street Police Station, where he asked to speak to Inspector Bleasdell, his old acquaintance from the San Juan days who was now in charge of the Bumper investigation. In the voluntary statement he made he blamed Bumper's death on Durant and Loomat. Both Bumper and Durant, he alleged, were "in love" with Loomat; Durant, apparently the more successful suitor, had already conspired to murder Bumper by giving him a poisoned roti. Boysie suggested that Loomat had lured Bumper to Point Cumana where the two of them had killed him and thrown his body into the sea. The prosecution was prepared to accept this story, with one alteration; that it was in fact Boysie who had used Loomat as homosexual bait in order to draw Bumper out of town to a place where he could be conveniently murdered.

The first witness for the prosecution was Dr. John McDougall, who had examined the body shortly after its removal from the sea, and who described in grisly detail the results of its five-day immersion. He was unable to specify with certainty the cause of death. The skull appeared normal and the heart healthy. Three days after burial the body had been exhumed and the stomach examined for evidence of poisoning, but with negative results. The body was too much decomposed for signs of strangulation to be evident. He was obliged to conclude, in default of other evidence, that death was due to asphyxia from drowning – a conclusion which fitted well with the Crown's theory of how Bumper met his end.

Dr. McDougall was followed by Bumper's niece, Pearl Stoute, who had identified the body. Such was its condition that she was able to do so only by the tattoo mark, in the form of a snake, which he had on his left forearm, and the ring on the little finger of his left hand. She also recognised Bumper's bandy legs.

Further evidence of identification was given by Sergeant Emmanuel Salandy, who was in charge of the Finger-Print Registry of the Trinidad Police Department. Sergeant Salandy had had over twenty-two years experience of fingerprint work, and had taken a training course in the subject at New Scotland Yard. Owing to the condition of the body he had found it extremely difficult to take prints. The outer skin of Bumper's fingers was hanging loose; "I just pulled it off," Salandy said, "it came off like gloves." Despite this he had managed to take impressions from the skin and found them identical with those of one Philbert Peyson, recorded in the Criminal Register as No. 7-12-61.

The evidence of both Pearl Stoute and Sergeant Salandy was hotly challenged by counsel for the defence, in particular Mr. Isaac Hyatali, who represented Coggins. But although they were able to pick out minor inconsistencies – Miss Stoute had said at the preliminary hearing that she recognised Bumper by his trousers; at the trial, that he had been naked when she saw him in the mortuary – there remained ample grounds for believing that the corpse was indeed the unfortunate Philbert's.

Joseph William Samaroo, garage and engineering works proprietor, now took the stand and gave evidence concerning his two motor launches, *Sam Super I* and *II*. These boats, with their original engines removed, had been placed in the care of Boysie, who had agreed to look after them in exchange for the right to use them for spreading his nets on. This had saved Samaroo the expense of a night-watchman, though if he had known of the other uses to which his boats were being put he might have considered it a false economy.

Next to give evidence was Clyde Clarke, a marine mechanic employed by Furness Withy & Co., a Port of Spain engineering firm which specialised in the sale of marine engines, and which, as the Trinidad agent for Johnson outboards, had often done business with Boysie. Clarke had been taken by the police to Samaroo's garage, where he had matched the piece of iron removed from Bumper against the base of a diesel engine in the garage. The holes in the iron corresponded to the holes in the base of the engine. The next day he was taken out to the launches. In one of them he found a wooden engine bed from which the metal plates had been removed. He had compared the iron in police possession with the engine bed and had found, once more, that the holes corresponded. He concluded therefore that the iron used to weight Bumper was one of the two engine extension plates on which the *Sam Super's* diesel had originally been mounted.

When the trial was resumed on July 19th, Robert Wilkie was called.

Wilkie claimed to be a painter, although as it afterwards turned out this was only one and by far the most respectable of his occupations. He had been standing outside a rum-shop at the corner of Queen and Charlotte Streets around ten o'clock on the evening of Friday, 14th April, waiting for a woman who never turned up – a claim which brought some facetious comments from the defence. While waiting, he saw a friend of his, one Hubert Rodney, a stevedore, better known as "Bag of Rice" because he had done a prison term for stealing one, and the two men got into conversation. Around 10.20 p.m., Boysie, Bumper, Loomat and the other four defendants had come down the stairs of No. 55 and got into the jitney. Wilkie was still there, still talking to Rodney, when around midnight Boysie and his party returned, minus Bumper, and shortly afterwards the strain of calypsoes had been heard floating through the windows of No. 55.

Then defence counsel Hyatali cross-examined Wilkie with devastating effect. The painter confessed that his gaol sentences totalled some twenty-six years; they included a year for shopbreaking, two terms of five and seven years for burglary, six years for entering a house to steal, and four years for the larceny of a pantry towel. In 1946 he was convicted for keeping a brothel. Moreover, there were discrepancies between his evidence at the preliminary hearing and that just given, which seemed to suggest that he altered his statements to fit the somewhat different statements given by "Bag of Rice".

Hubert Rodney, alias "Bag of Rice", was next to take the stand. Rodney's evidence was similar to that of Wilkie, although he had not seen Loomat get into the jitney. Under cross-examination, however, he broke down badly. He was uneducated and practically illiterate – if he had a watch, he confessed, he could not have told the time. Boysie's junior counsel, Johnston, asked him to account for the fact that, while at the preliminary hearing he had said he did not know Inspector Bleasdell, he now stated on oath that he did. Rodney explained that he "knew him by rank", a reply which caused Johnston to exclaim, not without reason, "How can I cross-examine a witness like this?" Boysie, Rodney declared, "was no friend of mine. I just said 'Right, right,' to him. Just as I say 'Right' to anybody. I say 'Right' even to my friends." (It should perhaps be explained that the greeting "Right" in Trinidad corresponds to "Hi" or "Hello" elsewhere, and is almost universal amongst the working class of Trinidad.) He was not worried by Bleasdell's questions about Bumper. "I had no cocoa outside and did not look for rain."

Tied into knots by defence counsels' probing, and upset perhaps by suggestions of collusion between him and Wilkie, Rodney closed the day's proceedings by denying that he had spoken to Wilkie at all on the evening in question.

By the following morning he had thought better of it, or, to use his own words, "recalled his brains" and remembered that he had indeed spoken to Wilkie. On the actual date of the occurrence, however, his testimony was shaky in the extreme. He asserted first that he knew exactly when he had last seen Bumper, and five minutes later admitted under pressure that he did not remember. In a rush of unwonted honesty he admitted that he did not know himself which version to believe. He also admitted that between 1923 and 1947 he had no less than forty-six convictions, for matters such as larceny, being armed with a weapon, assault, and wounding with intent.

The faces in the dock were looking brighter once more. If this was the best that the prosecution could do they had little to worry about. Unfortunately for them, it was not. The next prosecution witness was George Harper – the same Harper who, a few months before, had owed his life to the Singhs on their last and almost fatal fishing trip to the Hole.

Harper stated that Boysie had owed him two dollars for some repairs he had done to an outboard. The debt had been outstanding for some time but he had not asked for it as Boysie, though "a gentleman", quickly took offence if asked for money owed by him. But on the 14th he was "broken as a bat", having gambled heavily and lost; and when he said "lost" he meant "every cent". He went to No. 55, but Boysie was not there so he decided to walk back to his home in Carenage. Carenage lies on the Western Main Road beyond Cocorite. He passed through Cocorite around eleven – he knew the time because as he walked by the petrol station he heard Radio Trinidad signing off.

A little further on he had seen Boysie's jitney with "the little Indian boy" sitting in it. He went on to Boysie's home, No. 192, and, finding Boysie was not there either, had started back towards the parked jitney when he saw Boysie and the other accused coming up from the Leper Asylum jetty. Boysie promised him his money the next day, and he went home.

Although Harper admitted he had been a longtime associate of Boysie, the defence were unable to find anything discreditable in his record, and under cross-examination he stuck to his story with tenacity and even on occasions a kind of wry humour. Asked by counsel whether the night was dark – the implication being that he could not have recognised all the accused – he replied imperturbably, "Yes sir; all night is dark."

He was followed by a witness still more respectable – Isaac Bishop, nightwatchman for Contractors Ltd. at the Old Sea Plane Base at Cocorite, and an ex-policeman with sixteen years service. The premises occupied by Contractors immediately adjoined the Leper Asylum Jetty, and from them it was possible to see anyone passing along that jetty to the boats anchored off shore.

Bishop declared that around eight p.m. on the 14th Boysie had passed along the jetty with two other men and returned a few minutes later. At about eleven he had reappeared, this time with only one man, who rowed out in a rowing boat and returned to the jetty with Boysie's launch. Both men then disappeared in the launch, heading in an easterly direction. The launch returned half an hour later, this time with five men on board, and was anchored in the same place as before.

Bishop too stood up well under cross-examination, which was vigorous to the point of rudeness, and seemed largely based on the assumption that, as Bishop had once been a policeman, he was obviously going to be the mouthpiece of the prosecution in any case in which he was called as a witness. He was shaken on one or two minor details, but the substance of his evidence remained intact.

At this stage of the trial, the scales definitely seemed to be tilting in favour of the prosecution. And Worrell had yet to produce his star witness, his eyewitness – the boy who, if the Crown was to be believed, had seen the murder actually taking place.

18: "LOOMAT SAY HE SEE BOYSIE"

THE PROSECUTION'S star witness was none other than Rahamat Ali, alias Loomat.

He entered the witness-box wearing a dark brown shirt and flannel shorts. To the surprise of most observers, the five accused greeted his appearance with broad smiles. The smiles faded somewhat as his evidence unfolded. It supported in every detail the Crown's contentions – that Boysie had driven him, Bumper and the other four accused to Cocorite, that he had then fetched the launch, that Coggins struck down Bumper, that the others weighted him and took him out to sea, and that around half an hour later the five accused reappeared and they had all driven back to Queen Street.

As soon as his evidence in chief was completed, the lawyers fell on him like a pack of hungry wolves.

For the better part of two days he was subject to the most searching cross-examination. His evidence, if true, was so damning that the defence must at all costs shake it if they were even to hope for an acquittal. Time after time, by each counsel in turn, he was taken over his story in the hope that somewhere along the line he would be trapped into contradicting himself. But the only point on which his testimony looked really doubtful was his statement regarding the date. At the preliminary hearing he had said that the events he described occurred on a Thursday – he "couldn't remember" the day or the month. Now, however, some six weeks later, he was quite certain that the murder had taken place on Friday 14th April. In the interval he had "refreshed his memory" by consulting an almanac.

On the outline of his story he remained firm. Whenever he was caught on dangerous ground he would declare blandly, "I don't remember", and stick to that despite all the sarcasm his interrogators could level at him.

For an uneducated boy of fourteen to hold his own against learned counsel was indeed remarkable, and the defence sought to turn defeat into victory by alleging that no one of Loomat's attainments could possibly tell so consistent a story unless he had been elaborately coached beforehand. But here too Loomat countered with blank denials or inability to remember; devices which counsel in their turn claimed as further evidence of coaching.

So the trial dragged on, ticking up public money like a taxi-meter with every day that it lasted.

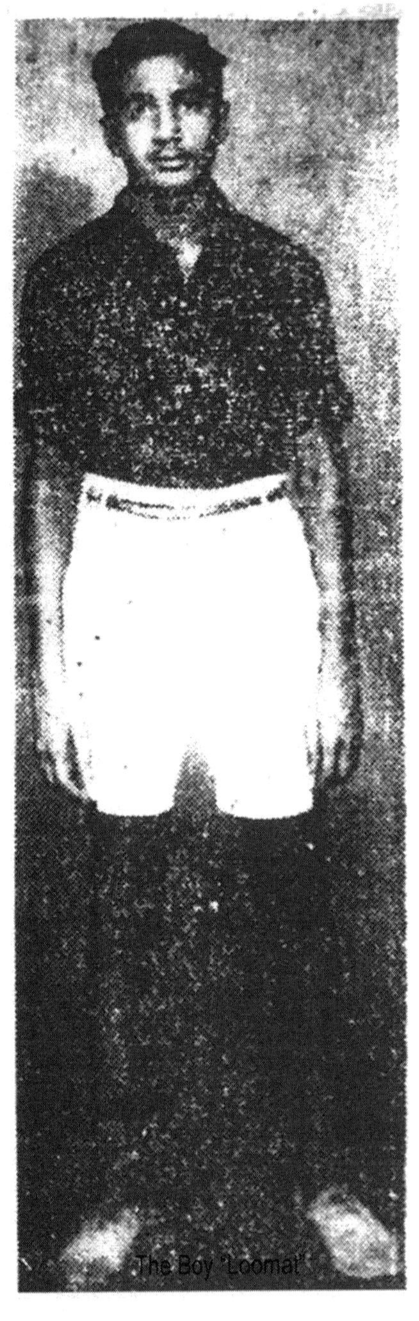
The Boy 'Loomat'

In a final bid to crush Loomat the defence resorted to ridicule. He was asked questions about religion. It transpired that he had never heard of the Koran. "What is your religion?" he was asked. "Indian," he replied.

But on one point neither the Crown nor the Defence questioned him. That point was the allegation of homosexual practices between Loomat, Bumper and Durant which had been a mainstay of the Crown case. One of the most curious features of this curious trial was the failure of the Crown to bring any testimony in support of its original contention that Loomat was the bait used to lure Bumper to his doom.

No matter how much scorn was poured on him, Loomat's evidence remained substantially unaffected, a coherent whole. It had to be either accepted or rejected entire; either you believed when (in the words of the calypso which was shortly to be produced) "Loomat say he see Boysie", or you dismissed his whole story as a fabrication. And though their accusations of coaching might seem plausible enough, defence counsel had been unable to produce any tangible proof.

The last witness for the prosecution was Inspector Bleasdell.

Bleasdell stated that Boysie came to him voluntarily on April 21st, the day after he (Bleasdell) had been put in charge of the case, in the company of a man whose name, at various times and by various persons during the trial, was given as Duencio or Junicio or Ignacio or Venetio Brown. This multinomial Brown had confirmed Boysie's story about the amorous entanglements of Loomat, Bumper and Durant, poisoned roti and all. On April 23rd, Bleasdell had seen James and Coggins, cautioned them and detained them pending further inquiries. He did not however arrest them until April 25th, the day when Boysie was arrested. Boysie had made a statement to Sergeant Blake which for some reason was never put into evidence, and which was actually refused by Bleasdell when the defence requested it, an action which the Judge rather curiously supported.

The other two accused had been arrested some time later; Durant on May 19th, with a warrant dated 11th May, Bruce not until May 27th, after he had been put in an identification parade with six other men and picked out by Loomat as one of the men in the jitney. Bruce was charged under the name of "George".

Under cross-examination by Boysie's counsel, Bleasdell denied strongly that the statement made by Boysie on April 21st had been obtained as a result of questioning; he remained silent when reminded that Besson Street Police Station was known throughout the Port of Spain underworld as "The Pacific" – "because there they 'pacify' people". The defence then turned their attention to the alleged coaching of Loomat. This was also denied; according to Bleasdell, Loomat had come voluntarily to Besson Street with his father to make a statement. This was on April 20th; between that date and April 26th, when Loomat was placed under protective custody and lodged at Staubles Bay, he had not visited Besson Street nor had he given instructions for Loomat to be detained there. As far as he was aware, Loomat had been at liberty throughout this period.

Throughout the course of the trial, Boysie's senior counsel, Archbald, had been insisting that the whole prosecution was baseless, as no boat could have come in to the shore by the Aquatic Club with the tide as it was on the night of April 14th; the water was much too shallow to take a boat with the draught of the *Marie Louise.* Time and time again Mr. Justice Brown had refused his plea that the jury should be taken to the alleged scene of the crime to judge for themselves; but now, in the middle of Bleasdell's cross-examination, he suddenly relented, and the case was adjourned for the day while the jury, watched by a large and curious crowd, sallied forth from the Red House in a hired bus, destination Cocorite.

Whether they derived any benefit from the outing – except a much-needed rest from what looked like an interminable vigil – it is impossible to say. On their return, the ordeal of Bleasdell continued. All the defence counsel were now working together to establish what had clearly emerged as the basis of their defence – the allegation that Bleasdell, alone or in company with other police officers, had fabricated the entire Crown case, and had with threats or enticements suborned the evidence of Wilkie, Rodney, Harper and Bishop; while Loomat, kingpin of the prosecution, was merely a ventriloquist's dummy through which the voice of Bleasdell could be heard speaking loud and clear. To lend colour to this accusation, Hyatali claimed on behalf of his client Coggin that Bleasdell had offered

Coggin his freedom if he would turn Crown witness against the others. The defence, while they might cast doubt on the Crown case as a whole and even demolish details of it, had made no sizeable breach in the closely-knit web of evidence which was steadily tightening round Boysie and his companions.

With Bleasdell's departure the case for the prosecution closed. It had lasted fourteen days, largely because of bitter and sometimes unduly repetitive cross-examination by the various counsel for the accused.

In any murder case, one of the main problems for the defence is to decide whether to risk putting their clients in the witness-box. Obviously it is better to do so if at all possible, for though they are not supposed to take this into account, the jury are obviously going to assume that a defendant who avoids taking the stand must have something to hide, and is therefore more likely to be guilty. However, the dangers of exposing a possibly guilty client to cross-examination by a keen prosecuting counsel are so obvious that no lawyer will risk such a course unless he is convinced either of his client's innocence or of his dialectical skill.

Mr. Rupert Archbald must have felt that his client possessed one or both of these qualities, for the defence opened with Boysie himself in the box.

If his situation was grave, Boysie gave no hint of that in his demeanour. He began with a calm summary of his current fishing operations. He had now only six boats – the rest of his Cedros fleet having been disposed of when he returned to Port of Spain – and these nowadays carried crews of two men instead of the original three. Harper, the prosecution witness, had been employed on one of these boats, and on the 14th had set out with a fisherman called Bamboozie at around 4. p.m. to go drifting for carite off Waterloo. They had not returned until 8.30 a.m. the following Saturday, so Harper could not have seen Boysie by the Leper Asylum jetty as he had claimed.

Boysie scorned to refute the evidence of Wilkie and Rodney, but that of the ex-policeman Bishop was another matter. He claimed that Bishop's testimony was motivated by personal malice. He had had a bitter quarrel with Bishop over the two *Sam Supers;* two Venezuelans had come to look over them with a view to buying and had almost made up their minds when Bishop approached them and told them the boats were rotten, as a result of which the Venezuelans had abandoned the deal. Boysie had taxed Bishop with this and harsh words passed between them, after which Boysie had ceased the allowance of free fish which he normally gave to Bishop.

As for Loomat, Boysie claimed he hardly knew the boy, had only met him on one or two occasions, neither of which was the night of the 14th. To the cry of "Loomat say he see Boysie" he returned an equally determined answer of "Boysie say he didn't see Loomat". According to his own account, he had spent part of that evening visiting one of his girls at No. 55;

after an hour with her he had returned home where he did some work and then spent the night. Even if he had not been so occupied, he claimed, he would have been unable to commit the crime in the way the prosecution said he had done, for three excellent reasons.

The first was that on Friday 14th April, 1950, high tide was at 3.30 p.m., low at 9.30. At eleven – the time at which he was supposed to have landed by the Aquatic Club – the tide would be just beginning to rise, but by the Aquatic Club there would still be a hundred and fifty to two hundred feet of mud exposed, and beyond that the water would only have been inches deep. It would have been impossible to bring a boat of the *Marie Louise's* draught into the shore, let alone get it off again with six men aboard.

The second was that on the night of the 14th all his boats, except one, were at sea, and that one – the *Marie Louise* – was out of action because of engine trouble.

The third was that Bumper did not die on the 14th at all. He personally had seen Bumper alive and well on the following day, and other witnesses would be called who would testify to the same fact.

He denied that he had gone voluntarily to Besson Street; on the contrary, Bleasdell had come to him at Queen Street, and had elicited a statement by means of questions. Moreover the statement read in court differed materially from the statement he had in fact made. The sentence, "I know that Bumper is in love with Loomat" should have read "I *don't* know that Bumper is in love with Loomat", and the sentence, "I know that both Bumper and Durant commit sodomy with Loomat" should have read, "I *don't* know that both Bumper and Durant commit sodomy with Loomat." It is hard to see what was his motive in claiming that these particular sentences had been changed, unless it was to cast doubt on the validity of the statement as a whole, for, if genuine, it was a rather unfortunate one. He would have been better advised, had he been able to think of a way of doing so, to challenge the sentence that said: "If Loomat ask Bumper to go anywhere with him he will go, so it is easy for Loomat to invite Bumper to go with him to Cumana and he was met there by Durant and they knocked him out and take one of the boats at mooring and took him to sea and left him there since."

This was virtually the prosecution's case, except that for Loomat and Durant they substituted Boysie, Durant and the three other accused. Admittedly, it contained no details about Bumper's fate that could not have been known or guessed from the press reports, but the passage was unpleasantly indicative of the way Boysie's mind worked.

Boysie claimed also that he had never read the statement, although he had signed it; he assured the court that he was unable to read. Bleasdell had interrogated him until 6.30 a.m. on the morning on which he was charged.

Under cross-examination, Boysie assumed the righteous indignation of a teetotaller on a drunk-and-disorderly charge. Asked to explain his goings-on at No. 55, he shouted, "I carry on that place for twelve years and I never have a charge for brothel!" He denied that he kept any henchmen there. "It is I alone and God!" The Solicitor-General cunningly led him on in order to establish in the minds of the jury the criminal milieu which Boysie inhabited; in quick succession he raised the issues of Fire Kong's shooting spree in No. 55, the whe-whe in San Juan, and the attempted murder of Joe Maynard alias Bam-Bam.

Worrell – "Was Maynard shot?"

Boysie – "Yes."

"A man went to prison?"

"Yes, he got five years."

"A gun was found in 55 Queen Street?"

"Yes."

"When one of your men gets uppish you will lick him out of the way?"

"I never murdered anyone since I was born!"

Boysie had to admit, though, that Bumper had frequently done odd jobs for him – how odd he did not mention. He was questioned further about his business methods. How was it, for example, that he could carry out complex business transactions, if, as he claimed, he could neither read nor write? "From the time I started business," he assured the court, "I have never kept books." "Have you ever paid income tax?" "None at all – all my business I run alone."

Every assault Worrell launched against him was deftly parried with this typical mixture of self-righteousness and semiconscious humour, and the score must have seemed to the observers equal or even slightly in Boysie's favour when he was at last allowed to leave the box. He might have proved himself a rogue, but everyone knew that already; he had definitely not been proved to be a murderer.

The first witness called to confirm his story was, of all people, Duncan Trotman.

Bage took the stand with his usual insolent smirk. The story he had to tell was superb in its effrontery; his picture of No. 55 made it look more innocuous than the rector's youth club, with the gunsels and their molls joining in a jolly songfest of calypsoes and Latin-American rhythm, while Bage played the chac-chac, Bumper the "Spanish boom" – a double-bass made from a tea-chest – and a couple of other hoodlums strummed guitars. This scene of innocent merriment had lasted through the night of the 14th and well into the small hours of the following day. Holding Bage's hand between chac-chac sessions had been Rosie, Bage's current girlfriend, who (he assured the court), would have confirmed his story in the fullest detail, had she not had the bad luck to die on July 5th.

So Bumper had been alive and well on the morning of the 15th. This was more than the Solicitor-General was prepared to take, particularly from the grinning Bage. In fact Worrell completely lost his temper and stormed at the witness, reminding him that he was an illegal immigrant, threatening that he would be expelled from Trinidad if he persisted in his testimony – a move which brought heated protests from the defence, but which Mr. Justice Brown did not seem to consider in any way improper for the representative of the Crown.

Bage, however, remained unshaken, and was followed by Boysie's son Chuncie.

Chuncie testified that the jitney which was supposed to have carried the murder gang had been in his possession throughout the evening and night of the 14th. He had in fact been the regular driver since February. On the afternoon of the day he brought several of Boysie's men back from Cocorite to Port of Spain – they had been engaged in repair work on the boats there – and then returned to Cocorite for a brief period, later going on to the house of his mother, Mana Lala, with whom he had always remained on very close terms. He had stayed there – at the corner of 12th Street and Second Avenue, Barataria – until the following day, and the jitney had remained outside the house all that time.

When it was suggested to him that he might have made a mistake in the date, he insisted that this was impossible, as April 15th was his birthday, and it was his custom to spend the eve of his birthday at his mother's, eating the special cake that she had prepared for him. This was perhaps an unfortunate choice of mnemonic, for, as Worrell was quick to suggest, it would be far more likely that he would spend his actual birthday there, and eat his cake upon the day appointed; it would have been easy for him and most advantageous for his father if he had simply retarded for twenty-four hours the events of the 15th. Chuncie however stuck to his story; others might celebrate their birthdays, he always celebrated the day before.

He also confirmed Boysie's statement that his launch could not have worked on the 14th; it was suffering from manifold trouble and had no exhaust. This meant that, even if the engine had been made to work, the boat would have been swamped within half an hour of setting out to sea.

Still heavier guns were brought to bear in support of Boysie's tidal theories. Montague Fahey, a licensed surveyor, now entered the box to prove by the measurements which he had carried out in person, that the *Marie Louise* could never have reached the shore by the Aquatic Club on that fatal evening.

19: THE JURY DISAGREE

FAHEY BEGAN with a confident summary of his researches. He based his evidence on a series of soundings he had carried out on April 30th, a fortnight after the date the murder was alleged to have taken place. It was, he assured the court, perfectly possible to work out the depth of water on April 14th from his figures.

According to these, the depth of the water off the Aquatic Club around 11 p.m. on that date would have varied between 14½ and 19½ inches. Off the Leper Asylum jetty it would have been around 19 or 20 inches. It had been assumed throughout the case – and the prosecution had not so far challenged the fact – that the draught of the *Marie Louise* was 2½ to 3 feet. Fahey's figures indicated that the launch would have run aground long before it reached the shore.

His manner carried authority, and it was clear that he had done a good deal to swing the case once more in Boysie's favour. But now it was the turn of Worrell – known to his profession as "The Bulldog" – to cross-examine the witness. Calmly he rose and with a deadly casualness asked whether from his figures Fahey would tell him the depth of water off the Aquatic Club on April 1st.

Fahey stared at him. "What has that got to do with the case?"

If he had taken off his trousers or sung an aria from Gounod's *Faust* the surveyor could hardly have undermined his testimony more completely. For a moment even Worrell seemed scarcely able to believe his ears; then he repeated his question, with a warning to Fahey that it was not his business to determine the relevance of the question. Once more Fahey insisted that it had nothing to do with the case. Here Mr. Justice Brown felt obliged to intervene and explain to the witness that it was none of his business to assess the relevance or irrelevance of questions addressed to him. But Fahey still hedged and refused to commit himself to any definite answer, leaving Worrell to drive home his point to the jury – that if Fahey could not estimate the depth of water a month before the 30th, it was hardly reasonable to suppose that he could do so for a fortnight before.

Having thus trumped the defence's ace, Worrell dealt comparatively lightly with the next witness – Raphael Eve, alias "Bamboozie" – who confirmed Boysie's statement that he (Eve) and Harper had gone out fishing on the night of the 4th, and had not returned till the following morning.

This completed Boysie's defence; the next of the accused was Durant, who also elected to appear in the witness-box.

Durant's defence, like Boysie's, was an alibi. On the 14th he had been nowhere near Cocorite, or Port of Spain for that matter; he had been staying – with Loomat – at a village called Bejucal, not far from Piarco. Here they had been guests of a nightwatchman and provision vendor called Rampat Bickramsingh. Durant and Loomat had spent the Friday afternoon helping to demolish a house which belonged to Bickramsingh; the next day Durant had accompanied Bickramsingh to a nearby sawmill to help him "select" some timber.

Asked by Worrell to give his qualifications as a timber expert, he was unable to do so; he insisted, however, that Bickramsingh had asked for his assistance in the matter. Several witnesses were called to confirm Durant's alibi. Among them was another nightwatchman, a man called Harry Dass who worked on one of the Public Works Department's irrigation schemes. Dass's testimony wilted somewhat when Worrell dug from him the admission that he had recently been charged with shooting a man in the Caroni Savannah Road; moreover he had been on night duty with the P.W.D. from April 6th to April 19th, and would therefore have hardly been in a position to swear that Loomat and Durant spent the whole night in Bejucal.

Worrell also pointed out that anything so strenuous as demolition work was equally out of character for Durant. Indeed, there was no record that he had ever done any work at all.

Bickramsingh too had been unfortunate in his contacts with the law. He had only just been acquitted on a charge of murdering one Mahabal, and it was alleged by Worrell that he and Dass had patched together their story as they exercised in the yard of the prison where they were held on remand. But Bickramsingh insisted that Durant's story was correct – Durant and Loomat had in fact slept at his home on the nights of the 14th, 15th and 16th April.

"How would you describe Loomat?" Worrell asked him.

"A big man in short pants," Bickramsingh said.

"Why?"

"Because he drinks and smokes more than I and he has more vices than I have."

None of the other accused had such an elaborate alibi as Durant. James entered the witness-box, Coggins and Bruce made statements from the dock, but the tenor of what they had to say was the same; all three of them had reached No. 55 at around 5.30 p.m. on April 14th and had remained there for the rest of the evening and night. Moreover, they all confirmed

Bage's evidence. At the late-night party the latter had so lovingly described, Bumper had been the life and soul, strumming happily on his Spanish boom at a time when, according to the prosecution, he should have been lying on the mud somewhere off the Aquatic Club beach.

Apart from that, they had little enough to say for themselves. Coggins repeated the story, told already by his counsel, of how Bleasdell had offered him his liberty in exchange for his evidence; Bruce hinted that there was something fishy in the length of time which had elapsed before his arrest, and that the identification parade at which Loomat picked him out had been a put-up job. Indeed their defence was so perfunctory that it seemed that they, or more likely their legal advisers, had realised that whatever they said would not have much influence on the outcome of the case. It was obvious to all concerned that if the other four had in fact taken part in the murder, they had only done so as Boysie's subordinates and under his instructions. It followed that their fate depended largely on how far the jury believed the evidence which Boysie had called on his own behalf. If they found him innocent his followers, too, would go free; if not, they would die with him.

Archbald, Boysie's senior counsel, was first to speak for the defence, and indeed his speech, which lasted two days, covered the ground so fully that the speeches of the remaining counsel were largely superfluous. He pointed out that the prosecution had failed to make out a consistent case; they had apparently abandoned their claim that Loomat was used as bait, while on the other hand Worrell's repeated hints that Bumper had been killed as an informer had formed no part of the Crown's original contentions, and indeed had not been substantiated by any evidence that the Solicitor-General had called. The prosecution had failed to show any motive for the killing. He recalled the unsatisfactory nature of the Crown's witnesses, and claimed that the whole case against Boysie and his men was a fabrication on the part of the police, who had blatantly secured false testimony by a mixture of threats and promises, or (as in the case of Bishop) by invoking the Old (Police) Pals Act. Even the identification of the body was far from certain. No jury, in the face of such evidence, could honestly believe that Boysie's guilt had been established beyond that "reasonable doubt" which, the law insisted, had to be satisfied before a verdict of "Guilty" could be brought in.

The other defence counsel followed Archbald's example and concentrated most of their efforts on blackening the characters of the prosecution witnesses.

At last Mr. Justice Brown began his summing up.

He reminded the jury that they should not take undue notice of the alleged absence of motive. In a murder case there was no obligation on the Crown to provide a motive; to prove the agency by which murder had been committed was quite sufficient. The defence had dwelt at some length on the unsavoury character of some prosecution witnesses, particularly Wilkie and Rodney. Admittedly, the jury would have to take such person's evidence with some care; but they should ask themselves what kind of people were likely to be found around Queen Street at such a late hour of the night, and whether they could reasonably expect decent citizens to provide evidence of goings-on in those districts.

Despite the attempts by the defence to cloud the issue, the case was really a simple and straightforward one. Either the jury would accept the evidence of the prosecution witnesses, in which case they would have no alternative but to find Boysie guilty, or they would have to agree with the defence that he was the victim of a police conspiracy. Mr. Justice Brown expatiated at some length on the vile nature of the latter suggestion, if it was untrue. However, it had been advanced by the defence as an essential part of their case, and the jury would have to consider it before coming to their verdict.

No one in the court that day – August 22nd – could doubt that Mr. Justice Brown's speech was a summing-up for conviction. When at last he had finished and the jury had retired, a great silence fell over the crowded room. It had rained that morning – the usual heavy lunchtime shower that falls almost daily in Port of Spain between May and December – and the hiss of car tyres passing along the roads outside could be distinctly heard. The environs of the Red House were packed with thousands of waiting spectators, kept in check by a hundred policemen on foot and sixteen mounted. In Woodford Square, fanatics held forth on the religious and political significance of the trial, while around them the thugs and layabouts who had followed in Boysie's train laid macabre bets on his chances of survival.

At 3.48 p.m., after the jury had been out for three hours, the door of the jury-room opened and the twelve men filed out. Mr. Justice Brown asked the foreman if they had arrived at a verdict.

The foreman of the jury regretted that they had been unable to do so.

Mr. Justice Brown then asked whether there was any further point of the law on which he could instruct them.

The foreman said there was not; he feared that the jury were hopelessly divided.

In that case, Mr. Justice Brown said, he had no alternative but to discharge the jury and order a retrial.

On this note of anticlimax ended the first Case of the Floating Corpse. The bets were void; the bettors, after hanging round hopefully for a last brief glimpse of the accused, gradually drifted away.

The trial had lasted twenty-six days. Disappointed though he might have been by the jury's verdict, Mr. Justice Brown felt obliged to excuse them from service for the next five years. The Trinidad government was the poorer by nine thousand dollars, and, at a hastily-called meeting, the

Finance Committee of the Legislative Council set aside a further seven thousand six hundred dollars for the retrial.

Reactions to the result varied. The respectable classes bemoaned times and manners which permitted such perversions of justice to take place; but many of the poorer people rejoiced that one whom, rightly or wrongly, they regarded as on their side had so successfully challenged the power of authority – for they regarded the hung jury as almost tantamount to acquittal. Surprisingly enough, Solicitor-General Worrell seemed also to consider that the trial had been a success. "Every sort of criticism," he declared, "has been thrown at my unworthy head, but, thank God! In this case I have blossomed forth like a rose. That honour I should wear lightly."

As for the accused, they were remanded in custody until such time as a new trial could be arranged. But a change had come over them. They were no longer the brash, slickly-dressed mobsters they had been at the time of their arrest. For Boysie the change began as early as the preliminary hearing. He had begun to pray – according to the death-cell diary he was to write seven years later – immediately after his arrest on April 25th; "but not sincerely". On June 6th, however, he made contact with an evangelical spirit. "The first psams [sic] was given me in the cell by a Prison Officer name Mr. Ford 1950 of the 12/6/50. Psalms 27." One wonders whether it was verse 3: "Draw me not away together with the wicked; and with the workers of iniquity destroy me not;" or verse 4: "Give them according to their works, and according to the wickedness of their inventions..." which particularly engaged his attention.

The five prisoners were lodged in separate cells but in the same prison corridor, so that it was possible for them to sing hymns and pray together; for the silence rule does not seem to be enforced in West Indian gaols, and besides what gaoler would have prevented such exemplary behaviour? Three of them continued vociferously to assert, not merely their innocence, but their total ignorance of the real murderers. If they had known, they declared, they would willingly have turned Crown witness. One, however, was less vocal. Though he himself was innocent, he happened to know the true story of what had happened to Bumper. There were powerful reasons that prevented him from speaking. He was prepared to go to his death if need be rather than tell.

The retrial was expected to commence shortly after the first trial had closed. But Boysie fell ill. The doctors found that he was suffering from a fairly advanced form of diabetes. This condition must have existed for some time, but until then it had probably been masked by his robust constitution. Now he had to spend several weeks in the prison hospital. It was not until November 6th that the second hearing commenced – this time before Mr. Justice S. E. Gomes.

20: ONCE MORE IN JEOPARDY

FOR THE FIRST FEW DAYS the second Floating Corpse trial followed the pattern of the first. Levy described his discovery of the body, Pearl Stoute her identification of it, Dr. McDougall repeated his account of its gruesome dilapidations. Evidence was in most cases almost word for word the same as at the previous hearing. This was as well, for the defence had appointed Mr. Bruce Procope, counsel for Durant in the first trial, as a sort of legal watchdog; armed with verbatim notes of both the first trial and the preliminary hearing, he was on the lookout for the slightest discrepancies between the three sets of testimony.

The monotony was broken at the end of the lunch adjournment on the second day. The accused complained that they were not being properly fed. Throughout the previous hearing they had been allowed to eat food sent in by their relatives; now this privilege had been withdrawn and they were forced to eat the prison diet, which Coggin described as "Salt fish and rice – not even good for a dog to eat." Boysie complained that they had "Not even a spoon to eat the stuff."

Proceedings were brought to a halt while Mr. Justice Gomes discussed the matter with the Solicitor-General. The Judge ruled that according to the regulations governing the care of prisoners, the accused were first-class prisoners and could have food sent in to them if they wished. Court was adjourned for a further fifteen minutes to give the five men the opportunity of eating the food which had been brought in for them that morning.

After this culinary interlude the trial resumed its remorseless progress. Now and then it was enlivened by flashes of mordant humour. Wilkie, asked if he was grieved at Bumper's death, looked puzzled a moment, then answered, "Grieved? No." "But you knew him from childhood?" "Yes." "And you weren't sorry about his death?" "Sorry? I am not sorry over nobody's death. Who dead, dead. I know I have to die." Loomat, who "maintained perfect calm and showed no sign of strain" throughout an eight-hour grilling by the defence, was asked, "What games do you play?" "Fly kite, spin top, play marbles," the fast-smoking, hard-drinking Loomat replied. "When last did you fly kite?" "Day before I gave my statement to Inspector Bleasdell at Besson Street."

With the cross-examination of Bleasdell on November 18th the trial swung suddenly into high gear. Archbald began by asking Bleasdell to give an exact account of his movements between April 20th and April 26th – particularly the occasions on which he had visited Besson Street Police Station. Bleasdell's answers were unnervingly vague. Under strong pressure he finally admitted that he had been there on the two dates mentioned; but of his precise movements between those dates he had no recollection whatever.

Archbald asked him to "refresh his memory" by reading certain extracts from the Police Diary of the Besson Street station.

The Police Diary is a record, kept by the duty constable and certified by the Station Sergeant, which contains notes of every occurrence which takes place at the station. Such occurrences would naturally include the admittance of persons in custody, the charges on which they were held, and the times at which senior officers arrived and departed. Bleasdell had no option but to do as Archbald requested. A subpoena issued on the Commissioner of Police had obliged the prosecution to produce the diary in court.

Entries in the diary indicated that, contrary to the evidence he had just given, Bleasdell had visited Besson Street on several occasions during the period in question, and might therefore be assumed to have had full cognizance of the state of affairs there.

But the Inspector insisted that he had no recollection of calling. The diary might be mistaken, or he might have dropped in for a matter of seconds only, long enough to enquire at the desk if there was any news for him. But in the face of the diary's "silent testimony" his assertions carried little weight. Loomat's lapses of memory were still too fresh in the minds of the court. Satisfied with the results so far obtained, Archbald switched his attack to the question of Loomat.

Loomat had insisted that in the first instance he had gone voluntarily to Besson Street to make a statement, and that he had not subsequently been detained there nor in any way kept in custody until he was removed for his own safety to Staubles Bay.

Entries indicated, however, that he had been brought to Besson Street on Sunday, 23rd April, in connection with the alleged theft of a pair of binoculars. Entry No. 29 for the following day, Monday 24th, showed that he was still in custody there and, entry No. 177, that later in the day Bleasdell had called for Loomat at Besson Street and taken him to the Divisional Detective Office. He had later been returned to Besson Street and remained in custody there until Bleasdell once more called for him and took him to Cocorite in order to identify the spot where the jitney was supposed to have parked on the 14th.

Bleasdell's answer – the only answer which in view of his previous testimony he could possibly make – was to deny all knowledge of the entries and insist that, while Loomat might have been held at Besson Street for the three days in question, it was not done on his instructions nor was he aware that the boy was being held. If an entry stated that he had called for Loomat on the 24th, that entry must have been made in error. He also denied knowledge of another of the entries which indicated that, after the binoculars charge had been abandoned, Loomat continued to be held "on enquiries on a charge of murder." He had been so busy, "on this and other matters", that although he was in full charge of the investigations into Bumper's death, he had not had time to keep track of the Crown's principal witness.

Even if one accepted this somewhat ingenuous plea, it did not alter the fact that Loomat was in police hands for three days.

Whether he was detained for stealing binoculars or suspicion of murder was beside the point; he had been detained, and in view of his subsequent evidence one could only assume that he had been detained for the purpose of bringing pressure to bear on him. Smoker and drinker he might be, but he was after all little more than a child, and to spend three days in "The Pacific", separated from everyone he knew, and with ominous threats of imprisonment hanging over him, would hardly be calculated to make him an unbiased witness.

That, at any rate, was what the defence alleged.

A somewhat chastened Bleasdell left the box, and the prosecution called their final witness, one Lance Murray, who lacked the professional qualifications of Montague Fahey, but had the advantage that *his* soundings had been carried out in full view of the jury when, on November 11th, the court had once more adjourned to view the scene of the crime. His figures, however, differed little from Fahey's. All of them gave slightly greater depths than Fahey had stated; none of them exceeded Fahey's soundings by more than eight inches. They might even have served to confirm Fahey's conclusion – that the *Marie Louise* could have landed neither at Leper Asylum nor Aquatic – but for one fact.

Previously both sides had accepted the Singhs' estimate of "2 1/2 to 3 feet" for the draught of their boat. But on the Court's visit to Cocorite the draught had been measured and found to be 18 to 19 inches at the bow, and 22 to 23 inches at the stern. Admittedly a loaded boat would need more than its actual draught of water to float, but even if Fahey's figures were accepted they no longer ruled out so completely the possibility of a landing at the points indicated.

So, with its position at least partly restored, the prosecution closed its case.

Once more, Boysie took first knock for the defence. Neither his six months' detention nor his new interest in religion had subdued the old Adam in him. He continued to insist on the purity of his motives and even the innocence of his actions. When Worrell, speaking again of Queen Street, asked him, "Is that a nice locality?" he answered imperturbably, "All places are nice to me. I do not know how other people look at it." He insisted that he had never read the statement he had allegedly given Bleasdell, for he could neither read nor write; though having signed the statement he had quickly to retract that and admit that "if you spell I can write." "If I call out letters to you, you can make them?" Worrell asked dubiously. "Yes – one behind the next," Boysie replied.

The next defence witness should by rights have been Bage; it was Bage who had followed Boysie at the first hearing. But Boysie's most faithful helper was no longer available. Worrell's threats had been put into action; in the interval between the two trials, Bage had been shipped back to his native island.

Instead a mechanic called Caspar Durant – no relation of the accused – took the stand. Caspar was foreman at Samaroo's garage, and had repaired several of Boysie's engines. He confirmed Boysie's statement that the launch's exhaust-pipe was missing and that any prolonged use would have swamped the boat. He admitted, however, that an ingenious person could have fitted a length of rubber hose to the exhaust so as to direct the water over the side, and that such a length was at present fitted to the exhaust. However, he declared, "When I saw that boat in April, the copper tubing was much longer and the rubber hosing was much shorter, being merely two inches..."

The inference hardly needed drawing. The *Marie Louise* had been seized by the police at the time of Boysie's arrest, and had remained in their hands ever since; if the exhaust was in a different condition it could only be because the police had deliberately tampered with it so as to discredit Boysie's story.

Then Montague Fahey was called.

Fahey repeated his findings with as much confidence as if he had never had that disastrous encounter with Worrell at the previous hearing. He should have learnt caution; the intervening three months had given the Solicitor-General plenty of time to enquire into his background. Was it not a fact, Worrell suavely enquired, that he had recently been suspended as a licensed surveyor? Fahey had to admit that it was.

Worrell: For misconduct as a surveyor?

Fahey: That is open to argument.

– Do you know Boysie Singh?

– No, sir.

– What!

– On one occasion...

– Oh, on one occasion now... Do you know Joseph Rennie?

– Yes.

– Did you occupy one of his rooms on one occasion?

– Yes, sir.

– With whom?
– With a lady.
– One of the prostitutes from Queen Street?
– Prostitutes?
Archbald: I OBJECT!

But it was too late. Any good Fahey might have done for the defence had been demolished in those few devastating minutes.

Much more effective were the police witnesses who were now called. Lance Corporal Collins, Corporal Lee, and Station Sergeant Munroe, all of Besson Street, admitted that Loomat had in fact been detained at that station from April 23rd to April 26th.

Last of all the defence took the unusual step of calling their watchdog, Bruce Procope, to give evidence. During the course of the trial Procope had noted a large number of cases in which the evidence given by witnesses conflicted with statements they had made at the first trial. In many of these instances the variations were trivial or such as could be explained by a quite innocent misunderstanding or lapse of memory; however, in sheer number they were quite impressive.

On the twenty-second day of the trial, Archbald opened his address for the defence.

He spoke without interruption for three whole days. The West Indian Bar has an unenviable record for verbosity, but in Archbald's favour one could say that he had a great deal of ground to cover. He had, moreover – despite the blowing-up of Fahey – a good case. He might have been excused for thinking that the *deux ex machina* of the Besson Street diary alone would turn the scales in his client's favour, particularly after the jury's disagreement in the first trial. Nevertheless he went conscientiously over the now-familiar ground of the doubtful identification, the unsavoury prosecution witnesses, the shortcomings of Loomat, the uncertain memory of Bleasdell, the tampering with the *Marie Louise* and the alleged distorting of statements of the accused, weaving all these threads into a vigorous denunciation of the police, whom, he claimed, had created the whole case against Boysie out of the murky recesses of their own imagination. Indeed, he covered the whole case so fully that the remaining counsel needed only a day – December 4th – to restate the defences of the other four accused.

Worrell wound up for the prosecution on December 5th; and on the morning of the 6th Mr. Justice Gomes began his summing-up.

He started by reminding the jury – as his predecessor had done – that there was no necessity for the Crown to indicate a motive; he quoted the saying, "The devil himself knows not what is passing in the mind of man." He went on to stress that discrepancies between evidence given at different hearings was not necessarily proof of a witness's dishonesty, and he indicated several ways in which such discrepancies might have quite innocently come about.

Next he dealt with the evidence of the various witnesses. He paid little attention to the inconsistencies of Wilkie and Rodney, and Loomat in particular was treated very lightly. "The pages I expected to be considerably marked in my notebook are the ones that seem to be the least marked," Gomes said of his testimony. He passed without comment Loomat's statement that he had gone to Besson Street voluntarily and had not been detained nor spent the night there. Moreover his survey of Loomat's evidence contained at least one error of fact – referring to Loomat's statement that he had first told his father of the alleged murder on Sunday, April 23rd, he said, "Presumably that was on the same Sunday on which we were told the body was found." In reality the body had been found on the previous Thursday – a fact which Gomes of all people should have remembered, unless the general uncertainty about dates was catching – and Loomat, even assuming his story was true, had had three days after the discovery in which to confess to his father; instead, he was asking the court to believe that he had only mentioned it on the day which, the defence alleged, he was hauled willy-nilly to Besson Street.

At this stage the court adjourned for lunch; when it resumed, Mr. Justice Gomes went on to deal equally leniently with Bleasdell. His only serious criticism seemed to be levelled at the unsatisfactory form of caution, one which included a garbled version of the charge, used by Bleasdell in arresting the accused; a typical sample (addressed to Boysie) went: "From information received it is said you drove your jitney to Cocorite in company with certain men. On reaching your home at Cocorite yourself and all the men came off the jitney and there Bumper was cuffed down to the ground." Apart from the dissimilarities between this version and the ultimate Crown case, even Worrell had admitted that "from this caution one would conclude the launch was actually sitting in Boysie Singh's yard ready to take the men out to sea."

Gomes, however, concluded by observing somewhat complacently that "this form of caution... has been dropped and will not be pursued in future," and went on to deal with the Police Diary. Far from dwelling on the inconsistencies between Bleasdell's testimony and the entries in the diary, he implied that in allowing the diary to be used at all he had – in the interests of justice, of course – gone beyond what was normally permissible in a court of law; he affected to believe that the defence had introduced the diary merely to permit Bleasdell to refresh his somewhat exhausted memory, and to have been completely unprepared for the use to which, "rather surprisingly", it was put. He seemed quite prepared to accept the reasons Bleasdell had given for the discrepancies.

Later, when dealing with the police evidence called by the defence in support of the diary entries, he explicitly warned the jury not to pay undue attention to the diary. "You cannot take an entry from the diary and say,

'That is the end of the matter, this is a silent testimony, it can't lie.' I state to you that the diary cannot be used for that purpose." He admitted that Munroe's confirmation of the diary proved that Loomat had been held against his will, but failed even to mention the possibility that, if Bleasdell and Loomat had been found lying on such a material particular, the rest of their evidence might be equally unreliable. Referring to the defence allegation that the whole prosecution case was a police frame-up, Gomes declared, "If that accusation is devoid of truth, it is the vilest accusation that could be made against any man, and I shall ask you to carefully consider this matter... What is suggested is that Inspector Bleasdell, within a matter of 24 hours or within a matter of a few days, devised a plot against five men accusing them of having murdered another man. Gentlemen, you must consider whether it is humanly possible to devise such a plot without its being detected."

He even called in blunders of the prosecution – such as the misleading cautions – to indicate that no such concerted plot could have been devised. Again ignoring the diary, he claimed that the only evidence called in support of the defence allegations was the fact that witnesses for the prosecution sometimes contradicted their testimony, and reminded the jury of his earlier ruling that minor discrepancies of testimony should not lead to the rejection of any witness's evidence as a whole.

The afternoon was already advanced when the summing-up closed and the jury retired.

They were out for two and a quarter hours. Throughout that time a profound silence reigned in court. The five accused seemed calm and confident. They felt certain that the revelations of the diary would have influenced the jury in their favour, and did not seem aware of how strongly the summing-up had gone against them.

It was not until they had re-entered the dock and the door of the jury-room opened that they began to show signs of uneasiness. Mr. Justice Gomes turned to the foreman. Had they this time agreed on a verdict?

They had. It was "Guilty."

21: AWAY WITH THE WICKED

FOR A MOMENT there was silence; then, like a wind suddenly rising, the sound of voices broke out and swept through the labyrinthine corridors of the Red House and away into the streets and the packed, motionless square, building swiftly as it travelled into one climactic roar of triumph and execration. In the courtroom itself officials struggled to maintain order as men clapped and cheered, women screamed, wept and fainted. The judge ordered the doors to be closed, and at last, when some semblance of quiet had been restored, turned and asked Boysie whether he had anything to say before sentence was passed.

Boysie's face worked; for a moment it seemed as if the extremity of his feelings had made it impossible for him to speak; then he burst into a passionate tirade against the forces which had brought him to the dock. "I am not sorry for myself," he shouted, "but for the people of Trinidad... I am innocent of this act and I have been framed. Since 1925 the police force is behind me either to kill me or get me a long sentence in prison. In this case the gentlemen have brought me in guilty. Later on these gentlemen will be sorry – perhaps six months after now! These witnesses have come in this court and swear us away! Murder cannot hide! There will be somebody to reveal this murder; it will be revealed six months after now. These gentlemen wherever they pass, in any form, in any way, in their clubs, in their homes, it will be whispered in their ears that I have been framed by Bleasdell – this man..."

For the second and last time in his life Boysie broke down and wept in impotent rage.

Calmly and impassively Mr. Justice Gomes pronounced sentence of death upon him.

This was too much for Durant, who was sitting next to Boysie in the dock; even as Gomes read out the sentence he collapsed.

He was lifted and propped on a chair so that he was facing the judge, but his head was tossing and rolling slackly from side to side as his own death sentence was read.

Next came Coggins' turn. As the judge reached the final words of the sentence: "... and may the Lord have mercy on your soul", the unregenerate Coggins snapped back, "Likewise yourself, sir." James was philosophical: "They find me guilty already. Nothing sir, nothing sir." Bruce was defiant:

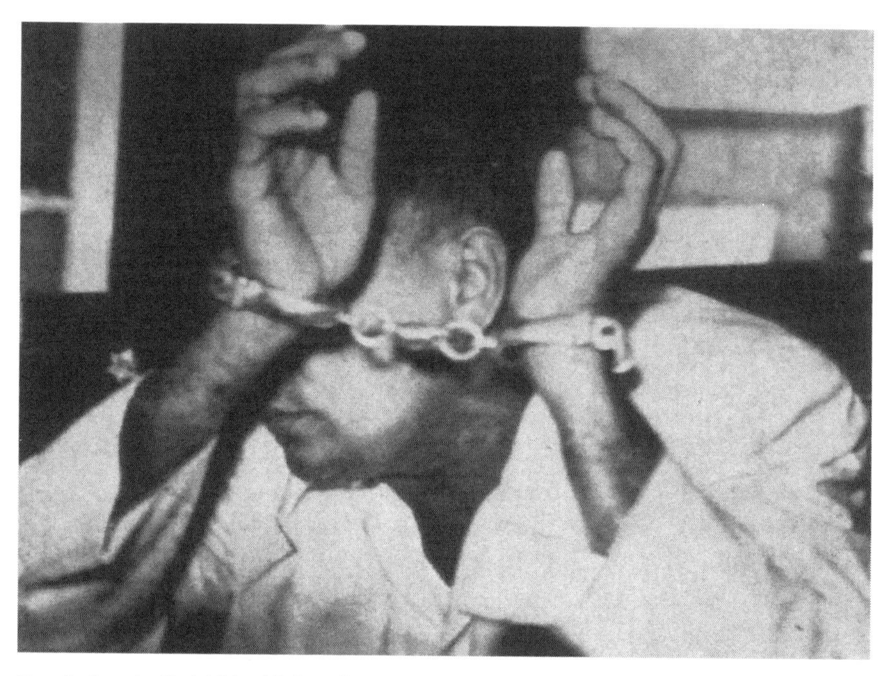

Boysie, handcuffed, hides his face from photographers after being sentenced to death in the Floating Corpse retrial

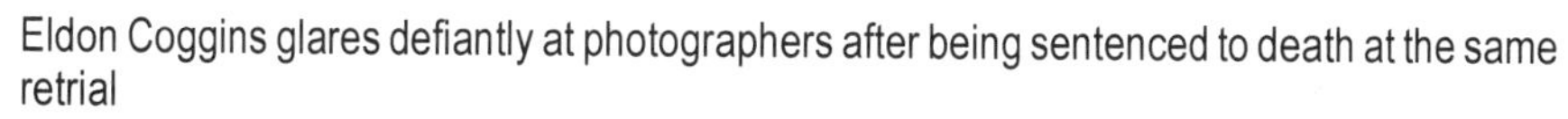

Eldon Coggins glares defiantly at photographers after being sentenced to death at the same retrial

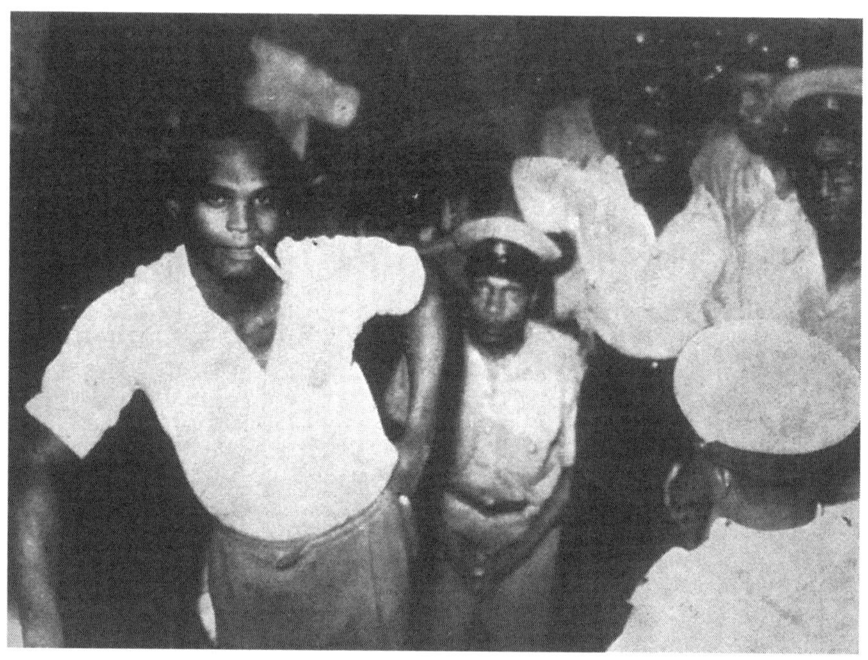

"Jesus Christ was sacrificed! Who is Bruce that he is afraid to die to save a man from murder?"

When sentence had been pronounced on all five men they were taken from the court. Outside, the crowd surged irresistibly forwards to catch a glimpse of them, to hurl abuse or shout commiseration. Again and again, the mounted police charged. Women collapsed and were trampled underfoot.

Somehow the courtyard of the Red House was kept clear while the prisoners filed out to the waiting van. Boysie came first, followed closely by the weeping Durant. A *Guardian* photographer aimed a camera at them, and Bruce, in a spasm of fury, tore off his shirt, ripped it in half and pushed it in the photographer's face. He then stripped off his trousers – the classic gesture by which, apparently, Trinidadians protest against what they consider acts of injustice against them – and walked to the van in his underwear. James also performed this symbolic striptease. The van was about to start when it was found that Coggins had left his Bible in the dock, and a policeman had to be sent back for it. While he was gone Coggins stood calmly smoking on the steps of the van and stared with contemptuous eyes at the sweating cordon of police which held back the mob. At last the policeman returned and the van drove away.

Boysie's counsel promptly lodged notice of appeal.

None of the five condemned men abandoned hope. Durant considered himself the most hard-done-by. At least Coggins, James and Bruce had formed part of Boysie's organisation, but he continued to claim that he had never had anything to do with Boysie and had only become involved in the case through his unfortunate association with Loomat. The one who knew the true facts of Bumper's death remained obstinately silent, even though his own end was now imminent.

For he, in common with the others, seems to have had a touching faith in the infallibility of justice. They all declared, both at the time and afterwards, that they knew they would not hang. The God whom they so industriously invoked simply would not let it happen.

While awaiting the verdict of the Appeal Court they passed their time singing and praying as before. These prayers were no longer merely for their own benefit. Also on Death Row was a policeman, Corporal Adolphus James – no relation to Boysie's co-defendant. Adolphus, a married man living with his wife, had been sentenced to death for the murder of his mistress, whom he had stabbed with a bayonet smuggled out of Port of Spain Police Headquarters. The Floating Corpse boys soon included him in their impromptu prayer-meetings, and the hymn-singing, bayonet-swinging policeman went cheerily to the gallows, armed with the consolations of his fellow-condemned.

Boysie was lodged in cell No. D2. On December 6th, the day of his conviction, he began – according to his diary – to pray sincerely for the first time in his life. The cynic may be forgiven for considering the degree of his danger the best measure of his sincerity. "I used look through the iron bars in the cells and pray to the virgin lady to take me to Jesus," he wrote. He prayed to the Virgin because the only form of Christianity with which he had ever come into contact was his wife's Catholicism. The Bible which he carried with him to prison was one published in Belgium by Brepols' Catholic Press, who advertise themselves as "Printers to the Holy See"; it was based on the editions published originally by the English College of Rheims and Douay, in 1582 and 1609 respectively – the proselytising Bible with which the Jesuits had tried to win back heretic England.

He also began to see visions. In Cell D2, he claimed, "I saw Jesus leading me out of prison. I also saw Jesus again in No. 10 cell. On the right side of the sun. When it was rising on the side of the sun was a block of mouroune [sic] colour and Jesus was going into the block. And my eyes open I got free from all my troubles."

Sincere or not, this story sounds too circumstantial to be an invention. Yet it would be too much to credit the Pirate of the Gulf with a genuine religious experience. One can only suppose that with the nervous strain of the long legal proceedings and the ultimate death sentence, his mind – if indeed he was sane at the beginning – had become a little unhinged. A man in his position might very well become subject to hallucinations, and the continual hymn-singing and Bible reading in which he indulged would condition the form which those hallucinations took.

That Boysie's perusal of the Bible was thorough indeed is attested by the numerous underlinings and annotations in his copy. Some of these were mere pickings-out of references to familiar things. Acts 12.5., for instance – "Peter therefore was kept in prison. But prayer was made without ceasing by the Church unto God for him." – is marked and underscored with the laconic note, "Prison". Another – John 7.71: "Jesus answered them: Have not I chosen you twelve; and one of you is a devil?" – bears no comment, but would seem to be a hit at Harper, whose life he had saved.

Others, however, show a greater degree of reflection. Luke 23.43-4, which recounts the saying of the robber on the cross next to Jesus – "And he said to Jesus: Lord, remember me when thou shalt come into thy kingdom. And Jesus said to him: Amen I say to thee, this day thou shalt be with me in paradise." – is heavily marked; it must have provided Boysie with much comfort. Several of the marked passages show his sympathy with the underdog and seem to indicate that he saw himself as a tropical Robin Hood. St. Luke 3.11 – "He that hath two coats, let him give to him that hath none; and he that hath meat, let him do it in like manner" – is marked with approval and bears the comment, "Communism" – a creed however of which Boysie's comprehension was as idiosyncratic as his spelling.

Support for the theory that Boysie was a straight case of megalomania can be found in the annotations scattered through the four gospels which seem to indicate that he actually identified himself with Jesus or at least considered Jesus primarily as a man in the same predicament as himself. The conspiracy of the priests in the court of Caiphas, as described by Matthew – "And they consulted together, that by subtilty they might apprehend Jesus and put him to death" – obviously reminded him of the case for his defence, for the word "Plot" is written beside it. St. Luke 4.29 is also heavily marked. "And they rose up and thrust him out of the city; and they brought him to the brow of the hill, whereon their city was built, that they might cast him down headlong" – this, though it bears only the comment, "Jesus", Boysie must have compared with his own fate in the Bumper case, and have consoled himself with the following verse 30 – "But he passing through the midst of them went his way."

Among the books of the Old Testament, it is hardly surprising that the one most heavily annotated is that of Job. Almost every page is marked. But if Boysie identified himself with Job he must have performed some remarkable feats of self-deception; for the first marked passage, Job 2.5, reads: "And the Lord said to Satan: Hast thou considered my servant Job, that there is none like him in the earth, a man simple, and upright, and fearing God, and avoiding evil, and still keeping his innocence? But thou hast moved me against him, that I should afflict him without cause." Nearer the bone was 6. 14 – "He that taketh away mercy from his friend, forsaketh the fear of the Lord" – was he thinking of Taitt when he marked this? Job 19.17 and 18 also struck a personal note: "My wife hath abhorred my breath and I entreated the children of my womb. Even fools despised me, and when I was gone from them, they spoke against me." For on Boysie's arrest, Doris Singh had deserted him and gone to live with her lover – Police Constable Harry Seurattan of Besson Street police station.

The sombre nature of Job's philosophy was all too appropriate for the death cell. The passage dealing with Job's disbelief in personal immortality – "But man when he shall be dead, and stripped and consumed, I pray you where is he? As if the waters should depart out of the sea, and an emptied river should be dried up: So man when he is fallen asleep shall not rise again." (Job 4.10-12) – is marked with the lugubrious comment: "Man not rise". The passage of gloomy splendour in which Job tells of his fear of approaching death – 10.20-22 – is also marked. "Shall not the fewness of my days be ended shortly? Suffer me, therefore, that I may lament my sorrow a little: Before I go, and return no more, to a land that is dark and covered with the mist of death: A land of misery and darkness, where the shadow of death, and no order, but everlasting horror dwelleth."

But while Boysie remained sunk in these graveyard meditations, events were moving rapidly outside.

Leave to appeal was granted, and the date fixed for January 10th, 1951. The Appeal was to be heard by Sir Cecil Furness-Smith, Chief Justice of Trinidad, Mr. Justice W. H. Irwin, and Mr. Justice E. Mortimer Duke.

Boysie's friends believed that the appeal would be successful. They had, however, considered the possibility of failure, and were prepared to meet it. For a long time a supply of dynamite had lain hidden at No. 55. Boysie had never succeeded in finding either a use or a market for it. Now his farsightedness was to be justified, for his gang planned – if the appeal failed – to blow down the walls of the gaol and liberate their leader by force of arms. Once free, a fast launch would be waiting to run him across the gulf to Venezuela – and Venezuela had no extradition treaty with Trinidad. If this fantastic plot came off, he would be in safety within a matter of hours.

At last, when Boysie and his four fellow-prisoners had spent five weeks in the condemned cells, the Court of Appeal began its hearing of their case.

The arguments of the defence were based mainly on Mr. Justice Gomes' summing-up which, they claimed, had gone against the weight of the evidence. He had shown himself biased in favour of the prosecution and had failed to direct the jury's attention to the many manifest inconsistencies in the Crown case. He had largely ignored the damning revelations of the diary, and had failed to draw the correct inferences from the discrepancies between Loomat's and Bleasdell's evidence and the diary entries, some of the most incriminating of which had been confirmed by the Besson Street police themselves.

After several days of legal argument the Court adjourned to consider its verdict.

On January 25th this verdict was delivered. After a long and careful consideration of the issues involved, the three judges found that the testimony of several of the prosecution witnesses was thoroughly unreliable. In particular they drew attention to the evidence of Loomat, which they described as "tainted throughout by inconsistencies, prevarications and failure of memory".

But their chief criticisms were levelled at the summing-up. Mr. Justice Gomes, they declared, had failed to give any direction to the jury on what they should do when the evidence of the diary and the police who supported it flatly contradicted statements made by Bleasdell and Loomat. Bleasdell had said he had not visited Besson Street, and the diary said that he had; Loomat had said that he had not been detained at Besson Street, and the diary said that he had. These points the defence had established beyond doubt, and the jury was therefore entitled to some assistance on them.

In view of these facts the Court had no alternative but to reverse the previous verdict and order that Boysie Singh, John Durant, Eldon Coggin, Alexander James and David Bruce be immediately set at liberty.

22: HOW BUMPER DIED

THE DECISION ROUSED a storm of controversy which raged around Trinidad for several weeks after the verdict was announced. The respectable classes could hardly believe what had happened; rumours were spread that direct pressure had been brought to bear on the Appeal Court judges, and were so widely believed that Sir Cecil Furness-Smith felt obliged to take the unusual step of writing letters to the Press in which he denied that he had received threats prior to the delivery of the verdict or had had to ask for police protection. But no sooner was this rumour scotched than another took its place – that Gomes had been railroaded in a political vendetta. Public bewilderment was so widespread that the wildest report could be sure of credence.

In other circles, however, the vindication of Boysie was greeted with unconcealed glee. The sinister tales of piracy were vague enough merely to cast a glamour over their central figure, but the countless "raises" distributed with a fine impartiality to the deserving and undeserving alike were fixed firmly in the public mind, swelling that fund of sympathy on which any West Indian criminal of working-class origins can count – a sympathy natural enough among people who, with some justification, regard the law as a thing arbitrarily imposed on them for the benefit of a ruling caste. To these people Boysie's release was a rare class victory.

Now that the case can be considered dispassionately it would appear that, on the evidence before it, the verdict of the Court of Appeal was reasonable and just. A jury does not exist to decide whether a prisoner is guilty in an absolute sense; if this were their purpose they might just as well use the rack or trial by ordeal. They exist to decide whether a prisoner is guilty *on the evidence that is put before them,* which is often a very different matter. In the case of the Floating Corpse that evidence was by no means conclusive enough to warrant a conviction. Justice must be seen to be done, and the onus of proving the case rests with the prosecution; these principles of English law were perhaps not so familiar to the Trinidadians who condemned the Appeal Court verdict as they would be to a British public, who might have more readily appreciated the point that where there exists "reasonable doubt" the defendant, no matter how notorious, is entitled to the benefit of it.

Just it might be, yet no one, not even the judges themselves, could have said that it was at all satisfactory. It left the case as obscure as it ever had been.

If Boysie hadn't killed Bumper, then who had? Certainly no one had suggested any likelier candidate. Perhaps, after all, the prosecution story was true. Yet in that case how could its inconsistencies be explained? And for anyone who knew Boysie's previous history there were still graver objections to be overcome. How was it that after disposing of at least twenty-one victims without trace, this particular one should have surfaced so opportunely? And how was it that Boysie had chosen the other four accused to help him with the murder, rather than the members of his pirate crew who were inured to bloodshed and would follow wherever he led?

Now for the first time the truth can be told.

Boysie did kill Bumper. But he did not kill him as the prosecution alleged, nor had the four men charged with him any connection with the murder.

When, after the Brooklyn Bar raid, Boysie had passed sentence on Bumper, Bumper was already as good as dead; there was no appeal from *that* court. Yet there are two facts that suggest he may not have informed on Boysie after all. One is the unsuspecting way in which he went to his death, though he must have heard the stories of Nugget and Bam-Bam and have had at least an inkling of what happened on Boysie's sea trips. The other is that if he *had* informed, the police would have been aware of the motive for killing him, and would surely have introduced this into their case; for though, as Mr. Justice Gomes had reminded the jury, there is no onus on the prosecution to provide a motive, it helps to get a conviction if a plausible one can be adduced.

But whether or not Bumper had informed – and the truth of that will perhaps never be known – Boysie thought he had; that was enough.

He was killed, as the prosecution had claimed, on April 14th.

That was about the only fact that they had got right. The car which carried him on his last journey left Port of Spain more than three hours earlier than Wilkie and Rodney had claimed; around 7 p.m. With him were Bage and Fire Kong. They lured him into the car, not with the promised joys of Loomat, but with the more mundane and plausible story that they were going to collect pirate loot which had been stored as usual in the *Sam Supers,* and needed a hand with it. Bumper had been asked to perform similar services before. He suspected nothing. All three drove down to Cocorite. However, they did not, as the prosecution had claimed, stop by the Aquatic Club; they went on to the Leper Asylum jetty. Boysie rode down from No. 55 on his autocycle to meet them.

It is ironic to think that when Bishop, night-watching at Contractors, said he saw Boysie and two men walk down the jetty at about 8 p.m., he was not merely telling the truth but had probably seen Bumper going to his death. The darkness which had prevented him from identifying Boysie's companions had probably also hidden the fourth man, or more likely one had already gone ahead to collect the 21-foot pirogue which was to carry then all out to the *Sam Super I*. When a few minutes later he claimed to have seen three men returning he was right again; this time there were only three.

In the meantime Bumper and his executioners had rowed quietly across the dark water to where the *Sam Super I* was moored. Not a word was spoken during the crossing. The four men climbed aboard the *Sam Super I* and went into the cabin quarters. It will be remembered that the launch carried two cabins on deck level with an engine-room beneath. The loot from the pirate raids was normally stored in the engine-room, so Bumper showed no surprise when Bage and Kong began to descend the companionway. He followed them down. Boysie came after him. Unseen by Bumper, he had ready in his hand a short length of rope.

As Boysie stepped off the last rung of the ladder he dropped the looped rope over Bumper's head and jerked it tight. Bumper, taken like most of Boysie's victims utterly by surprise, did not utter a cry. His back arched convulsively; his hands clutched at his neck and his feet beat a rapid tattoo on the engine-room floor, but soon he was still for ever.

Boysie went back up the companion way and rowed over to collect the *Marie Louise*. It was his intention to carry Bumper out to the Bocas, the deep channels between Chaguaramas and the Peninsula of Paria, where so many of his victims were already resting, and from which no corpse had ever been known to surface.

But when he reached the launch he found that its exhaust was still missing and the engine, though passed as fit by Caspar Durant, was out of action again with manifold trouble. There was no hope of fixing it that night. Boysie rowed back empty-handed to the *Sam Super I*.

Down in the engine room a bitter scene took place. Boysie wanted to leave Bumper there for twenty-four hours; during the following day the *Marie Louise* could be repaired again and used to drop Bumper as soon as it got dark. Bage and Fire Kong considered this course reckless to the point of stupidity. They argued that while the body lay in the *Sam Super I* anyone could come out and stumble on it. Boysie pointed out that only his own employees ever went on the *Sam Supers* and they could easily take steps to keep off unauthorised persons, but Kong and Bage insisted that it wasn't worth the risk. They wanted to row out and dump the body at once. Boysie warned them of the dangers of dropping a body in shallow coastal waters, but they insisted that if the body was weighted sufficiently, Bumper would never reappear.

Bumper himself took no active part in the argument, though his eyeballs gleamed unpleasantly under the lantern which was the sole source of light in that small airless room. But his mere presence worked a strange effect on Boysie's two henchmen. They did not mind killing when the evidence of their crime could be removed within seconds as completely as if it had never been; now that it lay staring them in the face they were for the first time overcome by fear.

Finally Boysie lost patience and gave a flat order that the body was to be left. All three took the pirogue to shore; Boysie rode back home, while the others stayed behind to moor the pirogue. As soon as Boysie was out of sight, however, they got out and rowed back to the *Sam Super.* They had decided for once to take the initiative into their own hands.

They did not need to look further than the engine-room of the *Sam Super I* to find the means of weighting Bumper's body. Neither of them had Boysie's scruples about removing Mr. Samaroo's property; they unscrewed the extension plate and lashed Bumper's body to it. Once he was securely tied, they lowered him into the pirogue, rowed out about three hundred yards further from the shore and there dropped him. Less wise in the ways of the sea than Boysie, they did not know that a strong current runs up parallel with the shore from Port of Spain to Chaguaramas. When Bumper surfaced – as he was bound to do, for the weight they had chosen was insufficient for the job – he would be carried up with it, not further out to sea, but if anything closer to the shore.

When Boysie learnt what had happened, he shrugged his shoulders. The damage was done. Perhaps after all the corpse would not rise, or if it rose it might be destroyed by fish before it was discovered.

It was not until he landed from the last pirate trip – the one on which Taitt, Meyers and the three Venezuelans died – that Boysie learnt of the discovery of the corpse.

He realised at once the danger he was in. Believing Bumper to be an informer, and knowing that the police knew Bumper was part of his organisation, he guessed that they would already have the motive for the killing, and that his arrest was only a matter of hours away. It seemed to him that his only hope of salvation lay in putting the blame upon someone else. He must have been encouraged in this belief by the fact that Inspector Bleasdell was in charge of the investigations. Bleasdell he knew of old, and he believed that the Inspector could easily be persuaded to switch his attentions elsewhere.

On the following day, the 21st, he went to see Bleasdell. It was not true, as he claimed at the trial, that Bleasdell came to see him at Queen Street or that his subsequent statement was extracted by questioning. The statement was perfectly voluntary. Moreover it was not true that Bleasdell had omitted the two "don'ts" that Boysie had included in the statement.

Boysie was forced to renounce his statement because Bleasdell would not act on it or even believe it. Once its genuineness was questioned, the mere fact of his making it became suspicious in the extreme; that was why he was at such pains to insist that Bleasdell had extracted it by unfair means.

But on the 21st, his sole aim had been to provide a scapegoat. There was indeed a certain basis of truth in what he said.

There *had* been bad blood between Bumper and Durant. Durant is even supposed to have given Bumper a poisoned roti.

I have heard more than one version of this incident, but the one with most support claims that Bumper and Loomat were at No. 55 one evening between the Mico and Brooklyn Bar jobs, and Bumper, feeling hungry, sent Loomat downstairs to buy him a roti. Loomat did so, and was on his way back, when, in the doorway of No. 55, he was stopped by Durant. Durant asked Loomat what he was doing, and, when Loomat told him, took the roti and slipped something inside it. Loomat then took the roti to Bumper, who ate it. Shortly afterwards Bumper was taken violently ill. Ignacio (or whatever his name was) Brown, who confirmed Boysie's statement, took him to the dispenser, Mr. Lincoln, on the corner of Prince and Charlotte Streets, but Bumper seems to have had as little faith as Boysie in orthodox remedies, for, according to Brown, "we went to the market and bought an Obee seed from a big fat lady." Whether the dispenser's prescription or the Obee seed proved effective no one can tell, but Bumper speedily recovered.

Whatever the truth of this story, it is certain that, shortly afterwards, Durant took Loomat to the country with him. This was the reason why Loomat took no part in the ill-fated Brooklyn Bar raid; Durant's alibi was in fact perfectly genuine.

But Bleasdell was convinced that Boysie had killed Bumper.

He knew also that it was unlikely Boysie had done the job alone. It remained to find out which of his henchmen had assisted him. All Bleasdell had to go on was Boysie's statement and his own knowledge of the men who were closest to Boysie. On the 23rd, he interviewed James and Coggins, at that time a purely routine measure, and had Loomat detained. It was not until Loomat had been detained at Besson Street – "The Pacific" – for forty-eight hours that James, Coggins and Boysie were actually arrested. What took place in those forty-eight hours can only be a matter of conjecture. It would hardly be surprising if Loomat, having been told that Boysie had shopped him – for on the police's own admission the binocular-theft pretext was not long kept up – had retaliated by shopping Boysie and such of his henchmen as were, to his and Bleasdell's limited knowledge, Boysie's closest associates.

This suggestion seems to be borne out by the affair of Bruce. Loomat – who if Boysie is to be believed had seldom or never visited No. 55 – had identified the fifth man in the jitney as Tobago George. Now there was a Tobago George in Boysie's organisation, but he wasn't Bruce. Bruce was known simply as Tobago, which happened to be his birthplace. Bleasdell, however, was not aware of this – and arrested the man whom from the similarity of nicknames he assumed was Tobago George. He then put Bruce in the line-up for Loomat to identify, and Loomat, in his own words at the retrial, said, "I pointed him out because I had known him before, and *because I knew he was associated in some way or other with Queen Street.*" Admittedly he was quick to supplement this by saying, "I pointed out David Bruce at the parade because he was connected with Bumper's murder", an explanation which, rather oddly, was accepted without question by Mr. Justice Gomes. It seems more likely that he had originally meant to implicate the real Tobago George, that Bleasdell was responsible for the mix-up, and that Loomat, faced with a line-up that did not contain Tobago George, but did contain *somebody* "associated with Queen Street", and nicknamed "Tobago", decided to take the line of least resistance and pick out the luckless Bruce; probably he was afraid that if he didn't pick someone he would be charged himself.

The only question that remains is why, if it was Bleasdell's policy to arrest Boysie's principal lieutenants, he did not also arrest Bage and Fire Kong. In Fire Kong's case there is a plausible explanation. The police were well aware that Kong had done the December shooting in No. 55; while Boysie's organisation was at large no one would testify against him, but once Boysie and the others were behind bars, they felt certain that witnesses would not hesitate to come forward. Kong was in fact arrested not long after Boysie, convicted of shooting with intent to kill, and, a week before his leader was found guilty, sentenced to ten years penal servitude.

It is not so easy to see why they did not charge Bage. Perhaps it was because he was an illegal immigrant; they did not need a conviction against him, they could have him deported at any time. One cannot avoid the conclusion that, throughout the Floating Corpse affair, the aim of the police was not so much to find the killers of Bumper as to smash Boysie's organisation by putting out of action as many of its members as possible. It was an understandable aim, though it is doubtful whether the police are ever justified in using immoral means, no matter how great the danger to society, since the use of such means tends to prolong the anarchy it is meant to suppress. The lawlessness of modern Trinidad may spring as much from past police irregularities as from the example of Boysie and his gang.

There is every reason to believe that if the Besson Street diary had never been produced, Boysie's appeal would have failed and he and his fellow-prisoners would have been executed. No one has ever satisfactorily explained how the defence came to hear of these crucial entries, none of which would in normal circumstances have been made public. Police appeared to suspect Harry Seurattan, the Besson Street constable who was now living openly with Boysie's wife Doris, though, according to reliable information, another policeman from the same station was in fact responsible. Indeed it is hard to see what Seurattan's motive could have been, for he should surely have been more anxious than anyone to see Boysie hang. Perhaps Doris, faithful to Boysie after her fashion, contrived to extract the story from him without his realising it. But nothing was ever proved against Seurattan. Shortly after the trials he resigned from the Trinidad police, and his present whereabouts are unknown.

Once the diary entries had been brought into the case, a verdict of "Not Guilty" was the only just one that could have been brought. Boysie was guilty all right – but he was not guilty *as charged,* and the four unfortunates charged with him were not guilty at all. Whatever their private feelings, the Appeal Court judges had to act as they did. No outside pressure was brought to bear on them. The gang preferred to rely on dynamite in the event of an unfavourable verdict. For while they knew well enough that witnesses could be bribed and intimidated, it never occurred to them that the same process might be applied to judges. The creation of such a belief among men actively opposed to the law is one of the unsung triumphs of British justice. But such beliefs can only survive if the courts continue to uphold the principles on which that justice is based – not the least of which is that it is better for a hundred guilty men to escape than for one innocent to be unjustly punished.

23: PIRATE INTO PREACHER

BOYSIES'S LIBERTY was short-lived. No sooner had he been officially released than he was arrested on a charge of receiving a stolen outboard engine.

The engine came from the boat of the two fishermen, Wilson and Cook, who had been killed on April 17th, 1950. Obviously the Crown would have preferred to bring charges of murder, but when Boysie had just been acquitted in a case where there was a perfectly good body, he was hardly likely to be convicted where no victims could be produced. At the preliminary hearing, in February 1951, Boysie was committed for trial. He returned to his cell in the Royal Gaol.

He had saved his life, but at an appalling price. His defence had cost him forty thousand dollars. At one stage of his career he could have paid this sum in cash, but after his disastrous losses of the mid-forties he never again succeeded in amassing a large capital sum. His income was high enough, but his expenses were heavy, and his luck at gambling no longer good enough to make up the difference. To pay for his defence he had to sell everything: his boats, including the *Marie Louise* – as soon as it was relinquished by the police – his trucks, the jitney, even such property as was left him, all had to go.

At first it did not look as if he would ever get out. The unprecedented length of his two murder trials had thrown the Trinidadian judicial calendar out of joint, and while the queue of held-up cases filed slowly through the courts, he remained in prison. After repeated efforts to secure bail for him had failed, application was made to a judge in chambers, stressing the length of time he had already been in custody. The season was propitious; it was just before Christmas 1951, and in due course the application was granted and Boysie was released on bail.

The world he entered was very different from the one he had left. Then he had been master of a powerful organisation, with an assured and substantial income. Now his organisation was smashed and scattered, his clubs closed down and the very premises let to other tenants; he was virtually penniless.

For a week or so he stayed quietly with his son, Chuncie. Then, in January 1952, he climbed on his autocycle – the only one of his vehicles that had not been disposed of – and set out on his preaching career.

Boysie Singh as a pirate, note the all-black costume

... as a business man

... and, all in white, as a preacher

Fantastic though this volte-face might appear to most observers, Boysie himself seemed to see nothing odd in it. His private behaviour was quite devoid of the hysteria or the sanctimonious speechmaking usually associated with bogus religious conversions. He would say simply that he was going out to hold a meeting at such and such a place, and he would go.

Trinidad, like the rest of the West Indies, has always been a fertile breeding-ground for the more exotic varieties of religion; the lack of a common tradition has encouraged an amoebic proliferation of sects, and made possible the setting-up of innumerable far-out, do-it-yourself churches. For example, there is living at the present moment in Trinidad's nearby dependency, Tobago, the proprietress of a bakery (a very successful one, incidentally) who describes herself as the Bride of Christ, and leads a cult which believes that Tobago is paradise, not metaphorically but literally; the souls of the blessed go there after death to be reincarnated as Tobagonians. This state of affairs has been encouraged by the eclectic attitude many people have towards the whole idea of religion. Like Boland Ramkissoon and his circle – whose part in this story has yet to be played – they church-hop from faith to faith, sampling what each one has to offer. Any would-be messiah is thereby assured of a hearing, even if he lacks the notoriety of a Boysie. Moreover neither training nor previous experience are needed. He can go to the nearest street-corner and simply start.

The religion which Boysie preached seems to have been of an undenominational kind, yet much closer to orthodoxy than one might have expected. Unfortunately, no copies of his sermons are available, but his doctrine seems to have been compounded of vague memories of his wife's Catholicism mixed with his own personal interpretation of Biblical texts made during his eighteen months confinement.

His equipment consisted of his Bible, a table, a white cloth, two coconut shells, some flowers, a large pressure lantern, and a candle. If the proposed site of the meeting was nearby, he would walk there, carrying these articles himself; otherwise he would travel by autocycle, borrowing the heavier items from sympathisers on the spot. Arriving at the site – usually a street corner or vacant lot – he would set up the table, cover it with the white cloth, place the coconut shells at either end of the table, arrange the flowers in them, set the candle between them and light it. He would then light the pressure lamp – for his meetings, which took place on weekdays as well as Sundays, usually began around six in the evening – and hang it in a prominent place. By this time a large crowd, sometimes several hundreds, would have collected. Trinidadians were naturally anxious to see for themselves Boysie's strange metamorphosis.

The meeting would then open with a prayer; the Litany of the Sacred Heart of Jesus is said to be the one he most frequently used. Then Boysie himself would speak. His sermons must have been remarkable feats of endurance, both for him and for his congregation, for they lasted as long as three or four hours. He spoke extempore, and without a microphone – his bull's voice carried to the furthest listener. His subject-matter was drawn largely from his own life; he would speak of his sufferings in prison and his earlier life of crime, ornamenting his discourse with scriptural citations which he quoted from memory. One report credits him with having said on a certain occasion, "I have killed two or three hundred Venezuelans", but such tales as these must be consigned to the Boysie Apocrypha; he was seldom so specific in his references to past offences, and while the outboard motor charge hung over him, he would indeed have been lacking in caution to refer specifically to his piratical career.

The moral of his sermons was plain enough. If such a sinner could repent, could be taken back into the arms of a forgiving Lord, who in all the world could consider himself beyond God's mercy?

Having continued in this vein for several hours, he would bring the meeting to a close with another prayer, announce the time and place of his next meeting, pack up his belongings and leave. Surprisingly enough, there was no collection. Boysie never derived any financial benefit from his preaching career. During this period he lived with unprecedented frugality on the little money left to him from the sale of his effects.

This scant allowance he would eke out with the proceeds of gambling. It is said by those who suspect Boysie's sincerity that he would often sit down to play whappie in the very spot where, a few hours before, he had come to preach. This is perhaps a slight exaggeration, but there is no doubt that he did continue to gamble during his preaching period. To be fair to him, one must remember that his orientation was towards the Catholic faith, which has always looked with an eye more tolerant than the Puritan's on such manifestations of human frailty.

From the evidence of those closest to him, at the time he seems to have taken his new vocation seriously enough. Naturally, no one in his circle questioned his reasons for adopting this new career. He was not – even in his regenerate days – the kind of man who would welcome or even tolerate any kind of enquiry into his motives. One indication of his sincerity he gave, and that was once more to change his entire wardrobe. The pirate's funeral rig was consigned to limbo along with the vice-king's zoot suit and the fisherman's merino and shorts. He now dressed entirely in white; white flannel trousers, white shirt and white jacket. He broke off relations with the former members of his gang. Admittedly, this was not difficult to do, for Fire Kong was in gaol, Bage in his homeland, and the others scattered. But police records and the memories of his associates both confirm that he undertook no criminal activities during his preaching days. To this extent, at least, he was sincere.

After six months his career was interrupted. Once more he appeared in the dock at the Red House – this time to answer the charge of receiving Wilson's and Cook's engine. The case was heard by Mr. Justice E. R. Ward, now Speaker of the Federal House of Representatives.

The prosecution, handled once more by the Solicitor-General, was clear and straightforward enough. On the night of April 16th, 1950, the two fishermen Gilbert Wilson and Sonny Cook had set out from Port of Spain on a routine fishing trip. The boat they used was not their own property; it belonged to one John Aquan who, like Boysie, owned several vessels. The net and the nine horsepower outboard which powered the boat were also Aquan's.

They were seen around midnight by another fisherman called Soliste Dedier, a man with forty years experience of the business; they were lying off the Waterloo Bank, to the south-west of Port of Spain, and were just lighting their lamps. Neither they nor their boat were ever seen again.

Worrell here tried to introduce allegations of piracy into the prosecution's case, but Rupert Archbald, once more defending Boysie, objected; Boysie was not charged with the murder of the two fishermen or even with stealing the engine, merely with receiving it knowing it to be stolen. Mr. Justice Ward upheld his objection.

Continuing the Crown case, Worrell told how, following a report, Corporal C. Maxwell of the Trinidad Police Force and John Aquan had gone to a house at La Lune, Moruga (about fifty miles from Port of Spain), which house was the property of one Ruthven Pegus. At this house were found both the missing engine and the net. Aquan was able to identify the engine by its serial numbers. Pegus stated that he had bought both engine and nets from Boysie.

In his defence there was little that Boysie could say. He admitted having sold Pegus an engine; Pegus, he said, had come to No. 55 Queen Street on April 14th (two days before Cook and Wilson set out on their last voyage) and asked him if he could buy an engine and a net. Boysie had told him he could sell him an engine but not a net. The engine he had sold was his own and not that of Cook and Wilson; if Aquan claimed the contrary he must have been mistaken in his identification or Pegus must have bought more than one engine. The net, Boysie claimed, had been sold not by him but by George Harper, for the sum of three hundred dollars. That part of the transaction was entirely Harper's business.

The jury were not impressed by his version. They returned a verdict of guilty, and on July 23rd, 1952, Boysie was sentenced to eighteen months hard labour. But for the long period he had already spent in custody, the sentence would probably have been heavier. This term he served in the Royal Gaol where he had been held during the Floating Corpse case and while awaiting trial in 1951.

His conduct in prison differed considerably from that of his previous long term, the 1928-31 stretch in Carrera. Then he had been sullen, rebellious and vindictive; now, whether impelled by his new-found grace or a maturer realisation that troublemaking didn't pay, he was a model prisoner. A good deal of the time he spent in the Prison infirmary, for it was only while in gaol that he troubled to have his diabetes treated. For the rest, he continued his Bible studies. It is hardly surprising that he earned the maximum amount of remission. Less than a year later – on July 6th, 1953 – he was discharged; the authorities, however, placed him under supervision for a period of three years.

As soon as he was released he went back to preaching.

Now his meetings became more elaborate. Shortly after leaving prison he made the acquaintance of a group with similar views to his own. He joined forces with them, and obtained the services of a female choir consisting of girls aged from fourteen to sixteen. Despite his history of womanising, no scandal was ever breathed against Boysie in connection with these girls. This, however, may have been due less to a change of heart than the total impotence which his untreated gonorrhoea had by this time brought about. After his last prison sentence he seems to have had no further sexual contact with women.

The choir would open the meeting by singing a hymn or hymns, in which a large part of the audience usually joined. Then Boysie, clad as always in the colour of chastity and innocence, would preach his sermon; he would now make this shorter than before, for the other adult members of the group had their pieces to say. More hymns from the girls and a collection would close the meeting. Boysie, however, took no share in the proceeds, which went to pay the choir and assist the needier of his co-religionaries.

Naturally the throngs which were attracted to Boysie's meetings were not composed exclusively of true believers. Many irreverent and cynical spirits who could not credit Boysie's reformation came to jeer at him or to ask provocative questions. Others more fervent sought to differ from him on knotty points of doctrine. To all interrupters or questioners, genuine or otherwise, Boysie's reaction was the same; he would tell them in vivid detail what, if he were not leading a religious life, he would do to them. Sometimes he himself gave considerable provocation. He insisted on preaching in San Juan, and it was hardly surprising that the San Juanese resented lectures on their spiritual welfare from a man who, a few years previously, had been throwing explosive charges at them and preventing them from marketing their produce. Yet Boysie in these days was not easily moved to wrath. His retorts remained purely verbal, and there is no record of his having been involved in violence throughout this period.

What is still more surprising is that at no time, either before or after his prison sentence, did he try to revenge himself on Loomat or any of the other witnesses who had testified against him during the Floating Corpse proceedings. Certainly this expectation was shared by the authorities. Throughout the trial, Loomat had been kept in protective custody at Staubles Bay, cut off from the rest of Trinidad by the U.S.-leased territory of Chaguaramas, through which only those with official passes were allowed. However, it was clear that he could not be kept there indefinitely. Arrangements were made for him to join the Merchant Navy; the necessary papers were made out, and a report appeared in the press stating that he had actually left. In actual fact he remained in Trinidad. His decision seems to have been voluntary; perhaps he preferred the known perils of the Trinidadian underworld to the unknown hardships of a sailor's life.

The event proved his judgement correct. Although the two are actually supposed to have met after the trial, nothing happened; Boysie merely laughed, asked after Loomat's health and then went on his way.

His failure to take revenge on Loomat is explicable enough. Throughout the trial all the prisoners had considered him merely a dummy of Bleasdell, in no way responsible for his actions. His extreme youth also told in his favour. There was no reason to suppose that he had acted either out of malice or in hope of reward, so it would have been unreasonable to punish him.

But all this does not alter the fact that in earlier days Boysie had killed men for one-tenth of the excuse Loomat had given. There remained, too, the other witnesses. For Bishop it might have been claimed that as an ex-policeman he was only doing what he conceived to be his job, and was no more deserving of retribution than any active member of the force; but Wilkie and Rodney were men whom Boysie, in his day of power, would have trampled contemptuously underfoot, and to the crime of treachery Harper had added that of gross ingratitude. One might argue that now Boysie's organisation was smashed, he was physically unable to revenge himself; but Boysie was always willing and indeed eager to do his own strong-arm work.

Repugnant though this may be in the light of his previous career, one is driven towards the conclusion that after his reprieve from sentence of death he did experience some sort of change of heart. In this matter, at least, he seems to have obeyed literally the scriptural injunction about turning the other cheek.

For the rest of 1953 and most of the following year he continued to travel through the island on his autocycle, preaching wherever he went.

It was this autocycle which brought his mission to an untimely end. He had failed to obtain a driving licence for motor vehicles in 1940, and from then on seems to have vowed to have nothing to do with the licensing authorities. Either he did not know that any permit was required for autocycles, or he just did not care; he was surprised and annoyed when, late in 1954, a policeman stopped him and asked him to produce his licence. In due course he was charged, convicted and fined.

It is hard to understand the wholly disproportionate outburst of rage with which Boysie greeted these trivial proceedings. Possibly he felt he had suffered enough from the law to have earned some kind of immunity for minor offences; this would certainly have been no less rational than a good many of his beliefs. Quick as in the old days to take offence, he seemed to believe that the case was just part of a pattern of police persecution. If such was the treatment accorded a reformed sinner, what was the percentage in righteousness?

Whatever his real feelings, he gave this case as the reason for his abandoning the preaching career. To quote his own words from his death-cell diary, "The Police arrest me for riding my Autocycle in 1954 late and that made me go back into the ordinary life."

24: "THE ORDINARY LIFE"

THE LAST TWO MONTHS of 1954 Boysie spent fishing with his son from a village called Erin on the east side of the island. But he seemed more than normally morose and sunk in his own thoughts, and at the end of the two months he packed up and returned to Port of Spain. Save for a single disastrous trip, he was never to return to the sea again.

Back in the city he had to support himself by some means, for what little had been left him from the ruin of his fortunes was by this time exhausted. However, for one of Boysie's reputation, those means were not far to seek. News had already gone round that he was back in the "ordinary life", and no one had any doubts about what was ordinary for Boysie. Even if he had been determined to go straight he would have found it difficult; anyone with an arson or beating-up job to be done was sure to go to him.

The first of these jobs was offered to him almost as soon as he reached Port of Spain; the burning of a bar called the "Rising Sun". Boysie was offered five thousand dollars for the job. He needed the money, but was too wary to plant the actual fire-raising device himself. This time, however, his very caution was almost the cause of his downfall, for he could no longer count on obtaining loyal subordinates; the three men whom he approached first not merely refused to have anything to do with the scheme, but also informed the police of his intentions.

In the meantime, Boysie had found a more amenable tool. On January 8th, 1955, under cover of darkness, he despatched this man with the familiar brown paper parcel and instructions about where and how it was to be placed.

The Rising Sun Bar occupied part of a single-storey building with a loft above; the other half was occupied by a clothing store. Boysie's man scaled the outside wall and entered the loft by a small window. At this stage, though so far unseen, he seems to have succumbed to nervousness; at all events, instead of placing the device square over the Rising Sun, he put it down in the middle of the loft over the division between the two premises. Then he made good his escape.

A few hours later the alarm went off, the matches struck and flamed, the petrol went up with a roar. In a matter of minutes both halves of the building were ablaze. The Fire Brigade could do little more than limit the outbreak to the one building; both bar and store were gutted to the tune of sixty thousand dollars.

Shortly after the fire, Boysie and another man were arrested and charged with arson.

The preliminary hearing took place before Magistrate A. N. Busby. It was claimed by the prosecution that the fire had begun with an explosion, and that Boysie had been seen running away from the bar. The other man in the case was barely mentioned, and Mr. Busby, finding that there was insufficient evidence against him, gave him an unconditional discharge. Boysie, however, was committed for trial. Bail was applied for; the police – rather surprisingly, considering Boysie's record and the fact that he was still supposed to be "under supervision", whatever that meant – did not oppose it.

And that, fantastically enough, was that. Eighteen months later, when Boysie was once more arrested on a capital charge, the case of the Rising Sun arson had still not come up for trial. No adequate reason for this delay was ever given; the reader, who should by this time be well versed in the vagaries of Trinidadian legal procedure, may perhaps be able to supply one for himself.

An ironical twist was that Boysie never drew his full fee. A cryptic note in his death-cell diary (in which he admitted responsibility for the "fire jobe", as he called it) indicates that he received only $3538 – the balance of $1462 remained unpaid at the time of his death.

On the proceeds of the crime he began to gamble again. Poker and whappie were his games during this period. His luck varied; sometimes he would find himself, like Harper, "broken as a bat"; somehow he would always manage to recoup himself. But he never again had those long winning streaks which had made his fortune in the late thirties and early forties. The man who had called himself the Vagabond King, who had strolled in state round the Savannah with his sinister retinue at his heels, who had distributed largess to half the destitute of Port of Spain, was often hard put to it to find the price of a meal.

His poverty was reflected in his scale of charges. Jobs which would at one time have cost thousands of dollars he was now prepared to carry out for the least sum that would put him back at the gambling tables. Later in 1955 he accepted a combined murder and arson job for the risible figure of $240.

It came about in the following manner. A woman from the Croisée district of San Juan was having an affair with a taxi-driver, but this had been ended by a violent quarrel; Trinidadian taxi-drivers, who are in general younger and more virile than their English equivalents, have a formidable reputation for sexual prowess equalled only by their promiscuity. The woman went to Boysie and offered him two hundred dollars to get rid of her ex-lover. Before Boysie had time to put the plan into operation he was approached by the taxi-driver himself, who, though equally vindictive, was less radical in his demands; he proposed that Boysie should simply burn down the woman's house. For this favour he was willing to pay the princely sum of forty dollars.

This put Boysie in a difficult position. It was his normal practice to secure a deposit of half the agreed sum before doing any of his "jobs"; on this occasion he had already received a hundred dollars for the removal of his new client. Broke as usual, he did not hesitate; with superb aplomb he collected a down-payment of twenty dollars from the prospective murderee, and promised to execute his wishes.

More than the wishes were to be executed; on pretext of casing the arson job, Boysie begged a ride in his client's taxi, a ride which was scheduled to be the driver's last. As they drove along a deserted byroad that led through the canefields behind the town of Caroni, Boysie asked the driver to stop a moment. Suspecting nothing, imagining no doubt that Boysie wished to relieve himself, the driver did so. The next second Boysie's fingers were round his throat.

Suddenly in the distance they heard the sound of a car engine. Boysie relaxed his grip. Sure enough, a car swung round the bend in the road and came swiftly towards them. Boysie let go, sprang from the car and plunged into the tall green sugar-cane. In the space of a second he was out of sight.

He made his way rapidly across country to Arouca, where he was then staying. As soon as he arrived there he took a piece of garlic and thrust it deep into his rectum. The violent irritation caused by the garlic set up a high fever, and he gave instructions that anyone who asked for him should be told that he was too ill for visitors. Indeed this was not far from the truth. He probably had in mind the aftermath of David Leach's death, when the pose of a sick man had saved him from a manslaughter charge.

But no one came. The driver had neither succumbed to Boysie's attack nor laid charges against him; he preferred to cut his losses rather than face a countercharge of instigating arson, while no doubt it seemed unwise to provoke Boysie to a second attempt. Boysie lay in bed for two days, at the end of which time he decided he was out of danger, got up and resumed his hand-to-mouth existence.

One rumour states that during this period he was asked by Dr. Dalip Singh, the wife-murderer, to dispose of his wife's body. In fact the good doctor – no relation of Boysie's – was already in custody at the time. A medical officer attached to the Colonial Hospital, Port of Spain, he was frequently required to give evidence in criminal cases, and should have appreciated the risks he was running. But he had bought perjured evidence to support his divorce petition, and feared exposure. His sole connection with Boysie lay in the means of corpse-disposal he eventually chose. He must have recalled the unexpected emergence of Bumper, buoyed up by the gases of decomposition. Profiting from his namesake's misfortune, he had removed his wife's intestines before committing her to the deep. However, he overlooked the elementary precaution of dropping her in deep water. Her gutted corpse was washed ashore, and Dr. Singh died on the gallows, on June 28th, 1955.

On several occasions in 1955 and 1956 Boysie had to have hospital treatment. On one occasion he was admitted in a diabetic coma. Though less intolerant of things medical than he had been in his youth – he went so far as to praise some of the doctors and nurses who attended him – he was still unamenable to hospital discipline and remained only as long as he was forced to do. At least once he walked out of hospital without waiting for his discharge papers. While at liberty he would neglect all treatment until his worsening condition obliged him to seek help once more.

Illness and poverty did not seem to embitter Boysie; rather they made him apathetic and indifferent to what might happen in the future. It would not perhaps be unduly fanciful to compare his situation, in these final years, to that of Macbeth; he too had supp'd full of horrors, and now, his perceptions atrophied by his career of crime, deserted by his friends, hemmed around by his enemies, he might well consider that his

...way of life
Had fallen into the sere and yellow leaf;

could indeed have echoed the sombre complaint of Shakespeare's doomed hero-villain:

I 'gin to be aweary of the Sun,
And wish the estate of the world were now undone.

Unknown to Boysie the chain of events which was to encompass his death had already been set in motion.

Early in 1956 he had made the acquaintance of a twenty-six-year-old fellow-Indian called Boland Ramkissoon. Boland worked as a lifeguard at Maracas Bay, and, like Boysie, had had religious experiences. It was not religion, however, which brought them together, but the fact that both were now residents of San Juan, and Boland seems to have developed almost a hero-worship for the older man. He addressed Boysie as "uncle"; he got into the habit of visiting his "uncle's" house more and more often, and once there he would talk for hours on end. A good deal of his talk consisted of a recital of his troubles. These were mainly domestic; and what was more natural than that he should ask the older man's advice?

25: BOLAND AND THELMA

BOLAND RAMKISSOON was to play such a vital part in Boysie's last year of life that it would perhaps be as well to consider his history in some detail.

He was born and raised in San Juan. His parents, though far from rich, owned a small tract of land on a steep hillslope above San Juan which was known as Ramkissoon Trace. In common with most Indian sons, Boland was treated indulgently, and seems to have been almost as rebellious a child as Boysie himself. In his early teens he was leader of a juvenile gang called the Phantoms. This leadership he won by feats of daring none of the others would emulate; on one occasion, for instance, he dived from a rock thirty feet above the Diego Martin river with a dagger between his teeth.

At seventeen he got involved in a fight over a girl and was slammed into unconsciousness by blows from a baseball bat. He was so seriously injured that it was a year before he fully recovered his health, and, as so often happens with those incapacitated at a critical phase of adolescence, the experience seemed to make him grow away from his contemporaries, to become introspective and morose.

In 1950 he married an Indian girl called Dorothy. They had one child, but the marriage was far from being a success. In 1952 they separated, and he was ordered to pay her maintenance of thirty-two dollars a month. By this time Boland was already employed at Maracas.

Maracas Bay is a mile-long semicircle of sand backed by tall coconut palms and steep-sided, densely-wooded hills, some fourteen miles north of Port of Spain. Until the early years of the war it was virtually inaccessible; the switchback of road that now leads to it was the work of the American forces, who, having by the Lend-Lease Agreement deprived Trinidad of its favourite bathing places, felt obliged in the interests of international friendship to make good the loss. They could justly claim that the new resort had clearer water than the old; unfortunately it was a good deal more dangerous. The bay faces north, and is therefore partially exposed to the prevailing north-easterly winds. Seas often run high there, the beach shelves sharply, the currents are treacherous; the job of lifeguard at Maracas is certainly no sinecure, and in fact Boland was only one of several employed there.

For Boland, however, it seemed an ideal way of earning a living. The hours were not long; the jitney which brought the lifeguards did not

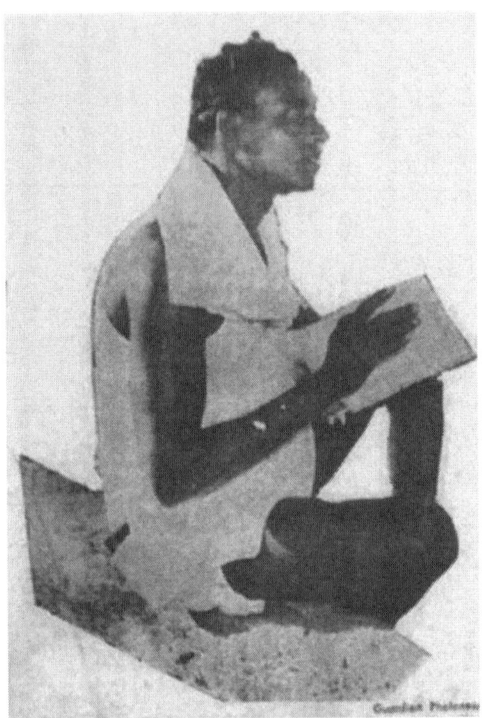

Guardian Photonews

Above is Boland Ramkissoon, self-styled Bible student, photographed last September in meditation on a log at Maracas Bay while the search went on for his sweetheart, Thelma Haynes.

DID SHE ESCAPE DEATH? This is Boland's wife Dorothy, aged 22, who Boland forsook for Thelma, and this is his daughter, six-year-old Bernice who was two when her father went to live with Thelma. Says Dorothy, "I don't know if I'll marry again. I'm getting big and fat."

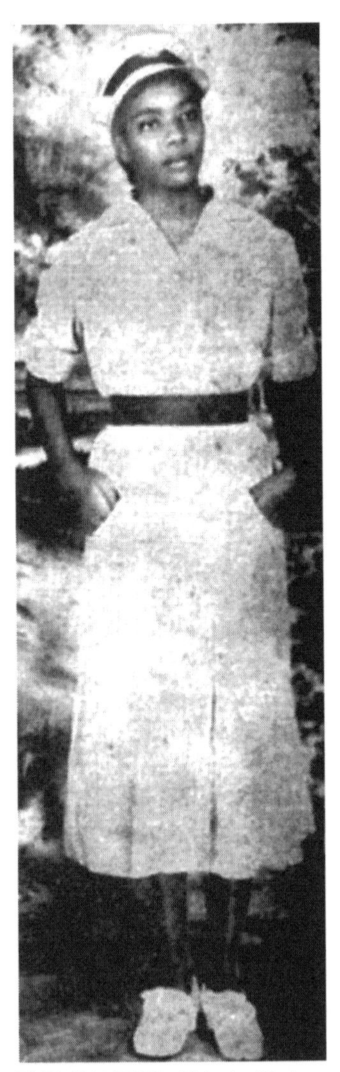

THE DANCER: This is Thelma Haynes, the vivacious folklore dancer for whose murder Boland Ramkissoon, her sweetheart, and Boysie Singh are to die. Exclusive photo shows the 23-year-old Miss Haynes as she appeared in her Red Cross uniform in the days when she and Ramkissoon lived together at Santa Cruz Old Road, San Juan. Then on July 30, last year, she left home, telling Ramkissoon's mother she was going to see her lover. She was never seen again. Neither was her body found"

usually arrive until nine-thirty or ten in the morning, and left again around four or five in the afternoon, depending on the presence or absence of bathers and the condition of the sea. For most of that time there was nothing to do but lie on the beach and take turns looking out for bathers in difficulty. The tall, dark, handsome Boland took every opportunity of showing off his physique, of which he was justly proud. His job, moreover, had just enough risk to shed glamour on its possessor without involving him in undue peril. Hero of the girls, he paced the dazzling sands through the brief tropical days, picking his admirers where he pleased.

Soon one in particular caught his eye.

When Boland met her she was working as a nurse at the first-aid post at Maracas. Her name was Thelma Haynes. She was of Negro stock, though the delicacy of her features suggests that there was some measure of European blood in her family. She was not a Trinidadian, but had been born in British Guiana. Nor was nursing her only occupation; when Boland met her she was a folklore dancer in Geoffrey Holder's troupe, and had been offered a contract to tour Puerto Rico with them. Those who knew her described her as a quiet, sweet-natured, affable girl.

Affairs between people of Indian and African origin are not common in Trinidad. Many Indians look down on the Negro with a hauteur worthy of any white supremacist, and the Negroes naturally resent this attitude.

The latter tend to go into civil service careers, while the Indians stick to private enterprise; one of the main causes of racial bitterness is that the police force, largely composed of Negroes, is believed by the Indians (I cannot say with how much justice) to bear down unduly heavily on Indian citizens. Boland and Thelma, like Boysie and Doris, proved to be exceptions to the general rule; they fell instantly in love with one another. Soon Thelma went to live with Boland in his tapia house at Ramkissoon Trace.

To reach it one ascended a precipitous dirt road, scoured by a torrent in the rainy season. Left of the road the house stood, a small whitewashed box with the woodwork painted blue. Two tall mango trees shadowed it with their matted foliage. In the days when Boland and Thelma lived there it looked neat and well-kept, but now its walls are peeling into brownish patches; tapia, of which they are made, is a kind of clay stiffened with twigs and grass, and like so many of the building materials used in the West Indies (which in consequence have everywhere an impermanent look, as if man's lease might at any time expire) its life is strictly limited.

In this house the lovers lived happily for the better part of two years. Boland's income – $142 per month – was hardly sufficient to maintain two homes; he gave up smoking and drinking, and Thelma in return gave up her dancing. This was a measure of her affection for Boland, as she thereby missed the tour of Puerto Rico she had been promised. But it was not long before dancing was out of the question anyway; Thelma became pregnant.

The child proved to be a girl, whom they called Joy. In the summer of 1956 she was eighteen months old.

By that time, however, a change had come over Boland. He had got religion. At first his interest in the subject was a general one, but after a period of shopping around the various churches he settled down as a fervent member of the Church of Pilgrim Holiness, an evangelical body with headquarters in the United States which maintains missions in many remote corners of the world. Nor was his conversion merely skin-deep. Boland no longer spent his time at Maracas showing off his muscular development to the girls. Instead, he would subject them to long harangues on their moral welfare, warning them against the evils of drinking, the use of cosmetics and immodest behaviour with young men, and larding his discourse with copious quotation from the scriptures.

Soon he became a notorious bore, and bathers would go to any lengths to keep out of his way. He was thrown back on the society of his fellow lifeguards. But these were as little desirous of a spiritual counsellor as the general public, and they too shunned him – with one exception.

This was Milton Rigoux, member of the Tacarigua branch of the Pentecostal Church, a body which peddles a somewhat different brand of evangelism to Boland's church, and which specialises in glossolalia – "speaking in tongues". The curious friendship which developed between these two began with an attempt at mutual conversion. Sprawled on the baking Caribbean sands, they would argue the merits of their respective faiths; Milton would try to get Boland to attend a Pentecostal service, Boland would urge Milton to visit the Pilgrim Holiness establishment. From this they proceeded by gradual stages to a discussion of their personal problems, and in this phase of their relationship Boland dropped his missionary role and humbly asked Milton for advice.

His trouble was that he did not know how to reconcile his current marital status with Biblical precepts. He was separated from his lawful wife and living in sin with another woman, and this was clearly wrong; yet one had to take into consideration the fact that, in the first place, his wife was allegedly living with another man – the driver of a hire-car called "Student Prince" – and, in the second place, he had a child by Thelma which would presumably remain his responsibility. What should he do? Milton told him that it was quite obvious that he was not living in accordance with the scriptures. His course was clear and admitted of no evasion; he must return to his married wife and "put Thelma away".

Boland seized eagerly on the ambiguity of Milton's remark. Milton had, of course, been speaking in the pseudo-Biblical jargon common among schismatics; Boland took the words in their colloquial sense, the more readily since he had an ambition which he had not dared to confide even to Milton. This was to become a minister of his church.

His unwillingness to discuss this with Milton – let alone Boysie – was probably because, as he knew all too well, he had no vocation for the task. His motives were purely economic. His job as lifeguard, while agreeable enough, just did not bring in sufficient money. After paying his maintenance he had little more than a hundred dollars a month to support himself, Thelma and their child. But as a minister he would command not merely a higher salary, but a rent-free house and the use of a car. To prepare himself for the position he was already taking a correspondence course with Billy Graham's Evangelistic Association. There was only one obstacle in his path – Thelma.

Obviously he had not the slightest hope of an appointment while he was living in sin. Milton was right, he would have to go back to Dorothy. But how was he to make Thelma go? He could not just tell her to do so. She would refuse. She was still in love with him, and if she had not been, there was still the child, Joy, and the fact that Thelma had given up her dancing career to live with him. To "put her away" in the most final and irrevocable manner began to look to Boland like the only solution.

It was hardly surprising that, as soon as he had conceived this idea, the first person he thought of was his new friend, his "uncle" – Boysie.

Boland, like all other Trinidadians, knew Boysie's previous history. He knew, or at least suspected, that despite the unfortunate exception of Bumper, Boysie had somehow been able to solve the killer's most critical problem, the removal of all traces of the crime. If he could enlist the help of such an ally he could enjoy the fruits with none of the risk. The prospect of being a murderer as well as a minister did not seem to deter him in the slightest; perhaps he took personally the text which informs us that "without shedding of blood there is no remission of sins."

So it was that Boland took to visiting Boysie with increasing frequency. As they sat together in Boysie's San Juan house of an evening, Boland would tell him – as he had told Milton – of the problems that beset him. But the facts that he gave Boysie were not the facts he had given Milton.

In the course of their acquaintance, Boland had arrived at a fairly accurate estimate of Boysie's character. He knew that Boysie would not, now that he was back in the "ordinary life", be interested in his friend's crisis of conscience; he knew Boysie was not likely to run the risk of a capital charge merely to make Boland Ramkissoon a Pilgrim Holiness pastor. Admittedly, Boysie's scruples might have been weakened by hard cash, but that was exactly what Boland hadn't got. His only chance seemed to be to persuade Boysie to do the job as a favour to a friend, paying him only what he was able to afford; but for this procedure it was necessary to present his situation in a more favourable light.

He told Boysie, then, that owing to the smallness of his salary he had fallen behind on the payment of his wife's maintenance. His wife was now threatening to put him in court and make him pay off the arrears, but this he could not do, and he was in danger of going to prison. Boysie pricked up his ears. He would do anything to assist a fellow-sufferer under the law. What did Boland suggest?

Boland's suggestion was that Boysie should help him to kill his wife and get rid of the body. There was no mention of Thelma.

Boysie thought it over. The money Boland offered – $160, and even that on the instalment plan – represented a new low in the liquidation market, and was hardly worth the risk of his neck. Sensing a certain reluctance on the part of his mentor, Boland hastened to add that he himself was willing to do the actual murder. It would be better that way, for his plan involved the decoying of Dorothy to some remote spot in order to kill her; if Boysie did this she would immediately become suspicious, whereas if Boland took her she would not realise his purpose until too late. Boysie's part in the plot would be limited to dumping the body, so that at worst he could only be charged as an accessory after the fact.

Both Boysie and Boland – and, as it subsequently turned out, a large number of Trinidadians – were under the illusion that a prosecution for murder cannot succeed unless the body of the murdered person is found. This belief, by no means confined to the West Indies, seems to arise from the use of the legal phrase *corpus delicti.* Unless the *corpus delicti* is produced, the law clearly states, murder cannot be proved. It is widely believed that *corpus delicti* means the corpse of the victim; in reality it means the fact of an offence having been committed. Obviously if ten people see someone throw a man overboard, that person could hardly expect to claim immunity because it proved impossible to recover the corpse. But this fact escaped the two friends. They had some excuse for their ignorance; never in the whole history of the West Indies had there been a prosecution for murder without a body to go with it, and the few cases which had occurred in the United Kingdom had received little publicity there. Moreover, there was the fact that, although the police knew Boysie had killed Wilson and Cook, they had not been able to bring any action against him, but had had to content themselves with the trivial charge of receiving.

They believed, then, that provided the murdered woman was never found they were both safe. Boysie was with reason confident that he could look after his end of the bargain, and his confidence dispelled whatever doubts Boland may have had about bearing the knife himself. The simplicity of the whole scheme finally overcame Boysie's doubts about the price; he agreed to give Boland his help.

Before they could put their plans into operation, Boysie was struck down by another diabetic crisis, and was admitted to the Port of Spain Hospital. Boland, anxious to demonstrate his friendship, went to visit him there. It was an unwise move. On July fifth, 1956, Neville Butler, a photographer on the staff of the *Port of Spain Gazette*, visited the hospital on a routine assignment and took a picture of Boysie. Boland, sitting at

Boysie's bedside, was included in the picture. It seemed a trivial incident at the time, but it was to have disastrous consequences for both of them.

Soon afterwards, Boysie was discharged from hospital, not cured, but capable of functioning once more. The preparations continued. On July 26th, Boysie paid a visit to an old acquaintance of his, a fishing-boat owner called Clifford "Dick" Smith. He had done Smith a favour once, had helped him to get back from Venezuela after Smith had drifted there and been imprisoned by the authorities. Now he had a favour to ask in return. He wanted the loan of a boat and engine for a few days.

Smith offered him an engine. He hadn't himself a boat to spare, but it so happened that, of all people, Boysie's son had recently brought him a boat and asked him to try and sell it. The boat was still in Smith's yard. No buyer had yet come forward and, till such time as one did, Boysie was welcome to the use of it.

Boysie bought two dollars worth of gas and oil for the engine, and set about making the boat ready for the sea.

Meanwhile Boland was nerving himself ready for the deed.

On the evening of July 30th a sacred concert was scheduled to take place at the Pilgrim Holiness church in San Juan. Boland was going to sing at this concert, and some days earlier he had asked Milton Rigoux to come and listen to him. Rigoux had decided to accept the invitation, and see what Pilgrim Holiness had that Pentecostal hadn't got. But when the day of the concert arrived, Boland seemed unusually preoccupied, and unwilling to talk. He did not even mention the concert. Milton wondered if Boland had forgotten the invitation; however, he decided to go along anyway.

The jitney dropped Boland back in San Juan as usual around six p.m. It was Boland's custom to go straight home to Ramkissoon Trace, and for part of the way he was usually accompanied by one of the other lifeguards, Lloyd Derryl. On this particular evening, Derryl, too, noticed a strangeness in Boland's behaviour. Not only was he unwilling to talk, he seemed unusually anxious to rid himself of Derryl's company. Finally, Derryl left him standing by the kerb, peering anxiously about him as if waiting for someone to turn up.

At about the same time he was seen by a neighbour, a Mrs. Maude French, who was on her way home. A few minutes later she saw Thelma Haynes. Thelma was walking in the opposite direction, towards the centre of San Juan. She was wearing a light brown nylon dress with a full skirt; the skirt had a white border with a flower pattern on it. Her shoes were black with wedge heels. On her left hand she had two gold rings, and on her wrist was a round gold watch with a cord strap. The keys of the tapia house swung from her fingers. Mrs. French immediately assumed she was going to meet Boland. She vanished in the direction of the Croisée – the San Juan crossroads that had already played a part in Boysie's destiny. Mrs. French thought no more of it and went on home.

As for Thelma, it was as if the earth opened and swallowed her up. She was never seen again: alive or dead.

Guardian Photonews

THE TURNING POINT TO FATE? – Miss Thelma Haynes, the missing dancer, went in one of the directions to which the arrows point, on the evening of July 30. The bridge she was seen crossing is about 100 yards up the line. The road at the left leads to Santa Cruz and Maracas, the other, to which the arrow points, to the Croisee. It is believed she was picked up by a vehicle at this junction and whisked away to a destination as yet unknown to the police.

26: THE CASE OF THE MISSING DANCER

AT 10.15 ON THE NIGHT of the 30th, Boland walked into the San Juan police station. Constable Carlton Bobb was on duty at the time, and even before Boland spoke he noticed that the Indian's manner was nervous and distrait.

Boland said that he had come to report that his common-law wife, Thelma Haynes, was missing. He had arrived home as usual to find that she had gone out. She had told Boland's mother, who lived only a few yards away, that she was walking into the town to meet Boland. But he had not seen her on his way up and, after waiting a little while, he had gone out to look for her. There had been no sign of her. He felt certain something must have happened to her.

Bobb did not take the matter too seriously. Four hours, he reminded Boland as he wrote out his report, was not a long time for anyone to be away from home; she might have bumped into an old friend or simply changed her mind and gone to visit some relative. He did not add, as he might well have done, that "disappearances", among a volatile people like the Trinidadian, were being reported all the time – the chance of a spree, an old flame, a fit of pique or simply the need for a change were ample excuse for almost anyone to leave home and turn up again, as if nothing had happened, a few days later. But despite Bobb's assurances, Boland remained as anxious as before; it was not like Thelma to be away so long, it had never happened before, she must have suffered some mishap.

Finally he went away, and the report was filed with all the similar reports.

The next day he did not turn up for work. Nor the next. Nor the one after that.

It was not until August 5th that he reported for duty. He had already sent Bertram Dufont, Supervisor of Lifeguards at Maracas, a medical certificate giving reasons for his absence. To the other lifeguards he confided that he had in fact been searching for his missing mistress. Since the 30th there had been no trace of her. He was afraid that someone had done away with her. She had not simply left him, as some of the guards suggested, for surely if she had gone of her own free will she would have taken her child with her. But Joy had been left behind at Ramkissoon Trace. During the day Boland's mother looked after her; at night she slept in the tapia house with her father; she was so attached to him that she would not go to sleep unless he was there.

August crept by. Nobody seemed to be paying much attention to the fate of Thelma Haynes. And indeed why should they? People were always disappearing. And a girl like Thelma, young, attractive, who'd had a taste of show business – for how long could you expect her to go on living in a tapia house with a married lifeguard earning $142 per month? So she'd left the child. Well, people were callous. And her clothes. They were impulsive too. That was how many people thought.

But not everybody. The police went on with their routine investigations. And it had occurred to David Prescod, crime reporter on the *Trinidad Guardian,* that this was one disappearance which didn't fit in to the normal pattern. He interviewed Boland, and Boland seemed far more nervous and ill at ease than one would expect a man in his position to be. It was almost as if he had a guilty conscience. The *Guardian* began to play up the story. From a brief item somewhere in the bowels of the 24-page paper it swelled to a column-and-a-half on the front page, with a picture of the Croisée ornamented with arrows showing which way each person had gone, and pictures of Thelma (in her dancing costume) and her lover Boland.

On August 21st – acting "on information received" – the police came with a search-warrant to the tapia house in Ramkissoon Trace.

The police had a brief moment of exultation when they thought the case was already solved. From among the clothes – Boland's and Thelma's – they pulled out a shirt stained with what looked like blood. Boland's explanation was unconvincing in the extreme. He had, he claimed, gone to Laventille – one of the hills outside Port of Spain where Boysie had run a whe-whe school – in order to pray. These prayers must have taken a form rather odd for a faithful sheep of the Pilgrim Holiness flock, for they involved the cutting of a branch from a "blood-sapped tree" – several West Indian trees do in fact bleed a viscous, reddish sap – and the shirt must have got stained in the course of this ritual. The police exchanged knowing looks and took it to the office of the Government Analyst. But their triumph was premature; analysis revealed that, whatever the stain was, it wasn't blood.

There can be nothing more unnerving in a police investigation than to imagine one has found positive proof of some person's guilt, only to find that the evidence is quite valueless. The natural human reaction is to suppose that one has made a mistake and the person is in fact innocent. But the man in charge of the case – Superintendent Leslie Slater, now Assistant Commissioner of Police – was not so easily discouraged; he continued to keep Boland under surveillance.

It was here that Boland made his fatal mistake. If he had had the presence of mind to act naturally and go on acting naturally, it is more than likely that he would have escaped detection and be living – with Boysie – to this day. For after all there was nothing tangible against him. The photograph which showed him with Boysie did not in itself constitute evidence, though it might give a strong indication of guilt. He did not benefit in any obvious way from Thelma's death, and all the available evidence seemed to indicate that they had been on good terms until the day of the disappearance. There was nothing the police could do except hope for one of two things: that some new piece of evidence would turn up, or that Boland, given enough rope, would eventually hang himself.

This he proceeded to do.

The trouble with Boland was that his personality was unstable. He could not stand up to the knowledge that everything he did was noted and reported by the watching police. He began to dream.

His dreams took a strange form. They revealed to him what had happened to Thelma – a revelation so startling that he felt obliged to take it to the San Juan Police Station the next day.

"Let us go to Waller Field" (an abandoned U.S. military airfield, favoured resort of car-burning thieves), "I think they have part of Thelma's body buried there," he told them. The police were sceptical, but they took him by car down the Churchill-Roosevelt highway till they reached the Mausica River. There Boland told them to stop. If they searched, he told them, they would find the body hidden somewhere among the feathery bamboos that bordered the river.

The police searched among the bamboos for some time, but without result. Their suspicions deepened; they kept Boland under closer watch than before.

On September 5th, Boland spoke to Police Constable Ethelbert Atwell. He seems to have met Atwell, whom he knew slightly, quite by chance, but he did not hesitate to unburden himself; he had developed an irresistible impulse to speak to any policemen he saw, whenever and wherever he saw them. His earlier statement had been pointless enough, but what he said now was suicidal folly.

He told Atwell that Boysie had killed Thelma.

The only explanation one can give of his action is that his nerve had broken under a fortnight of police suspicion. Probably he did not realise that fish and decay by that time would have left nothing of Thelma that could be identified; he must still have feared that her body would rise to confute him with its "silent testimony", and that his only hope of safety lay in accusing someone else. Anyhow, he told Atwell that a "short black man" had helped Boysie kill her and "cut her entrails"; they had then taken her out to sea and dumped her. How he had obtained this information he did not say.

P.C. Atwell hurried to give this information to his superiors, and Superintendent Slater went to have a few words with Boysie.

As soon as he learnt Slater's business, Boysie realised not merely that

Boland Ramkissoon emerging exhausted from the mangrove swamp near Cocorite after his unsuccessful search for his missing mistress Thelma Haynes.

Harbour police dragging for Thelma Haynes corpse off the north-west coast of Trinidad.

Boland had betrayed him, but that unless he did something quickly Boland would escape justice altogether and he, Boysie, would pay the penalty alone. There seemed only one course open to him, and that was to repay the betrayal with interest. He immediately produced a pair of trousers, a gold wrist watch and two gold rings. These, he said, had been given him by Boland on the morning of July 31st. Boland had asked him to look after the watch and rings and to have the trousers washed. Boysie had noticed that there was blood on the front of the trousers, but added, with the feigned innocence he was so fond of assuming, that he "thought it was the blood of an animal or bird." He had therefore got one of his relatives to wash the trousers for Boland.

Slater took the articles and set in motion further enquiries, particularly in stores which sold jewellery and watches.

Boland did not seem content even now that the police had switched their attention to Boysie. On September 8th he made a further statement, this time to Police Constable Clarence Basarath, the purpose of which seemed to be to place the blame still more squarely on his partner's shoulders. Boysie, he said, had described himself as "King of the Sea and Rajah of the Land"; he had added that he made "an annual sacrifice to the sea to remain in good health" – Thelma being the sacrifice for 1956. Boland went still further and said he was now ready to give the whole story of how Thelma had died.

It had happened as follows. On the evening of July 30th he had indeed met Thelma in San Juan – contrary to the original statement he had made to P.C. Bobb – for he had arranged to go with her and visit her aunt, a Mrs. Ashmead, who lived in the suburb of Diego Martin. Diego is some twelve miles from San Juan by road, and lies on the far, western side of the capital. Boland and Thelma had therefore taken a taxi (public transport is virtually nonexistent in Trinidad) and travelled into Port of Spain. As they drove through the city the taxi was hailed by Boysie, who claimed to be going to his old base of operations Cocorite (which also lies on the San Juan-Diego Martin road).

When the taxi reached Cocorite, Boysie told the driver to stop and asked Boland to help him with a parcel which he had (presumably) put in the boot. Boland and Thelma both got out. No sooner had they done so than a man appeared from the shadows and seized Thelma from behind, locking his arm about her throat so that she could not cry out. The gallant Boland then rushed to Thelma's defence, but was prevented by Boysie, who pulled a gun on him and ordered him to keep quiet. Human sacrifice, it appeared, was not Boysie's only motive in disposing of Thelma; he had a solid cash inducement in the shape of $500 from Boland's wife, Dorothy, who had told Boysie that "she didn't want any negro woman to make style on her". Boysie and his accomplice had then laid Thelma (still alive) in a boat – "Oh

God!" she had said as they lifted her on board – and put out to sea; that was the last Boland had seen of her.

He had kept silent about the whole affair, he told Basarath, because he was afraid of Boysie and his gang. If he talked to the police they would kill him too. This was the explanation for all the curious twists and turns he had made since the disappearance.

In support of his story, Boland claimed that he had had further dreams about the present position of the body, this time indicating that it had been washed ashore somewhere between Cocorite and the Yacht Club, around the mouth of the Diego Martin river. He seemed so convinced of this that on the following day a police officer, Corporal James, was despatched with him to search the coast at Cocorite.

On the way there his manner seemed more than usually nervous. Turning to James, he asked, "Suppose we see Singh guarding the place?" "What is man that thou art fearful of him?" the Corporal replied with dignity, a retort to which the evangelical Boland could find no answer.

West of Cocorite the coast is mangrove – a foreshore backed with hundreds of yards of mud, puddled with stagnant, brackish pools, haunted by land-crabs of every shape and size. From the mud rise the mangroves, stunted, twisted trees seldom rising more than eight or ten feet, but with their corky buttress-roots merging into an impenetrable tangle of tough, finger-thick strands. Into this desolation Boland, followed by the faithful James, half-walked, half-waded. The hours passed, the sun declined, but still he searched on, his singlet and shorts soaked in sweat, his legs mired to the thighs with the viscous silvery-grey mud. While he searched he kept crying out, "Oh my wife, Thelma my wife, I love her." But there was no trace of Thelma's body. All he could find were a few pieces of cloth and a piece of nylon, almost colourless through long immersion in water and mud, which he claimed had formed part of the clothes Thelma had been wearing on the night of her disappearance. At last, after five hours, Corporal James had had enough; but Boland, exhausted as he was, refused to give up the search, and had to be dragged bodily from the water by the impatient police. The latter now had almost too much to go on; the two suspects were doing all their work for them. Both stories could not be true, and it seemed more than likely that neither was true, for each of Boland's statements had served merely to contradict the last. Moreover, the inquiries among the Port of Spain jewellers were already bearing fruit, and other witnesses were coming forward. On September 11th both Boysie and Boland were arrested.

They took Boysie in the Crystal Palace restaurant in San Juan. There was a billiard room behind the restaurant, and Boysie was playing billiards – a sport he had taken up since his last prison sentence – when the police came for him. As befitted Boysie, his opponent was no ordinary player, but Slim

Sahadar, currently billiards champion of Trinidad. Boysie had just asked Slim to go out and buy him a CC Mel, a type of malted drink popular in the West Indies. He got back with it just in time to see Boysie stepping into the police car. "I had to drink the CC Mel myself," Slim said disconsolately. Boysie was taken to Police Headquarters in St. Vincent Street and lodged in the cell next to Boland.

What happened next was an act of folly so fantastic it would be hardly credible if it were not confirmed by so many independent witnesses. No sooner had the key turned in the cell lock than Boysie began a shouted conversation with neighbour Boland. First he abused Boland for having betrayed him, then advised him that his only hope was to swear that the statements he had made had been extracted by third-degree methods. The police, he went on, had not found and never would find Thelma's body, so that if only Boland would withdraw what he had said they would both be invulnerable. All this was carried on in a tone so loud that he could be heard, not merely by the police in the corridor – who, scarcely able to believe their luck, were industriously taking it all down – but by ordinary citizens walking in the street outside Police Headquarters. What made Boysie behave in this way it is impossible to tell; one can only assume that illness and poverty had sapped his judgement and anger at Boland's weakness overcame what little was left of it.

While Boysie and Boland were held on remand, the police continued their search for the missing girl. Police launches patrolled to and fro, dragging the shallow waters off Cocorite and Chaguaramas, but without success. They were looking in the wrong place, though they were not to know that.

At the preliminary hearing, despite the submission of defence counsel Hyatali and Johnston that there was no proof that a crime had occurred and therefore no case to answer, both the accused were committed for trial at the next assizes.

27: THE FINAL VERDICT

THE TRIAL of Boland Ramkissoon, 27, lifeguard, and Boysie Singh, alias the Rajah, 48, fisherman, for the murder of Thelma Haynes, began in the Central Criminal Court before Mr. Justice F. J. Camacho on February 4th, 1957. This time Mr. C. T. W. E. Worrell was not there to lead for the Crown; in the interval between Boysie's murder trials he had died in hospital, after a long illness. His place was taken by Mr. Malcolm Butt, Q.C., assisted by Mr. Ralph Hercules. Mr. Isaac Hyatali (Goggins' counsel in the Floating Corpse case) represented Boland, while Boysie was defended by the junior of the two counsel who had represented him in his last murder trial – Mr. Edgar Gaston Johnston.

Once again the crowds swarmed round the Red House to catch a glimpse of the accused, and the daily report of the proceedings filled two or three pages of the *Trinidad Guardian*. The accused was the first to be tried a third time for murder; the case was the first murder-without-a-corpse in the British Caribbean; the crime was the first of Boysie's in which a woman was involved. All these facts added to the news value of the trial; but the last-named seemed the most potent to the press, who unanimously described it as the "Case of the Missing Dancer".

The crowd round the court contained far fewer sympathisers than that which had collected during the "Floating Corpse" case. In the six years that had passed since his acquittal – nearly half of them spent in custody – Boysie had experienced what is experienced by anyone, respectable or disreputable, who falls suddenly from power or riches. Now that there were no more raises, no more reflected glories to be won by being seen in his company, his hangers-on had deserted him, and those who had reluctantly admired his success now felt only contempt for his failure. No longer was he the gangster king with his new suit for each day of his trial – a living advertisement that crime did pay if you were smart enough; the face glimpsed briefly through the glass of the police car carrying him to the Red House was marked with the lines of penury and disease, and, though the deep-set eyes blazed almost as fiercely as before, all the fine plumage was gone.

He took his place in the dock next to Boland. "Well-groomed," a *Guardian* reporter wrote that day, "Ramkissoon wore a smartly tailored light-blue gabardine suit, white shirt and matching tie." His soft, rounded face – the face of a man who gives way too easily to his emotions – seemed "tired, expressionless", and wore a "dreamy faraway look". He presented a vivid contrast, in both clothes and deportment, to his fellow-defendant. Boysie wore "A well-worn cream shirt showing his hairy chest, and sporty flannel trousers." His manner, however, was "calm and concentrated". The proceedings opened with a long legal argument, for Johnston and Hyatali submitted that the two accused should be tried separately. Mr. Justice Camacho, however, considered that the interests of justice would best be served by a joint trial.

The Crown case was that Boland and Boysie, acting in concert, had conspired to murder Boland's mistress. Although no body could be produced, there was in the Crown's opinion no question that Thelma had been killed; in fact, the very method chosen by the accused was designed precisely to preclude any possibility of the body being found. Thelma was last seen alive on July 30th, 1956; witnesses would be called who would testify that she had been with Boland in San Juan that evening; proof would be forthcoming that Boysie and Boland not merely knew each other but were on intimate terms; the articles handed by Boysie to Superintendent Slater would be shown to be identical with those worn by Thelma at the time of her disappearance; and all these proofs were quite independent of the statements by the two accused incriminating one another, and, in Boland's, actually indicating the means by which Thelma had been killed and the reason why her body had never been recovered.

Any prosecution which is unable to produce the victim's body labours under obvious difficulties. Not only is it unable to state the cause of death, and unable therefore to build up the chain of evidence that so often leads through the murder weapon to a clear indication of the guilty party, but there must inevitably exist in the minds of all those present – particularly the jury, on whom alone the fatal responsibility rests – the thought that, after a verdict of guilty and the execution, the supposed victim might suddenly turn up alive and well. A jury in such a case might be understandably anxious to avoid the irrevocable.

In the Case of the Missing Dancer, however, the Crown had almost everything except a body. It was not surprising that the defence rested its main arguments on the impossibility of proving that the crime had been committed; for, if it had been committed, there could have been little doubt in anyone's mind that Boland and Boysie had committed it.

First witness was Neville Butler, who had snapped Boland on his luckless errand of mercy to Boysie's hospital bedside. There was nothing the defence could do about that. Bertram Dufont, the Lifeguard Supervisor, then came forward to give details of Boland's working life. Boland had apparently complained to him also about his financial difficulties; the $32 maintenance he paid Dorothy was too much, he had said, for a man of his limited income. After giving details of the lifeguards' daily routine, he confirmed that from the evening of the 30th July to the morning of the 5th August Boland had been absent from work. Cross-examined by Hyatali, he admitted that Boland had provided a medical certificate, but the prosecution's inference was obvious; that Boland's sickness had been faked to cover up the state of nervous shock into which Thelma's murder had thrown him.

The next two witnesses tied Boysie into the plot. Clifford Smith told how on July 26th Boysie had come to him for a boat and engine; his account of the incident was confirmed by Cletus Millington, a carpenter who had been present during the interview. Defence counsel tried to shake their version of the incident without success; in this trial there were none of the lapses of memory so common in the Floating Corpse case, and the prosecution had not to rely on so many witnesses of doubtful character.

Most telling of the witnesses against Boland was Milton Rigoux. Neither their former friendship nor Milton's religious principles prevented him from entering the witness-box and giving a long and detailed account of all that had passed between them on the subject of Thelma. He now claimed that, before the decision to "put away" Thelma was taken, Boland had boasted of his friendship with Boysie and claimed that he could at any time call on Boysie's assistance to get rid of Thelma, or Dorothy, or Dorothy's lover, or all three if need be. This would seem the most dubious part of Milton's testimony, for it sorts ill with the high religious tone of their usual conversation; but to one as unstable as Boland any kind of conduct was possible, and it was not a matter that the defence could very well disprove.

Eventually, Milton confirmed, it was Thelma Boland decided to put away "to please the scriptures". He went on to the fatal 30th, recalling Boland's odd behaviour and the invitation to the Sacred Concert: Milton had turned up at that concert, as arranged, but Boland never came; while waiting for him, however, Milton claimed to have seen Boysie passing by.

The defence tried to undermine Milton's testimony by attacking his religious pretensions. How long had he been a member of the Pentecostal Church? About two years. And before that? Nothing. Nothing? Surely he must have had a religion of some sort? Mohammedan, Buddhist, Confucian? "That's right, I was a confusion," Milton cracked back.

Evidence of seeing Boland in San Juan was given by fellow-lifeguard Derryl and Mrs. French. Cross-examining her, Hyatali sought to establish another of the defence's points, the absence of motive. Was it not a fact that Boland and Thelma had been on the best of terms? Mrs. French had to admit that they had; she had never known them to quarrel, they were always "loving and nice".

But the most conclusive evidence for the prosecution was provided by the eleventh witness, Richard Hugo Gittens. Gittens was now a draughtsman, but previously he had worked as a salesman in the watch and clock department of a Port of Spain store. A gold watch was produced in court and shown to him. Had he seen it before? He had. He had himself sold that watch in 1954. To whom? Thelma Haynes.

It was in fact the watch which Boysie had given to Slater, saying that Boland had given it him to keep.

Another of Boland's neighbours followed Gittens. This was Mrs. Matilda Charles, another neighbour of Boland's, who had seen Thelma at 5.30 on the afternoon of the 30th. She was also shown the watch, together with two gold rings, and stated that Thelma had been wearing both watch and rings just before she set out to meet Boland.

The rest of the evidence was perhaps less damning, but impressive in its sheer quantity. Altogether twenty-one witnesses were called by the prosecution. Other lifeguards and residents of San Juan testified to Boland's movements on the 30th. According to lifeguard Kelvin Herbert, Boland had said quite openly he intended to meet Thelma in San Juan that evening. A man called Ezekiel Samuel had actually seen them together there. In fact Boland could hardly have got more publicity for his movements if he had hired a brass band to accompany him. Yet just after six he, too, it seemed, had disappeared, not to surface again until his visit to P.C. Babb in the San Juan police station four hours later.

What had happened in those four hours was never satisfactorily established. Boland claimed he had been searching for Thelma, but no one had seen him doing this, and if he had already met Thelma, as Samuel had stated, it was pretty obviously untrue. The Prosecution claimed he had spent the time murdering Thelma and presumably helping Boysie to dispose of the body, but as to where or how the murder had been committed they remained silent; on this point the only evidence they had was Boland's accusation of Boysie, and they could only leave the jury to assume that something similar to his account of the crime had actually happened, though with Boland as willing participant instead of shocked but impotent observer.

Indeed the link between Boland and Boysie was still tenuous; so far it existed only in Thelma's ornaments, for try as the prosecution might, they could not make out that to visit a man in hospital or borrow a fishing boat were evidence of conspiracy, let alone criminal intent. But now there took the stand a man whose testimony, if true, materially strengthened that link; Mookoot Maraj, who described himself as a restaurant-keeper with premises in George Street, not far from Boysie's old stamping-ground in downtown Port of Spain. He had, it was said, a still closer connection with Boysie, for he was married to Boysie's niece, and had been chosen to pass on to Boysie the pay-off for the crime.

His story was that early in August, not long after Thelma's disappearance, Boysie had called at the restaurant and Maraj had overheard him talking to his niece. Boysie had told her he had done "a big job for a man for small money". A few days later Boland had called and left an envelope with $60 in it. This was to be given to Boysie the next time he called.

The rest of the prosecution consisted of police testimony. Despite the objections of the defence, all of the numerous and frequently conflicting statements made at various times by both accused were admitted as evidence. Superintendent Slater told of receiving the watch, rings and trousers from Boysie. He had to admit, however, that the trousers (which like Boland's shirt had been analysed for bloodstains) had, also like the shirt, proved innocent of human blood. Either the washing had been unusually thorough, or Boysie's story was rubbish. Before the result of the analysis was known, Slater had confronted Boland with the trouser story, and Boland, perhaps from a desire to embroil Boysie still further, declared that Boysie, while holding him at gunpoint on the shore at Cocorite, had ordered him to take off his trousers and had then thrown him another pair which he was forced to put on. The pair he had given to Boysie was the pair Boysie gave to Slater.

Presumably Boland's intention was to show that Boysie had deliberately tried to incriminate him. But all that emerged from this treble- and quadruple-crossing was a growing conviction in the minds of the jury that the two accused were equally involved and equally guilty.

P.C. Basarath followed his superior officer and gave Boland's original account of the crime, while further statements from Boland were recounted by two other constables. Their evidence concluded the case for the prosecution.

There was little that the defence could do to refute the facts that had been set out. Against the prosecution's twenty-one witnesses they called only three, and one of these had his testimony ruled inadmissible. Neither Johnston nor Hyatali allowed his client to take the stand or even to make a statement from the dock.

It was a wise decision; their conflicting statements had laid both of them wide open to a skilled cross-examiner, while the unstable, over-emotional Boland was just the type to break down completely under pressure. Besides, they could easily be made to attack one another, and, as the mainstay of the defence was the assertion that no crime had been proved, it would hardly do to have both defendants, by their mutual accusations, tacitly admitting that one had.

But this left them only the evidence of Boysie's niece and Harry Persad.

The former came out with a forthright denunciation of her husband. She had, she admitted, been married to him for twenty years, but that was as far as their connection went. For several years they had been separated.

Mookoot, whom she described as a loafer and a liar, came only rarely to the restaurant – which was her property, anyway, not his – and then merely to cadge money from her. It was not true that Boysie had used the words Mookoot alleged, nor had Boland left money at the restaurant; moreover, as Mookoot was no longer resident, he was hardly likely to have known what went on there.

Persad's evidence was just as forthright. He too, by an odd coincidence, owned a restaurant – indeed the catering profession was almost as fully represented in this trial as that of night-watchman in the Floating Corpse case. His restaurant, however, was in San Fernando, second largest town in the island, and by all accounts he was a fairly substantial citizen there. Persad stated that he had visited Boysie in Boysie's home at San Juan on the afternoon of the 30th. When he arrived there, at 4 p.m., he found Boysie ill in bed. Persad remained at the house until 8.30 the following morning, and Boysie was there all that time. He was vigorously cross-examined by the prosecution, but refused to give an inch; nor was it possible to discredit his character. His record was good and he had no convictions. Butt did however extract one crumb of comfort; Persad turned out to be Boysie's cousin.

No alibi could be established for Boland; on his own admission he had been wandering round San Juan in search of Thelma. The only other witness the defence called was David Prescod, whose articles had first focused public attention on the Missing Dancer. By a curious blunder – the subpoena was made out, not in Prescod's name, but for "the crime reporter of the *Trinidad Guardian*", and Prescod was on holiday at the time – the wrong man appeared in court, and the mistake was not discovered until he had actually been sworn. The next day Prescod himself appeared. The defence had intended to ask him certain questions about the sources of reports which he had written in the *Guardian*, particularly those which dealt with what Thelma had worn on the night of her disappearance. But the prosecution objected, and after a prolonged legal argument, Mr. Justice Camacho ruled that newspaper reports were not admissible as evidence.

Johnston and Hyatali spoke in turn for the accused. They contended that no person should be called upon to answer a charge of murder unless proof of the *corpus delicti* was furnished either by direct evidence – the presence of the victim's body – or on "irresistible grounds of presumption". These grounds they claimed, did not exist in this case. There was no body. No blood had been found on any of the clothes of the accused or on Thelma's jewellery, the only belongings of the missing girl – except for the scraps found by Boland among the mangroves, which were anyway of doubtful identification – which had so far been recovered. Moreover it was quite possible that Thelma had disappeared of her own free will.

She had been born, not in Trinidad, but in British Guiana. It was quite possible that she had gone back to her native land, for no enquiries had been made there. Admittedly her passport had been found in the tapia house, but that was not conclusive proof that she was still in the island. Everyone knew that there were ways of avoiding the immigration laws – Boysie most of all, Johnston might well have added.

Johnston also echoed Boysie's familiar claim that the police were out to "get" him. Some of Boland's statements, he alleged, had been obtained by unfair means for precisely this purpose – at one time he seemed even to be hinting that the police had promised Boland immunity if he gave evidence against Boysie, and had later retracted this promise. Finally there was the absence of motive, which, though in itself not conclusive, tended – when taken in conjunction with the absence of a body – to bear out the defence contention that no crime had taken place.

On the eighteenth and last day of the trial Mr. Justice Camacho summed up.

He referred to the extensive press reports of the trial. "Learned counsel for the accused called attention in his address to the streaming headlines in the papers which he says aroused public passion and prejudice. He went so far, gentlemen, as to say that the headlines and reports of evidence in the press were unprecedented." Camacho expressed his confidence that the jury would not allow their decision to be influenced in any way by this publicity.

Next he dealt with the absence of the victim's corpse. Having explained the law to the jury he told them categorically, "There *can* be a conviction for prosecution of murder if no body has been found." All that was necessary was for the jury to decide whether the facts set before them could be accounted for by any rational hypothesis other than murder. If there was no other possible explanation they were fully entitled to bring in a verdict of guilty, body or no body. They would, of course, first have to be satisfied beyond reasonable doubt that the missing girl was dead. The defence had suggested that Thelma might be in British Guiana, and that possibility would have to be considered; but, referring again to the publicity the case had received, not only in Trinidad, but throughout the Caribbean, he asked whether anyone could seriously believe that Thelma, if still alive, had not heard of the proceedings, or, if she had heard of them, would not have immediately come forward.

The jury withdrew. Boland looked restless and unhappy; Boysie maintained his air of calm composure. But this time there was little doubt as to what the verdict would be. There were none of the demonstrations that had followed the Floating Corpse retrial verdict, no weeping women or applauding men, when the jury returned at last to find both the accused guilty of murder.

Mr. Justice Camacho turned to Boysie. Had he anything to say before sentenced was passed upon him?

He had. More in sorrow than in anger he rose and said, "I am very happy, my lord, standing here again and given the privilege to say something to the people. I have observed that you done your best in your summation and the gentlemen of the jury also. You will find that I am a man with a very large reputation in this country. And where a man goes out in a launch and take a hook and put a piece of bait on it and after a while when he takes the hook back up from the water the bait is gone, he can only say that a shark has taken it away.

"I am a land shark. Nothing happens in this country that is not put on me. Whether I am sick in bed, whether I am dead or out to sea, they will say it is me, Boysie Singh."

The police, he said, were "tyrants existing in this country (who) have the country corrupted. For wanting promotion they will do anything in this country... God bless the Englishmen! They sent two English Commissioners down here some time ago and they found out that Trinidad had so much corruption... I was placed on trial before... I spent twenty-one months in gaol waiting trial. After it was told to me that the police had gone away with my wife. That was well-known all over Trinidad."

Coming back at last to Thelma, he said, "I am prepared to face death. I am not afraid of anything because I know my conscience is free and my hands are clean... No one saw me with this girl. I don't know whether she is black, white, yellow, pink or red. But there you are! They say Boysie Singh killed she!"

He sat down, and for the second time in his life saw a judge drape on the stylized convolutions of his wig, the little square of black silk so oddly miscalled a cap; for the second time heard that judge pronounce sentence of death upon him.

Mr. Justice Camacho then turned to Boland. Had he anything to say? Almost in tears, Boland addressed the court. "I do not believe in this whole world. I, Boland Ramkissoon, who has saved sixty-four lives, stand in this court convicted of something I know nothing of. I know nothing of it, nothing at all!" He too was sentenced to death.

Once more crowds were surging round the Red House. Throughout the trial public feeling had run strongly against Boysie; on the fourth day a mob of schoolboys had tried to storm the car which carried Boysie and Boland to court, and, every day after that, howling children had surrounded the building and greeted each appearance of the accused with treble screams of loathing. This sinister chorus gave some indication of how, in the years of eclipse, Boysie's reputation had developed. Doubtless many of those who shrieked childish abuse at the fallen gang-leader had had him presented to them, when they were naughty, as a menacing ogre – if you do that again I'll let Boysie Singh take you. At last the ogre was in their power, and they could take their revenge on him.

But the crowd which now smashed through the police cordon was composed mainly of adults, and the police could wade into it, truncheons swinging, without compunction. They cleared a path to the waiting van, and Boland and Boysie were off on their final journey.

28: THE LAST DAYS OF BOYSIE

BOYSIE WAS SENTENCED to death on February 25th, 1957. But he still had nearly six months to live.

On March 1st both defence counsel applied for leave to appeal and this was granted. Two months passed before the Trinidad Court of Appeal – which on this occasion consisted of Sir Joseph Mathieu Perez, Chief Justice, Mr. Justice Archer and Mr. Justice Watkin-Williams – met to consider the case. Chief grounds for the appeal were misdirection and the judge's refusal to grant a separate trial.

If Boysie hoped for a repetition of the Floating Corpse verdict, he was in for a disappointment. On May 6th his appeal was dismissed. The court held that there was no substance in the criticism of Mr. Justice Camacho's summing-up, and declared themselves satisfied "after close and critical analysis of the evidence that the discretion of the Judge in refusing a separate trial was correctly exercised in the interests of justice."

There was one last hope; an appeal to the Privy Council in London. Both men's funds were long since exhausted, so that the appeal had to be made *in forma pauperis;* owing to the unusual nature of the murder this privilege was granted. In July 1957 the case was heard by the Judicial Committee of the Privy Council, consisting of Lord Jowitt, Lord Denning and Lord Cohen. Grounds were the same as in the Trinidad Court of Appeal, with the additional one that the circumstantial evidence adduced in the original trial was not sufficient to link either defendant conclusively to the murder.

After due consideration, however, this appeal also was dismissed.

So Boysie's last chance of life had vanished. Oddly enough, while he still maintained his innocence, he no longer seemed to feel bitterness, either towards his gaolers, the police, or those whose testimony had secured his conviction. Some at least of this unwonted resignation may have been due to his failing health. Even if he had been acquitted, it seems unlikely that he would have lived much longer; rheumatism, diabetes and gonorrhoea had between them ruined his strong body, and he had never spared himself either exertion or indulgence. During this last sojourn in prison he was ill with increasing frequency. "I have to be thankful," he wrote in the diary which he now began to keep, "for Mr. Munro Dept Commiss comming to my cell on Monday 15th of July 1957 when I was lying on my bed with fever then I compliant to him that my bowels did not move for 6 days. Which was complaining about before."

He received the news of his approaching death with a composure which contrasts oddly with the frantic rage he had shown after his previous death sentence. Yet perhaps it was a natural enough reaction. On the first occasion he had been at the height of his power when he was struck down; he had lost the world; but now there was so little to lose, nothing but a life of increasing pain and privation, with no hope of relief except in death. "I read in the Gurdian [sic]," he wrote on August 14th, "that I am to Hang I felt happy. Death is a sweet thing to me. If you read the life of Josep [sic] in Genesis from Chp. 37 to Chp. 50 v. 20. You all think evil against me. And out of evil cometh good."

It is not clear what he saw in the life of Joseph that he connected with his own life. Was it that Joseph, too, had been imprisoned? In what way had Boysie returned good for evil? The pages of Genesis are starred with the familiar ragged crosses and gnomic comments, but the passages marked – the story of Onan, the dreams of the butler and baker in Pharoah's prison, the embalming of Jacob, even the fact that Pharoah speaking to Joseph "called him in the Egyptian tongue" – seem to indicate merely the wanderings of a mind too unsettled by thoughts of the past and doubts and fears of the future to attend very closely to what it was studying.

His behaviour throughout these months was generally docile and co-operative. As in his previous spells in prison he studied the Bible and gave moral lectures to his fellow prisoners. Much of his time was spent in going over the events of his life in a mood which fluctuated strangely between complacency and remorse. At one moment he might be writing smugly of his "Fire Jobe" or "Paricey days"; at another he might think self-pityingly of the long-ago whipping for kite-flying which, he claimed, began his career of crime; at a third he might express his repentance in a tone which, despite his other attitudes, somehow carries conviction. "Thank God that I knew when I had to Die. That I had time to Prepare for my Death. Some people die. and never have the time to say Oh God." Three or four days later he confessed, "Son, I have offended God most Greaveous… I whent back and join my hands with Wicked Persons. I must be punished by God and this is my Portion."

In this latter mood old grievances were forgotten or ignored. He wrote affectionately of Doris: "She was a very good wife to me If I had taken her Advice I would Be a better man… my wife told me that if I leave the life I am living and my Friends and live a different life I will be a better man And she said if I sick she will Work and mind me."

Even the warders came in for this new benevolence. "All the officers where very kind to me in all my Trials until my Execution … the officers are well Train men. And all the officers are Polite and Nice to all Prisoners... Though I am in the condemn cell I was never Hungry nor had I ever one day to beg bread." Could this have been a calculated piece of hypocrisy, meant to curry favour with the prison staff? Perhaps; and yet such an action would have been just as much out of character – his previous character – as genuine praise.

Once or twice traces of the old Boysie peeped through. "Public enemy No. 1 is dead," he wrote with smug irony. "I only hope there will be no missing Person in Trinidad." But the most constant threads in his diary are his readiness for death and the deep affection which he felt for his son Chuncie. "Son you must go to Church," he wrote. "Pray to God go often as you can to Church. God will bless you. You is a very good son but I made you Shame manny Times. Son I leave my blessing from God to you. I pray God he will send his angel to guide you and keep you upon this earth. from evil I leave my kisses and Love for you my son."

Although he mentioned several of his crimes – even referring to the "Big fight" twenty-five years before in which Leach the gambler had died – he was careful to avoid definite admission of any of his murders. Perhaps he still hoped for clemency. But at last he realised that there was no possibility of a reprieve. "Son when they read the Dead Warrant to me it was on a friday at 4 PM on clock and Rain began to fall with dark clouds." Only a couple of days before the date scheduled for his execution, he applied through his lawyers to the Governor, requesting that he be allowed to dictate his full life story, with a complete confession of his crimes, to his son. This last request, strangely enough, was refused him. The Governor, Sir Edward Betham Beetham, K.C.M.G., C.V.O., O.B.E., giving reasons for his decision, stated that he had taken it in case Boysie might implicate innocent persons, who, once he was dead, would have no means of clearing themselves. The cynical were quick to find other, less charitable explanations; that if Boysie told the whole story he might reveal the names of highly-placed persons who had been involved in his criminal activities; that he might produce chapter and verse of police corruption which would include the names of high-ranking officers who had at one time or another received bribes from him.

Boysie took the news stoically. He had hoped to be able to leave his son a full account of his crimes, which would, he believed, realise a substantial sum and ensure that Chuncie would never be tempted by poverty to imitate his father's career. Still, he had confided most of the facts to Chuncie already, and perhaps the latter would write his life-story. "Son," he said in his diary, "you will Put in the Life of P.O.S. Yankey days. Paricey days. Preaching days. Glamour days. Fishing days. Fighting days. Prison days."

He signed it with his long, scrawling, palsied signature, and then closed the diary for ever.

Nothing remained now but the last few hours of waiting. These he bore

From Boysie Singh to my Son
When I was Sixc years old
I Was Flying kite and Back
into a Paile of ashes next fire Behind the
Pomping station Then I Walk home
at albertha St. no 10 I was treated
by my Mother.
From 1950 When I was
arrested 1950. 25 to Aprual
I used to Pray but not Sin-
cerelyon till 6th of December
1950 I used look Through
the iron bars in the cells
and Pray to the virgin
Lady to take me to jesus
that I shauld be given
a chance of my life that chance Was
given to me

The first page of Boysie Singh's prison diary, written while under sentence of death for the murder of Thelma Haynes

Son I have offended God
most Greavious
on my Last trial I Prayed
very hard for freedom
I got it.
In Prison D.2: No.2 cell
I saw Jesus Leading me
out of Prison.
I also saw Jesus again
in No10 cell.
~~I Prayed~~ on the Right
side of the Sun.
When it riseing ~~in~~
on the side of the Sun
~~thin~~ was a klock of
moorowne colour
and Jesus was going into
the block

Boysie's own acount of his "mystical experience" while under sentence of death.

with the same icy composure he had shown during the trial; but now he had help that had ever been denied to him. Ever since his marriage to Doris the Catholic faith had loomed, huge and vague, cloudily understood, on the periphery of his life. Now, in his last prison sojourn, he asked for and was given instruction in that faith from the prison chaplain, Father Tiernan. On the very eve of his execution he was received into the Catholic Church.

The morning of August 20th dawned at last. Mornings are very calm, very still in Trinidad; no wind stirs the air, air that is cool after the long night, and the sky is almost always a placid blue, barred near the eastern horizon with dove-coloured cloud. This morning was no exception, though little of its clear light penetrated to the cell in the Royal Gaol where Boysie was waiting. The hangman was waiting also; for him the day was indeed fortunate; Boland was to die as well as Boysie, and for the double execution he would draw double pay, $144 – more than Boland had earned in a month, guarding life, though less than Boland had offered Boysie for his fatal services. And outside the gaol, the crowds were waiting, dark in the morning light like the shabby black vultures that scavenge the outskirts of the city; their faces, bored, impatient, death-loving, greedy, all turned with a strange longing towards the prison walls.

Feet sounded in the corridor; a key turned in the lock of Boysie's cell. He looked up to see the warders, the Prison Governor, Father Tiernan. Suddenly with a flash of the old Boysie, the Boysie who had to lead at whatever the price, he said, "I want to go first – I'm not afraid, I'll take it like a hero." They made way for him, and he walked unassisted to the place of execution. He did not speak again. Only the low drone of the priest's voice could be heard; then the trap sprung, the rope jerked tight, and Boysie, Pirate of the Gulf, most ruthless of murderers, died in a state of grace, having received the last sacraments.

But the story was not quite over. The crowd outside did not leave after the execution; they stayed on until the hearse that was to carry the bodies to the General Hospital drove out through the prison gates, and as it drove they streamed after it, screaming and running, struggling to climb on board. On reaching the hospital, the attendants tried to get the two coffins to the mortuary, but the crowd poured in after them, and among the stacked corpses and smells of formaldehyde a macabre battle took place: the mob fighting for a last sight of the hanged men, police and hospital orderlies fighting to prevent them. At last they were driven out, and some semblance of order restored; but they did not disperse, some continued to hang round outside the hospital, while others more knowledgeable made their way towards the place of burial.

Later that day a hearse left the General Hospital and drove towards St. James's Cemetery. Here is Trinidad's Potter's Field; here the paupers and murderers are buried in unmarked graves. By the time the hearse arrived there, a crowd of several hundreds had assembled. Once more disorder broke out. As the crowd surged forward, five mounted policemen went into action; dodging the flying hooves, people crashed into one another, tripped, fell; several rolled into the open graves. Hastily a cordon was formed and the police held back the mob while Father Tiernan read the burial service. Then the gravediggers swung their spades and with the most final of all sounds the earth began to rain down upon the two coffin lids. Slowly, reluctantly, the crowd broke up. "He must have been moved by God," one bemused citizen was heard to murmur. Soon there was no one left save the police guard which had been instructed to remain in case anyone tried to remove the bodies.

Amongst the retreating crowd there were two men – David Prescod, who had first drawn attention to Thelma's disappearance, and Boysie's son. Their eyes met. They had little cause to love one another, but at that moment such things did not seem to matter. "He was not a man like you or I," Chuncie said. Then he too turned away.

Guardian Photonews

THE FINAL SCENE. – Here is the final scene in the sensational drama of Boysie "The Rajah" Singh and Boland Ramkissoon. It is the Murderers' Cemetery, St. James, where hundreds of people flocked to witness the burial of Trinidad's "historic" killers after they were hanged at the Royal Gaol. The van (right) brought their coffined bodies to this open plot of ground from the Port of Spain Mortuary where postmortem examinations were made. The eager, talkative crowd make use of every vantage point to catch a glimpse of the proceedings, while mounted policemen, almost hidden among them, hardly have room to manoeuvre.

Police guard the grave as Boysie's coffin is lowered into it.

The inset photograph is of the flowering shrub that now marks Boysie's grave in Murderers' Row.

29: PORTRAIT OF A MURDERER

IF HE WAS NOT A MAN "like you or I", what kind of a man was he?

In an ingenious study entitled "Murder by Numbers" – apparently the only one on the subject – Mr. Grierson Dickson makes out an excellent case for considering mass-murderers, or multicides as he calls them, as belonging to a category totally distinct from other types of killer. A multicide, according to his definition, must in addition to having committed the necessary number of crimes, fulfil certain other qualifications. His killings must be spaced out over a length of time – otherwise anyone who ran amok would have to be included. He must operate in a civilised community, where murder is not merely illegal but actively abhorred by society – otherwise killers in duels, blood feuds, Western gun-fights, revolutionary causes and fanatical religious movements would qualify also. He must be sane, or at least sane in a legal sense.

This reduces multicides to a select club – Mr. Dickson black-balls all but some forty-odd candidates over the whole of modern history. These he divides further into those who kill in the course of sexual perversion – Christie, or the "Monster of Dusseldorf", Kurten – and those who kill for direct financial gain – Haigh or Petiot. One of the most striking facts which emerges from his investigation is that almost all these multicides – unlike one-shot murderers, who often have clean records, or other professional criminals, who almost invariably stick to one type of crime – have criminal records dating back to adolescence or early manhood, covering a period of about twenty years, and comprising a wide variety of offences, often of a petty nature.

Now at first sight it would appear that Boysie fits in perfectly with the foregoing picture, and that his place is with murderers-for-profit of the Haigh-Petiot type. He even corresponds with Mr. Dickson's findings on the ages of multicides. Mr. Dickson finds that the first theft-convictions of murderers-for-profit take place between ages seventeen and thirty-six, with a mean figure of twenty-four. Boysie was eighteen when he was first convicted for theft. Their age at execution ranges from thirty-two to fifty-three, with an average age of forty-two. Boysie was executed at the age of forty-nine. His resemblance to Petiot is still more striking. He was a year younger than the French multicide when first convicted; the same age when he was executed.

However, if we compare Boysie somewhat more closely with Mr. Dickson's findings, a number of dissimilarities begin to emerge. "The majority of multicides," he declares, "had a consciousness of physical inferiority, which the psychiatrists reasonably argue tends to create a defensive aggressiveness." Could this be true of Boysie, undisputed boss of the toughest town in the Caribbean, a man who was never known to lose a fight? Admittedly his health had begun to deteriorate by the time his murderous career commenced, but changes of health in later life seldom if ever have the psychic impact of lifelong infirmities. The multicide, Mr. Dickson states, is "probably the product of a bad home and a fairly good education." The reverse would be truer of Boysie.

The differences between Boysie and the typical multicide become still more marked when we consider Mr. Dickson's portrait of the latter specimen. "He is probably a small, dapper, well-dressed man in his forties. He is a fairly sociable type, speaking quietly and correctly, perhaps with a trace of self-satisfaction at his own achievements, but with an undeniable charm of manner. He is abstemious, probably a teetotaller and nonsmoker, he does not swear, and the vicar of his parish probably believes him to be a good Christian... He is probably rather mean in small financial transactions... (he) is a type we are apt to meet in a shop or office, at parish whist-drive or tennis-club dance... such a horrifyingly ordinary little man that in his lack of outstanding qualities lies the secret of his success".

Apart from the nonsmoking and teetotalism it would be hard to find a description more inappropriate for Boysie.

But the most remarkable difference between Boysie and the multicides lies in nature of the killings themselves. Nearly all those committed by true mass-murderers are performed by a single person in circumstances of absolute secrecy. Sexual killers occasionally operate with a partner – Haarman and Grans, for example – but here the picture is more one of a *folie a deux* than of the master-and-man violence of Boysie and his accomplices. Almost the only profit-murderer to work in company seems to have been William Burke. But Burke's crimes were only profitable because of an anomaly in the law which was of comparatively short duration, and Burke himself was a character who had never made a success of anything; one could not compare his makeshift organisation with Boysie's smoothly efficient machine.

Clearly then one cannot classify Boysie with the Haigh-type multicides. There exist however obvious similarities between his career and the careers of classic American gangsters of the Al Capone-Dutch Schultz type. As far as organisation is concerned, the parallel is fairly accurate and quite helpful. Both Boysie and the Chicago School worked through a group of subordinates closely bound by desire for profit, need for protection, mutual guilt and fear of kangaroo justice. These groups usually conform to a pattern – the tightly-knit nucleus of regular executives, to whom all the important tasks are assigned, surrounded by an amorphous and frequently-changing body of hangers-on, who may engage in legal or illegal enterprises of their own, and who form a pool from which can be drawn operatives for specific tasks, or, more rarely, recruits for the executive group. To this pattern Boysie's mob also conformed. (It is perhaps worth noting that the rigidly-centralised gang beloved of crime-writers, controlled in its every function by some "mastermind of crime", and tricked out with oaths, passwords and suchlike flummery, has no equivalent in real life.) There is reason to believe that Boysie deliberately based his gang on what he knew of organised American crime, just as his Yankee-day clothes were based on the further-out American styles of the period. Indeed the flamboyance of dress and behaviour which marks this phase of his life is another typical characteristic of gangsterdom.

When one comes to consider the killings, however, the pattern breaks down once again. Most American gang murders derive directly from the gang's *raison d'être,* bootlegging, the numbers game, prostitution or trade union racketeering; Boysie's were quite separate from it. His organisation was formed to handle and control a chain of gambling, drink and vice clubs, and the switch to piracy represents a change of intention more radical than can be paralleled from the annals of British or American crime.

The contrast will, perhaps, be more clearly understood if we consider the victims of the respective groups. The vast majority of men killed by gangsters are other gangsters; apart from police (in emergencies) or crusading journalists, these are the only people the average gangster needs or wants to kill, for they alone are in a position to threaten his livelihood or his security. Indeed the more successful and better-organised gangs try – as Boysie in his earlier periods tried – to avoid causing any harm to the ordinary citizen; for such bodies are governed by the laws that govern all business enterprises, and good public relations can be as important to the racketeer as to the manufacturer. Boysie, however, when he took to killing, killed mainly the general public. Only the murders of Bumper and Leonard Olivera conform to gangster orthodoxy. Granted some of his victims may have been smugglers, but it was not because they were smugglers that he killed them; they had the advantage as victims that their movements were clandestine and they could the more easily disappear, but we have no evidence that he ever took this into account. Others – his clients for the chute – may have been criminals, but it was not because they were criminals that they died; they died because they had cash and easily-disposable property on them, and they could be removed without trace.

Moreover gangsters do not normally kill for direct profit; but rather to ensure already existing profits by the elimination of competition or of treachery within their own group. Boysie's pirate killings were in every case self-contained episodes; leaving aside his motive for the moment, if there had been no deaths there would have been no money.

It would not even be accurate to compare his activities to those of an organisation such as Murder Incorporated, tempting though this analogy is made by the history of his last few years. For Murder Incorporated also existed mainly to get rid of gangsters, and should be considered merely as an example of another business trend – the tendency of specialist firms to take over from larger and more general enterprises certain non-profit-making functions, such as catering, cleaning, debt-collecting, or, in this case, killing, in return for a cash-down or contract figure.

More similarity might seem to exist between Boysie's gang and the smaller, more mobile groups which specialise in crimes such as bank robbery – not to mention out-and-out bandits of the Jesse James breed. But bandits and bank-robbers, careless of civilian life as they often are, seldom set out deliberately to kill for money. Their murders are ancillary to the main purpose of the bank-raid, payroll job or armed hold-up; they do not normally kill unless they meet with resistance. None of Boysie's victims resisted, but they were killed anyway; moreover there are several facts, such as the placing of irons in the launch and the macabre jests on the outward journey, which indicate that the killing of victims was a preconceived and predetermined part of his criminal pattern.

It would seem, then, that Boysie took a type of crime – mass murder for profit – previously carried out only by the lone-wolf type of killer, and adapted to it the means and methods of Chicago-style gangsterism. If so, this alone would suffice to make him unique in the history of modern crime. Whether in fact he is as unique as he appears will be considered in a moment.

First, it is necessary to dispose of one or two points. The first concerns his sanity. When any more than normally horrible crime is committed – horrible by reason of its attendant details, or, as in this case, its sheer ruthlessness – there are always those who will insist that its author cannot be sane. On closer examination, their main reason for this belief turns out to be the particularly horrible nature of the crime. Leaving aside this circular argument we can consider the question from two viewpoints – the legal and the psychological.

Legally – at least according to the McNaughton Rules which applied at the time of his cases, and apparently still apply, throughout the West Indies – there is little doubt that Boysie was sane. The amount of planning which went into his trips proves that he knew what he was doing. As for knowing it was wrong, the law has always interpreted that less in an absolute sense than as the equivalent of "knowing-society-will-punish-you-if-it-catches-you", and Boysie's anxiety to conceal his crimes indicates that he was aware at least of this. The English law relating to diminished responsibility has been in operation for too short a time for one to be certain how Boysie would have fared under it.

Assuming he would have been willing to make such a plea – and, in the West Indies, any form of mental ill-health still carries the stigma of the snakepit – it is hard to see what evidence could have been brought in support of it. His business operations were successful enough to remove any suspicion of feeble-mindedness.

The one attempt in legal history – Haigh's; admittedly under the old law – to adduce number and weirdness of crimes as proof of insanity was a total failure; indeed it is hard to think of a single mass murderer who has escaped the supreme penalty on mental grounds, partly because of the consistent purpose which such a career implies, but also, one suspects, because most jurymen take the commonsense view that it is foolish to give such confirmed enemies of mankind the opportunity of escaping and taking up their old profession again.

To the psychiatrist, Boysie would no doubt have appeared a dangerous psychotic. This is, of course, the most difficult type for him – or anyone else – to deal with. Psychotics are usually well enough adjusted on a superficial level not to feel the need of expert assistance; indeed they often consider themselves models of sanity, and grow furious at the mere idea of medical intervention. At the same time they exhibit such pronounced and antisocial variations from the norm of human conduct that it is impossible for a psychiatrist – and hard for a layman, if he sees them in action – to consider them as in any meaningful sense of the word sane. Their danger lies precisely in this capacity to alternate between socially acceptable and socially unacceptable conduct.

Here the layman might well stop and ask, is not this simply what in less sophisticated days one used to refer to as an "evil" person? The answer is a qualified "yes"; qualified because it was then assumed that an evil person chose evil deliberately, being able if he wished to choose good, while it is nowadays assumed that a psychotic has no control over his own actions. The similarity is, however, close enough to make one wonder how much one gains by changing the terms, or whether either is particularly helpful when one is discussing an individual such as Boysie; for although both might be applied as labels, one tells us no more than the other what kind of man he really was.

It may be more profitable to begin from another angle, and consider the forces which in the first place made Boysie a criminal. We have his own account, but that, as I have suggested already, should be treated with caution. It is unlikely that a single act of injustice, however severe, would condition the development of a whole lifetime unless other pressures were being exerted in the same direction. Even if one accepts the fact that it could, two other facts must be taken into consideration; first, that even before his birching Boysie had exhibited the aggression and love of dominance which were to characterise his behaviour throughout his life, and second, that the explanation is a little too similar to the explanations he produced for his piracy (the confiscation of his boats) and his return in 1954 to "the ordinary life" (the licence conviction). He seems indeed to have been unduly fond of such self-exculpatory rationalisations.

Yet, if we examine his early life, we find little trace of the patterns believed nowadays to be conducive to crime. He did not come from a broken home; indeed, ties within Indian families tend to be stronger than elsewhere, and if Boysie seemed to set little store by them, his rejection was deliberate and voluntary and in no sense a result of neglect by either of his parents. The role played in his upbringing by his elder sister, though unusual by European standards, is by no means uncommon amongst Indian families. Nor could it be claimed that his crimes were due to what is nowadays euphemistically described as an "underprivileged background". The Singhs admittedly were poor, but there is no indication that they ever suffered physically or mentally as a result of their poverty; moreover, being poor in the tropics is by no means so unpleasant as it is in a temperate climate, where physical discomfort and lack of anywhere to go are added to the universal drawbacks of the condition.

Those who seek the origins of crime in the criminal's social surroundings will no doubt point to the peculiar conditions governing the Indian community in Trinidad which were described at some length in an earlier chapter of this book. Admittedly such conditions might produce an environment favourable to crime, but if they tended specifically to produce criminals of Boysie's type one would expect to find a large number of embryo Boysies circulating around Trinidad in the twenties and thirties. In fact there were none. Boysie had things all his own way for so long precisely because there was no competition.

The lawlessness which undoubtedly existed amongst sections of the Indian community, and to which the conditions mentioned above undoubtedly contributed, was of a kind very different from Boysie's. It has already been pointed out that the Trinidadian Indian is a strong individualist as far as his career is concerned, and this individualism extends into his criminal activities. He seldom forms gangs on the American pattern. Apparent exceptions such as the San Juan mob of Mano Das are, in fact, organised on completely different lines: loose regional federations, they exist through communal rivalry rather than criminal intent, and engage only sporadically and incidentally in gang violence or crime.

Indeed, apart from the crimes of passion common to most citizens of hot-blooded countries, offences committed by Indians fall usually into one of two groups: acts of violence directed against personal or family enemies, often arising from disputes over property, or fraudulent business transactions which are little more than commerce carried on by other means. Both types are carried out by individuals or families rather than gangs.

This helps to explain why so many of Boysie's henchmen were of African descent. For the Trinidadian Negro's criminal pattern is distinct from that of the Trinidadian Indian. As regards the former's choice of offences, it is hardly surprising that the various forms of larceny are the commonest. The descendants of slaves naturally tend to regard any property they can "win" or "liberate" as legitimately theirs, whereas the business-minded Indian, even on a criminal level, has a much sharper sense of *meum* and *tuum*. Moreover the tendency to avoid individual responsibility while accepting collective responsibility, shown in the Negro's preference of a civil service to a commercial career, is reflected on a lower level by his unwillingness to act alone in criminal matters, even when the only alternative is to work with untrustworthy associates. In consequence, his gangs are usually loosely-knit, short-lived organisations, for no one will bear for long the onerous tasks of leadership. On the basis of these facts alone one could have prophesied that Trinidad's first successful gang would be composed of Negroes and controlled by an Indian.

But we are no nearer an understanding of Boysie himself.

This is perhaps because we have been considering him from too strictly criminal a viewpoint. There is still a strong tendency to treat the criminal and respectable worlds as totally separate entities; whereas in fact they not only shade into one another as imperceptibly as (say) sanity and insanity or "normal" and "abnormal" sexual behaviour, but are more intimately connected in other ways, some of which have been suggested in the course of this book. In fact, one of the writer's objects has been deliberately to blur the distinctions normally drawn between legal and illegal activities, with the aim not of encouraging the latter, but of trying to gain a deeper insight into both, and more particularly into the relationship that exists between them.

If, then, we compare Boysie, not with other criminals, but with types in the world at large, we may succeed in finding a closer analogue.

Now the most sustained comparison between the criminal and non-criminal life is found in Henry Fielding's *Jonathan Wild*. This novel is generally taken as an ironical debunking of crime, a reaction to the sentimentalising of the underworld found in *The Beggars Opera* and ballad broadsheets on the lives of highwaymen. But leaving aside the whole question of intention – too large for a work of this kind, and anyway Fielding isn't around to be asked – the parallels drawn between crime and political life cut both ways; the book could as easily be taken as a satire on politicians. Take the scene in which the youthful Wild discloses his ambitions to the rascally Count la Ruse:

> I have an awkward pride in my nature, which is better pleased with being at the head of the lowest class than at the bottom of the highest ... (I) should be as well satisfied with exerting my talents well at the head of a small party or gang, as in the command of a mighty army, for I am far from agreeing with you, that great parts are often lost in a low situation... the same genius, the same endowments, have often composed the statesman and the prig, for so we call what the vulgar name a thief. The same parts, the same actions, often promote men to the head of superior societies, which raise them to the head of lower; and where is the essential difference if the one ends on Tower Hill and the other at Tyburn?

Later, having acquired one or two confederates, he meditates on the human condition in the following terms:

> Mankind are first properly to be considered under two grand divisions, those that use their own hands, and those who employ the hands of others. The former are the base and the rabble; the latter, the genteel part of the creation... And now indeed the merchant should seem to challenge some character of greatness, did we not necessarily come to a second division, viz, of those who employ hands for their own use only; and this is that noble and great part who are generally distinguished into conquerors, absolute princes, statesmen, and prigs. Now all these differ from each other in greatness only – they employ more or fewer hands... Now, suppose a prig had as many tools as any prime minister ever had, would he not be as great as any prime minister whatsoever? Undoubtedly he would. What then have I to do in the pursuit of greatness but to procure a gang, and to make the use of this gang centre in myself? This gang shall rob for me only, receiving very moderate rewards for their actions; out of this gang I will prefer to my favour the boldest and most iniquitous... and thus... convert those laws which are made for the benefit and protection of society to my single use!

I have quoted at such length (a length which I hope did not seem excessive) partly because, in this age of undue respect for the great, the resemblances between national leaders and criminals are not sufficiently noted, but mainly in order to prepare the reader for what, without some kind of support, might have seemed to him a far-fetched and implausible conclusion. It is that one can only appreciate the true nature of Boysie Singh if one considers him, not as a criminal, but as an aborted dictator.

Some people might deny the very existence of such a category. This is because we are still insufficiently schooled in the thought of Machiavelli, and in consequence persist in paying more attention to what people say than to what they do and are. All those who seek to achieve absolute power by revolutionary means speak in terms of "the National Destiny" or "the Will of the Masses", but one would be incorrect in deducing from this that they have any genuine interest in the causes which they profess to represent. To adopt for a moment the near-meaningless phraseology of politics, it is significant to note not only that such types are to be found as frequently on the "left" as on the "right", but that many have been known to switch effortlessly from one to the other; Mussolini is of course the most notorious example.

The picture one gets is in fact not of overeager politicians putting ends before means, but of aberrant psychological types pursuing a destiny as compulsive as that of, say, sadists or exhibitionists. It matters nothing what side they are on as long as the force that drives them is satisfied. But whereas the satisfactions of sadists and exhibitionists are easy to come by, and depend on their own efforts, the opportunities of becoming a dictator are limited, not merely by the shortage of vacancies, but by the countless obstacles, social, political and personal, which must be surmounted before the desired apotheosis can be achieved.

It follows, therefore, that even if the dictator-type is comparatively rare, it must have a high percentage of frustrated members, mute inglorious Hitlers for whom there can never be room at the top. Doubtless some achieve positions of minor authority, and work out their disappointment by bullying their unfortunate subordinates. But if we accept Fielding's analysis it is only reasonable to suppose that many of them would take to crime.

What must be the most outstanding characteristics in such a type? Obviously a desire to excel amongst one's fellows, to lead and dominate them in all circumstances, and to allow no obstacle to stand in one's way once one has decided to pursue a particular course of action. That Boysie possessed all these to an abnormal degree, countless incidents in this book bear witness. Assuming these characteristics to be innate, or at least early acquired – for there is abundant evidence that he possessed them in childhood – one must next ask what opportunities he had, in the Trinidad of thirty or forty years ago, to put them to legitimate use.

At this point it may be argued that ambition and ruthlessness alone do not automatically qualify their possessor for distinction; that in those who succeed they are usually accompanied by exceptional intelligence; and that Boysie, far from exhibiting such intelligence, left his primary school with the bare rudiments of the three R's. All this is true, but we first must consider the barriers that existed to prevent a person of Boysie's background from educating himself. These were psychological rather than material. Admittedly it was difficult enough, in the virtual absence of scholarships and government grants, for a poor boy to reach a university, but it was by no means impossible, given a strong enough desire; the present Governor of Trinidad, Sir Solomon Hochoy, was born in very humble circumstances in a village in northern Trinidad. But the island was then under Colonial Office rule, all positions of authority were held by people from the Old Country, and, as the era of nationalism and political disquiet had not even dawned, this state of affairs looked like going on for ever. It followed that the only road for advancement – whether one was educated or not – lay in servile kowtowing to the ruling class, and even this would bring only such crumbs as the mighty ones cared to let drop from their table.

To one of Boysie's independent temper, such a career would have been nauseous in the extreme, scarcely thinkable. It is therefore hardly surprising that he took so little interest in education; nor can his low level of academic attainment be attributed to lack of intellect, for the success of his business ventures and his long immunity from police interference prove that, in practical matters at least, his ability was well above the average.

But without an education, what could he do? The professions were closed to him; legitimate business, with its long period of apprenticeship at low pay and its enforced subservience, was no more attractive than government service; while any form, of manual labour – other than his beloved fishing – he considered beneath one of his parts. The only way he could achieve distinction was to acquire a Reputation, and the means by which such a Reputation was acquired – the single combats, the gang fights, the contemptuous disregard of other people's persons and property – served not merely to confirm him in his antisocial tendencies, but revealed to him the means by which he could extend his power far beyond the limits of his own district.

I am not suggesting that Boysie thought consciously or acted deliberately on these lines. It would have been remarkable, indeed, if someone of his background and education had reached such a level of self-awareness. But because he lacked the ability to verbalise or perhaps even clearly conceive such thoughts, it does not mean that they did not exist or had no effect on his conduct. It is often possible to observe in the lives of the inarticulate a logic and purpose far beyond their power to state, yet too clear to be mere coincidence – the fruit of a nonverbal thinking, intuitive and obscure, yet not necessarily less precise than the more conscious, communicable kind.

Let us assume, then, that what Fielding's hero in the tongue of the Age of Reason lucidly stated, Boysie cloudily but powerfully felt. It has been pointed out that during Boysie's first long prison sentence, the Carrera stretch in 1928-31, his conduct and attitude to life underwent a change, a change of a kind that would have been regarded as highly improbable by anyone who knew his earlier history. If his outlook in youth was that of the young Wild, "better pleased with being at the head of the lowest class than at the bottom of the highest", then his outlook on leaving Carrera corresponds closely to Wild's maturer beliefs as expressed in the second passage

I quoted. Like Wild's, his earlier crimes were committed with his own hands; like Wild's again, his later ones were carried out through the agency of subordinates, who took the punishment if anything went wrong. His objects were the same as before; it was just a question of employing "more or fewer hands".

Had Boysie been born a few years later, it is quite possible that at this critical stage of his career he would have chosen politics rather than gambling and crime. The connection between crime and revolutionary politics has never been adequately studied – Stalin's bank robberies and the activities of the F.A.I. [Iberian Anarchist Federation], that bizarre mixture of murderers and idealists, are two of the more obvious examples that spring to mind – but it is certainly a close one; and Boysie, throughout his life, was far more conscious of his proletarian origins than the average gang leader. He was always available to the humblest of his followers, and a large slice of his income was distributed amongst them; money that, in the hands of most *nouveaux riches*, would have gone towards the accumulation of status symbols. But, clothes apart – and these were essential costume for the role Boysie sought to play – he showed little or no interest in material possessions. The properties he bought were purely investments; he had hardly a house that a prosperous shopkeeper would not have scorned; at the height of his prosperity he would sleep on a bench and dine off flyblown pastries from a wayside stall, not from deliberate austerity or meanness, but a genuine indifference to his personal comfort. His one apparent departure from these standards – his membership of the high-type poker club that cost him his fortune – is not really a rejection of them; for what is the purpose of achieving eminence if one's achievement is to go wholly unrecognised? But Boysie was determined to succeed on his own terms, not on other people's.

More overt evidence of his social preoccupations is to be found in his marking of Bible passages that favoured the underdog – his note, "Communism", has been mentioned already – and in certain passages of his death-cell diary, particularly the following: "... if you have Food you must give your Brother you find today you will eat your Brother the Country is based upon survival of the Fittest. So a Poor Man haven't a chance, in my experience."

But the most outstanding fact about Boysie is that he possessed a charismatic personality. This I know will be disputed by many people, particularly those who knew him in the later years of his life. Assistant Commissioner Slater, for example, who investigated the Thelma Haynes case, spoke of him as "that wretched creature", and could not understand why I wished to write about him rather than the bourgeois, respectable wife-killer Dr. Dalip Singh. But Slater never met Boysie until after the Floating Corpse case. In the course of my investigations I interviewed a number of people who had known him at the height of his power. All of them spoke of him in terms of affection and respect. Some admittedly were confessed criminals whose admiration is easily explicable, but others were old associates who for many years had gone straight, and there were a few who had never been involved in his illegal activities. All of them, even the criminals, deprecated the pirate atrocities, but each found in his character something to praise.

The point is made with the intention not of exonerating Boysie, or showing that he was a nice murderer as murderers go, but of illustrating the peculiar hold he had over those who came into contact with him. One of them told me, "When he was there people could do things they couldn't do when he was away. I have tried to lift a boat by myself, and I couldn't do it; then when he stood by me and told me to lift it, suddenly I could." If the reader thinks this is far-fetched, let him consider the curious nature of the murders themselves. To my certain knowledge at least six other people took part in these, probably more, of whom more than half had no prior knowledge of what they were about to do. Yet none of them ever betrayed him. Admittedly Fire Kong's revolvers must have deterred them. But even when Kong and Boysie were both under arrest, when a denunciation would have brought immunity and official favour at no personal risk, when the example of Loomat and Harper, Rodney and Wilkie was there to prove that one could testify against Boysie and still live, not one of those who had taken part or of the greater number who knew of the murders ever came forward to accuse him.

Perhaps even more significant than the fact they did not is that he cannot have imagined they ever would. One who commanded by virtue of his power to terrorise alone would hardly have dared to take unblooded members of his gang on pirate raids without prior indoctrination. That Boysie was able to do so so bespeaks a confidence rare in the underworld and as seldom justified. Many mass-murderers have had personal charm, more have been sexually attractive, but hardly any have had Boysie's capacity for arousing feelings of loyalty, a capacity found more often among the idols of revolutionary movements than among professional criminals.

That his mind did at times run on political matters is shown by his interest in the course of the European War, and his admiration for his fellow-Arian, Hitler – a choice of hero significant in the extreme. Yet this interest never seemed to extend to local affairs, even in the late thirties when the discontents of the age finally reached Trinidad. A contemporary of Boysie's was Uriah (Buzz) Butler, the union leader who was interned on Chacachacare after the bloody riots of 1937. But by this time Boysie was already committed to a criminal career. Butler had organised labour behind him, while labour, organised or disorganised, was what Boysie's followers most wished to avoid.

But the real reason why he had never tried to dominate his fellow-men by means of politics lies in his limited education. The idea that he could simply did not occur to him. Indeed, one of the things which must strike any impartial observer is the contrast between the strength and flexibility of the organisation he built up and the pettiness of the ends to which he set it. Even the total proceeds of his piracy probably did not reach thirty thousand dollars, while his thefts of engine differentials and folding metal chairs are ludicrously disproportionate to the effort involved.

With the armed force at his disposal he could have cleaned up Port of Spain's banks, or put hundreds of rioters on the streets to overthrow public order and create a climate for any coup, criminal or political, that he had in mind. But his education and background were against him; luckily for society, he never learnt to think big. Even at the height of his power he would walk into shops and lift balls of fishing twine from the counter, daring the assistant to stop him – a sure sign that his picture of himself could not outgrow the Woodbrook Reputation.

A more searching test of the Dictator Theory is to see how far it explains some of the more puzzling episodes of his life.

In the light of this theory, several features of the murders begin to make sense. The two pictures which remain most vividly in one's mind – the trussed victims, helpless, knowing their fate, being told to pray, and the unwilling executioners, on their way home, being asked what it felt like to kill – are only explicable in terms of a desire to achieve power over men, power greater than Boysie had hitherto been able to obtain by legal or illegal means. He progressed from routine crime to mass murder in the same way that dictators progress from internal revolution to external war, and for similar reasons. One is that weapons that are made have to be used; having perfected an organisation that was powerful and loyal enough to carry out the pirate raids, it would have been remarkable if he had refrained from using it for that or some similar end. Another is that the dictator-type cannot stand still; driven less by conscious ambition than by the relentless, lunatic logic of his own character, he must progress from one enormity to the next until death or failure stops him. But the greatest of all is perhaps simply the will to obtain a higher degree of power over more people, irrespective of the cost in life or happiness which this may entail.

In all probability Boysie himself was unaware of these motives. No doubt he sincerely believed that when he killed Wilson and Cook, Taitt and Meyers, he was doing so merely for the few hundred dollars worth of equipment their boats would yield him. Yet it is impossible to avoid the feeling that this, plausible though it might seem, was simply another of his rationalisations. The cash-motive and the revenge-motive were comprehensible to him, and served therefore to justify his actions; whereas if he had accepted the Dictator Theory he would have seemed to himself a monster.

The curious workings of his mind are shown even more clearly in what is perhaps a still more baffling phase of his life – his "Preaching days". Probably no other criminal of his stature has ever taken up an evangelist's career, still less abandoned it and returned to crime. Yet the obvious questions – was he a fake? Was he sincere? If he was sincere how could he go back? If he was a fake what did he hope to gain? – are not so much unanswerable as irrelevant.

Let us assume he had indeed chosen a criminal career as the only feasible expression of his will to power. But after the Floating Corpse case, his empire was irrevocably shattered. When he was released on bail at the end of 1951 he was nearly forty-four years old, and had a record extending over the last thirty of them.

Now if he had been a true criminal he would almost certainly have gone back immediately to a life of crime. For the dyed-in the-wool crook, the confirmed recidivist, goes on getting into trouble, not because he is essentially evil, or because he is more stupid than the mass, or even because the wicked Prison Commissioners failed to teach him a trade, but because he *thinks of himself as a criminal and nothing else.* It is as absurd to expect him to change overnight into an honest man as it would be to expect a monk to become a bookie's runner or a fire-eating colonel the editor of a pacifist weekly. That the change is occasionally made is a tribute to the limitlessness of human flexibility rather than any reformative efforts on the part of authority.

But Boysie did not conceive of himself as essentially a criminal; he was merely a man who had taken to crime as one of several possible outlets for the forces that drove him, and once that failed, the natural thing was to choose another. It is therefore irrelevant to discuss his "sincerity"; doubtless he himself was convinced that he was sincere, but the motives of our actions are seldom what we think they are, and preaching happened to be the only means by which a man with no formal qualifications and no money could succeed in dominating the public – or at any rate that section of the public which came to hear him. For his congregations played in Boysie's life a part similar to that played earlier by the retinue of hangers-on which had attended his every appearance – they formed at once the natural complement of his personality, the fuel for his egotism and the outward and visible symbol of his success. He had to have them, in some shape or form, because he had a message to deliver to the world, the message of his own turbulent spirit:

> A fiery soul, which working out its way,
> Fretted the pigmy body to decay,
> And o'er informed the tenement of clay...

and since this message was so strictly personal, it mattered little in what terms it was delivered, whether it was "Save Your Souls" or "Kill and Spare Not".

His abandonment of the preacher's career is equally explicable in the light of this theory. His own reason was his conviction for driving without a licence, but this is the least plausible of his rationalisations. If the incident had any effect at all, it was probably only to crystallize a state of mind that had been developing for some time. Preaching might make it possible for him to master the minds of those who heard him for the three or four hours that he spoke to them; but that was all. As a gang leader he had been supreme in his field; as a preacher, once his novelty value had worn off, he was no more influential than dozens of other churchless prophets all flourishing in the schismatic hot-house of Trinidadian religion. Gradually this fact must have been borne in upon him, but he could not admit it even to himself, for to do so would have been to cast doubt on the genuineness of his conversion, in which he genuinely believed. He had therefore to give himself some external cause for abandoning his vocation. The driving conviction was timely and it served. If it had not been that it would have been something else; Boysie never had to look far for a grievance.

Where now was he to go? Even if the hard cash temptation of the Rising Sun job had not been offered him, there could only have been one answer; back to crime. Hopeless as it seemed, it was now the only thing he could do. He could no longer go back to the sea. He was a shadow of the man he had been. Enfeebled in body and mind, racked by disease, penniless, almost friendless, haunted by injustices fancied and real, he had to go on treading the sombre path that led to the execution shed and the stoneless, nameless grave.

It is ironic to think that he was probably innocent of the crime for which he died.

Nothing was produced at the trial that linked him with the actual commission of the murder; that he was so linked was merely a reasonable supposition in view of his record – which everyone in the case knew, even though they were supposed to ignore it – and the proven closeness of his relations with Boland. But even the most damning pieces of evidence – the borrowing of the boat, the production of Thelma's jewellery, Boysie's own indiscretions in the cell at Police Headquarters – were equally consistent with his having merely disposed of the body. If he had pleaded guilty to being an accessory it is probable that he would have escaped the gallows. But he was certain that total destruction of the body gave him immunity, and he preferred to gamble the chances of acquittal against the certainty of a long sentence which such a confession would have brought him – a sentence which in all probability he would not have survived. In the event, the very mystery that surrounded the crime worked against him; since no one could prove how Thelma had died, no one could prove that he had not killed her.

According to his own account, what actually happened was this.

It will be remembered that Boland, when discussing the murder, had told Boysie that it was his wife Dorothy who was to be killed. Boysie believed this, for he had not the slightest reason to doubt it; and, the cynic might add, more men kill their wives than kill their mistresses. On the evening of July 30th, Boysie had gone to Cocorite and got the boat ready, while Boland met Thelma in San Juan and persuaded her to enter a car which he had borrowed for the purpose. He then drove her along the mountainous Saddle Road that forms a secondary link between San Juan and Port of Spain, and up the road that branches off it towards Maracas. Boland knew this route well; he travelled it every day. It climbs in a series of nerve-racking hairpins to the crown of the three-thousand-foot ridge that separates the north coast from the rest of Trinidad. But the car in which Thelma was riding never reached the top. It stopped a few hundred yards up from the Port of Spain fork.

How Boland persuaded her to get out – for by this time it must have been nearly or quite dark – or whether he forced her out at knife-point, will never be known. At any rate he is alleged to have taken her up a narrow, soggy path which pierces the dense jungle by the side of the road to the clearing at the end of it; an open space no larger than a small room, backed by a stand of bamboo like huge vegetable organ-pipes. There in the quiet and the dark, with its strange forest smells and the perpetual dropping of water from the leaves, Boland thrust the knife into his lover's heart. When she was dead he put her in a sack and tied it and carried it back to the car, which he turned and drove down the twisting road to the sea at Cocorite. There Boysie was waiting. They carried the sack to the boat, and without another word Boysie pushed off and started the outboard.

This time there were no irons in the boat; either he had learnt the lesson of Bumper, or feared that someone might notice them and deduce their purpose. But this time he was going to make sure that the body disappeared by gutting it and then dropping it in deep water. For an hour he sailed westwards through the night, passing the American base at Chaguaramas and Staubles Bay, passing through the chain of islands that lies off Trinidad's north-western tip, until at last, some four or five miles north of the Bocas, and in ninety to a hundred fathoms of water, he stopped the engine, took out a knife and cut open the sack.

He was not easily surprised, but what he now saw in the feeble light of his lamp caused him to start back in bewilderment. For the dead girl who for the first time lay exposed to his sight was the wrong colour. He had expected to see the brown skin of Boland's Indian wife, Dorothy; instead he saw the black skin of Thelma. But it was too late to do anything about it by then.

He got down to the gruesome job of removing the murdered girl's intestines; when this was done he threw her over the side, and she sank instantly. He restarted the outboard and headed for Cocorite.

He found Boland still there. Already the would-be minister was feeling the pangs of conscience or pure funk which were to lead both of them to their deaths. For two hours he had paced the shore, biting his nails, unable to leave the spot until his accomplice returned and he knew that the job was successfully completed. He may really have believed that Boysie had dropped Thelma only a little way out and that she would be washed ashore in the mangroves as his dream had told him. Lifeguard though he was, he knew nothing of the sea, he would not even know how far two dollars worth of fuel would take Boysie in his two hours away from shore. And, as our fears themselves so often bring about what we dread, so did Boland's fear that Thelma would rise again bring death not only to him but to his accomplice, the man who – though he claimed a score of victims and escaped all penalty – was, this one time, innocent of the deed.

30: AFTERMATH

SOME OF THE MEN who had worked with Boysie themselves came to violent ends.

Fire Kong – Gerald Miller – never got out of Carrera. He went there in December 1950, found guilty of shooting with intent to kill, and began his ten-year sentence. But he was determined not to complete it. Prison lore stated that if you ate the blue soap used in Trinidad gaols, you would give yourself diabetes. Kong realised that in some such device lay his only hope of escape. Nobody gets away from Carrera itself; you might as well serve out your sentence in this Caribbean Alcatraz as chance a mile and a half through the sharks to the nearest shore. But if he became ill he would be transferred to a hospital on the mainland, from which his escape would be relatively easy.

So he began to eat soap. But Fire Kong was never one to do things by halves; he ate too much. The soap did indeed contain lethal ingredients. In a matter of hours he was on his way to hospital, but for the last time. He died of caustic poisoning.

Bage – Duncan Trotman – died, like his master, on the gallows.

He was deported from Trinidad – unwisely, one might think, considering that he was a witness in a trial for a capital offence which was still *sub judice,* and on the result of which the lives of five men depended – between the first and second Floating Corpse hearings. The rest of his brief life was spent in his native Barbados. Here he holed up in Nelson Street, most notorious in Bridgetown, a hundred-yard strip by the Careenage packed with brothels and bars, and frequented by the toughest criminals of which this relatively unsophisticated island can boast. Here, from his long absence and his known connection with Boysie, he had already a reputation, which he proceeded to embellish with such tales of his buccaneering ventures that he soon earned a new nickname – John Pirate.

On January 17th, 1958, towards midnight, he took a boat and with two accomplices rowed out into Carlisle Bay, the open roadstead where (prior to the construction of the Deep Water Harbour) all ships discharging cargo in the island had to drop anchor. Bage had his eye on one particular vessel – a Royal Netherlands ship called the S.S. *Hermes.* Silently his accomplices rowed him alongside; he caught hold of a rope and swung himself aboard.

As the ship was in the process of unloading, the hatch covers were off and the cargo was exposed. The uppermost crate contained what might seem hardly the most valuable of pirate loot – it was filled with cardboard cartons of Carnation Evaporated Milk. Bage, however, was not fussy; he opened the crate and had removed twenty cartons, preparatory to passing them over the side, when some noise he had made or the movements of his dim figure alerted the lookout.

The lookout snapped on the ship's lights.

Spotlighted by the glare, Bage stood alone. His hand went to his chest. Unknown to his accomplices – or so they afterwards declared – he had under his shirt a revolver attached to a length of string round his neck. From all corners of the deck the ship's crew moved in, silently surrounding him. One of them – a sailor called Stanley Astwood – was standing only a few feet from him. Bage drew his revolver and told them to stand back. Most of them obeyed; only Astwood remained. Bage repeated his order, but Astwood still stood his ground. Bage shot him at point-blank range.

Astwood took a couple of steps as if he had decided belatedly to give in to Bage and then his legs doubled under him and he sprawled on the deck. Bage leapt over the side of the ship, slid down the rope to the waiting boat below. His accomplices rowed him swiftly away.

Within a couple of days all three were under arrest. Astwood had died of his wound; the charge was capital. Bage might still have hoped to get away on grounds of doubtful identification, but one of his accomplices turned Queen's evidence against him. This man's lawyer failed to inform the other defence counsel of the fact, so that on the morning of the trial their case was cut from under them. There was nothing Bage could do except launch into an impassioned tirade against his companion's treachery. The judge directed the jury to find his second accomplice not guilty, and Bage alone was convicted, on April 18th, 1958, and sentenced to death. He was executed three weeks later in Glendairy prison.

Most of the others are still alive. Many are still to be found in and around Port of Spain. Some are going straight. Some are in and out of gaol. There are few, even among the honest ones, who do not sneakingly regret the old days, the days when for a time they had the exhilarating sense of being beyond the law.

One evening before I left Trinidad I went to see Boysie's grave.

The Potter's Field is a long, gently-sloping expanse of grass, like an ill-grazed meadow, which ends abruptly in a steep grassy rise, pediment of the jungle-covered hills which climb, one on top of the other, to the heights of the Northern Range. Just under this rise is Murderers' Row. A footpath leads through it, and people are passing all the time; if you weren't told you would never know it was a graveyard, for there are no tombstones, no memorials of any kind, and the only signs of burial are low mounds here and there, that might be the work of moles or incompetent ploughmen. A suburban street runs along one side of it, with the one-storey concrete boxes looking westwards over the nameless graves.

Boysie and Boland are buried close to one another and only a few yards from Boysie's namesake, Dr. Dalip Singh. When the doctor was buried, relations planted on his grave a tree known to Trinidadian Indians as "madar" ; its leaves are applied as poultices for swellings and pains in the joints, its flowers are used in the making of wreaths. Two years later cuttings were taken from Dalip's tree and planted on the graves of his two fellow-country-men. The tree planted over Boland, the lifeguard who saved sixty-four lives and only took one, withered and died; but those on the graves of Dalip, wife-murderer, and Boysie, killer of uncounted victims, are thriving and flourishing to this day. Both are now about the height of a man. They have thick, rather flabby silvery-green leaves, and a pale mauve flower without scent, which, when I saw it, was just breaking into bloom.

And a stone's-throw from them the swarming life of the island went on. A few yards away were the neat concrete houses, with a view from their front windows that might give the fanciful some unquiet nights; but here no one thought anything of it. Behind the houses were thick, pale-green banana plants and stumpy, shaggy palms, shading by imperceptible degrees into the jungle that backs the city. On the road, children were running and screeching, their cries muted somehow by the blueness and lateness of the hour. A man in shirtsleeves and drab trousers carrying a corded bale of wood set the wood down on end in the middle of the road, squatted upon it and carried on a shouted conversation with the people in one of the concrete boxes. A goat staked by the roadside uncurled its chain from the stake, cropped slowly nearer and nearer to Boysie's grave. The sky over the mountains was limpid with evening. In a little while it would be quite dark.

As I walked away in the deepening darkness, I thought of the man who lay buried there. What kind of man had he really been? Tyrant, psychotic, criminal, victim of circumstance? All I could really feel, echoing in my mind, were the words that his son had spoken, words that might serve, if such a thing were allowed him, for an epitaph: –

HE WAS NOT A MAN LIKE YOU OR I.

ABOUT THE AUTHORS

Derek Bickerton had several careers. He was born in England in 1926, spent several years in the Caribbean, including surveying trips into the unmapped interior of Guyana and work as a journalist in Barbados in the late 1950s and early 1960s. It was in this period he wrote *The Adventures of Boysie Singh* (1962) and a novel about the Caribbean, *Tropicana* (1963). Thereafter he developed a distinguished academic career as a linguist who advanced the study of creole languages. After a spell teaching in Ghana, he spent four years as a senior lecturer at the University of Guyana. Out of this came his *The Dynamics of a Creole System* (1975). From 1971-1995 he taught at the University of Hawaii where he developed his theories on the origins of languages, writing such books as *Roots of Language; Language and Species; Adam's Tongue* and *More than Nature Needs: Language, Mind, and Evolution.* He continued to write works of fiction. He died in Hawaii in 2018.

Kenneth Ramchand is Professor Emeritus of West Indian literature at the University of the West Indies, St Augustine, Trinidad. He is the author of *The West Indian Novel and its Background* (1970, 2004) and many other titles. A collection of his essays will appear with Peepal Tree in 2020.